From Now On

Amelia Henley

ONE PLACE. MANY STORIES

HQ
An imprint of HarperCollins*Publishers* Ltd
1 London Bridge Street
London SE1 9GF

www.harpercollins.co.uk

HarperCollins*Publishers*
1st Floor, Watermarque Building, Ringsend Road
Dublin 4, Ireland

This edition 2022

1
First published in Great Britain by
HQ, an imprint of HarperCollins*Publishers* Ltd 2022

Copyright © Louise Jensen 2022

Louise Jensen asserts the moral right to be identified as the author of this work.
A catalogue record for this book is available from the British Library.

ISBN: 978-0-00-851199-9

MIX
Paper from
responsible sources
FSC
www.fsc.org **FSC™ C007454**

This book is produced from independently certified FSC™ paper
to ensure responsible forest management.

For more information visit: www.harpercollins.co.uk/green

This book is set in 10.9/15.5 pt. Caslon by Type-it AS, Norway

Printed and Bound in the UK using 100% Renewable Electricity at
CPI Group (UK) Ltd, Croydon, CR0 4YY

9030 00008 0035 2

Amelia Henle   for
exploring the intricacies of relationships through writing heart-
breaking, high-concept stories. Her first two novels, *The Life We
Almost Had* and *The Art of Loving You*, have been international
bestsellers.

Amelia also writes psychological thrillers under her real name,
Louise Jensen. As Louise Jensen she has sold over a million copies
of her global number one bestsellers. Her stories have been trans-
lated into twenty-five languages and optioned for TV as well as
featuring on the *USA Today* and *Wall Street Journal* bestsellers list.
Louise's books have been nominated for multiple awards.

Also by Amelia Henley

The Life We Almost Had
The Art of Loving You

Kai Jensen!
Get your dreams just right . . .

PROLOGUE

Charlie

There are many different kinds of love.

Charlie watches her as she lies beside him, the rise and fall of her chest. Outside, there's the thrum of a passing car, but here they are, cocooned in their own world.

He wishes they could remain in this moment.

The afternoon sun pushes through the window, casting a small circle of light over her heart which he knows beats for him. He doesn't want to break it, and the thought that he might is the source of infinite sorrow.

The clock ticks.

Time marching forward.

Time running out.

I love you.

He feels the shape of those words stuck to his tongue, heavy and cumbersome, weighted with the memories of the last time he uttered them. Charlie's chest tightens painfully.

He takes three slow, measured breaths.

This is not the same.

She shifts her weight, her mouth lifting at the corners before relaxing again. He doesn't need to study her features to commit them to memory; every time he closes his eyes, he sees it all: the curve of her smile, the sweep of black lashes framing light blue eyes, the smattering of freckles across her shoulders. It doesn't seem fair that now he has found love, now that he is certain of it, it is, perhaps, too late. Still Charlie cradles the feeling carefully on the palm of his hand, knowing it is something rare and fragile and beautiful, not wanting to release it. She is blissfully unaware, her face slackened with sleep, the taste of her still on his lips. The inevitability of goodbye is torturous, but he has made a promise to his family. His family who he has let down in the worst kind of way even though, he thinks, he is not the worst kind of person.

Or is he?

It has been an age now, but he still deliberates whether it was all his fault. Sometimes he's convinced it was but often the memory is as hazy as the muted recollection of a dream, not entirely tangible and open to interpretation. Although some of the details are a blur, he does remember with clarity the way the fabric of his universe had been ripped apart at the seams. Afterwards things were never quite the same however hard he had tried to repair the tear with clumsy stitches, looping the coping techniques he had been taught over and over his pain until it was barely visible. The inexorable truth was that he had endlessly questioned who he was, what he felt. How had his life been built on a lie? It didn't seem possible and yet, somehow, it was. Even into adulthood he had found himself constantly scrutinising his reality, reaching out to touch it with his fingertips, trying to fathom what was real and what wasn't.

She.

She is real and his battered heart isn't quite ready to let her go.

She sighs and rolls over onto her back, her head lolling to one side, her blonde hair fanned across the pillow.

Charlie dips his mouth towards her ear, the smell of her coconut shampoo drifting towards him as he whispers his secrets; the hopes and dreams he had for them.

He tells her it all.

Everything.

And that is how he unequivocally knows she is the one.

He trusts her in a way he hasn't trusted anyone in years and years; not since that inimitable day.

Gently, he brushes her hair back from her face; her skin is warm and soft.

The light changes in the window. Rain patters against the panes as the sky cries ceaseless tears.

It's almost time to make an impossible decision that will end in heartbreak.

Charlie's heartbreak.

He loves her but can love be enough?

She is going to leave unless he makes her a promise that will be impossible to keep.

He thinks of the threads that tie him to this house through his tangled past and his complicated present and, for a single blissful moment, he imagines cutting himself free. Floating between his family and her. Which way would the wind blow him?

There are many different kinds of love and if he has to choose one . . .

He *has* to choose one.

Today.

Now.

SIX MONTHS BEFORE

CHAPTER ONE

Charlie

Charlie is a terrible son.

This thought runs through his head as he knocks on the front door as though he is a stranger, as though this hadn't once been his home. It's been so long since he was last here, he can't quite remember if he still has a front door key or where it might be. Not hanging from his key ring where he might see it every day, where it might remind him of this house.

Of everything.

Reassuring himself that there is good in the world – his world – he glances at Sasha as she stamps her feet against the cold beside him, her breath billowing a white cloud in the freezing air. The sight of her still makes his heart flutter, which isn't a very macho thing to say, but then Charlie isn't what you'd describe as an alpha male. Sasha flashes him a smile – the smile that made Charlie fall for her – and again he thinks how lucky he is that he's finally found happiness. Finally ceased endlessly questioning whether he deserves it.

The front door creaks open and there she is, his mother, looking the same and yet somehow different. Her long brown hair now streaked with more grey than when he last saw her. How long has it been since he last visited? Easter, he thinks. He bought tubs of sweets for his younger siblings, which they loved.

Mum's eyes crinkle around the corners with delight as she gestures them into the warm hallway. It still has a shabby brown carpet although years of thundering footsteps have trodden down the pile which is interwoven with white animal hair.

On cue, a dog – the same dog he can smell despite the vanilla air freshener lingering in the air – hurtles towards Charlie. He sets down his case and crouches, opening his arms, and she flings herself at him, paws scrambling for traction as she attempts to fit her too-large body onto his lap, her rough tongue covering his face with love and licks. Some of the tension he's been carrying begins to dissipate as he scratches her behind her ears, her eyes closed in rapture. She's a mongrel, part poodle they had ascertained from her curly coat when she became part of the family several years ago. Nowadays she'd be given some fancy name, some sort of 'doodle' or 'poo' he supposes.

'This is Billie,' Charlie says to Sasha as he wipes the drool from his cheek with his sleeve. 'And this is my mum, Ronnie.' He stands. 'Mum, this is Sasha. My . . .' he trails off. Girlfriend seems too small a word, but he can't say fiancée. Not yet. In his pocket he fiddles with the ring box, small and hard. He's been carrying it around for weeks, but it never seems like the right time. Tonight, New Year's Eve, is perfect, but they are in wholly the wrong place. This tiny Derbyshire village isn't where he wants to form new memories, good or bad. Besides, he hasn't yet shared the shame of his past with her and this he must do before asking her to spend the rest of her life with him.

Mum squeezes past Charlie and reaches for Sasha, sweeping

her into an enthusiastic greeting, not the obligatory peck on both cheeks that is the way in his London life but a genuine I'm-delighted-to-meet-you hug.

'Charlie hasn't brought a girl home before.' His mum grins.

Irritation shivers down Charlie's spine. He has taken plenty of girls – well, three if you're counting – home but this . . . this isn't his home. That is apparent from the way he stands awkwardly in the cramped space, still wearing his coat, still wearing his shoes. He is thirty-three but here he reverts to being a child, awaiting instructions.

'Charlie!' His stepdad sticks his head around the door from the lounge, his booming voice filling the silence. 'Don't stand on ceremony, lad.'

They traipse a crocodile line into the living room. 'Hello, Bo.' Charlie and his stepdad fold themselves into a bumbling one-armed hug. Bo has raised Charlie since he was a teenager; a difficult age for most, an impossible one for Charlie. They draw apart and Bo gently pats the bristles that spike Charlie's chin.

'You need a shave, lad.' A smile passes between them, and, Charlie thinks, a shared memory. Charlie at fifteen carefully lathering shaving foam onto his skin for the first time under Bo's watchful eye, the scratch of the razor as it sliced at the hairs that had begun sprouting above Charlie's upper lip.

'Oh, I quite like a beard.' Sasha bestows a beaming smile as she shrugs off her faux-fur coat, teetering on her heels on the parquet floor. 'You have such a cosy home, Ronnie.' Sasha is never tongue-tied, searching for conversation. She has an easy way with people.

'Take a pew.' Bo settles himself on the black leather couch, which is criss-crossed with duct tape covering the places Billie has broken the ageing material with her claws or teeth.

Sasha sits, crossing one denim-clad leg over the other.

'Tell me about yourself, Sasha,' Mum asks. 'Where are you from?'

'London. I've never lived anywhere else.'

'It's funny but I never think of people being born there, more moving for work. Do your family still live there?'

'There's just my parents, but yes.'

'No siblings?'

'No.'

'It must be lovely for your mum and dad to live so close to you and see you regularly.'

There's a beat before Mum turns to him, a too-bright smile on her face.

'How's city life then? I can't imagine living anywhere so busy.'

'Same as usual,' Charlie quickly replies. He had asked Sasha not to mention his forthcoming transfer to New York next month. He doesn't want to upset his parents before their big night. They don't need to know yet that he's here to say goodbye.

'You made good time this morning? We weren't expecting you so soon. You must have caught an early train?' Mum asks.

Charlie glances at Sasha. He doesn't want her to think he's a natural liar – he's not; there had been enough lies in his childhood – but it would hurt his mum immeasurably to learn they'd travelled up last night but had chosen to stay in a hotel instead of here, with her, his family. 'Blended' they'd be categorised as nowadays, but Charlie still views them as two separate entities. Them and him.

'London isn't too far really,' Sasha says as she places her hand on his knee, deflecting the question. 'Not like your trek today. How long does it take to get to Cornwall from here?'

His mum pulls a face. 'Colesby Bay is about six hours away.'

'Must be some party you're going to.' Sasha tucks a strand of blonde hair behind her ear.

'It's a gig. On the beach, so we'll probably freeze but there'll be a fire and food and fireworks.'

'That sounds so cool,' Sasha says. 'Who's playing?'

Mum's eyes flicker towards Charlie before settling on Sasha again. 'We are.'

'Seriously?' Sasha elbows Charlie. 'You never told me your parents are in a band.'

'Were,' Charlie corrects.

'We have the photos to prove it.' Mum crosses to his nana's old sideboard and slides open the doors.

Charlie inwardly shrinks. 'We don't want to make you late—'

'Nonsense.' His mum cuts him off as she squeezes between him and Sasha, her arms laden with photo albums. 'Marty isn't picking us up just yet; besides, if we don't spend some time with you now, when will we, if you've got to rush back to London tomorrow night?' Her eyes, the same brown as Charlie's, fix on his. 'We missed you at Christmas, Charlie.'

'Sorry.' He doesn't offer transparent excuses, instead focusing on softly stroking Billie's muzzle with his index finger as she bumps her head against his ankles as though, if she doesn't make a connection every three seconds, he might disappear again for months on end.

Mum opens the album, the photos suffocating under tight plastic, and lovingly smooths out an air bubble with her knuckles before she angles the page towards Sasha.

'That's Bo when I first met him.'

'Wow.' Sasha's eyes flicker between the picture of the younger

Bo, the tan, his hair falling past his shoulders, sunglasses pushed on top of his head, to the man he has become with his short back and sides and pale skin, his stomach overhanging the waistband of his trousers. The guitar Bo is holding in the photo is plastered in stickers, a peace sign, a cannabis leaf – it was all very seventies, but the fashion was all wrong for that era. 'When was this?'

'Eighteen years ago. After . . . I'm sure Charlie told you about . . .' Mum falters.

Charlie gives an imperceptible shake of his head, glances at Sasha, worried she might probe into what his mum is leaving unsaid, but she's too engrossed in the photos to notice.

'We went to Cornwall,' Charlie picks up the story. 'On holiday.' *Running away.*

'Yes,' Mum carries on. 'We'd only been there a couple of days when we saw Bo's band playing on the promenade—'

'I'd like to say she couldn't resist me,' Bo jumps in, 'but I think it was the jazz that lured her over.'

'They were playing "Summertime" and I couldn't help joining in.' She begins to sing it, eyes half-closed, back in that day, taking Charlie with her. The screech of seagulls, the smell of hot doughnuts, the warmth of the sun on his skin.

'I sang with them for the rest of the summer,' Mum says.

Oh, that endless summer. Sitting at the Cliff Top Café, feeling like he was on top of the world, head almost touching the clouds. Bottles of Coke speared with red and white striped straws; chips doused in vinegar. Charlie kicking his legs against the harbour wall, watching various dads scoop sand into buckets, kids collecting feathers and pebbles to decorate their castles. Mum had pushed two-pence pieces into his hand so he could amuse himself in the arcade while she practised with the band. Dropping the coppers into the coin pusher. Waiting for the clatter of tumbling coins to spill out of the machine. He wouldn't say he was happy exactly, that seemed too far out of reach after . . . but he had begun to feel a contentment when everything had changed.

Again.

'Why did you stop playing?' Sasha asks.

'When Ronnie and Charlie came back here, I moved with them. I tried, but . . .' Bo shrugs. 'Had to get a proper job. Who knows, there might be a talent scout there tonight. This could be our big break.'

'Bo has never given up on his dreams,' Charlie says. Even on jam nights at the local pub he was optimistic he'd get his big break.

'Ah, Charlie lad. You know your mum is my dream.' It's true. They're devoted to each other, never stopped showing affection the way that some couples do. A touch of the hand. A brush of the lips. 'But music is a close second. Anyway, we're a happy family now, aren't we?'

Bo doesn't reference what it took to get here. Charlie's own dreams broken. His spirit broken.

Family.

Charlie thinks about what that word means to him. He fingers the ring box in his pocket.

Family is hope, a future, a choice.

Love.

'But you're playing again tonight?' Sasha asks.

'Yeah, putting the band back together.' Bo grins but then his smile slips. 'Our drummer, Marty, has been diagnosed with prostate cancer. He's based in Sheffield now but Fingers, our keyboard player, lives in Cornwall, and he's organised a fundraiser.

We thought a beach party would be fun and . . .' Bo's voice drops. 'It might be the last time . . . you know.'

For a moment they sit in silence until Sasha asks if there are any photos of Charlie in the album.

Ronnie turns the page and points out a younger him, not quite a child but not yet a man. If you look past the mop of curly dark hair, which nowadays is tamed with product, you can see the sadness shadowed in his eyes. His jaw tightens as his mum tells Sasha that after that picture had been taken, he had eaten so much candyfloss he'd felt sick for the rest of the day but it wasn't the sticky spun sugar that had made his stomach churn; it was the fear, the confusion, the knowing that they had come here because he had lost something, and recognizing that, from the adoring way his mum and Bo were gazing at each other, he'd also found something and he wasn't sure it was something he wanted.

Still, as Sasha screams with hilarity at his too-short-shorts, his protruding knees, his unkempt hair, he laughs good-naturedly.

He's a world away from that child who had been thrust into an unfamiliar and uncertain situation; he is the man he'd *chosen* to become. Sasha is the swirl of vanilla buttercream on top of the perfect cupcake. His happily ever after. He reaches for her hand and gives it a squeeze.

'Where are Duke and Nina?' He throws a distraction Mum's way before she can turn the page again. For a second Sasha looks blank as though she's forgotten they've come to babysit Charlie's half-brother and -sister rather than to poke fun at the ungainly teen he'd once been.

'They're next door baking with Pippa,' Mum says. 'They shouldn't be too long.' She checks her watch just as a horn beeps outside. She cranes her neck to peer out of the window. 'That's Marty, we must get going.' She stands. 'We can drop into Pippa's to say goodbye.' She turns to Charlie. 'The kids might want to stay up for "Auld Lang Syne".'

'That's okay. It will be nice to see in the new year together,' he says, although inwardly he's disappointed. He wants that midnight kiss with Sasha without an audience; he's already planned an inordinately romantic speech, but then if they aren't alone he won't do anything stupid like propose tonight, here.

They all bustle back into the tiny hall again.

Mum and Sasha hug their goodbye, exchanging a premature 'Happy New Year'.

'Charlie.' Mum opens her arms to him.

He bends down and fastens his fingers around Billie's collar on the pretence she's about to bolt through the front door.

'See you tomorrow.' He tilts his head upwards, not quite looking at her face, as he crouches on the floor among the dog hair and his resentment which, even now, he can't quite shift. It wasn't her fault. He *knows* that and yet he still can't release his grip on the bitterness he's been carrying around for so long it feels like part of him.

And yet as she gazes down at him with tenderness, he knows she'd be devastated if she had any inkling how conflicted his feelings towards her are. How complicated.

'Look after them for me, won't you?' she whispers. 'And look after yourself too,' she adds but not as an afterthought. It's as though this is what she wanted to say all along.

'I promise.' He crosses his chest with his finger the way he used to when he was small. Not a hug, but enough.

For a moment their eyes meet, and he feels held. The way

he had when he was younger, before Bo and Nina and Duke. Before any of it. The way he had when he'd had a nightmare, a tummy ache, a fear of the monster living under the bed. There is a split second when he longs to hurl himself into her arms, tell her that he loves her, that he knows she loves him really and has done her best and that he's sorry he has brought her so much shame, but his words are tangled up with his emotions and his memories, and he can't unpick them before she turns away from him and walks down the path. The garden gate creaks open. She spins and raises her hand in a wave but before he can free his fingers from Billie's collar and wave back, she's disappeared from view.

Sasha has healed the crack in Charlie's bruised heart, but in that moment, suddenly he wants to make it right, all of it. He vows that when he sees his mum tomorrow, he will tell her everything, the way he felt all those years ago, the way he felt until recently. He wants to say goodbye properly. To promise that he'll call her every week and mean it. Leave for New York with a clean slate, a clear conscience. He doesn't want to feel like he's running away.

Again.

As yet, Charlie does not know that he will not get the chance to put things right. If he had known what was to come, he would have gone after her, stopped her from leaving, reassured her that he understood the choices she had made.

He would perhaps have told her that he forgave her.

At the very least he'd have whispered that he loved her. Those three words would have meant everything to her, and she had not heard them from him in such a long time.

Now, she never would.

But Charlie, of course, does not know that he'll never see her again as he turns around and closes the front door, his fingers on the handle, unknowingly touching the last thing at home that his mum would ever touch, the warmth from her hand already faded.

CHAPTER TWO

Duke

Duke loves being at Pippa's house. He sits on a stool at the breakfast bar and swings his legs impatiently. Pippa's baking batches of biscuits and cakes to take to her party later. She says round food is good luck on New Year's Eve because a circle indicates the old year has come to a close and a new one is about to start. Duke doesn't care about all that – he just wants to eat them.

'I can smell the cookies are nearly ready,' he says.

'You can't *smell* something is nearly ready.' Nina doesn't look up from her newly painted pink fingernails, which she's filing into curves.

Pippa smiles. 'You've a sensitive nose.'

'A sensitive everything,' Nina says, which is pretty much what Mum might say but when Mum says 'sensitive' it sounds like a good thing. Nina makes it sound bad but then ever since she'd turned fifteen she made everything sound like the Worst. Thing. Ever.

A rush of cold air blasts into the kitchen as his parents slip through the back door.

'We're off now.'

Duke jumps down and wraps his arms around Mum's legs, his nose pressing against the fabric of her skirt. He breathes in deeply, a heavy perfume filling his throat; she doesn't usually wear any. She doesn't usually go anywhere that isn't with him. 'Do you have to go?'

'We'll be back tomorrow.'

'Why can't we stay here? With Pippa?'

'I've told you. Pippa's going to a party of her own tonight. Besides, Charlie's come up from London to spend some time with you.'

'But I hardly know him.'

'He's your brother,' Mum says, like that means Duke automatically knows him, which is stupid because he rarely sees him. 'You should go home and say hello.'

But Duke can think of several reasons why he shouldn't.

1. Charlie always pays more attention to Billie than to him.
2. Last visit, Charlie bought him a tub of jelly sweets for Easter that he couldn't eat because they contained gelatine. If he was a GOOD brother, he'd have remembered that Duke is a vegetarian and bought a chocolate egg.
3. Nina acts weird around him like she hates him but at the same time she is always trying to impress him.
4. Mum always secretly cries after he leaves even though he promises he'll visit again soon.
5. He ALWAYS breaks his promises.

'I'll be back before you know I've gone,' Mum says, which is another stupid thing. He'll know she's gone the second she walks out of the door. How will she be back before that? 'I love you.' She drops a kiss on top of his head. 'Love you too, Nina.' She opens her arms and steps towards Duke's sister, but Nina flaps her away with 'wet nails'.

Dad rolls his eyes behind her back and mouths 'hormones' at Duke, which he's been doing a lot lately whenever Nina is stroppy. He had asked Mum whether he'd get hormones too and she had said that's part of biology he is still too young for, but sometimes she says he's such an old soul for an eleven-year-old so he doesn't know whether he's too young or too old. Nina often calls him a baby because he doesn't live in the *real world* but he likes his world. The lists he makes and the random thoughts that filter through his head make him smile to himself and, when he does, Nina laughs and calls him weird, but if being happy makes you weird then he's okay with her calling him that.

Duke hugs his mum and dad, telling them he loves them, before they then leave. He is sad for about five seconds until Pippa asks him if he wants to eat the remnants of the cookie dough, which is stuck to the mixing bowl. He scoops it out with his fingers and has put half of it into his mouth when Nina says,

'It's got raw eggs in it. You'll probably die if you eat that.'

He hesitates, glancing at Pippa for reassurance. 'Nobody's going to die,' she says, adding, 'I promise.'

'If they do it's your fault now,' Nina says.

'Nina! Don't be unkind to Duke.'

Duke knows if Dad were here he'd roll his eyes and mouth 'hormones' so Duke tries not to let her words worry him but they still do. He carries on chewing, but the mix doesn't taste as sweet anymore.

*

Duke's tummy feels fluttery as he steps into his lounge. Charlie is sprawled on the sofa, his arm around a woman who he supposes is his girlfriend. He sits up quickly when they come in as though he's been caught doing something wrong like when Duke should be learning on the computer but instead is playing Minesweeper because it's more fun.

'Pippa.'

Duke doesn't know why Charlie looks so surprised to see her. She's lived next door like forever.

'Sasha, this is Pippa. We went to school together.' Charlie doesn't say hello to Duke or Nina at first. It's like he can't see anyone but Pippa, which is stupid because it's not as though they're each wearing an invisibility ring like the one in *The Hobbit*.

'Hello, Charlie.' Duke gives a little wave.

'Hello. Sorry, Sasha, this is my brother, Duke, and my sister, Nina.'

He can't be that sorry because he immediately focuses on Pippa again but Duke supposes that's okay because Charlie has two days with him and Nina and Pippa will be leaving in a minute. She isn't looking at Charlie though, she's too busy arranging the plate on the table, sliding it to the left and then the right until it's in the middle.

'How are you, Pippa?' Charlie asks.

'You know.' She shrugs, which isn't an answer at all. 'Fine. Doing okay.' She straightens up.

'Good. And how's your grandma?'

Now Pippa stares at Charlie. 'She died.'

'I didn't . . . I'm so sorry.' He crosses to the table, his arms moving as if to hug her but Pippa turns away from him. Instead, he reaches out with his hand to touch her shoulder, glances at

Sasha, leaving his arm hovering in the air in an awkward way until he lowers it and chooses the biggest cookie as though that's what he meant to do all along.

'Six months ago,' Pippa mumbles.

Charlie does this strange stepping forward and stepping back thing.

'Mum did tell you,' Duke says. 'You weren't picking up the phone, so she had to leave you a voicemail with details of the funeral. She was cross with you for not coming.'

'I don't . . . I can't have listened . . . I should have been there. Sorry.'

Pippa has tears in her eyes now. Duke doesn't like that Charlie has made her sad thinking about her grandma but while no one is looking at him he sneaks a couple of the still-warm cookies into his pocket.

'Anyway,' Pippa says too loudly as she turns to Duke. He can feel the blood rushing to his cheeks. His fingers twitch to put the cookies back but then she says, 'I've got to go and get ready for my party so Happy New Year everyone.'

It's a bit weird when she's gone but then Sasha says, 'Your manicure is very pretty,' to Nina and rather than rolling her eyes and saying something sarcastic his sister mumbles, 'Thanks.'

'I've got some baby pink lip gloss that should match,' Sasha says. 'Do you want to try it?'

Nina throws a death stare to Duke but he's hardly going to say Nina isn't allowed to wear make-up when he has stolen cookies in his pocket, is he? Duke won't tell on her the way Nina tells on him sometimes like if he'd stuck a star on his chart without doing his chores, with an 'you're not the golden boy now', which is stupid because his hair is dark, the same as Charlie's.

Sasha fetches a glittery gold bag and unzips it. 'Shall we go the whole hog? Eyes, cheeks and lips?'

'Can you teach me how to highlight properly?'

'Of course! You have gorgeous skin,' Sasha says.

Nina sits on a chair and Sasha begins dipping a brush into a pot. Duke perches awkwardly on the sofa – he wants to go to his room, but his mum always says it's rude to disappear when visitors are here but is Charlie a visitor? He is family, even if he doesn't feel like it.

Duke looks to Charlie. He's an adult; he should know what to say, what to do, but it seems he doesn't.

'Have you made any books lately?' Duke speaks first. They can't just *sit* here.

'I don't make the books, Duke. I'm a literary agent. Remember, I explained it to you last time?'

Duke shakes his head. Last time was ages ago and Duke doesn't remember the details.

'Writers send their books to me and I read them and if I think they're any good I send them to a publisher to ask if they might like to print them.'

'Why don't people send their books straight to the publishers?' Duke doesn't quite understand the point of Charlie.

'Because the publishers are very busy and they don't have time to read everything.'

Duke is sometimes very busy – he thinks of the endless columns on his reward chart on the fridge – but he always has time for books. He even gets stars for reading, which is silly because it isn't as if it's boring like the washing-up or folding his clothes.

'What if you like something and the publisher doesn't?'

'That happens sometimes. Then—'

'And what if you don't like something and don't send it but the publisher would have loved it?' It doesn't make sense to Duke. 'Mum said you wanted to write a book once?'

Charlie looks surprised. Duke wonders if this is a secret like when Nina snuck out of the window at night last week to meet someone and made him promise not to tell.

'Yeah, but . . .' Charlie shrugs.

'I didn't know you wanted to write?' For some reason Sasha is combing Nina's eyebrows – girls *are* stupid.

'When I was younger but then . . .'

'Then what?'

'Something. Nothing,' Charlie says but that doesn't make sense. How can something be nothing? 'Sasha works in publishing too.'

'I'm an editor,' Sasha says.

'What's one of those?'

'It's like when your teacher corrects your work with a red pen.'

'I don't go to school.'

'Why not?'

'It wouldn't suit me. I'm not the right personality. Nina goes because Mum says she needs the stimulation but I'm better off at home. I wouldn't be happy there.'

'But you went to school, Charlie?' Sasha asks. 'Yes, you must have because you said you went with Pippa. It's strange I know literally everything about you now but hardly anything about your childhood. Did you—'

'Nina!' Charlie says in a fake voice. 'You look so grown-up now.'

Nina glows under Charlie's praise. Sasha beams too. They don't seem to realize that he is just trying to change the subject. Mum does that a lot and Duke is well-practised at recognizing it and trying to change it back. Sasha hands Nina the mirror.

'I don't look like me.' Nina's fingers touch her face as though she's reassuring herself that she is real. When she tears her eyes away from the mirror she glares at Duke.

'What are you laughing at?' But Duke isn't laughing; he's smiling because Nina had been too, and she doesn't smile as much as she used to. It's as if Sasha has painted over the hormones and Duke can imagine them struggling to break free under the sparkly silver that surrounds Nina's eyes. Their tiny hormone feet sticking to the shiny stuff on her lips.

'All dolled up and nowhere to go,' Sasha says. 'Shall we order some pizza for lunch and watch a movie? Have our own party.'

'We don't have a TV,' Duke says.

'So . . .' Sasha asks, 'what do you do for entertainment around here?'

'I'll show you,' Duke says excitedly.

'No, it's okay,' Charlie begins but Duke is already racing into the hallway, turning to beckon the others as they follow him.

Duke pushes open another door. 'This,' he announces, 'is what we do.'

'Wow.' Sasha spins around taking everything in. The piano, the saxophone, guitars, a microphone. Everything crammed together in the space where a dining table should be.

'Yes. Wow,' Duke says proudly, wondering why Charlie and Nina aren't saying anything.

'And that?' Sasha points to the words on the gold wall written in large, black swirling letters. 'That's a bit different to Live, Laugh, Love.'

'"All The Things You Are" is Mum's favourite song. She sings it to us. Ow.' Duke rubs his ribs where Nina has jabbed her elbow. He doesn't think there is anything wrong with Mum singing them her favourite song. There are lots of different versions. When Ella Fitzgerald sang it, she made it happy, but Sarah Vaughan made it feel sad. Mum would sing it fast in the day and then slow before bed, changing the words to suit them all. They weren't a promised kiss or a breathless hush but other things; clever, funny, kind.

'Who are all these people?' Sasha studies the framed black and white photos hanging on the walls.

'They're all jazz musicians.' Duke points to one. 'That's Duke Ellington; I'm named after him although his name was Edward really. He was a pianist, but I prefer the saxophone.' Duke sticks his finger towards another. 'That's Nina Simone. She was a singer. Our Nina can sing, and I think she's just as good although sometimes she'd rather just play her clarinet. And that—' he leads Sasha to another photo '—is Charlie Parker. He was a saxophonist but Charlie's better at guitar and piano, aren't you, Charlie?'

'I don't play anymore,' Charlie says.

'You don't play?' Duke's mouth drops open, his hands on his cheeks.

'We're not all as obsessed as you,' Nina jumps in. 'Honestly—' she rolls her eyes at Charlie '—Duke is basically always playing. It's because he hasn't got a life.'

'Music *is* my life. Well, music and Billie. I would literally die without them.'

'Dramatic, much,' Nina mutters.

Duke stares intently at Charlie, trying to understand him. 'So, you don't play *and* you don't write anymore?'

'No.'

'This is so cool,' Sasha claps her hands together. 'Can you play something for me?'

Charlie says no at the same time Duke says yes.

26

'Please.' She smiles at Charlie, but he doesn't smile back.

'No.'

She glances at the wall again. 'All the things you are, Charlie: boring—' she counts them on her fingers '—secretive, party-pooper . . .'

Duke imagines someone on the toilet pooping out a party. The bowl overflowing with balloons and streamers. His dad trying to clear it with his plunger. He smiles.

'What are you smiling at?' Sasha asks him.

'Oh, he's always smiling to himself. He's weird,' Nina says.

Duke forgets his daydream and looks to Charlie to ask him again if they can play a song but he has left the room. He *is* a fun sponge.

'Nina?' Sasha asks. 'I'd love to hear you sing?'

'Umm. Okay.' Nina switches on the amp and Duke picks up the saxophone. It's heavy but he's stronger than he looks.

'"I Wan'na Be Like You"?' he asks his sister.

'No. That's babyish—'

'From *The Jungle Book*? I love that film!' Sasha says. Duke loved it too. They'd watched it at the house of one of the other home-ed kids.

Nina tucks her hair behind her ears. 'Okay.' She begins to sing a slowed down version, not the fast tempo one they'd sometimes do with Dad on guitar and Mum batting a tambourine against her thigh where they'd all dance and shake their bottoms like Baloo the bear.

He doesn't enjoy it as much.

*

Later, they eat Veggie Volcano pizza straight from the box and afterwards Billie licks the grease from Duke's fingers.

'Billie Holiday!' Sasha suddenly shrieks, making them all laugh. 'Your mum really goes all in, doesn't she?'

'Not always, no,' Charlie mutters.

Sasha asks if they have any games. Duke suggests KerPlunk but Nina complains it takes too long to set up. She loves Twister but Duke's arms and legs aren't as long as everybody else's – he's small for his age – and so they play Monopoly. Duke is the banker because Mum always says he's good at maths.

Charlie wins.

Duke had been determined to stay up until midnight, but he must have fallen asleep because he wakes up in his own bed. At first, he isn't sure what has disturbed him. It is still dark outside. But then there's the sound of the bell, quickly followed by a frantic knocking on the front door. Duke pulls his covers up to his chin and clutches them tightly. His stomach spins like the washing machine churning up the fiery jalapeños he had eaten. But it isn't just the chillies making him feel this way.

He's scared.

The banging brings with it a sense that somehow his life is about to be forever changed. No one ever knocks on the door in the middle of the night.

Something is wrong.

He closes his eyes and tries to imagine his mum perching on his bed, her hands smoothing his hair as she softly sings 'All The Things You Are'.

Funny.

Brave.

But this isn't funny and he doesn't feel brave.

Somehow, he knows that his world is disintegrating, turning to dust, just like the stolen cookies he had forgotten to eat that will now be just crumbs in his pocket.

The knocking comes again, loud and urgent.

Duke hides under his covers but he can still hear it.

CHAPTER THREE

Charlie

Charlie cannot sleep.

By the pale moonlight penetrating the thin curtains he watches Billie, curled in her basket, snoring gently. Her legs twitch furiously. He wonders what she is chasing in her dreams and whether she'll catch them. Charlie's dreams have always seemed so far out of reach, unobtainable, but then he'd met Sasha who is his future. However, lying on the uncomfortable sofa bed he can't help turning over his past.

Pippa had been friendly albeit distant earlier but then what did he expect? He had hurt her immeasurably once and that, coupled with not coming home for her grandma's funeral, is inexcusable, unforgivable. It isn't only that he should have been here to support Pippa; her grandma was such a big part of his own childhood.

Sasha rolls over, clutching the duvet to her chest. Although not their usual London party, she seemed to have had a good time playing board games, eating pizza, more relaxed around Duke and Nina than he was.

It saddens him that he barely knows his siblings. What they

think. What they feel. What makes them happy. Separating himself from this house, distancing himself from the memories of what had happened to him when he lived here has meant he has missed out on so much.

He only sees Duke and Nina two or three times a year and each time they have changed enormously.

On the surface today Duke had reminded him a lot of himself and it was this that had created an awkwardness between them. Charlie didn't want to think of the child he had once been.

He had softened when Duke had fallen asleep on the sofa, his head lolling against Charlie's shoulder. He'd tenderly scooped up his brother, thankfully not as heavy as he'd feared, and carried him up to his bedroom, the space that used to be Charlie's before Duke came along. Charlie had been twenty-two and had already left home when Duke was born but it still stung that his mum had given his room away. Now it was decorated a bright blue rather than grubby white, but bookcases still lined the walls. After settling Duke into bed, Charlie had crouched and scanned the spines, squinting in the dim light that rolled in from the hallway. The shelves were groaning under the weight of tatty paperbacks, faux-leather hardbacks, even some old encyclopaedias. Duke had eclectic taste. Charlie made a mental note to send him some books when he returned to London.

He hadn't been sure how to relate to Nina, but Sasha had bonded with her in a big sisterly sort of way. They haven't planned children of their own. He isn't cut out for parenting and that is his last thought before someone raps sharply, insistently, on the front door.

He sits bolt upright, his stomach churning with both the fizzy elderflower they had drunk and a creeping sense of fear.

Nothing good ever comes from a 5 a.m. visitor.

The banging comes again and again and he rushes to answer the door before it wakes Nina and Duke, flicking on the hall light as he runs. A rush of cold air blasts into his face as he blinks in the brightness. In front of him are two men. He steps backwards away from their uniforms, their sombre expressions. It is the second time he's been faced with the police and after that first time his life had changed immeasurably as he knows it will again now.

After tonight, nothing will ever be the same.

He shakes his head.

Don't tell me.

'Mr Johnson?'

'Walker.' Charlie had never changed his surname when his mum had married Bo.

'Can we come in?'

Don't tell me.

Charlie's legs shake as he leads them into the lounge. Sasha is pulling on a jumper. Before he can cross to her side Nina and Duke pound down the stairs. They run to Charlie and he offers them each a hand, and their smaller fingers squeeze around his.

United as siblings for perhaps the first time ever.

Don't tell me.

'Veronica and William Johnson are your parents?'

'Ronnie and Bo.' Charlie never understood how Bo came from William. He had asked him once but he can't remember the answer. He does remember, though, that Bo had once told him if he were to pick a stage name it would have been Woody. Woody Shaw. But Bo . . . This isn't the thing that his racing thoughts should be focusing on, but it is, somehow believing that if he can solve the puzzle of the name before the officer speaks again Bo might appear. His mum might magically materialise.

Don't tell me.

'I'm afraid I have some bad news.'

CHAPTER FOUR

Nina

It is the sharp wind whipping against Nina's face that causes her eyes to stream. It isn't tears. She cannot cry.

Her parents are dead.

She doesn't believe it. She won't believe it.

Once she'd spent a holiday here in Colesby Bay. She remembers the vibrancy, the colour. Staking their claim on the crowded beach, spreading a tartan picnic rug and laying out the thick sandwiches they had made together in their caravan. Dad shelling eggs, Duke mashing them with a fork, Nina mixing in the mayo while Mum buttered fresh white bread. Later, Mum had been starfished on an orange towel soaking up the sun while her dad shrieked with mock fear as Nina and Duke advanced towards him, freezing sea water sloshing out of red plastic buckets.

Now it's bleak, almost deserted.

They always said they'd return but it was such a long journey and Duke got carsick, and instead they'd spent the last few years alternating between Cleethorpes or Mablethorpe.

Now she is back and it's the last place on earth she wants to be.

Again, her eyes scan the ocean as she wills her parents to

appear. How could they have gone out on a boat at midnight to watch the fireworks? It's ridiculous, all the things her parents told her that she should not, that she could not do, and then they go and throw away their own rule book and . . . In her head she can hear her mum humming 'All The Things You Are' and she shakes the sound away. It turns out that all the things her parents are, were reckless, stupid, selfish.

Dead.

She won't accept it until their bodies are found. The coastguard here, Alan, has repeated the same things as the police had when they'd stood uncomfortably in her house early this morning.

The tide and the weather pattern had swept her parents out to sea when the rickety rowing boat they had foolishly gone out in to watch the midnight fireworks had capsized. Bodies – *bodies* – aren't always washed up but this is unpredictable; there is no way of knowing. What they did know with certainty was that the temperature of the freezing air and frigid water would have killed her parents along with the bass player and keyboard player of the band – Hal and Fingers – who had been with them. It would have been quick, they were told, as though that was some comfort. It was only Marty, the drummer who had cancer, who had survived. The one who had chosen to stay on the beach.

Marty stands by their side now. He's told them what had happened over and over; sometimes they've asked questions and sometimes they've just listened. Eventually they have all run out of words. None of them speak. Not Charlie, her brother, who is an adult but doesn't seem to know what to say. Not Duke who is silent, face white, dry eyes wide. Not Pippa who drove them here at 6 a.m. after the news. Luckily, she'd been the designated driver last night so she hadn't consumed any alcohol at her party.

Not like her parents who had apparently been drunk.

Her parents are dead.

Alan, the coastguard, eventually wanders off, followed by Marty who wants to get back to his family in Sheffield. He promises to keep in touch. Nina, Charlie, Duke and Pippa remain clumped together on the beach, their sight trained on the horizon, the grubby sky merging with the grey, choppy sea, watching, waiting. Billie, sensing something is wrong, doesn't tug at her lead to be free; instead she sits on Nina's foot but Nina's extremities are so cold she can barely feel her fingers or toes.

Seagulls screech out their sorrow for the fractured family. The odd passer-by stumbles across the uneven sand, wellington boots crunching over shells and pebbles. Sometimes they call out 'Happy New Year' to the group. Nina wants to tell them to fuck off but her teeth are clattering together so hard she can't speak. She can't stop shivering. The dampness in the air sneaks between her skin and her clothes, chilling her flesh until there isn't a single part of her that feels warm. She wishes she were home. She wishes she could pretend the last few hours have never happened. That she'd been able to run away to London like Sasha had after the police had left. That's probably not a fair way to put it; she'd offered to come to Colesby Bay but she has an important meeting tomorrow in London and, because there is limited public transport today, Charlie insisted she leave. Nina wishes she were anywhere but on this beach with the biting wind and the myriad footprints imprinted on the damp sand. She studies each one wondering if they belonged to her mum and dad, but although she can dismiss some as too big or too small, with others she just can't tell and she wants to hold back the tide, order the sky not to rain, so she can preserve them all.

Her parents are under that freezing grey water along with the seaweed and the fishes. As she thinks this it sparks a memory. She glances at Charlie. Longing to slip her hand inside of his. He is only inches away from her, but emotionally they're an ocean apart.

When she was small she had idolised him. He'd called her 'little sis' once and she'd misheard. Misunderstood.

'Little Fish?'

He had laughed, ruffled her hair as she'd smiled up at him, asking, 'Does that make you Big Fish?'

It had stuck for a while, those nicknames for each other. Their own private joke. But once Charlie had moved away he'd seemed to forget about her. He probably can't even remember the affection that was once between them.

Or perhaps she's remembering it wrong.

He hadn't thought twice about abandoning her. He hadn't called her Little Fish for years. He probably doesn't even remember that he once did.

Big Fish.

Big fucking disappointment more like, and now her parents have abandoned her too, or that's what it feels like. Charlie's gaze is still fixed on the horizon. Oblivious to her pain. Oblivious to her.

She crosses her arms and seeks out Duke.

He is crouching down, picking up shells and dusting the sand from them before he stuffs them into his pocket. He wanders down the beach, growing smaller until Pippa calls him back.

'Let's go and get some food.' Pippa's hand rests gently on her arm but she shakes her head. She can't leave here; she can't leave *them* here. Out there. Alone.

Her parents are dead.

She hadn't even bothered saying goodbye to them last night.

She clamps her lips together, afraid she might say it now; it sounds so final.

She doesn't believe it. She won't believe it.

'Nina?' Charlie touches her arm. 'It's time to go.'

She shakes her head but he gently tugs at her arm and numbly she allows him to lead her to the steps, which carry her away from the sand and the sea and the memories of holidays past: her and Duke digging a moat for the castle they had made; Dad fetching ice creams that were half-melted and dripping down the cones by the time he reached them; Mum tipping her face to the sun – *it feels good to be alive* – rubbing cream into her skin. Nina doesn't say goodbye to any of it as they settle themselves on wooden benches on the pier. She clings tightly to her memories as Charlie and Pippa fetch chips. Cardboard cups of hot chocolate, clumps of powder rising to the surface. Duke cuddles up to her, wrapping his arms around her waist and resting his head on her shoulder and, for the first time in a long time, she lets him.

Only Billie has an appetite and after she's sampled each of their chips, licking her lips in delight at the unexpected treat, there is nothing left to do but go home, but home is where the heart is and Nina's heart is here with the big expanse of sea and her lost parents but still she trudges on her tired, heartbroken legs to the car.

'I'll be back in a sec.' Charlie dashes into a seafront shop, the yellow and orange bunting outside flapping furiously in the wind. He returns minutes later with a box of fudge as though they're on some sort of day trip. It is this, more than anything else today, that springs tears to Nina's eyes.

He doesn't care.

She ignores him the next time he speaks, and the time after that, until he stops speaking at all.

On the way home Duke sleeps, his head jerking upright every now and then before settling back against the window. Nina wishes she could at least doze. Block out what happened.

Forget.

Her parents are dead.

Pippa fiddles with the radio, settling on Classic FM before switching it to an eighties pop station five minutes later. Madonna is *True Blue*. Nina is too.

'Do you mind?' she asks. 'I'm so tired. I need the noise to stay awake.'

Nina does mind. In this moment, she hates music. She hates the way it has torn her life apart. Why couldn't Mum and Dad have stayed home with them last night? 'Putting the band back together' – her dad had grinned as though he was a teenager. He had responsibilities. A life.

Them.

She glances at Duke and she suddenly hates him too. Remembering the way he had hugged Mum and Dad goodbye, telling them both he loved them. She thought of the way she'd dismissed them, shooing them away when they'd tried to hug her, prioritising her manicure over them. In a rage she began to scratch furiously at the pink nail varnish, her nail slipping onto the soft skin of her fingers, making it bleed.

She welcomes the pain. Forgetting the polish, she scratches at her forearms, feeling the release of pressure in her head as her nails rake her skin.

The haze has lifted and the sun shines brightly welcoming in the new year, white clouds blow across the sky with speed. They drive past a hill teeming with families, many walking dogs. From the boot drifts a soft whine from Billie letting them know that she too would like to be running over the sodden grass, feeling the wind against her fur.

Nina reaches behind her headrest and Billie pushes her nose against her palm before licking the remains of the salt and vinegar from her fingers. A red and green kite bobs across the sky and she thinks of her parents' bodies bobbing in the sea.

What will happen to them? She both wants and doesn't want to know.

'Charlie, can I borrow your phone?' Against her jeans she wipes her hands dry from Billie's saliva.

'In a sec, I'm just replying to Sasha.'

Typical that he's putting someone else before her.

Pippa's hand leaves the steering wheel. She picks up her mobile from the centre console, unlocks it with her thumb before passing it back to Nina. Their eyes meet in the rear-view mirror and the panic in her subsides momentarily. At least somebody still cares about her.

Nina opens a webpage and googles. Horror rises in her stomach as she reads that if her parents remain in the sea then in about a week their skin will absorb the water and it will peel away from the underlying tissue. Fish and crabs will nibble at their flesh.

'Stop!' She clasps one hand over her mouth as she begins to open the door, not caring that the car is still moving.

Pippa swerves onto a grass verge. Nina only just makes it out of the car in time before she vomits.

It is Pippa who rubs her back in circular motions, Pippa who scoops her hair away from her mouth. Charlie remains in the car, his head in his hands. She despises him. She despises everyone.

At last she stops retching, her stomach muscles aching. Her

legs are shaky but Pippa settles her back into her seat, fastening her seatbelt.

They begin to move again, this time slower, the window cracked open, Nina knows she stinks. She has globules of sick down the front of her shirt. Incredibly Duke is still asleep.

They've been travelling for hours when her brother wakes up. There is only about forty-five minutes left of their journey.

Duke yawns and wipes his mouth with the back of his hand before he asks, 'What's going to happen now?'

'We're nearly home,' Nina says.

'I mean after. Who's going to look after us?'

'I think . . .' Nina pauses and waits for Charlie to jump in. He doesn't. She glares at his profile as he stares out of the window. From the stiffness of his shoulders, the flush that spreads across his neck, she knows he's heard but he isn't saying anything.

Why isn't he saying anything? Panic beats a drum on Nina's heart.

'Charlie,' she says sharply. 'Who's going to look after me and Duke?'

CHAPTER FIVE

Charlie

By the time they are home, the sky has darkened to the total blackness that only winter brings. The stars are invisible although Charlie knows they are still there, hidden by clouds. You don't always need to see something to know that it exists, do you? All the time Charlie has lived in London he has known that Mum and Bo are in the house he grew up in, living out their lives. It's inconceivable that now, suddenly, they are gone.

Pippa cuts the engine. 'Let's get the kids inside.' She sounds exhausted, looks exhausted. She has driven for twelve hours today after scant sleep last night. Charlie experiences a flush of shame that it hadn't occurred to him to offer to take over. He had spent much of the journey silent and shocked. Unable to comfort Nina when she was being sick at the side of the road, unable to reassure Duke when he'd asked who would look after him.

What is he going to do?

They traipse inside. In the lounge, the lights on the Christmas tree twinkle. A breeze from Pippa closing the front door causes a card to sway on the mantlepiece before it flutters to the floor. Charlie picks it up. On the front a fat robin on pure white snow;

inside it wishes 'Ronnie, Bo, Nina and Duke a Very Merry Christmas'. There is no mention of him. Rationally he knows this is because he is an adult living away from home but he is not feeling rational. He snaps the rest of the cards down; this family of four is now a family of two, or are they a three? Charlie doesn't know where he fits. Where any of them belong now. Their world has changed forever.

'Charlie—' Pippa lightly touches his arm '—what do you want to do?'

His head throbs as he thinks about funerals and childcare and all of the things he doesn't feel equipped for but then Pippa adds, 'The children are tired but they haven't eaten since the chips and they only picked at those,' and he realizes she is asking about now, not the future, which stretches out undefined and uncertain.

Duke and Nina are in the hallway. Still wearing their coats, still wearing their shoes, the way he had yesterday. They are now the strangers in their own home, awaiting instructions.

He crouches and unzips Duke's yellow anorak, eases his arms from the sleeves. He unlaces his brother's trainers and tugs them off before lining them up on the shoe rack next to matching tartan slippers that his parents will never wear again.

Nina pulls off her own things before moping into the kitchen, clicking on the light and staring around as though she has never seen it before.

Charlie gathers the pizza boxes that are strewn across the worktops; they need to go in the outside bin. It's unfathomable that just twenty-four hours ago they had been playing games.

Laughing.

Had they been laughing when his parents had slipped under

the icy surface of the brutal sea? Had they made jokes as salt water had filled their lungs?

'Charlie?' Pippa gently takes the boxes from him. He has gripped them so tightly in his hand that his thumb has punctured the cardboard.

'Right.' He turns to Nina and Duke. 'Shall I make some food?'

'Food?' Nina glares at him as though it is all his fault. She turns and storms upstairs. He hears her thundering footsteps and then the creak of springs as she hurls herself onto her bed.

'Duke?' Charlie asks.

'I'm tired.'

'Let's get you upstairs then.'

Charlie leads his brother up to his room. Helps him into his pyjamas. Tucks him under the duvet. Duke hasn't cleaned his teeth but Charlie thinks that's the least of his worries.

'What's going to happen now?' Duke whispers.

'I'll read you a story,' Charlie says, deliberately misunderstanding.

He scans the bookcase; Duke has the complete set of J. R. R. Tolkien books but they're too weighty and he doesn't have the focus. Instead, he settles on Roald Dahl's *Charlie and the Chocolate Factory*. There is a comforting familiarity about the story that his mother used to read to him that momentarily eases the ache in Charlie's chest. His eyes flicker between the pages and Duke's face, noticing the way his mouth lolls open when he finally falls asleep.

In the hallway, Charlie closes the door gently behind him. He can hear anguished weeping coming from behind Nina's door. She hasn't cried all day and now it seems that she cannot stop. Charlie raises his hand to knock but then lets it fall to his side. What can he possibly say to make this any better?

Still, he doesn't feel he can leave her so he sits on the carpet, his spine hard against the wall waiting until her sobs grow quieter until, finally, they stop altogether. She has cried herself to sleep and her silence is a huge and shameful relief for Charlie who pulls himself to his feet and trudges downstairs. Pippa is sitting at the table, a plate of crumbs and discarded crusts in front of her.

'I made myself a sandwich. Didn't know how long you would be. I've fed Billie too. Drink?'

'Please.'

Pippa automatically makes him a tea while his taste buds scream for a whisky, vodka, oblivion. But he cannot drink, empty stomach or otherwise. He feels the pinch of guilt for even thinking about eating but the gnawing hunger in his stomach is making him feel sick. He makes toast, spreading it thickly with butter, thinly with Marmite, but every bite feels tasteless and terrible in his mouth.

'Do you want to talk about it?' Pippa asks when he pushes his empty plate away.

'Yes. No.' Charlie links his hands behind his head and stares up at the ceiling.

What is he going to do?

'I'll help. Any way I can. I'm here for you.'

'I can't ask that of you. I wasn't there for you. Your grandma. I'm sorry.' Charlie doesn't offer an excuse; there aren't any. Pippa is his oldest friend; there was a time she was his only friend, and missing the funeral was reprehensible. He doesn't always reply to texts from Mum or listen to his voicemails, instead placing messages into the box marked 'home' he keeps in the furthest corners of his mind and firmly closing the lid. Now that he is here the box is wide open once more. Is there ever any escape from the past?

'It's okay. She was eighty-six.'

'That doesn't make it hurt less.'

'No. But it didn't come as a terrible shock though. Not like . . . this.'

'I'm sorry,' he says again, his eyes conveying that he isn't just apologising for her grandma but for everything. All of it. Her eyes hold his, telling him that she understands.

But does she forgive?

'It's late,' she says, although it's only ten o'clock. It has seemed an interminable day and part of him hopes it never ends because, if it does, he has to wake up tomorrow and live it all again. The shock, the sorrow, the worry. A Groundhog Day of grief.

What is he going to do?

He walks Pippa to the door.

'I'll come back in the morning and help you with breakfast.' She pulls him into a hug.

Her kindness causes tears to form behind his eyes. After giving her a gentle squeeze he pulls away. He cannot fall apart. Pippa wends her way down his garden path, and then her own, not running like she used to when they were six, pigtails bouncing, gap-toothed grin wide.

When she is safely inside, he heads back into the kitchen and pours himself a large measure of Bo's whisky, raising the glass to his lips, salivating at the smell, before he changes his mind, tipping it down the sink.

He cannot fall apart. Not today. Not now.

In the lounge, he collapses onto the sofa. Billie jumps up and lies next to him, her head on his stomach. Rhythmically he strokes her, dislodging the particles of dried sand imbedded in her fur from her roll on the beach. Smelling of damp, she gazes at him, trustingly, until her eyelids droop and she begins

46

to softly snore, oblivious to the fact that her life has also changed immeasurably.

He takes out his phone and calls Sasha. She picks up on the fifth ring. He can hear music in the background, chatter.

Laughter.

'Just a sec,' she says. Charlie waits until she is somewhere quieter.

'You went to Simon's then?' Charlie had forgotten about the New Year's Day party. London seems a world away.

'Yes. I was sitting in the flat driving myself crazy thinking about you, the meeting tomorrow about New York. What I'll do if I don't get the transfer when you have yours. Sorry, this isn't what you want to be talking about right now. I . . . I'm not sure what to say to you.'

'There's nothing you can say. Have you told everyone about . . . you know?'

'I've told everyone you're sick. I wasn't sure if . . . How are you anyway?'

'Tired. Sad.' Small words but he can't describe the enormity of the emotions that sweep through him on a loop from his head to his toes, making his scalp tight and his body hot.

'And the children?'

'Nina is angry. Duke hasn't cried yet and that's a worry but . . . I don't know. It's such a shock.'

'It's . . . they seemed like lovely people, your parents. I am so sorry, Charlie. I wish I'd stayed with you. It was all such a rush.'

'That's okay. I insisted you left. The meeting is important. There's no point both of us taking time off work. You've a pile of manuscripts to read.'

'Yes. Back to normal in the morning.'

But Charlie can't ever imagine anything feeling normal again. He hears someone call Sasha's name in the background.

'I've got to go. I'll call you later,' she says.

'I'm going to crash. Let's catch up tomorrow.'

'Okay. Do you know when you'll be home?' she asks but Charlie doesn't know where home is now.

Nina. Duke. Billie. Somebody has to take care of them, but it doesn't have to be him, does it?

What is he going to do?

CHAPTER SIX

Nina

Nina feels as though she has woken in somebody else's skin. Somebody else's life. Her arms sting from her self-inflicted scratches. Her house full of unaccustomed sounds. Not Mum singing as she dresses, or Dad whistling as he shaves but Charlie speaking in a low voice while a different radio station to the one her mum listened to plays.

Her parents are dead.

She turns the thought over but all she feels is . . . disbelief. A small seed of hope begins to unfurl inside her mind. Perhaps Charlie is talking to them on the phone right now. She flings back the duvet, still wearing yesterday's clothes, and pounds down the stairs. They'll laugh about this one day: *remember the time we thought you'd drowned.* Not yet, of course, but one day, when they are all sitting around the table, shaking cornflakes into bowls, arguing over who should fetch the milk.

'Charlie?' She runs into the kitchen. Pippa is humming softly along to 'Don't Look Back in Anger' while she whisks eggs.

'He's in the garden.'

It's freezing outside. The lawn sparkles with frost, the sky almost white.

Charlie leans against the wall under Nina's window.

'Is that—'

'Sasha,' he mouths, and that seed of hope curls tightly into itself once more.

Nina trudges back inside and slumps into a chair. Pippa places a mug of hot chocolate in front of her and gives her shoulder a squeeze. That one, small gesture says more than words could. It says *I'm sorry. I'm here. I wish I could change things, but I can't.*

It is only when Duke climbs onto her lap that she notices he is there. She wraps her arms around him and he leans back into her. They haven't sat like this for years but she feels that he's all she has and she clings to him tightly. What will happen to them now? Will they be sent to a children's home? Separated? She supposes somebody might want to adopt Duke; he's small for his age and, she grudgingly concedes, cute. But her? Who would want a moody teenager? She wants to ask Charlie again but she is afraid of the answer.

After breakfast they go for a walk because they can't think what else to do. They go to the pocket park because no one ever goes there when there's a much larger space five minutes down the road. Duke holds Pippa's hand. Charlie unclips Billie's lead but she doesn't run off and explore like she'd normally do, twitching nose sniffing everything, she stays close to them, her head down. Instinctively, in the way animals do, she knows something is wrong. She too is sad.

At home Pippa tells them she's going to peel some veg for lunch.

'Want to help?' she asks Duke and he nods, his hair sticking up at all angles. Nobody has reminded him to brush it this morning.

'I suppose we should start . . . you know . . .' Charlie looks to Nina. 'Telling people. Have you got a piece of paper and a pen?'

Nina fetches the pad from the kitchen and a biro. On the first page is a shopping list. Mum's writing. The same swirling script that Nina would find inside of her birthday and Christmas cards – **lots of love** – but now Mum will never write anything new again. She runs her fingers over each word – aubergine, courgettes, mozzarella, basil – and wonders what Mum was planning on cooking.

'So . . .' Charlie trails off.

'There's the home-ed lot,' Nina says. 'I haven't got any numbers but they've got a group on Facebook. There's . . . umm, Dad's work, I guess. There's couple of people from there he used to go to the pub with occasionally but . . .' she screws her face as she tries to recall the names but she's never paid attention and for that she feels ashamed. 'Neither of them had any friends really. They preferred to be with each other.'

'In their own little world. It's a comfort that . . . you know, they were together,' Charlie says.

'A comfort?' Nina tries to force a sarcastic laugh but it sticks in her throat.

'Not . . . you know what I mean. They couldn't bear to be separated, could they?'

Nina thinks of the embarrassment they caused her at parents' evenings, sports days. The way they kissed, held hands constantly. Their love was complete. She doesn't have to think very hard about who she'd choose to spend her last few days with but this is not the right time and they are not the right person for a million different reasons. Still, for a brief moment she had thought she too might have experienced love but it is now buried under a mountain of grief and regret.

'There's Aunt Violet, I suppose,' Charlie cuts through her thoughts.

'She hated Dad.'

'I know, but—'

'She called him a failed rock star. Do you know how much he was hurt by that?'

'I do, yes. I know how much Bo dreamed of—'

'And it wasn't like he didn't provide for us. He got a *proper* job, didn't he? In the end. So what if it didn't pay a lot. We managed.'

'I think Violet just wanted more than *managed* for Mum. After my dad . . . I don't know, she just wanted better.'

'*Better?*' Nina knows she is directing her anger at the wrong person.

'Sorry. That came out wrong. Look. Let's not fight. Violet is Mum's sister and she has a right to know.'

'Please don't call her.' Nina hears the desperation in her voice but the last thing she wants is that . . . cow here. She'd overheard Mum talking to Dad about her before, how she'd always said 'she knew it would end in tears'. It would all end in tears. 'She'll gloat.'

'Nina, she won't gloat. She'll be devastated.'

Nina glares at him.

Charlie sighs. 'Let's just put a pin in Violet—'

'Like a voodoo doll?' Nina asks.

'Like we'll talk about her later. Now who else is there?'

'I can't think of anybody. There's no family and . . . God, that's pitiful. Work, home-ed and Aunt Violet are basically all the people Mum knew.'

'I don't believe that. There was a mantlepiece full of Christmas cards.'

They read each one, mostly common names that could belong

to anyone, a few that Nina recognizes but she doesn't know how to contact them.

She has seen her parents for every single day of her fifteen years but, when it comes down to it, it's sad how little she knows them.

'Does Mum have an address book?' Charlie asks.

'What's that?'

'You know. Before the days of technology people would write down their contacts somewhere.'

'Oh. I dunno.'

'I'll look downstairs. Can you go and check her room?'

'I don't want—'

'Please, Nina.' Charlie sounds so tired. So desperate. 'Okay,' he says when she doesn't answer. 'I'll do it.'

'No,' she snaps. As much as she doesn't want to rummage through her mum's things, she doesn't want anyone else to touch them, ever.

'Thanks,' Charlie says.

'Whatever.' She tries to stomp up the stairs to demonstrate she is still not happy but she doesn't have the energy.

Sickness swells in her stomach as she stands outside of her parents' bedroom. She has to take three deep breaths before she can even push open the door. Her eyes are drawn to the bed she would clamber onto as a toddler, a Beatrix Potter book tucked under her arm, often dragging her cuddly Peter Rabbit by the ear. He wasn't really a proper Peter. She had fiercely, vocally and repeatedly expressed her desire for one but her parents couldn't afford branded merchandise. Instead, Mum had picked up a plain-looking bunny from a second-hand toy stall on the local market.

'No,' Nina had stamped her foot. 'Not Peter.'

Her mum had smiled and paid for him before dropping him into her bag.

'I hate him,' Nina had said.

Later, she had seen him, pegged on the washing line, water drip-drip-dripping from his fur. Her memories are hazy but she knows that while she had lain in bed that night there had been the thrum of the sewing machine coming from downstairs. She recalls her delight when she had woken in the morning to find the rabbit on the end of her bed, wearing a smart blue jacket – looking very much like Peter. She had pressed him to her chest, whispering that she loved him into his long ears. What she can't remember now is whether she said thank you to her mum. Whether she told her that she loved her with as much enthusiasm she'd shown her soft toy.

She collects Peter now from the bottom of her wardrobe where she had stuffed him when she grew too old to have him on display but didn't quite feel ready to throw him away. She pads back to her parents' room and this time she crosses the threshold. She climbs on the bed and curls her knees to her chest, her arms wrapped around the rabbit.

'Thank you,' she whispers. But it's too little. Too late. The pain of regret builds. She trails her fingers down her arms before digging her nails in hard, dislodging the scabs that had formed yesterday, but the release doesn't last as long as it had the day before and so she presses her face against her mum's pillow and breathes in the smell of her; not perfume and not shampoo, just . . . Mum.

'I'm so sorry.' She begins to cry. She is sorry for it all, for not telling her parents how much she loved them. How much she appreciated them. Most of all, she is sorry she never said goodbye. It is a long time before her body stops shaking, both the rabbit and the pillowcase drenched with her tears.

Eventually she sits up, rubs her sore eyes. Slowly she drinks it all in. The make-up spread across Mum's dressing table. She only ever wore it on special occasions.

A birthday.

A party.

A drunken midnight boat trip.

In front of the mirror, Nina twists the lipstick and coats her mouth with the almost imperceptible nude. Mum had made such an effort – had Dad told her that she looked beautiful? Probably; he adored her. Why hadn't Nina told her mum she had looked nice instead of flapping her away with still-wet nails, as though she was nothing? She runs her finger over the bronze eyeshadow with the gold flecks and tries to imagine it on her mum. There is a brief, horrible moment when she can't quite recall the colour of Mum's eyes before she remembers they were the exact shade of Cadbury's milk chocolate. She sinks onto the stool, her heart beating furiously. Realizing that sometime in the future, not today, but sometime, the nuances that make up her parents will fade from her mind. The sound of their laughs. The tone of their voices. It will all gradually slip away until all she is left with is a 2D image, a flat snapshot in her mind of the people they once were.

Her dad's clothes are heaped on a chair in the corner – and he told her to be tidy. She picks up his navy cable-knit jumper and slips it over her head, feeling the scratch of wool against the cuts on her arms. The sleeves hang down over her hands.

On the back of the bedroom door are matching dressing gowns, white and towelling.

Everything is just as they left it as though at any moment they could come back. Nina feels uncomfortable. Intrusive. She pulls open her mum's bedside cabinet drawer and half-heartedly rummages through it for an address book. She is almost certain her mum won't have one. Her world was made up of this house, this family. Her heart and head always full of Dad, no room for anyone else. She slides the door shut. She doesn't want to do this. She doesn't want to inadvertently uncover anything personal that might make her think about her mum any differently.

Nina's mind turns to morbid thoughts. What if she has an accident? Who would go through her room?

Nina has secrets of her own.

Things she wants to keep hidden.

CHAPTER SEVEN

Duke

Duke wakes, his legs sticky, pyjamas and sheet soaked.

He hasn't wet the bed in years and he doesn't know what to do. Who to tell? His parents aren't here anymore and that is because of him, he thinks. His fault. Nina calls him weird sometimes and she is right. He still hasn't cried – not because he doesn't feel sad but because the sadness is stuck somewhere and it won't come out. Not out of his mouth anyway.

He begins to peel his pyjamas off. Nina hasn't stopped crying. He hears her now, through the wall, and he knows he can't ask her how to work the washing machine. He's too embarrassed to ask Charlie.

Duke dresses. His skin itches as it dries. He should probably have a bath – he hasn't had one since the day before New Year's Eve and that's four days ago now but nobody has told him to have one.

He bundles his sheets and pyjamas in his arms and creeps out onto the landing. Downstairs he stuffs everything into the machine and then he puts the green balls in that Mum uses that are supposed to get your clothes clean but don't always. He jabs at the buttons, watching the numbers on the display jump from thirty, to forty, to fifty, wondering what they mean.

'Hey.' Pippa touches his shoulder. He spins around, feeling his face glow hot. He hadn't heard her come in but then she's here pretty much all of the time at the moment. 'What are you washing?'

He can't think of a suitable lie. 'My sheets,' he mumbles.

'Did you have an accident?' she asks. Duke wonders how one word can mean so many different consequences: wet sheets; a capsized boat. He nods.

'I won't tell anyone. I promise,' she says but how can Duke trust her? On New Year's Eve when they had made cookies and he began to eat the dough Nina had said, 'It's got raw eggs in it. You'll probably die if you eat that.'

Pippa had promised him, 'Nobody's going to die,' but they did, didn't they?

'If they do it's your fault now,' Nina had said and so he must be to blame, mustn't he? If he hadn't been a greedy pig and eaten that dough, then Mum and Dad might still be here? Mum always talked a lot about karma and fate. He isn't quite sure how it works but she had always said the universe listened to everything.

'Duke, why don't you go and have a shower and I'll see if there's any more laundry and make your bed?'

'And wash my hair?' he asks.

'And wash your hair.' She ruffles it.

Showers aren't fun, not like baths, and it doesn't take Duke long. In his room he dresses before heading downstairs. The kitchen is empty, the lounge too.

'Charlie? Pippa?' There's no reply.

Duke runs back upstairs. All the bedroom doors are open.

Where is everyone? Every time Charlie, Nina or Pippa are out of sight, a jumping bean of anxiety hops around his tummy at the thought they might never come back.

From the bathroom he can hear a noise. He sits cross-legged outside of the door and waits.

When Nina opens the door, she snaps, 'You could have used the downstairs loo.'

'I don't need the toilet,' he says.

'Weirdo.' She's cross but he doesn't know why. He has only heard the tinkling of wee. It isn't as though she was having a poo or anything.

He heads back to the kitchen. Pippa opens the back door with her elbow, her arms full of vegetables. 'I just nipped home to fetch supplies.' She smiles.

'Where's Charlie?'

'He's outside, Sasha's here.'

'Is she staying?'

Pippa shrugs. 'I guess so.'

Duke is glad. He hugs Sasha around her waist when she steps inside the hallway. 'I've missed you,' he says. He knows it's a stupid thing to say, he's only met her once, but what he really means is that he misses the way his life was when he met her. It's all muddled inside of his head but it's like she is a connection to the time before his parents died, as though she might have the superpowers to bring them back. She stands stiffly for a moment but then her arms tighten around his shoulders, 'It's nice to see you too, Duke.' He gazes up at her as though she might have brought some answers with her but, if she has, she keeps them a secret.

'Nina's eyes are all red from crying,' he says. 'You could put some of that glittery stuff on them.'

'I don't think Nina is really in the mood for a makeover.' Charlie gently eases Duke away from Sasha.

'But it made her happy the last time.'

'I've got a little something for you both.' Sasha crouches down and unzips her bag, pushing Billie's inquisitive nose away. She pulls out Samsung smartphone boxes. 'One for each of you.' She passes Duke his. 'I know your parents didn't let you have mobiles but . . .' her cheeks flush pink. 'Sorry, I should have checked . . .' She glances up at Charlie and he squeezes her shoulder.

'It's very thoughtful of you. Isn't it, Duke?'

'Yes. But . . .' he remembers his manners just in time and says thank you rather than the 'who would I call' that was slipping from his mouth. He doesn't have any friends but the fact that Sasha thinks he might makes him stand a little taller as he rushes down the hallway to show Pippa. From behind him he can hear Charlie mutter 'you didn't need to do that,' and Sasha saying something about 'living in the dark ages'. He knows from the history lessons Mum gave him that means something to do with the Roman empire, but he feels they are all living in dark times right now, and Sasha, the only one without red, swollen eyes and a forced smile, might be the one to make it all a little brighter.

'Look. Sasha bought me a phone.' He skids to a halt. On the kitchen table are a pile of shells. His shells. The ones he collected from the beach on New Year's Day. He picks one up and runs his finger over the bumpy surface, watching as grains of sand sprinkle onto the pine tabletop, which is punctured with grooves of cutlery, marks of family life. Mum could have touched this shell that night. She was always gathering and discarding things. A pile of daisies to make a chain, a bunch of pine cones to spray gold for Christmas. What if . . . Duke closes his palm around it, concentrating hard, trying to feel the imprint of her fingers, her soft skin.

'I found them in your pocket when I collected the laundry,' Pippa says gently, placing her hand on his shoulder. 'We can wash them and do something with them.'

'Like what?'

'Put them around the flowers underneath the bird feeder; your mum loved the garden.'

Duke shook his head. 'A big fat pigeon might steal them.'

'We could put them on the kitchen windowsill so everyone can see them every day.'

'They might get knocked off and broken.'

'We could . . . Remember that wind chime I have hanging outside of my front door?'

'The one made of coloured beads?'

'Yes. Those beads belonged to my grandma and when she died I didn't want to leave them in her jewellery box gathering dust so I made the chime and now I see it every time I come home and it's like she's greeting me.'

Duke thinks about this. 'How will we make a hole in the shell without breaking it?'

'I'm sure if we set up your new phone and go on YouTube, we can learn how to do that.'

Duke eyes her suspiciously. He isn't sure he can trust her after the whole cookie thing. She had promised that no one would die.

Grown-ups don't know everything.

'What if we watch a video and find out what's involved before you decide?' Pippa asks.

Duke shrugs. 'Yeah. Okay.' Because what else does he have to do? Usually if he had free time he'd play his sax but he vows to never play again. He doesn't deserve the joy it brings him. He ate the cookie dough. He caused this and he deserves to feel terrible forever.

'Come on, Duke—' Pippa gently nudges him '—let's set your mobile up and see what it can do.'

Duke hands it to Pippa, not really caring what it can do, because the thing he wants it to do the most of all is impossible. It's a piece of plastic, not a magic wand.

It'll be rubbish.

Everything is rubbish.

His phone is brilliant. It doesn't matter that he doesn't have anybody to ring, although Pippa has put her own, Charlie's and Nina's numbers in the contact list and he's going to ask Sasha for hers. It plays music and games and taught him and Pippa how to make a wind chime from the shells. They had to boil them first and then carefully make a hole with a drawing pin. His heart beat so fast as Pippa twisted the sharp point around the edge of the first shell sure it would shatter, but it didn't. Now the chime hangs outside of their front door. It doesn't really make a noise but it looks good.

Afterwards he helps Pippa cook lunch. He's a good cook. He's been helping Mum for years, peeling their home-grown vegetables. Growing stuff was one of the 'fun' activities Duke's mum came up with to make learning interesting. At first he didn't like the way his shoulders ached after digging or the damp feel of the earth under his fingernails but then his carrots began to grow and he still remembers the elation he felt as they served them up for dinner.

'Three small sticks each? What are we, miniature rabbits?' Nina had muttered.

But the next year they'd made their patch larger and the vegetables had grown bigger and he'd added cabbages and runner beans and courgettes. They'd also grown potatoes in a bin that his dad called 'Dusty', for some reason.

Today, the carrots Duke washes under the tap are in a plastic bag – something Mum wouldn't have approved of – and have come from Tesco. As he scrapes them he wonders if he will plant anything this year, if Charlie will help with the digging.

Thoughts of life continuing without Mum, seeds sprouting, vegetables growing, are so incomprehensible, so confusing, that he drops the carrot in the sink and stares up at the sky. How can it still be there? Still be blue?

The world is still turning and he wants to shut it out.

He runs towards the stairs, wanting to hide under his covers. He slows when he passes the music room. Those swirling letters on the wall taunting him.

All The Things You Are.

Scared. Scared. Scared.

Pippa had persuaded Duke to come downstairs for lunch. They all sit around the table. Sasha talks too much, filling in the silence. She tries to engage Nina in conversation about music, but music is the last thing any of them want to be reminded of. Pippa changes the subject, asking Sasha what new books are being published this year.

'I had a new series of wizard books but they all fell on my head,' she says, eyes on Duke.

'Fell on your head?'

'Yeah. I only had my *shelf* to blame.'

Duke laughs.

Then he remembers why Sasha is here and his parents aren't and he shovels a forkful mashed potato into his mouth and wishes he could stuff his laughter back inside. Miserably, he spears a piece of leek and it flies from his plate, landing on the floor where a grateful Billie hoovers it up.

'How long have you been an editor?' Pippa says.

'Eight years now. I started off as an assistant and worked my way up. What is it you do?'

'I'm working in a care home right now, it's only temporary though. You'd have thought I'd have had enough nursing after Grandma but . . . it's not a vocation but I do enjoy it and it gets me out the house.'

'I like being in the house. Working from home is one of my favourite things about being an editor. The fact I can read any-where.'

'So, you'll be working from here?' Duke is hopeful.

'Sorry, kiddo—' Sasha ruffles his hair – why do adults keep doing that? It's annoying. '—I've got a breakfast meeting on Monday. I'll be leaving tomorrow night.'

'Can't you stay?' Duke can't bear to lose anyone else.

'I'm afraid not, we have jobs to do.' She glances at Charlie.

'But Charlie's not going back to London.' Duke notices the look that passes between Charlie and Sasha and he feels those jumping beans in his tummy again. It must mean something bad or they would just say it out loud.

'Are you, Charlie?' Duke asks in a smaller voice.

Before Charlie can answer his phone begins to ring. He answers it as he stands, strides out into the hallway, pulling the door to behind him but they can still hear his voice.

'You've found . . . Oh God . . . they're gone. They're really, actually, gone.'

They hear him begin to cry.

CHAPTER EIGHT

Charlie

Charlie sinks on the bottom stair, feels Sasha's hand on his shoulder. He still clasps his mobile in his hand although the call has ended.

'Charlie?' It's an effort to raise his head, his mind weighted with the terrible news he has been given. The terrible news he must now share. Pippa stands in front of him, one hand holding Duke's, the other Nina's.

'That was the . . . They've found . . .' It feels as though someone is jumping up and down on his chest, his lungs grappling for air. 'They've found Hal and Fingers.'

'Are they . . .' Nina pleads with her eyes for a different answer to the questions she can't bring herself to ask.

Charlie nods.

'But Charlie—' Sasha crouches, taking both of his hands in hers '—you know they are all . . .' she lowers her voice '. . . dead. There's no hope. The conditions . . . the weather . . . the tides. You know that, right?'

And Charlie does know but knowing the facts hadn't stopped him wishing for a different outcome and he knows from the hope that has diminished from the eyes of his siblings that they too felt the same.

How do you accept death without a body?

Grieve?

Move on?

But he must. Mum and Bo aren't coming back.

What is he going to do?

Charlie's stiff and uncomfortable from sleeping on the sofa bed. Sasha had slept peacefully beside him, and Charlie had envied her for the ability to switch off, wherever she was. He envies her because she can walk out of this house without any guilt or regret. He envies her because she can live her London life or transfer to New York. She has choices. A future. Right now, Charlie doesn't feel he has either.

They skipped breakfast and have eaten lunch and now Charlie sits in the kitchen with Sasha, his hands nursing a cold mug of instant coffee that would taste infinitely more palatable with a slug of whisky but alcohol isn't the answer, although he doesn't know what is.

Duke is playing on his phone, the game making pop-pop-pop noises that jab at his headache. The household is missing two vital members but it still feels too crowded. There's no space Charlie can escape to; Duke has his old room. He can't bring himself to claim Mum and Bo's room but if he were to stay here full-time . . .

What is he going to do?

Pippa and Nina are doing one of Pippa's grandma's jigsaws. He doubts in normal circumstances it would be their first choice of fun but it's a good distraction. He doesn't know what he'd have done without Pippa these past few days. They've fallen back into their friendship, their early friendship anyway, without the tragedy that came later which she had tried to support him through. Now, it's a different situation, a different tragedy, but she is still here.

Charlie needs to apologise to her, for everything he once did, everything he was, but now is not the right time. He thinks that soon he will have other people to say sorry to. Other apologies to make. He rises to his feet, the desire to run away from his siblings driving him to the door.

'Let's go for a walk,' he tells Sasha. 'We need to talk,' he adds before anyone else can ask to come with them.

But Billie has heard her favourite word and is spinning joyful circles, so Charlie quickly clips her lead onto her collar and they slip out of the back door.

They walk mindlessly. Charlie unaware where his grief-heavy legs are subconsciously leading him, even when they are trudging up the incline. It isn't until they reached the top of Briar's Hill he realizes where they are. It was here his parents would bring him for a picnic when he was small, him balanced on his dad's shoulders when he'd grown tired, Mum carrying a wicker basket crammed with egg sandwiches and fruitcake. He had felt he could stretch his pudgy arms up and touch the clouds with his fingertips. It was here he'd hung out with Pippa after school – they'd tried their first cigarette, their first swig of vodka – in the days before he'd shut her out, shut out the world.

'Wow.' Sasha shields her eyes from the bright winter sunshine as she drinks in the brown, yellow and deep green patchwork fields sprawling below them, stretching as far as they could see. 'You don't get this in London. It's beautiful.'

It is. The perfect backdrop. He still carries the ring box in his pocket; if he pulls it out now, the diamonds will sparkle in the sun, but it's not the right time.

It never seems to be the right time.

Charlie pulls her to him and hugs her tightly, her hair blows against his face and just for a moment he imagines he is invisible.

'So,' Sasha says when Charlie has released her. She sits cross-legged on the grass and pats the space next to him. 'What next?'

'Tea, I suppose when we get back; we've had a cooked lunch so an egg sandwich—'

'I wasn't talking about today, Charlie.'

'I know.'

She waits for him to speak but he doesn't know what to say.

'I've had my transfer confirmed for February,' she says quietly.

New York always seemed so far away but now the distance is immense. It's not just oceans he would have to cross to get there but grief, guilt.

'Our five-year plan.' She slips her hand into his.

'Our five-year plan.' They'd both known what they'd wanted. Building their respective careers in London, purposefully choosing a publisher and an agency that also had New York offices. They'd marry – that remains unspoken but acknowledged it would happen before they returned to the UK by which time they'd have enough of a nest egg to invest in property. They have it all figured out.

Had.

'Simon wants you to phone him and confirm you're definitely still going.'

'How can I go?'

'How can you stay? A change of scene—'

'Don't. Just don't. It's not just me, is it? There's Nina and Duke.'
He rips a handful of grass from its roots before allowing it to slip

through his fingers along with his ambition and his dreams. He feels his throat closing, the space growing smaller. He is shrinking too, his life, his hope.

'I bought them the mobiles so you can video call. Keep in regular contact. They're lovely kids,' Sasha says. 'But we never—'

She doesn't finish but he knows. Children aren't part of their five-year plan; they'd come later, if ever. Charlie needs to tell Sasha the truth about his own childhood before they make any decisions and he's had ample time to do that but hasn't been able to find the right words. And now here they are, discussing children, only not *their* children.

'Surely you're not expected to raise them?' she asks.

But there's no one left to expect anything from him and that in itself is the problem. Charlie is the adult now although he does not feel it.

He had made a promise and he endlessly replays the memory, searching for hidden meanings.

'Look after them for me, won't you?' Mum had whispered. 'And look after yourself too.'

'I promise.' He had crossed his chest with his finger.

Had she known then that she wouldn't be back? It was ludicrous to think that she had and yet she had looked at him so earnestly, so intently.

Look after yourself too.

If he looks after himself it means going to New York. If he looks after Duke and Nina he would have to stay here. He had unknowingly made two promises and only one of them would be possible to keep.

'If I don't—' he clears his throat '—then . . . who?'

'There must be someone else? A relative?'

'Not really.' He shakes his head. 'No one who would want to take them on and no one they'd be happy with.'

'But what about your happiness?' She rests her head on his shoulder. 'Our happiness?'

'I can't just leave them.' Although he wants to. He wants to roll down the hill the way he had when he was a child. To feel that sense of freedom. Already, Nina and Duke are heavy chains around his ankles.

'But . . . are you thinking of bringing them to New York?'

'I don't know.'

'What about the house—'

'I said I *don't know.*'

Sasha sits up and leans forward, her elbows resting on her bent knees. She stares into the distance. Charlie doesn't know whether she is watching the tatty straw stuffed scarecrow moving in the breeze or whether she is seeing their future slip away.

'Sorry for snapping. It's just . . . Christ. I don't even know where to start.' The thoughts in his head tumble from his lips. 'What do I do? How can I afford New York and the mortgage on the house here, if there even is a mortgage and . . . can I pay it anyway? It's not in my name. With no bodies there are no death certificates. How can I speak to the bank, the energy providers when *nothing* is in my name? And legally—'

'Charlie, breathe.' Sasha crouches in front of him, her hands on his shins. He realizes his words have fallen out in a garbled rush and he hasn't inhaled for probably a minute at least.

'It's . . . a lot.' He's negotiated seven-figure deals but right now he feels helpless and hopeless.

'You're not on your own. I'm here. And there's people who can help. Social Services.'

'You mean, put them into care?'

'I didn't say that. I was thinking of advice. But . . . perhaps . . . It's an option and . . .' she doesn't need to say he doesn't have too many of those. 'I'm sorry. I feel so useless.' Her voice thins and he knows this is not easy for her either. Not what she'd signed up for. But then he feels the ring box again and realizes she hasn't signed up for anything, not yet.

'If you want to leave, I don't expect you to—'

'Shh.' She presses her lips against his and they fall back on the grass. He rolls on top of her, and her legs wrap around his waist. He kisses her harder as his hand slips under her coat, her jumper, his cold fingers on her warm skin. She tugs at his belt, his zip. He doesn't stop her. He is desperate to feel alive but, instead, he feels nothing.

At home, he rings Marty from the band. He isn't sure if he'd have been told about the discovery of Hal and Fingers but he has.

'I couldn't help but think that somehow they might all be . . . I dunno . . . on an island or something,' Marty says. 'Stupid.'

'I had hoped the same. That Mum and Bo were out there, together.'

'It'll have been . . . not a comfort. I dunno what the right word is, Charlie, but Bo being with Ronnie right up until the end . . . he loved the bones of her, you know.'

'I know. And having played a last gig. He never lost hope that he might make it. I wonder if he regretted anything, at the end. They say your life flashes before you. Whether he wished he'd never met her and me and . . . Sorry, Marty.' Charlie sniffs.

'He loved having a family. He was never happier than when

he was with your mum. He . . . he didn't want her to know this but, shortly after he moved up to Derbyshire with you, he had an offer. Have you heard of the James Patrick Ensemble?'

'Hasn't everyone?' They're the most successful jazz group touring today.

'They weren't quite as big then but definitely on the up and up. They lost their guitarist and the trumpet player recommended Bo and . . . well . . . they invited him to join the band.'

'He . . . he turned it down? But it was everything he wanted.'

'Ronnie was everything he wanted. He couldn't bear the thought of being on tour for months at a time. Away from her. From both of you. He didn't feel it was right for you both to join him travelling. He wanted you to have the security of a fixed home, the stability of school. He never regretted it. I've never seen a couple more in love.'

Charlie hadn't either. Mum and Bo just . . . fit. They glowed when they were together. Finishing each other's sentences. Knowing instinctively what the other needed, sometimes silence and space, sometimes a conversation, a touch. There was something just so right about them. Is that how love should be? Is this how it is for him and Sasha? Charlie turns this over long after he has said goodbye to Marty and hung up the phone.

It's dark by the time Charlie drops Sasha at the station that night, even though it isn't yet seven o'clock. It's the last train to London.

They have talked again during the journey and Charlie is a little clearer about what he is going to do.

'I'll miss you,' she says as she hugs him goodbye. 'I'll text you and let you know when I'm back.'

'I'll see you soon.' He kisses her softly.

'Don't forget you need to ring Simon, Charlie. Clarify what's going on with New York. He's waiting.'

'I know.'

He stands on the platform, hands stuffed into his pockets, waving as the train pulls away. He doesn't run alongside it, shouting his love, as they do in the movies. He thinks Bo would probably have done that for Mum.

At home he slips into the bathroom and locks the door. Runs the taps on the bath so no one can hear him as he makes the call he doesn't want to make.

Says the things he doesn't want to say.

CHAPTER NINE

Nina

Violet.

Charlie's fucking rung Aunt Violet.

CHAPTER TEN

Charlie

Charlie buries his face in Billie's fur. He'll miss her. He'll miss them all but he can't do this, he can't put his life on hold to be a substitute father. He's not ready. He's already been here for three weeks and it's been awful, awkward. On top of failing miserably as any sort of role model, working from home is not working for him. Nothing is working for him.

He stands.

'So . . . I'll give you a ring. Soon.'

'Don't bother,' Nina spits. Charlie can't look her in the eye.

'Duke?'

Duke rushes towards him and wraps his arms tightly around Charlie's legs.

'Please don't leave us. Please don't leave us.'

Violet peels Duke away from Charlie and clasps him by the shoulders. He shrugs her off and huddles next to Nina instead.

'It's better if you just go,' Violet says. Since he called her she's been like a whirlwind, spinning everything out of his control, asking that he stay until she'd organised her annual leave and then arriving with a suitcase, telling him to return to London. 'And give them a few days to settle before you get in touch.'

This is what Charlie wanted. Someone who would take charge, who would know what is best. Someone who would raise the children and it isn't as though Violet is a bad person, she's just . . . different to Mum.

Still, it's a wrench to open the front door and, when he steps outside, he feels four angry eyes boring into his back.

He hesitates for a moment, his head hung low, purposefully not looking at Pippa's house. Again, he is walking away from her after she has been there for him through the worst of times.

Charlie's emotions are tangled and he can't unpick the guilt he feels from his shame and loss and he hasn't yet left but he feels he will miss them, but is he telling himself this to ease his conscience?

If this is the right thing for him, it has to be the right thing for them too, doesn't it?

Stuffing his hands in his pockets he strides away from the house, away from his siblings, away from the memory of his mother.

Away from Pippa.

He leaves them all.

CHAPTER ELEVEN

Duke

Duke can hear Nina and Aunt Violet arguing downstairs. He can't make out what they are saying but their words are fast and angry. He doesn't need to hear what they are shouting because he knows what it's about.

The same thing it has been about for the past two weeks.

Duke picks up another book – *Tiddler*.

He is way too old for this one but he remembers the time he had chosen it for his story every single night, shifting over on the bed so Mum could stretch out her legs, his head resting on her shoulder as they both read the story aloud. He had loved rhymes, the rhythm of the words; it felt like everything made sense.

Now, nothing makes sense. He is that small, lost, frightened fish in an unknown ocean, wishing desperately that everything can go back to the way it was before.

It can't.

Duke drops the book into the box. It's nearly full and he hasn't even begun to pack his Lego yet. Aunt Violet said not to bring too much stuff as his bedroom at her house is much smaller but how much is too much? She has only given him four boxes and all of those are full. Perhaps his new room isn't a room at all but a cupboard under the stairs. He looks around sadly; there's his green light shade covered in dinosaurs his dad had bought after their visit to the Natural History Museum – 'so you don't forget our trip,' he had said, but it was the only time Duke has ever been to London and he'll never forget the constant noise, the people. He had shrunk into his mum's side, clutching her hand tightly.

His curtains are blue and have trains on them and he doesn't like trains anymore so they don't matter quite as much but Mum had still made them for him on her sewing machine. There's a glass lighthouse filled with different coloured sand he had carefully collected on the Isle of Wight, layers of orange, yellow and purple. Nina had one too. He'd liked it there, the waterfall and Carisbrooke Castle where Dad had bought him a wooden sword and shield, and he'd pretended to be a knight, but he had been sick on the ferry on the way home, and again in the car.

What will happen to the rest of his things? To this house? Will it be sold? Will this be someone else's bedroom one day?

The thought makes his stomach feel sort of empty and he wonders for the first time if Charlie had felt that way when Duke had moved into this room that used to be Charlie's.

Perhaps if he says sorry, tells Charlie he understands, he might come back; he could even have this room – and then they could all still live here and everything would be . . . not the way it was before but better, he thinks, than it will be at Aunt Violet's. He doesn't know what Aunt Violet said to Charlie to make him leave. She might be scary but she's not exactly Gollum.

He picks up the phone that Sasha bought him. There are still only three numbers in his contact list and Charlie is one of them.

He presses the green button and waits and waits, listening to the ringing loud and unanswered against his ear.

Charlie doesn't pick up.

There's a slam. Through the paper-thin wall that separates their bedrooms he hears Nina howl with rage and the heavy thud as she throws something.

Duke tentatively taps on her door before pushing it open. 'I've finished my packing. Do you want me to help you—'

'I don't need to fucking pack because I'm not fucking going anywhere.'

'But—'

'Go away!' she screams as she hurls a glass towards him. Duke begins to shake as it shatters against the doorframe, shards of glass splintering the carpet. He wants to tell his sister that he is not the enemy. The enemy is sitting downstairs, looking too much like his mum, the same eyes and the same full lips, but Aunt Violet's mouth never seems to smile. He quickly retreats.

Duke creeps downstairs. He can help Billie get ready at least. She'll want her favourite toy, the cuddly penguin she got for Christmas. She has long since pulled the stuffing out but she takes the scrap of material to her basket every night. He hopes Aunt Violet has a big garden, somewhere Billie can run around in and perhaps somewhere where he can grow vegetables.

Aunt Violet is sitting at the kitchen table, her head in her hands.

'I . . . I've filled the boxes,' he says.

She raises her face to his. She looks like she's been crying. 'At least one of you does as they're told. I don't know, Veronica has let you both run wild.'

'Nina's upset. This is her home. Our home.'

'I know that—' she pats the chair next to her and he slips into it '—but I have my own home. Really good neighbours.'

'We have Pippa—'

'I have a life. It isn't fair to expect me—'

'We don't expect you to do anything. You could go back to your house, Charlie could—'

'Charlie can't—'

'I know you probably think we're better off with you because you're old . . . older,' he quickly corrects, as he sees the frown line on the bridge of her nose deepen, 'but Charlie did look after us really well and—'

'You have to come and live with me—'

'But Charlie—'

'Charlie didn't want you,' she snaps.

Duke feels himself crumple inside. Charlie isn't here because he doesn't want to be here. With them. Of course not. Why would he? Duke feels an idiot for ever thinking his brother might take them on. Him with his weirdness and Nina with her hormones. Why would he choose them over London? Duke has lost another person and inside he feels as though his stomach has stretched open really wide and something heavy has dropped into it, but still he can't seem to cry.

'I'm sorry. That was blunt.' Aunt Violet pats his hand. 'We'll get used to each other, learn to rub along together,' she says but Duke knows there is more to being a family than getting used to each other and rubbing along together.

There's love.

And, right now, it feels he doesn't have any.

*

It is much later and three more arguments before Nina's bag thud-thud-thuds down the stairs; she follows it, stamping angrily, her rucksack slung over her shoulder.

'I need to get my clarinet.' Nina kicks open the door to the music room. Duke follows her.

They both stand frozen in the doorway, eyes trained on those swirling black letters on the golden wall:

All The Things You Are . . .

Broken

Lonely

Orphaned

Duke's fingers find Nina's but she snatches her hand away, picking up her clarinet case.

'Grab your saxophone,' she orders.

'No.'

'You can't just leave it here. Dad—'

'I don't want to play anymore,' Duke says but what he really means is he doesn't want to play without his parents. He wants to explain to Nina that he ate the cookie dough and caused all of this, so he doesn't deserve the happiness music brings but if she hasn't figured out for herself that it's all his fault he is too scared to tell her. His world has already shrunk so much. She is the only constant he has left.

Actually, not the only one.

'Billie?' He heads back into the hallway. 'Billie. Time to go.' But she doesn't come running.

'Billie's already gone,' Aunt Violet says.

'To your house?'

'To her new home.'

'You've given our bloody dog away!' Nina yells.

'Nina, do stop swearing. I can't believe your parents let you be so feral.'

'Where is Billie?' Something strange is happening to Duke; he can feel his body begin to shake, can feel his skin turn icy cold and he doesn't feel as though he's in his own body.

'That girl next door has taken her.'

'Pippa.' Duke begins to run out the front door but Aunt Violet grabs him around the waist.

'I told Pippa to stay inside with the dog. Less stressful for everyone. You can visit her when she's settled in.'

'Billie.' Duke can feel he is screaming from the rawness in his throat but there's a funny whooshing sound in his ears and he can't quite hear. 'Billie!'

Aunt Violet half drags him to the car, the frigid February air, along with his tears, stinging his throat. She bundles him in the back. He scrambles to get out.

'Duke.' Aunt Violet speaks sternly. 'You're only going to distress the dog if she sees you like this. You love her, don't you?'

Duke loves her so much he feels his heart will burst. 'Yes,' he whispers.

'Then don't upset her. Get back in the car.'

Duke does as he is told.

Nina throws herself on the backseat next to him, her eyes wet, lips trembling.

Aunt Violet pulls away. Duke twists around in his seat. Pippa is at her window, wiping tears from her cheeks with her sleeve, Billie next to her, paws on the sill, her tongue lolling out the side of her mouth, a confused expression in her eyes.

Come back. Come back. Come back.

Duke watches as she grows smaller, as they travel away from

the dog he has loved since she was a puppy and the only home they have both ever known.

He releases a howl of anguish – the howl of the wounded animal that he is.

Finally, wrenchingly, he begins to cry.

CHAPTER TWELVE

Charlie

Charlie had begun his career as an intern thirteen years ago. At the end of his interview he'd been asked if he had any questions and he'd leaned forward and earnestly asked,

'What's the greatest attribute I need to succeed in publishing?'

'The capacity to drink huge volumes of alcohol,' came the reply with a laugh.

That wasn't strictly true, of course; he needed patience, a rational head, a confidence to tackle awkward conversations. Ironic, really, when he has spent much of his life shying away from awkward conversations but still he has called Nina and Duke twice a week. Still he hasn't told them that at the end of this month he's moving to New York.

In business he needs to know when a deal is good and when to walk away.

He tries to apply the same logic to his private life, but it doesn't sit right with him. Moving to the other side of the world.

He's a coward.

He takes another glug of sparkling water wishing it were champagne, and scans the room. This book launch isn't for one of the authors he represents but for a Young Adult novel Sasha has edited. It's been nominated for a literary award, the writer – a debut – touted as the next best thing. He watches her now, the broad grin that stretches across her face, oblivious to the fact that next month there will likely be another 'next big thing' and her career could end up solely comprising of this one book. He flicks through a copy. It's almost all dialogue and there's no punctuation, making it difficult to figure out who is speaking.

'Brave' is the cover quote provided by the 'next big thing' from a couple of years ago who he does represent and he knows that behind the scenes she's frozen with fear, unable to complete her second book, scared it will never live up to the first.

A hush falls across the room as Sasha taps the microphone and begins her speech, explaining why she immediately fell in love with the story the second she read it. Sasha is passionate about books but more level-headed about everything else, including him. Theirs was a gradual coming together, their paths crossing at events, stilted small talk turning to lingering at the bar at the end of the night, swapping phone numbers, dreams. Realizing they wanted the same things.

It isn't that Charlie feels she doesn't love him but he sees the way her eyes light up when she talks about stories, she feels the way he does about words, and he feels . . . it's silly to say jealous but theirs was never a 'I knew the second we laid eyes on each other' story, but that doesn't mean they can't have their happily ever after, does it? They want the same things. Their five-year plan meticulously drawn.

Charlie gently pats his pocket, feels the ring box he still carries with him. Tonight isn't the right time, despite the champagne she is drinking and the canapés and the table he has booked them later at Sasha's favourite Italian restaurant.

He'll propose in New York. Perhaps on top of the Empire State Building. Somewhere memorable and photogenic. Sasha loves to Instagram.

Charlie wanders around the room. In the corner there is a table covered by a crisp, white cloth, stacked with proof copies of books for people to take. Charlie thinks of Duke with his studious round glasses that magnify the sorrow in his eyes; he might like one. Before he can pick up a copy his phone vibrates.

Duke.

His heart sinks as he reads the text, his brother's distress dripping from his words. Momentarily he begins to compose a reply – *Billie is having a great time with Pippa!* – but it sounds fake and patronizing and everything he doesn't want to be. He doesn't know who he wants to be. He switches off his phone, drops it into his pocket and plucks a glass of orange juice from the tray of a passing waiter.

He tries to tune into the conversation buzzing around him, focus on the faces, but all he can see is Duke forlornly clutching his handset programmed only with three numbers, waiting for a reply that will never come.

They aren't his problem.

So why does it feel like they are?

Sasha is asleep. Charlie stands among the packing boxes in the flat, which next week will likely have new tenants. It never gets properly dark in London, not like the blackness in Derbyshire, which is absolute. Charlie rests his forehead against the window as he watches the steady stream of headlights pass beneath him. The bright blue 'Kebab' sign opposite competing against the neon red 'Cocktail' that flashes from the bar next door.

He will miss this.

They call New York the city that never sleeps but it's possible to still be awake without the noise and the people and the hustle and the bustle. He knows this because Nina frequently messages him at 3 a.m.

She hates the new house.

She hates Aunt Violet.

She hates him.

He doesn't reply. He tells himself it's because he thinks Aunt Violet is right. The children need time to settle but really it's because he is ashamed and, worse still, he thinks that if his mum was here she'd also be ashamed of him but then hasn't she been ashamed of him for years?

Charlie runs his fingertips lightly over the scars on his wrist.

He still has the box of fudge he bought from Colesby Bay on New Year's Day. He eats a piece, feeling the sweetness dissolve on his tongue.

He remembers when his mum gave birth to Nina. Her exhaustion. The way he'd watched his sister to give her a break. He'd helped with the relentless stream of nappies, sterilising bottles, warming formula. His conflicted emotions. The love he'd felt as he'd gazed at his new sister tempered with a feeling of envy that she had two solid parents who loved her, that, for her, his mum had chosen a better father than she had for him. The way Nina had splashed him as he'd bathed her, the smell of talcum powder after he'd dried her. The resentment he'd felt when Mum had scooped her up, cradling Nina protectively to her chest, covering her damp, newly washed hair with kisses. At the time he'd run his fingers over his scars on his wrist and wonder if she loved him that much, why she hadn't protected him. He'd tried to lock that love away, forget his family existed most of the time but now they occupy every waking thought. He recalls leaning over Nina's cot as she'd wrap tiny fingers tightly around his thumb and he'd whispered that he'd be the best big brother ever.

He had tried but, as she'd grown, he'd felt more and more set apart. She called Bo 'Dad' when Charlie never had. She had a different surname. Bo doted on her. Charlie told himself he treated Nina so tenderly because she was a girl. A daughter. He didn't compare them and find Charlie lacking. By the time Duke was born, Charlie had left home, and when he came to visit, that was what he felt like: a visitor. Bo had a son now, a *real* son. Bo didn't treat Charlie any differently but, with Duke, there was a softness in his eyes; he cradled him as though he was gold. Each time Charlie left to return to London, they all stood on the step, waving him goodbye until they stepped back inside, a family, and he was left, catching the train. Alone.

With the passing of time, Charlie can now see that perhaps the gentleness he saw in Bo was because Nina and Duke were babies, not because they were biologically his. That if Bo had been around when Charlie was small perhaps he too would have been swept into Bo's arms. Showered with kisses.

He thinks perhaps he has got so much wrong.

Too much to put right?

He switches his phone back on. Immediately it buzzes. It isn't Nina but Pippa. Charlie had messaged her earlier to ask how Billie is and her one word reply tells him 'fine'.

She is disappointed in him too. They have had one brief, curt conversation since he returned to London where she told him that she can't keep Billie long-term.

'Can't or won't?' Charlie had asked, his tone defensive.

'It's not just you that has life plans.' She was equally tetchy.

Long after their conversation had ended, Charlie had wondered what Pippa's plans are. He hadn't asked her anything about herself. She must still be devastated over the loss of her grandmother who had raised her but he had been too wrapped up in his own problems to ask her about her own. She had been there for him. She had been there for him *again* and he had let her down.

He has so many people to say sorry to he doesn't know where to start.

The sun is beginning to rise. The sky smudged with pink and orange.

Sasha slips her arms around his waist, nuzzles her chin against his shoulder.

'You're up early.' She kisses the back of his neck.

He turns to face her, his lips finding hers. His hands slip under her camisole top. She pulls back. 'I've a breakfast meeting.'

She showers and dresses, leaving before he does. He's sorting his bookcase into two piles, one for the charity shop and one to put in storage, when the post drops onto his mat. He rifles through the envelopes, junk, junk, and then something else.

Something official.

He has to read it twice to make sense of it. Have Duke and Nina received one too? They must have . . .

He reaches for his phone.

CHAPTER THIRTEEN

Nina

Nina pushes the knot in her school tie up to her collar. There's a familiarity in putting on her uniform, stuffing her pencil case into her rucksack, even though she's getting ready in unfamiliar surroundings. She actually cannot wait to get to school, to see Maeve who has been her best friend since primary. Get out of this place.

Her new bedroom is stark and soulless – a bit like Aunt Violet herself. The walls painted white, she hasn't been allowed to put any of her posters up. Her cork board, covered in pictures of her and Maeve, Mum and Dad, Billie, rests against the pine wardrobe door and she has to move it every time she wants to pull out something to wear. The room is too small for her things, too small for her emotions.

At least she's going to the same secondary. Before, she'd approached from the east and it would take twenty minutes to walk there; now she'll come from a different direction and it will take her thirty-five minutes. Learning that Aunt Violet lives in the west like the Wicked Witch in *The Wizard of Oz* had made her briefly smile but realizing that she lived so close to them all these years and had never repaired her relationship with Mum seems even more tragic now.

This is what is on her mind when her phone begins to ring, Charlie's name flashing on the screen. She's tempted to ignore it but they need to talk.

Still, she leaves it until the last second before the answer service will cut in to pick up.

She sits cross-legged on her bed, which is too hard and gives her backache. The one at home – she still thinks of her old house as home – had never been replaced and was too soft. She wonders if she'll ever find her 'just right'.

'You got it then?' she says before she even says hello.

'The form N208. Yes. Did—'

'Me and Duke have one too, in case we want to object. And we do want to object, don't we, Charlie?'

'I . . . I don't know. What does it all mean?'

'Missing presumed dead. I think it's quite explanatory, Charlie.' She's being deliberately unkind. She knows it's a shock for him, at least Violet had explained the process to her and Duke but then she would have told Charlie too if he ever answered his phone. 'But . . .' She tries to recall all the things Aunt Violet had told her. The fragments of fact whirl around her head and she tries to catch hold of them, to pin them down in the right order. 'It's the first step. Aunt Violet has put an advert in the paper too. The court has had a copy of her form and there's going to be a hearing.'

'And then what?'

'And then Aunt Violet can apply for a death certificate and then she'll be able to access Mum and Dad's bank account, claim their life insurance, that sort of thing.'

'I saw on TV once that you had to be missing for seven years before you could declare someone dead?'

'Aunt Violet said there are exceptions if people are missing and there has been some sort of natural event and it's certain they couldn't have survived.'

'It just seems so . . . final.'

'It's horrible.' Rationally she knows that her parents can't, that they won't come back, but she wants to retain that smidgeon of hope. All of the times the words 'Mum' or 'Dad' have tripped from her tongue must add up to hours, days, maybe even weeks, months, years. Now she will never utter their names again and impatiently wait for their reply. For their attention. She doesn't want to believe it but this form states in black and white the hurtful truth that they are really gone. She can't accept it. She won't.

She never said goodbye.

She pushes away the thought which batters her again and again, the way she had dismissed them so readily New Year's Eve, so focused on her nails.

She never said goodbye.

They can't be declared dead. Not without bodies. No matter what the experts say, there has to be a chance they are wrong.

Has to be.

'You have to stop her, Charlie.'

'But . . .' She hears Charlie breathing, tapping his fingers against something while he thinks. 'I'll call you back, Nina.'

'But I've got to go—' He's already hung up.

Seconds later her phone rings again; it's Maeve.

'So . . . it's going to be so weird not calling for you this morning. I hate that you've moved.'

'Me too. I feel like I live on the other side of the world. We'll meet halfway though?'

'Yep. At the park.'

'Can't wait to see you. Know who also can't wait to see you?'

'Not Miss Rudd.' They both laugh; Nina has never got on with their form tutor. She had missed the first couple of weeks of term but had found sitting around at home with Charlie and Duke, and then Violet and Duke too depressing. Miss Rudd hadn't been any kinder to her when she had returned though.

She guesses again.

'Umm. You. You'll be pleased to see me?'

'Obvs me idiot but . . . Ryan Martin. I bumped into him at the shop last night when I went to buy my weight in Dairy Milk to distract myself from you moving into Violet's.'

'Right.' It seemed like a lifetime ago Nina had snuck out of the house to go on a double date with Ryan, Maeve and Lenny. She still feels sick when she remembers what happened. What Ryan did. What she did.

'Do you like him?' Maeve asks.

Nina had always told Maeve everything but she hadn't told her . . . that. How could she? Maeve might look at her differently. Realize that she doesn't know Nina as well as she thinks.

'Gotta go,' she says. 'Laters.' She ends the call.

The memory of that night isn't all bad. Nina recalls what it felt like to be carefree, to be desired. To desire.

She doesn't want to speak to Ryan ever again but still she coats her lashes with mascara, draws a thin black line under her eyes before she pencils over it again until it is thick and angry-looking. She slicks her lips with deep-red lipstick. She'll get into trouble but she doesn't care. She stares defiantly at her reflection, her outside matching her inside.

Nina is pulling on her shoes, which painfully crowd her toes, when her phone rings.

Charlie.

'I've spoken to Aunt Violet.' This time it is him who skips pleasantries. 'I think . . . I think this is the right thing to do. We know Mum and Bo aren't coming back. It's only a matter of time before they're found. Violet can't afford to raise you both and she shouldn't have to struggle to buy you the things you need.'

Nina swallows hard; she needs new shoes but the things she really needs, really wants, can't be bought.

'But, Charlie—'

'I know it's upsetting but there are practical things—'

'Fuck practical things, Charlie, and fuck you.' She hangs up before the tears she is constantly struggling to contain fall freely. She feels herself shrinking under the weight of anger and guilt and confusion until she's a tiny figure standing in one of the snow globes she used to collect, her emotions a frantic flurry of flakes. Without conscious thought she feels her nails ripping into the skin at the top of her thigh again and again. The sharp sting of pain makes her wince but then a calmness, everything settling until the next time she is shaken again.

She slings her rucksack over her shoulder and stalks from her bedroom.

'Nina?'

She doesn't acknowledge Duke. She knows today will be terrifying for him, and not because of the stupid form N208. She knows what's to come for him but she cannot help him. She has nothing left to give.

'Nina?' he pleads as she walks away the way Charlie had walked away.

Perhaps it runs in the family.

Selfishness.

Spite.

But still, as she slams the front door behind her, she feels a pinch in her heart.

How will Duke cope with what he must go through today?

CHAPTER FOURTEEN

Duke

'Nina?' Duke calls after his sister as she stomps down the stairs but she doesn't answer, doesn't even turn around, and then she is gone, slamming the front door behind her.

It is his very first day at school today, ever, and terrified is too small a word but he doesn't know a bigger one.

His blazer doesn't fit him properly, the sleeves covering his hands. He pushes them up as he runs to the toilet and hunches over the bowl for the third time, thinking he might be sick.

Aunt Violet taps on the door. 'Time to go, Duke.'

'I don't feel well. Can I go tomorrow instead?'

'You'll still feel like this. I know this isn't easy and that isn't your fault – God knows what that sister of mine was thinking teaching you at home, letting you run wild – but you have to go to school. It's important to get some qualifications.'

'But I'd have taken my GCSEs anyway.' If he were running wild, he'd be an animal with sharp teeth and claws and he'd scratch and bite anybody who tried to make him do something he didn't want to do like go to school. 'I told you the home-ed group—'

'Duke, I can't home-school you—'

'But you could; I could help you—'

'It's a complete change of lifestyle and this is hard enough for me. I've already taken two weeks of annual leave to look after you and I . . . I've missed my job. I don't want to leave it. Now you and Nina are both living here we can all try and move forward.' She doesn't say this unkindly. 'And I really do want what's best for you—'

'You don't care,' Duke says sadly.

'That's not true. If I didn't care you wouldn't be here. You'd be—'

'With Charlie?'

'No. Somewhere else. And perhaps not with Nina either. I'm doing my best to keep you both safe, together. Now dry your eyes. You're eleven, Duke. It won't be as bad as you think. You might even make some friends.'

A space hopper like the orange one abandoned in his garden leaps around in Duke's stomach as they walk. He intermittently breaks into a run to keep up with Aunt Violet as she marches along. It's all so different to those long, languid strolls with Mum where they would stop to let Billie sniff everything she wanted to, which was pretty much everything. He misses Billie so much, more than he misses Charlie. Pippa had sent him a video message that morning of Billie waving her paw and wishing him luck.

Along with his stomach feeling all fluttery, there is now a strange feeling in his chest as they arrive outside the black, wrought-iron gates. He hasn't been here for a couple of years. Nina had begun to travel to and from school with her best friend Maeve once she had turned thirteen but before that, when he

98

and Mum would wait for her outside, with Billie sitting patiently, her wagging tail brushing against the pavement. He hadn't taken much notice then, but now he notices everything, making a mental list of all the reasons the other kids stare at him as he coaxes his reluctant feet through the gates:

1. His hair is longer than all of the other boys'.
2. His shoes are shinier.
3. Everyone else has a battered old rucksack clinging to their backs like the shells of snails; he has a faux leather satchel hanging across his body.
4. His uniform is neat, trousers in sharp creases, shirt buttons done up to the collar, tie pushed as high as it could go without strangling him (it still feels as though it is strangling him).
5. Nobody and that means *nobody* is carrying a plastic lunchbox.
6. Nobody and that means *nobody* is being dragged across the playground by their aunt, or is holding hands with an adult AT ALL.

He is taken to his class by the school receptionist and left in the care of his teacher, Miss Greenly – at least he hasn't got Miss Rudd who Violet hates. She gestures him to an empty desk near the back and he scurries towards it, glad he hasn't had to speak, but then,

'If you want to come to the front and introduce yourself,' she says.

Duke shakes his head.

'Come on. We all want to know who you are.'

'Do we?' quips a boy from near the front.

'Any more of that, Jayden, and I'll be keeping the whole class in at morning break.'

Angry muttering snakes around the room. Some kids turn to glare at Duke as though the detention they haven't actually got is all his fault.

'Duke?' Miss Greenly smiles warmly.

He stands slowly, feeling slightly sick as he picks his way to the front, head down, his mind humming 'All The Things You Are' to block out the other kids.

'Don't rush, we have all day,' that boy, Jayden's mean voice cuts through the song. A wave of laughter crashes over him. Duke picks up his pace and is almost, almost there when Jayden sticks out his foot. Duke trips. For a few seconds he is suspended in mid-air and he feels like a superhero and wishes he has the power of invisibility. Then he crashes to the floor, hears the crunch of his nose and feels the warmth of the blood, and he thinks at least now he'll be able to go home. Then he remembers he doesn't really have a home anymore and there, sprawled on the floor in front of thirty strangers, he begins to cry.

It is lunchtime. Duke has spent the entire morning with the school nurse. She has cleaned the blood from his face, held an icepack to his nose, and although she hadn't sent him back to class, she hadn't sent him home either. She's brought him to the cafeteria and just . . . left him here. It's noisy, full. Long grey tables with benches stripe the hall in straight rows like someone has measured them with a ruler to space them evenly, the way Duke had carefully calculated the distance between the furrows he would dig with his trowel in his vegetable patch before he planted his seedlings.

He has been somewhere like this once before, a day trip to the zoo where he'd been given a red balloon that tugged against its string and had his face painted like a tiger. He remembers how he'd growled and acted fierce and he tries to replicate this now as he stalks over to the table, eyes swivelling from left to right seeking out danger but danger is everywhere he looks.

He isn't sure where he's supposed to sit, so he slides onto the nearest empty bench and opens his lunchbox. Wrapped in clingfilm is a sandwich. He unwraps it and separates the pieces of bread, pulling a face when he sees a pink slab of ham atop of a thick spread of butter.

Gross.

Aunt Violet feeds him meat almost every meal despite him telling her that he's a vegetarian, that Mum was a vegetarian.

He never eats it.

Whatever, he isn't hungry anyway. His nose is still throbbing.

There is also a yoghurt, strawberry, which is okay, and an apple.

'Duke, isn't it?' It's that boy who tripped him up, Jayden, with his two friends. 'I think we got off to a bad start. This is Luke and Brandon.' He gestures to two boys but Duke doesn't grasp who is who. They look identical with their soft pudgy faces and hard stares. They plonk themselves down on the opposite bench and the bench Duke is sitting on lifts. Wouldn't it be cool if he was catapulted into space and never has to come back to earth? The thought of this makes him smile.

'Something funny?' Jayden's voice is hostile, his eyes too.

'No. I was just . . .' Duke lowers his gaze. 'No.'

'What you got for lunch? Anything good?' Jayden pokes around in the lunchbox. 'Want to swap your sandwich and yoghurt for some custard creams?'

Duke nods. Aunt Violet doesn't believe in snacks. He thinks of the New Year's Eve cookies and how they had turned to dust in his pockets. Jayden helps himself to Duke's lunch and then stands.

'Where are my biscuits?' Duke asks.

'Biscuits? What biscuits? Oh . . . you thought . . .' he laughs, looking at his friends until they laugh too. 'Nah, it's cockney rhyming slang. Custard creams is dreams. I've swapped your lunch for my dreams and my dreams are—' he tilts his head to one side in the gentle way Billie does but there is nothing gentle about this boy '—that you'll piss off.' The three of them wander off, laughing.

At a loss, Duke picks up his apple and crunches into it so the chunk of fruit can push down his emotions but the space in his throat is closing and he begins to choke. While he grapples for breath, he swipes at the tears that stream down his cheeks, not wanting the other kids to think that he is crying, even though he is.

He is dying and nobody cares.

Was this how his parents felt when they were drowning, their lungs burning as they tried to draw in air?

There isn't enough air.

He is dying and nobody cares.

All around him is chatter and noise. Laughter. Nobody asks if he is all right. He feels his eyes bulge like the frog that lived under the rockery as he seeks out a teacher, a dinner lady, anyone who might help him but nobody notices him.

He is dying and nobody cares.

Pressure builds in his skull and just when he thinks his head might explode, splattering the walls and ceiling with his brains and blood, there is a hard thump between his shoulder blades. The lodged piece of apple flies from his mouth and lands on the middle of the table with his saliva and his fear. He wipes his mouth with the sleeve of his blazer and warily studies the freckled face who has saved him.

'Hi, I'm Evie,' she says as she sits down next to him. 'I'm in your form, not that you probably noticed as you spent most of the time you were there face down on the floor.' She pulls a half-eaten bag of beef crisps out of her pocket and offers him one.

'I'm vegetarian,' he says, almost apologetically, expecting her to get up and walk away.

'Me too. There are no animal products in these.' She shakes the bag.

His throat is sore from the choking but she is the first person who has been kind to him all day, so he takes a crisp and pops it onto his tongue, letting it dissolve so it won't be so sharp when he swallows it.

Evie tips the packet up to her mouth and empties out the crumbs. 'Where did you go to school before here?'

'I didn't. I was home-schooled.'

'Why?'

'Mum said I don't have the right personality for school.'

'You are a bit . . . different,' she settles upon. 'Have you had an assessment to see if you're on the spectrum?'

'What do you mean?' To Duke, spectrum means rainbows. The band of colours which aren't really colours at all but all to do with light. How can he be on a rainbow? He thinks of himself balanced high about the sky and smiles.

'See. This is what I mean. You're smiling to yourself. You're a bit weird.'

'Nina thinks I'm a lot weird, but I don't mind.'

'Who's Nina?'

'My sister. She goes here too but she's the right type for school so she's okay.'

'I don't have any brothers or sisters. I don't have many friends either but that's because most people here are boring. Not you, you're interesting.'

Duke straightens his spine and feels a Ready-Brek glow surround him.

'You owe me a favour now that I've saved your life, you know?'

Duke nods.

'You're going to help me with something but we can't tell anyone or we'd be in trouble. Promise you'll help?'

Duke thinks; perhaps he has found a friend and so he doesn't think too deeply about what Evie might want him to do or the trouble he might get into.

'Yeah, I'll help.'

What's the worst that could possibly happen?

CHAPTER FIFTEEN

Charlie

Charlie video calls Pippa, an ache deep inside him as she comes into focus, curled on the sofa, Billie snuggled next to her. February has been freezing so far but they look so cosy.

'I wasn't sure if you'd answer,' he says pitifully, grateful that she has after he'd texted her that he is leaving the country.

'I wanted to say goodbye before you leave for New York tomorrow,' she says, a finality in her voice. Charlie wonders whether this is giving her the closure she didn't get last time he had left.

'We can still . . .' he trails off. Her attention is now on Billie who has leaped off the sofa and is barking at the sound of the doorbell.

'Sorry, Charlie. I've got to go.'

'Duke and Nina won't pick up my calls since I told them about my transfer,' he blurts out his confession and his shame. Telling them had been one of the worst things he'd ever had to do. The timing was particularly terrible, moving into Aunt Violet's house had been rough on them both. Duke having to adjust to school life. He thought they might shout, cry, but instead they hadn't said anything and that was worse somehow. As though they'd never expected anything better from him.

'Give me ten minutes and then try them again.' She holds the phone up as she walks, her face sliding in and out of focus. She stops at the front door and looks directly at the camera.

'Goodbye, Charlie.' And then she is gone and he wants to call her back but she has her own life to lead and so does he.

He waits, checking his watch frequently as the minutes tick painfully past.

After ten minutes he calls Nina, knowing that Pippa will have kept her word.

'Hey.' He smiles brightly as the video connects. Nina glares at him. Her face is full of heavy make-up. Mum would hate it. Duke is next to her, pale, withdrawn, his arms crossed over his chest. 'How are you both? Any news?'

'Duke nearly got expelled for spray painting "meat is murder" on the side of the school,' Nina says, a what-are-you-going-to-do-about-that-then expression on her face.

'Right.' Charlie doesn't know what to say. Whether to tell him off for graffiti, praise his principles, ask him why he did it but then he realizes that he doesn't have to do anything. That's Violet's job and relief floods through him. He knew he wasn't cut out for raising kids.

'Evie asked me to,' Duke says. 'She's my friend. *She* likes me,' Duke says in a tone that implies Charlie doesn't.

Charlie makes stilted conversation for another couple of minutes before he tells them they can come and visit in the holidays.

'We can go to the top of the Empire State Building,' he says.

'Whatever.' Nina picks her nails, bored. Duke doesn't say anything else except goodbye in the smallest, saddest voice that Charlie has ever heard.

*

Charlie wakes early. The boxes are packed, their flights are booked. They really should get up and strip the bed; it's almost time to leave. This is it. Everything they both want.

Or is it?

Next to him, Sasha links her fingers through his. Her other hand splayed across his chest.

'Do you think . . . we're doing the right thing?' he asks. He isn't only referring to leaving the children. He's questioning their relationship.

Charlie has been going over what Marty told him about Bo giving up his dream of earning a living as a full-time musician. Turning down the opportunity to be in the James Patrick Ensemble because he had a new dream – Mum.

Would he give everything up for Sasha?

Would she give everything up for him?

Would he want her to?

He feels the weight of Sasha shift in the bed, knows she is propped on her elbow staring at him. He opens his eyes but he doesn't reach for his glasses, not wanting the blur of her shape to sharpen. Knowing what will be written on her face.

'Of course. Don't you want to go?'

'I do but I'm wondering if this is the right time. Duke got into trouble at school and—'

'He's a kid. That's what they do.'

'It isn't only that. The "Missing Presumed Dead" application should be approved soon and although I've said to Aunt Violet it's okay that she uses Mum and Bo's money to raise the kids, I'm worried that when they are both older there might not be anything left for them, financially.'

'So, speak to a solicitor and sort it all out.'

'Aunt Violet works for a solicitors. She knows what she's talking about.'

'You can't just take her word for these things. Surely siblings are the next of kin? Shouldn't the estate come to you?'

'It's complicated. With Aunt Violet fighting for custody—'

'There isn't exactly a fight for Nina and Duke, is there?'

She's right. Should Charlie have fought for them? He thinks about the promise he made to his mum.

Look after them.

Look after himself.

Contrasting and conflicting.

He's supposed to be getting on a plane in five hours.

Sasha is watching him, trying to read his thoughts. He tucks her hair behind her ear and kisses her, thinking back to their first kiss – awkward and accidental – and then travelling back further. His first kiss at six, which felt thrilling and embarrassing, and then his first real kiss at thirteen, which had felt . . . everything. It had felt like everything.

Should it always feel like that or does time naturally wear the sharp edges of attraction down to a dullish blade?

Is the indecision he feels over leaving Nina and Duke partly because, deep down, he feels indecisive about Sasha?

His mum and Bo were always touching, kissing. Laughing. He'd never heard them base anything on a five-year plan.

His relationship with Sasha has been centred around them wanting the same things but what if he wants something different now? What then?

'You haven't changed your mind, have you?' Sasha asks.

'No. It's just . . . the children. What if we—'

'Exactly. *The* children. Not *our* children. Charlie, there will always be a place for Nina and Duke in our lives. They can come and visit when we're settled and we can see them when we get back but I don't . . . I don't want to be their mother.'

'I'm not asking you to be.' He leans forward. 'You can just be their friend. You got on well with Nina, doing her make-up—'

'That was a one-off, Charlie. Not a lifetime.'

'It wouldn't be a lifetime. Nina will be off to uni in three years, Duke will be—'

'Always dependent on you. If you go back, they will both *always* be dependent on you.'

'As an older brother, perhaps they'll turn to me for advice but I'm not their father.'

'But if you take on that role you would be, Charlie. Don't you see?' She takes his hand but he finds no comfort in it. 'And it's very commendable but it's not . . . not what I want. We've talked about this so many times. I want New York.'

'With or without me?'

There's a long silence. Charlie thinks of that ring in his pocket. The glittering diamond he thought was a substitute for those three words he can't say. He can't even say them now. He could pull out the box. Offer it to her now. Offer her everything.

But he doesn't.

'With or without you,' she says eventually, but not easily. Charlie sees the pain etch into her face. Feels it.

Part of him falls away. The part that thought he could be happy and in its place is an unutterable sadness.

'You want me to choose between you and my brother and sister?'

'You want me to choose between you and my career?'

Again, they both shuffle that little bit further apart. The space in the bed widening between them. There's a cold stretch of sheet in the middle of them now, where their bodies were once pressed together.

'I'm sorry,' he says.

'Me too. I wasn't expecting . . . this. But . . . sometimes I think I don't really know you. Not really.' She trails her fingertip over the scar on his wrist.

She has never asked him about it. She doesn't ask him anything now but he's a musician. He understands the meaning behind the words, the beats of silence. She never really wanted to know about his past because their future was all mapped out. If he rips that map in two now what is he left with?

'I'll be okay when I'm there.' He forces a smile.

'You're coming?' Her face lights up.

'Of course.'

She covers him in kisses, his neck, his shoulders. She dips her head lower and he gently places his hands on her cheeks and guides her mouth back to his. A perfunctory peck and then, 'We need to get moving, the Uber will be here soon.'

In the shower Charlie lathers his hair with the last of the shampoo before he watches the suds drain down the plughole, hoping they will suck his doubts and fears away too but long after he is dried and dressed they still linger.

Does he want to stay for Nina and Duke, or does he want to stay so he doesn't have to be with Sasha?

He just doesn't know and it isn't fair to use his siblings as an excuse. To let them think he wants them if it's solely because he may not want . . . this.

*

At the airport Sasha chatters away excitedly about the experiences they can share, catching a show on Broadway, catching a cab.

'They'll be bright yellow like in the movies.'

She talks about anything and everything except for the children.

'Anyway, it's nearly time! I'll just nip to the loo.' She kisses him before she leaves. Her lips are dry.

It's a relief when she's gone. Charlie's head throbs but he knows it isn't really her voice, or the sound of the suitcases being dragged along on wheels or the frequent announcements of the Tannoy that's causing him pain.

A tinny voice declares that their gate is open for boarding.

He takes out his mobile to switch it onto airplane mode so he doesn't forget later. There's a message alert.

Pippa has texted him a photo. He studies it; it takes a second for him to realize what it is.

What it means.

In an instant everything has changed, again.

CHAPTER SIXTEEN

Nina

Milk splatters over the table as Nina plunges her spoon into her bowl, her cornflakes sinking under the force.

'Don't play with your food,' Aunt Violet snaps.

'I've told you, like, a million times, I don't eat breakfast,' *you silly cow*, Nina adds, but only in her head. 'Mum never made—'

'Your mum never made you do a lot of things, letting you run wild.'

'Not forcing me to eat cereal I don't actually want isn't actually letting me run wild,' Nina says.

'It's the most important meal of the day.'

'Whatever. Gotta go or I'll be late. It takes me longer to get to school from here.'

'Yes, you've mentioned that.' Aunt Violet turns towards the sink and Nina thinks she hears her mutter '*a million times*' but she isn't sure. 'Duke, go with your sister. It's vital I'm at work a little earlier for a critical meeting.'

Nina rolls her eyes. You'd think Aunt Violet was a solicitor not a legal secretary the way she makes out her job to be so important; she probably only makes the tea and hands out biscuits.

Still, she knows Aunt Violet's boss, David, helped her with all the 'Missing Presumed Dead' forms, which will allow her to control . . . everything.

But not her; Nina will not be controlled.

She watches as her aunt lifts her hair off of her neck and clips it into place. Perhaps she fancies David. Hopes he'll slip off the glasses she wears for reading and let down her hair and say, 'Why Violet, you're beautiful,' except Aunt Violet isn't. She's ugly on the inside and that shows on the outside.

Nina doubts her aunt has ever been in love in her life, not like she is. Nina feels the buzz of excitement, which quickly fizzles out when she remembers her parents have gone and she shouldn't be feeling all the things she's feeling, a desperate need to be touched, kissed.

'Come on, squirt,' she says to Duke and they leave the house that does not in the month that they have been here, will never, feel like home.

On the corner, Nina balances her rucksack on a garden wall and unzips it, pulling out her make-up bag. She opens the camera app on her phone and switches it to selfie mode.

'Hold it still,' she instructs Duke as she uses the screen as a mirror, sweeping black mascara over her lashes, painting her lips caramel. She could have done this in her bedroom; it's not like she's scared of Aunt Violet or anything, but it's less hassle this way and, besides, she is used to it. Mum never liked her wearing make-up either but then a lot has changed in the few weeks since Mum was here.

'My arm aches,' Duke complains.

'That's because you haven't got any muscles,' Nina says.

'If I had I'd punch Jayden in the face,' Duke says fiercely.

'Is he still giving you hassle?'

'Only when Evie isn't around. I think he's scared of her.'

'Christ, Duke, learn to stick up for yourself. And find some new friends. Evie does nothing but get you into trouble.'

'She doesn't.'

'You got detention for that graffiti!'

'But I owed Evie for saving my life.'

'Dramatic, much. Only you could almost die eating an apple.'

'You can almost die doing anything.'

Nina's eyes meet her brother's; they are both thinking about the boat. The sea. Their parents. She feels the connection between them. The connection she used to feel with Charlie until he abandoned her. Charlie can't be relied upon. He isn't the big brother she adored when she was small, her Big Fish, but perhaps it is her turn to be the Big Fish for Duke.

'Look. I know we hate Violet but . . . we're lucky really we have somewhere to go and we're not in foster care. If you get expelled—'

'Charlie could—'

'Charlie couldn't. Besides, he's probably on the plane already.'

Her anger rises again. Nina rummages around for her blusher, lowering her face so Duke doesn't see the sting of tears in her eyes that she fights to hold back. She doesn't want to ruin her carefully drawn eyeliner.

'Hello.'

Nina's spirits sink. She hadn't heard Evie approach, that girl is like a bloody ninja without the fighting, of course, because Evie deplores violence. She's against pretty much everything as far as Nina can tell.

'Do you know,' she says to Nina now, 'that women expose themselves to approximately two hundred chemicals every day through make-up and beauty products?'

Nina throws her a scathing look. It's fine to be all fresh-faced and natural at eleven when you don't care about being attractive. Try it at fifteen when you're desperate for someone to fancy you.

'Really, you're pretty as you are,' Evie says. 'You don't need to try and attract boy—'

'And that's what you think every girl . . . every *woman* who wears make-up is doing?'

'It's just that I believe that women should be free from—'

'Fuck's sake. Feminism is about more than burning your bra, not that you'd have that problem yet.' Nina lowers her gaze point-edly to Evie's chest. 'Feminism is about choice. About being in control of your body, what you wear and how you wear it.'

'Did you know that the average woman spends almost ten thousand pounds on cosmetics during her lifetime? Imagine the good you could do, *choose* to do, with that instead.'

'Yeah, well, you go spend that on saving a dolphin or whatever and don't judge those of us who don't want to look like . . . you.'

Nina stalks away, feeling mean. What is wrong with her argu-ing with someone in year 7. Evie is young and idealistic and Nina knows that losing her parents and her home has made her cynical and bitter. She thinks about apologising, explaining that she really does love dolphins but, when she turns around, Duke and Evie are laughing at something; her words haven't affected Evie at all. Nina wishes she had her confidence, her certainty. Evie has a purpose, a place in the world, and Nina is still cast adrift, unsure of who she is. Suddenly she is aware of the layers of make-up covering her skin like a mask. She considers rubbing it off but then Miss Rudd is in front of her, hands on hips, and she's glad she has painted on a face that isn't hers.

'I hope you've brought in your English essay, Nina?'

Since Nina had returned to school Miss Rudd hadn't once said 'I'm sorry to hear about your parents' or 'You must be finding it hard to focus' instead asking about that bloody essay all the bloody time.

Bitch.

Before the bubbling anger she feels spews out of her mouth, putrid and poisonous, Maeve is next to her, linking her arm through hers. Nina feels herself calmly speak.

'I still haven't finished my essay yet, sorry.' She isn't sorry and knows she doesn't sound it.

'Nina!' Maeve says in a bright voice. 'Miss Rudd won't expect you to have done your homework from last term *under the circumstances*, when none of the other teachers have, will you, miss?' Maeve stares at their teacher, unflinching.

'No.' Miss Rudd offers a tight smile. 'Of course not.' She stalks away.

'What a cow,' Maeve says. 'Ignore her. Want to hang out with Lenny and Ryan later?'

'Nah. Boys of our own age are so immature.'

'What do you want to do then?'

'Avoid Vile Violet. Is there anyone at yours?'

'No. Empty house until Dad gets home.'

Nina feels a fluttering deep inside, the corners of her mouth lifting into a smile.

'Cool. I need to walk Duke home but then let's go to

yours and maybe Sean . . . your dad, I mean, can drive me home after?'

Nina mentally runs through her wardrobe. When she drops Duke at home she can get changed. Her black top perhaps. Something lower cut anyway. Something sexy.

Something to prove she is no longer a child.

CHAPTER SEVENTEEN

Charlie

Charlie stifles another yawn. There's nothing to see out of the window but darkness. He checks his watch again, nearly there.

There's a slowing as the train slides into the station. Charlie gathers up his rucksack and steps out into the night. It's still, peaceful, quiet. Nothing like the hustle and bustle that would have greeted him at JFK Airport if he'd caught his flight. Guilt warms his cheeks at the thought of Sasha flying alone, struggling with her own suitcase along with his, navigating her way without him to the vacant apartment owned by a friend of her father's that they'd only ever seen online.

He had seen myriad emotions cross her face at the airport as he'd told her he was staying: disappointment; anger; frustration; worry, but the one she'd settled on was resignation as though she'd never really expected him to leave.

'Yet, I'm not coming *yet*.' Charlie had tried to show her his phone, the photo from Pippa, to explain but she'd waved him away.

'I've got to go.'

'Ring me when you're settled. We'll talk everything through properly,' he had said but she'd been looking over his shoulder, not really listening and, instead of one of the big emotional movie good-byes with fierce hugs and endless tears, she'd given him a hurried kiss almost as an afterthought as she'd rushed towards the plane.

There's a single taxi at the rank, not a sunny bright yellow one, but one as black as his mood.

'You up from London?' asks the driver.

Instead of answering him, Charlie gives him the address. He's not in the mood for talking. He's not in the mood for listening either. He wants to shout and rage and . . . oddly, cry.

The journey is short but long enough for Charlie to have dozed. He starts awake when the driver loudly clears his throat, jerking his head upright, cricking his neck.

The sight before him is a deft blow to the stomach. After Pippa's picture he'd been expecting it, but it is still a shock.

He trudges down the path to his family home glaring at the 'For Sale' sign that spears the February frost on the lawn.

Inside, he heads straight for the kitchen, dialling Aunt Violet as he walks.

'You've put the house up for sale,' he says as the call connects, kicking himself for starting this way instead of asking about the children.

'Yes. I was going to tell you when you'd settled in New York. Legally we can't sell it yet but it could take months to find a buyer in this market. We'll need to sort through everything in it at some stage but I can—'

'I'm not in New York. This is rather sudden, isn't it?'

'We talked about finances, about me taking over everything when I filed the "Missing Presumed Dead" order.'

'I know but . . . the house?'

'What do you think I should do with it? I've a perfectly good home. Of course, you're entitled financially to—'

'I'm not ringing about my share.' Charlie grips the worktop in front of him. 'I want us to keep the house. To rent it out. It's already fully furnished. The monthly income can—'

'And who's going to collect the rent?' Violet asks.

'There are management companies—'

'Who take a hefty cut. Have you even looked into the potential income?'

'Not yet—'

'Or what being a landlord entails? The criteria a property has to meet? Fire exits? Boiler service? Energy performance certificates? Carbon monoxide alarms?'

'No, but—'

'Well, I have because I've researched it. This isn't a decision I've taken lightly, Charlie. But there are furniture and furnishings fire regulations, electrical safety standards. Not to mention—'

'Violet, please.' Charlie lowers his voice. 'I'm trying to do the right thing for Duke and Nina.'

'And I'm not?'

'I'm not saying that but . . . it's their home.'

'*Was*,' Violet says but with kindness. 'Was their home, Charlie, and hanging on to it, hanging on to the past, I really don't think it's in anyone's best interests. Not the children's. Not yours.'

'I want them to have the security of—'

'Charlie. Other kids sleeping in their old bedrooms won't give them security. It will be confusing.'

'It isn't just the money.'

'I understand that. You'll always have your memories, Charlie, and nobody can take those away. They're not dependent on bricks and mortar. But . . . keeping a house Duke and Nina can't live in won't make them happy because, really, the house isn't what they want, is it? You or I are not what they want. What they really want is Ronnie and Bo, but they can't have them.'

Charlie swallows hard, knowing that she is right.

He has a quick shower before heading over to Pippa's, his head clipping the beads from her home-made wind chime as he presses the bell and waits.

She's wearing black and white polka-dot pyjamas, her hair twisted in a towel on top of her head, fluffy pink slippers cover her feet. Her skin is make-up free and she looks about fourteen – the age they were when her grandma put a stop to their weekend sleepovers because, 'You've reached the age you'll have urges,' she had said.

'Urges?' Pippa had asked innocently. 'What are they then?'

Grandma had shot a look towards Charlie and he had quickly turned his snigger into a cough.

'It's like when you want a chocolate biscuit and you know you shouldn't but you can't help yourself,' Grandma had said.

'So . . . is Charlie the chocolate biscuit, or am I?'

'It's okay.' Charlie hadn't been able to bear Grandma looking so uncomfortable. 'We've already taken sex-ed at school.'

Grandma had shaken her head. 'Sex didn't exist in my day.'

'I think you'll find it did or I wouldn't be here,' Pippa had replied.

'Well, we didn't talk about it, only . . .'

'Urges?'

Unable to contain his laughter, Charlie had tugged Pippa's arm and under the hot summer sun they'd run up to Briar's Hill, flopping onto the dry and brittle grass. Pippa had shyly told him that she'd started to develop feelings for someone and Charlie had felt his tender heart beat faster.

Now, again, he feels his heart beat faster but he cannot pinpoint why.

'I . . . I didn't go to New York,' he says.

'No shit, Sherlock.' She gestures him inside. He squeezes down the hallway and it's like stepping back into his childhood. The wallpaper is exactly the same – faded rose print – the muddy brown carpet too but the stairlift is a newer addition.

The second Pippa opens the lounge door, Billie bowling-balls herself at him, licking his hands, his face, her frantic tail wagging so fast it lifts the pages of the magazine that's slung onto the sofa.

'How's she been?' Charlie asks.

'Fine. She's unsettled, of course, but she's comfortable with me. It's not like I'm a stranger.'

'And how are you?' It's important to Charlie that he knows. He hasn't asked her enough questions about her life since he's come back.

'I'm okay. Surprised to see you. Why aren't you in New York?'

'I couldn't get on the plane after your text. When I saw the house was up for sale, I panicked. I just can't see another family there. I see . . . us. Me, Nina, Duke and Billie. Our family.'

'So, you haven't agreed to sell it? I wasn't sure if you knew, that's why I sent the photo of the board.'

'I had no idea. It's not like it's ours to sell yet but Aunt Violet has applied for a "Missing Presumed Dead" certificate.'

'How do you feel about that?'

Charlie pauses. How *does* he feel about that? 'I don't know. I don't think I've properly accepted it yet. But I can't expect Aunt Violet to bring up Nina and Duke without any financial help.'

'There'll be things she can apply for: child benefit and tax credit.'

'I guess. I haven't really looked into it. With Violet working at a solicitors she seems to know what to do. She started the process back in January as soon as I'd rung her asking her to take the kids. Her boss is helping her, pushing things through as quickly as he can. I think . . . And I'm not sure but I think with her applying for the Missing Presumed Dead and then after that the death certificate, it gives her the right to control all of Mum and Bo's affairs because there isn't a will, not one we've been able to find anyway.'

'But surely children are the next of kin?'

'I don't know. I didn't mind when it was the savings, the life insurance. She's told me there'd be paperwork for me to sign and I agreed, I don't want Nina or Duke to go without, but—'

'She's put the house up for sale.'

'Yes. It's not like I think she's after the money but . . . I thought it made more sense to rent the house out. Have a regular income.' Charlie crosses to the window and lifts the curtains, checking that the board is still there. It doesn't seem . . . real. None of this seems real. 'I've just called Violet and suggested it and she said that I want to hold on to the house so I can hold on to my memories.' He turns, hands splayed. 'What do you think?'

'What I think,' she says carefully, 'is that perhaps you need your own solicitor. You could have spoken to one from New York. You didn't need to miss your flight.'

Charlie stares out into the darkness. His own pale face reflected back at him.

He could have spoken to a solicitor on the phone.

Why didn't he get on that plane?

He settles himself back on the sofa, and Billie nestles beside him, her head on his lap. He strokes her ears finding comfort there, and courage too.

'I guess I've been pretending that everything is okay. That Mum and Bo are still here with Duke and Nina but seeing that For Sale sign really brought it home to me. Mum will never potter around the garden again. Bo will never perch on the sofa, carving his wooden figures. Nina and Duke . . . The music room.' *All The Things You Are.* 'Whoever buys the house will probably turn it back into a dining room.' He shakes his head, sadly. 'It isn't okay, is it? Nina and Duke can't be okay because . . . because . . .' He covers his face with his hands while he composes himself and, when he lowers them, he can feel his eyes are wet with tears. 'I . . . I've felt that . . . that absolute misery, Pippa, that comes with having your childhood ripped apart.'

'I know.' She crouches before him and takes his hand. 'I was there.'

'I pushed you away,' he whispers.

She shakes her head. 'It isn't important, it's—'

'But it is. I want to make it up to you.'

'It's not the right time to go over the past, Charlie,' she says sharply.

'But . . .' He takes a breath. He doesn't know what she needs because he doesn't know her anymore. 'I'd like to be friends again. Get to know you. What you've been doing. What your plans are for the future?'

Pippa takes the towel from her head and her damp hair falls around her shoulders. It smells of the strawberry laces they used to eat as kids.

'I don't really know what I'm going to do. Grandma left the house to me and Mum – you know my parents lives in Scotland now? Now Dad's out of the army he wanted to settle near his parents.'

Charlie shakes his head. He used to know everything about Pippa and now he knows nothing. 'I'm not even really sure how you ended up living here again?'

'I only stayed in Birmingham after uni because . . . because of Rick really.'

Rick.

Charlie remembers how he had felt when Mum had told him that Pippa had fallen in love, was living with someone.

'How do you feel about that?' Mum had asked.

'Fine,' he had replied but the truth was the thought of Pippa being somewhere else, with someone else, had made him feel sick, which was ridiculous and unfair because he had left first. He'd told himself it was because she'd been his best friend since he was five that he worried about her, never admitting, not even to himself that, perhaps, it was more than that.

'So, you and Rick . . .'

'He wasn't right for me.'

'But he treated you okay?'

'Like a princess.'

Charlie feels his fingers curl into fists and he forces himself to straighten them again.

'But I don't believe in fairy tales, happily ever afters. Do you?' Her light blue eyes hold his along with an unspoken question.

'Ninety-nine per cent of the manuscripts writers submit to me end with happily ever after; it's what everyone wants, isn't it?'

'Yes, but my story isn't finished yet and I'm ready for the next chapter. I came back here because Grandma needed me, but now? I don't know. You seem to have this clear path all mapped out but—'

'I really don't. I still feel about twelve on the inside.'

'Glad you don't look it on the outside. It wasn't your finest age. All that hair!'

'What was my finest age then?'

'You're not looking too shabby right now.'

Is she flirting with him? Is he flirting with her?

What is he doing?

'I think we're all just making it up as we go along,' she says. 'I once thought adults had it all figured out, but we don't, do we?'

'I certainly don't.' He is overcome with a feeling of helplessness. 'Pippa, I really don't know what to do.' He can't untangle whether he's referring to the house, the kids, Sasha, New York . . . It's such a lot.

Too much.

Tears trickle down his cheeks, but he makes no move to brush them away. He has never felt so confused.

'Charlie.' Pippa moves to sit next to him on the sofa. Her hand reaches across his lap and she pats Billie's head, before her fingers find his. He grips them tightly. 'Remember what my grandma used to say?'

'You are capable of more than you think.' He can almost hear her, smell the lavender talcum powder she used to sprinkle over herself, the sofa, the carpet, to try and eradicate the bad smell that Buttercup, the Jack Russell she used to have, would leave behind.

'It's true. You are capable of so much more than you know. But you're exhausted. You need a decent night's sleep and then you can come up with a plan before you speak to Violet again.'

'Fail to prepare . . .'

'. . . prepare to fail.' Pippa finishes another of her grandmother's favourite sayings.

Charlie remembers the times they would often finish each other's sentences, realizing that, despite the years and the miles that had come between them, Pippa still knows him better than anyone else. He finds that both sad and comforting.

Achingly familiar.

Their eyes meet. Her gaze flickers towards his lips before travelling back upwards once more. His thumb begins to stroke the back of her hand, her skin warm and soft. She gently eases it out of his grasp.

'You should go. I'm tired too.'

'Can I stay here?'

'I don't think that's a good idea.'

But still, she doesn't pull back; if anything she moves closer.

It is then his phone begins to ring.

Sasha.

It's late. His conversation with Sasha had been short and curt, more on her part than his.

Yes, she'd arrived okay. The apartment is tiny but thanks to the owner being a friend of her father's it's rent free for six months and she's very grateful. She's tired. They'd talk tomorrow.

She hadn't wanted to hear his apologies or excuses. Thankfully she hadn't asked if he had a plan.

He still hasn't.

Pippa had walked him to the front door, her hand on Billie's collar, using her as a barrier between them as she wished him a swift 'goodnight'.

Now he's lying in Duke's bed that creaks each time he turns. His feet are hanging over the end and the single duvet barely covers him but there is something soothing about being back in his old room. He remembers lying here as a child, unable to sleep. Pippa would be in her bedroom opposite and they'd communicate via torchlight.

He tries it now, using the flashlight app on his phone.

One blink – *are you awake?*

No response. He thinks she probably doesn't even sleep in the same box room anymore, which used to be plastered in posters of New Kids On The Block and NSYNC.

He remembers another code, three flashes – *Do you want to meet tomorrow?*

Darkness.

He tries five flashes – *I'm sorry.*

Finally, he receives a response, two flashes in return.

Go to sleep.

But he can't sleep.

What is he going to do?

Tomorrow he will sort everything out, somehow.

CHAPTER EIGHTEEN

Duke

Duke can't sleep. He can't stop thinking about Charlie in New York. He said he'd text Duke when he got there but Aunt Violet makes him and Nina put their handsets in the kitchen drawer each night before bed so he can't check. It's a stupid rule.

'What if there's a fire and I need to call nine-nine-nine?' he had asked Violet.

'The smoke alarm will make a noise and wake me and I'll call them.'

'What if there's a bomb in my room and I need to call the army?'

'Who would leave a bomb in your room? Now you're just being silly.'

Jayden might want to blow him up, Duke had thought, but Aunt Violet didn't want to listen to him anymore. Not like Mum, who at least used to let him get his worries out of his head before dismissing them. It's one of the things he hates about living here. He makes a list of the others.

1. Billie isn't here
2. Going to school
3. Meat on his plate every dinnertime
4. When he flushes the toilet, the water is green

He hears Nina creep out of her room and downstairs. He wonders what she is doing. Whether she's sneaking out again the way she had when they lived at home.

He wonders where she went then. What she's doing now.

CHAPTER NINETEEN

Nina

Nina scurries back to bed, clutching her phone to her chest. She'll put it back in the kitchen drawer before Aunt Violet checks tomorrow.

There's no text from Charlie but she doesn't care. He abandoned her before and he has again, so what?

Everybody leaves her.

But however flippant she tries to be, she cannot calm the throb of loneliness she feels.

Charlie left her to be with Sasha.

Her parents left her and Duke behind on New Year's Eve to be together.

She has no one.

What if she did?

She compiles a text:

I love you

Her feelings laid out before her in black and white. Should she send it? She runs her thumb over the letters before deleting them. A rejection would sever the last strand of hope she clings on to that there is somebody, somewhere, who will love her.

Who won't leave her.
She opens a webpage.
How can you tell if someone fancies you?
She reads the responses becoming more disheartened.
She begins a new search,
How can you make someone fancy you?
This is more helpful. These are all things she can do.
Will do.
Tomorrow.

CHAPTER TWENTY

Charlie

Charlie rubs sleep from his eyes. Dawn is dragging colour into the sky as he rolls out of Duke's single bed. Every part of him aches. His back. His shoulders. His heart. It's still the middle of the night in New York. Sasha will be curled up, snug, in the double bed that was meant for them both, resting before she begins her new life, her new adventure. Without him.

He pads downstairs. Last night after he'd left Pippa's he'd gone straight upstairs to bed but now, as he opens the lounge curtains, he can see how sorrowful the house looks. It's only been empty for a few weeks but a film of dust coats the sideboard, the photos. He picks up a silver frame that contains a photo of the five of them – six if you count Billie. It isn't a recent shot. Mum's hair isn't streaked with grey and Bo doesn't have his paunch. Duke is missing his front tooth as he beams into the camera, Nina has her hair in pigtails, and Charlie . . . Charlie is glancing to the side as though he can't wait to get away. He gently places the picture back down and leaves them there, frozen in time.

Halfway down the hallway is one of Billie's tug toys, the orange rope frayed at the end. It's like one of those weird documentaries

133

that investigate sudden disappearances. A family stepping momentarily out of their lives never to return.

In the kitchen he searches for food. He had barely eaten yesterday, a chocolate chip muffin at the airport and a soggy egg sandwich on the train. The fridge is empty, as he'd expected, but there are still some tins left in the cupboards, baked beans and spaghetti hoops, things he is guessing that Aunt Violet doesn't approve of. He opens a can and scoops congealed macaroni cheese into a saucepan and while it heats he studies the things pinned to the cork board. A letter from Nina's school from the teacher she hates – Miss Rudd – reminding her that her English essay is overdue and she must hand it in on the first day back. He guesses all the teachers will now cut her some slack. There's a list of spellings that must be Duke's along with his home-ed timetable, which is exhausting just to read. There's a couple of photos – Bo barbecuing, a baseball cap pulled low over his face, while Mum lounges in a red and white striped deckchair with a glass of wine, Nina and her friend Maeve in the background, and one of Billie, panting into the lens, Duke's arms wrapped around her neck. How he must miss her. Finally, in Mum's scrawl that acts as a magic wand vanishing his appetite away, 'Happy New Year!!!' is written on a pink Post-it note. He traces the letters with his fingertips. The hopes she must have had when she'd written this not knowing that she'd barely see in the new year and it would be anything but happy for them all.

He sits at the table. There are prong marks in the soft pine. He remembers Nina as a toddler banging her hard plastic fork in frustration as she waited for her dinner.

There are other dents too.

Scratches from a biro in front of the place that Charlie still thinks of as his. He would sit here and write what he grandly referred to as his novel but was really a jumble of pretentious thoughts staining the A4 paper.

Dried paint is crusted around the edge of the table. He picks at it with his thumbnail until the blue flakes away. He thinks this probably came from Duke.

The grooves of a family. The map of their ordinary lives.

How can he get rid of this table where they had eaten meals for as long as he can remember? He wants to keep this at the very least. What about the rest of their things?

He wanders around the house. There's so much stuff here.

In the music room he closes his eyes, hearing his mum's soulful voice singing 'Why Don't You Do Right'. She sang that a lot in those dark days after Dad had gone, when all her love had poured into Charlie instead until he too had let her down, brought her so much shame she had packed him off to a therapist to try and 'fix' him.

As he leaves the room he notices Duke's open saxophone case, instrument still inside. He frowns. Why hasn't his brother taken it to Violet's? He remembers Nina teasing him on New Year's Eve.

'Duke is basically always playing. It's because he hasn't got a life.'

'Music *is* my life. Well, music and Billie. I would literally die without them,' Duke had said.

Charlie's throat closes. His poor, poor brother.

He picks up the case; he'll take it to Violet's when he visits.

In the garage, he puts the saxophone in the boot of the family's baby blue VW Beetle.

He glances around. It is here that Bo taught him how to whittle.

'See this, Charlie lad?' He'd passed Charlie a lump of wood.

'You can give it a shape. Make it anything you want it to be. All you need is patience, imagination and a bit of faith.'

'But it doesn't look like anything.'

'Not yet, maybe. But smooth away those rough edges and, in time, you'll be left with something beautiful.'

'Do you think I can do it?'

'All you can do is try your best, lad.'

Charlie had never been as good as Bo, but he remembers how he had held the wood in one hand, knife in the other, persevering until he had something resembling a fish. Then he had taken a small piece of wood and fashioned another.

'Big fish, little fish!' Nina had clapped her small hands in delight and had insisted on carrying them everywhere with her. He wonders where they are now. Even if Nina still had them, she probably wouldn't remember the meaning behind them. His little sis.

His little fish.

He wonders where Bo's tools are now. He scans the shelves. There are three large, plastic boxes, labelled with names: Charlie, Nina, Duke.

He lifts his down, carries it back into the house.

In the kitchen, he removes the lid. Takes out the contents one by one. They are out of order. Muddled.

Photos of him as a baby, Mum gazing at him tenderly as he slept in her arms. A tiny box containing a tooth and a lock of hair. A postcard from Frankfurt; he had sent that after he became a literary agent during his first ever visit to a book fair.

Even after he left she had never stopped collecting things.

Then clippings from *The Bookseller* announcing deals he has made throughout his career.

She was proud of him.

The realization is bittersweet.

Too late.

The regret Charlie feels is unquantifiable.

He rifles through the rest of the things.

Pictures he had drawn: stick people holding hands, in front of a boxy house. A brilliant yellow sun shining in a light blue sky. School reports; 'English – A – Charlie shows a natural talent for writing.' Something unidentifiable fashioned out of clay with googly eyes.

A letter in a childish uneven scrawl.

Dear Mummy,

I am very sorry I broke your favourite vase and then blamed it on the wind. Cross my heart promise I won't lie to you again.

Followed by a sad face.

But then, underneath a reply from his mum,

Accidents happen. It's what you do afterwards that counts. Thank you for making a cross-my-heart promise you won't lie again. I know they are your best promises and you will keep them. Love you lots Charlie and nothing you do will ever change that.

Charlie can barely see the smiley face inside of a heart she had drawn at the bottom of the page through his tears.

He crosses his arms on the table and buries his face into them, shoulders heaving.

She had loved him, had taken pride in his achievements, always, and it had been his guilt, his shame, that had made him blame her, so he didn't blame himself. She had sent him to a therapist, not to 'fix him' but to try and help him.

How had he got it all so wrong?

He cries for her, for seeing things clearly when it's too late.

His eyes are sore, throat raw, by the time he composes himself. Packing everything back into the box except the letter.

Accidents happen. It's what you do afterwards that counts.

Mum and Bo aren't here anymore and Charlie had run away. Left the house. Left his siblings. He had promised his mum New Year's Eve he would look after them.

Thank you for making a cross-my-heart promise you won't lie again. I know they are your best promises and you will keep them.

Should he be the one to raise them? Could he?

He takes a shaky breath. Begins to pace to work off the adrenaline. He cannot make a life-changing decision based on the overwhelming emotion he feels in this moment.

It wouldn't be solely his life he would change.

He stalks down the hallway, pausing at the music room, Duke's saxophone.

He should be here playing it. It's what Mum and Bo would want.

But what does *he* want? Charlie cannot get his thoughts in order.

He hadn't got on that plane for a reason.

Upstairs, in Duke's room, the shelves are still crammed with books. He doesn't seem to have taken too much. In Nina's room, pieces of Blu Tack are stuck to the wall where posters used to be. An empty shelf – at least she had taken something.

A Coke can crumpled on the floor. He picks it up and takes it over to her bin but when he sees what she has already thrown away the can slips through his fingers. He covers his lips with his fingers, tries to quell the tears that threaten once more. Crouching down, he lifts them out. The wooden big fish and little fish he had carefully whittled all those years ago.

She had kept them.

Until now.

He puts them on the empty shelf before changing his mind. She doesn't want them. Doesn't want him.

It confirms the doubts he is wrestling with. He has no idea how children think. What they want.

But he could learn?

All you need is patience, imagination and a bit of faith.

Can he bring them together, not to recreate the family they have lost, but to form something new?

'But it doesn't look like anything.'

'Not yet, maybe. But smooth away those rough edges and, in time, you'll be left with something beautiful.'

Dazed, he stumbles back to the kitchen. There is an emotion he can't identify in the pit of his stomach and he doesn't know whether it is excitement or fear.

Perhaps deep down this is what he wanted all along, he just hadn't realized it because the thought of becoming a substitute father is huge and terrifying. Bo is such a lot to live up to.

'Do you think I can do it?' he whispers.

'All you can do is try your best, lad.'

He is back at the table. The one with the dents and the scratches he had been so desperate to hang on to an hour before. Now, he realizes it isn't the table with the marks on that he wants but the family who made them.

His family.

He'll fight for them if he has to.

CHAPTER TWENTY-ONE

Nina

Nina expects a fight when she comes downstairs for breakfast, mobile in her pocket, but Aunt Violet is distracted. If she's noticed Nina had taken her handset she doesn't mention it.

While Duke shakes cornflakes into both of their bowls she revisits the webpages she had read last night.

If you have feelings for someone. Tell them. Be honest.

In the cold light of day she questions whether she can really do that. What if she is laughed at or rejected or worse?

But . . . what if she isn't?

Before she can decide either way the doorbell rings.

CHAPTER TWENTY-TWO

Charlie

Accidents happen. It's what you do afterwards that counts.

This.

This is what Charlie is doing afterwards. Ringing Aunt Violet's doorbell. Intent on telling her that he has made a huge mistake. That he wants to take Nina and Duke home where they belong, with him.

He hasn't been here for years. There had been a distance between her and Mum once Bo moved in, a gap that Charlie didn't understand and didn't try to bridge.

He has spent his life not asking enough questions. Not trying to understand.

Today, now, he is making a change.

'Charlie.' If Violet is surprised to see him she doesn't show it.

She invites him in and they walk towards the kitchen. The kids are sitting at the table eating breakfast. His heart lifts when he sees them. How could he have walked away from them? They are a family, bound and tethered by their own grief.

'Charlie!' Duke jumps down from his chair and runs straight at him, wrapping his arms around his waist. Charlie hugs him tightly.

Nina doesn't move, appraising him over her suspended spoon of cornflakes, which drips milk back into her bowl.

'Not in New York then?' He can't tell whether she is pleased or not.

'No.'

'Go and get ready for school,' Violet says.

'But I haven't finished—'

'Now,' Violet cuts Duke off.

'You complain I don't eat breakfast and now I am—'

'You too, Nina.'

'Whatever.' Nina makes a painstakingly slow exit from the room.

Violet closes the door after her and gestures for Charlie to take a seat. She doesn't offer him a drink. His mouth is dry; his tongue feels too big for his mouth.

Perhaps he should have waited until he had rehearsed what he wants to say, how he wants to say it. Until the children were at school at the very least.

'I'm here about Nina and Duke. I've come to get them. I think they should live with me. In the house.'

'No.'

'But I think—'

'You *think*?'

She crosses her arms. The hope he had had that she would be pleased to relinquish the responsibility trickles away from him. Sweat prickles in his armpits. He knows the importance of language, decisiveness, he negotiates for a living for God's sake, but there is more at stake than a publishing deal and he already feels it slipping away from him.

'I *know* it's for the best. I want them to live with me.'

'Why?'

'Mum would have—'

'You, Charlie. What do *you* want? A loss of freedom, to be financially supporting Duke and Nina for years to come. It doesn't end after school you know, parenting. There's university. And that's without everything in-between. The tantrums, the hostility. You really want all of that?'

'Do you?' he snaps and then begins again. 'Yes. I've thought about what's involved—'

'When? When have you considered it? When you were running back to London? Accepting a job in New York? Are you still going? Will you be dragging the children halfway across the world? What if you don't? What will you do?'

He is silent because she is right. He stares down at the black and white chequered floor tiles, a chessboard. It's his move but he hasn't thought this through properly. He hasn't spoken to Sasha. To Simon, his boss. He doesn't know if he can pass on New York and keep his job in the London office. How practical will it be to jump on the train to the city? Can he even do that within Nina and Duke's school hours? He works from home sometimes, reading manuscripts, answering queries, but there's a large portion of his job which is composed of face-to-face meetings.

He clears his throat. 'I haven't worked out the finer details.'

'Which proves you're not ready to be a parent. You can't provide the stability they need. I'm best placed to bring them up. I'm in my fifties, Charlie, I'm never going to have children of my own. I'll likely never live with a man, I'm too set in my ways, but you . . . you have your whole life ahead of you. The girlfriend Duke keeps talking about . . . Sasha, is it?'

Charlie nods.

'You should be in New York with her. You only get one life, Charlie. Do you want to spend it here? In a legal battle – and don't forget where I work, and then what? You're stuck. Tied to the place you couldn't wait to move away from.'

'But—'

'What if you turn out like him? Your dad?'

Charlie's stomach tightens as her words land with a hard punch. 'I don't think . . .'

'*Think*. There's that word again, Charlie. I know you don't want to be like him but sometimes it's inevitable. There's that genetic link. You went through such a lot, Charlie. Is that what you want for Duke and Nina?'

The floor seems to tilt beneath his chair. It's his move again but it's already checkmate.

His dad falls into the forefront of his mind. His dad who he had thought loved him once but then had failed him in the worst imaginable way. Part of the reason Charlie was so pleased children didn't feature in his and Sasha's five-year plan was because, if he's honest, he is scared he'll turn out the same. Scared he'll crumble under the weight of everyone else's needs. Memories strobe. His dad pushing him away when he brought him a book to read. His dad screaming at him to be left alone. His dad packing a suitcase, leaving. And then . . . what came after.

'The children will be late for school and I need to go to work. Go home, Charlie.'

Charlie stumbles as he stands. He opens the kitchen door; Duke and Nina are on the other side.

How much have they overheard?

'I've got to go back to London for . . .' he falters.

'Whatever,' says Nina dragging Duke down the hallway. 'We're going to school.'

He wants to call them back to explain, but he really doesn't know what to say.

Half an hour later, Charlie is on the platform waiting for a train. A boy wearing a 'Seven Today' badge pushes in front of him.

'Sorry,' his mother says. 'It's his birthday. We're taking him to the Tower of London. He's overexcited. You know what kids are like.'

Charlie nods, even though he doesn't, not really. But he watches as the boy smiles as his mum and his dad both take one of his hands and he wonders if it's the things he will see at the Tower of London that will stick in his mind or the being together. He thinks it is time, love, that children need the most, and, although Charlie didn't receive either from his dad, he knows as he watches the boy's mum lick the edge of a tissue before dabbing away something at the corner of the boy's mouth that he had that in abundance from his own mother.

Time.

Love.

He is half of Mum.

He has her hair, her eyes, her musical talent, so perhaps she is his stronger half and this is a comfort. Whatever Violet says, Charlie is not like his dad.

He is not running away.

Family is hope, a future, love.

Not only, and not always genetics, but a choice.

Nina and Duke are his choice.

He couldn't tell them that at the house because he doesn't want to get their hopes up but he is going to London to meet with a solicitor he knows.

To find out where he stands.

Accidents happen. It's what you do afterwards that counts.

This.

This is what Charlie is doing afterwards.

Fighting.

CHAPTER TWENTY-THREE

Duke

So, this morning had been awful. Terrible. Horrible.

Duke had come downstairs, and Aunt Violet had asked, 'Have you done your homework?'

'Yes,' Duke had lied. He hadn't been able to because, as it turns out, Mum telling him that being banker at Monopoly made him brilliant at maths wasn't true at all. He didn't understand prime numbers or factors or literally anything.

Duke had concentrated intently on tipping cornflakes into his bowl and Nina's, flooding them with milk, hoping that was the end of the conversation.

It wasn't.

'How did you find it?' Aunt Violet asked.

'Fine,' Duke had replied because, although she'd asked a question, he knew she didn't really want to hear his answer. 'Fine' seemed to avoid her going off on one of her long speeches about how lucky he was to live here and go to school and how he didn't know he was born, which was ridiculous, because if he hadn't been born he wouldn't be here, now, so of course he knew it. Fine seemed to be the word to use when you wanted to avoid a proper conversation. No wonder adults said it so much.

Surprisingly, she hadn't said anything else though. Just stared out of the kitchen window with a faraway look in her eyes until the doorbell had rung. She'd bounced up and down on her toes a few times like boxers do before she'd strode down the hall.

It was Charlie! He wasn't in New York!

Aunt Violet had bundled him and Nina out of the kitchen and closed the door although they had remained in the hallway, their ears pressed against the wood.

When Charlie had said he'd come to get the children, Nina had actually squeezed Duke's hand so hard he'd pulled away and tried to give her a glare but she'd been smiling and then so was he.

They were going home!

Except they weren't.

Aunt Violet said some stuff and Charlie didn't say much at all.

Afterwards he had come out the kitchen and told them he was going back to London. Before Duke could ask any questions, Nina had dug her fingers into his arm and yanked him away.

Now, when they get outside, he pulls his arm away from Nina. 'But we need to talk to Charlie, tell him that we want to live with him. He might change his mind and stay.'

'He won't change his mind. You heard him. He barely put up a fight. He's only here to ease his conscience.'

'He didn't go to America. That has to mean something.'

'It means he can go now and tell himself he tried.'

Duke has to half-run to keep up with his sister.

'What was that stuff about Charlie's dad?' He's never thought about him before, even when Charlie called Dad 'Bo', he'd never really wondered where Charlie's real dad was.

'I dunno. Mum said he was "troubled", whatever that means. I think the scars on Charlie's wrist are something to do with him.'

'What did he—'

'I don't know!' Nina shouts. 'I don't know anything except we're stuck at Aunt bloody Violet's forever. Christ, I'd rather have drowned too.' The minute she says this she clamps her hands over her mouth as if she wants to stuff the words back in but Duke's ears can't unhear them.

'It's okay,' Duke says quietly. 'I know you didn't mean that.'

'Shut up, Duke,' she snaps.

He swallows back his tears as he trots after her into the playground. Nina never used to be so mean. Before Mum and Dad died she used to sometimes laugh at his jokes and Duke wishes he can make her happy again but he can't do that when he has forgotten how to laugh too and can't think of anything funny to say.

'Don't walk with me now,' she hisses, shoving him away. Duke thinks that sometimes Nina is embarrassed to have him as a brother and that makes him sad because, although Nina looks odd now, a bit like a clown really with her thick make-up, he knows that inside she is just the same and he loves her anyway.

The second he is on his own, Jayden saunters over, flanked by Luke and Brandon. Duke no longer uses his satchel because he got laughed at; instead, today, he has an old black rucksack that Aunt Violet used to keep her swimming kit in. It smells a little of chlorine but Duke thinks it's cool.

'What's this piece of shit?' Jayden wrenches it from his shoulder and tosses it to Luke who turns it over in his hands before saying,

'It ain't even branded.'

'Branded with what?' Duke asks. He thought only cows were

branded. Is it kinder when they have a tag through their ear rather than when they are marked with a red-hot iron? Duke imagines branding Jayden's forehead with 'idiot', and he begins to smile.

'Freak.'

A hard shove sends him sprawling to the floor. His knees and palms sting.

'You, boy!' The deputy head is crossing the playground and Jayden quickly offers his hand to Duke and pulls him to his feet.

'He tripped, sir.' Jayden smiles.

The teacher walks away and Jayden moves his fingers onto Duke's wrist, twisting, hurting. He struggles to be free. But then, suddenly, Nina is there, and Duke doesn't see her school uniform but a mask and a cape.

Super Sister to the rescue.

'Oi. Dickhead.' Nina slaps Jayden around the head. 'Leave him alone.'

Jayden releases his grip and slinks away.

Duke puts his arms around Nina's waist but she pushes him away. 'I'm sick of sorting your shit out.' She stalks away. Hero to zero in seconds.

Tutor time is awful. Terrible. Horrible.

Everyone traipses to the front and hands in their school trip money to Miss Greenly except Duke who hadn't given the letter to Aunt Violet because the thought of being stuck on a coach for hours with Jayden is not fun even if Evie would be there. She's at the dentist this morning and she's the only one that Jayden, Luke and Brandon seem to be scared of.

Miss Greenly asks him to stay behind after the bell has rung.

'Duke—' she smiles '—we don't want you to miss out on the trip. Is there a reason why you haven't brought your slip in?'

He shrugs.

'The school can help out families if they can't meet the cost. It's nothing to be embarrassed about.'

'It isn't that.'

'What is it?' She looks so kind he almost tells her about the bullying but then he remembers when he'd waited until after class to confide in her before. Jayden had stood in the doorway. He'd mimed slicing his throat with his index finger. Snitches get stitches, he'd mouthed and every time Duke thinks of his throat being cut he feels sick.

'Duke?' Miss Greenly prompts gently. 'Is there something you want to tell me?'

'I'm ill,' Duke blurts out. 'I mean, not now, but I get really travel sick.' It isn't exactly a lie. If he was trapped on a coach with Jayden he would absolutely vomit. 'Please don't make me go. I'll bring a letter in explaining.' He thinks Nina might help him forge one but then she'd said she is 'sick of sorting his shit out' so he doesn't know what he'll do.

'Can I go now, please?'

Miss Greenly nods and Duke hurries out into the corridor.

Jayden is waiting.

'Has everyone seen the weirdo's rucksack?' he says loudly. His friends snigger.

Duke tries to ignore them as he hurries to the science lab while they continue to laugh about his bag, his hair, everything.

So, he's weird . . . so what? It's something Nina has been calling him for years so it *shouldn't* hurt but somehow it does. Not quite as much as the Chinese burn Jayden had given him. He can still feel the sting on his wrist where his skin had been twisted in two different directions.

Insults snap at his heels like dogs, and not friendly ones like Billie. At the thought of her Duke wants to cry but he doesn't want the other kids to think Jayden is the cause of tears and so he begins humming 'I Wan'na Be Like You' inside his head and thinking of happier times.

He is calmer now. Jayden is in a different class for science. He sits on a high wooden stool on the bench. The class are told to partner up for experiments and everyone pairs up immediately leaving Duke alone. He's put with two girls and the double lesson passes quickly.

At breaktime the wind blows the rain across the playground. Duke huddles against the wall, trying to keep warm and dry. No one comes over to talk to him but that means no one is calling him names either so he takes that as a win. Frequently he checks his watch as though he is waiting for someone or has somewhere important to be, rather than counting the minutes until the bell rings and he can return to the safety of his classroom where, other than the odd insults or the scrunched-up pieces of paper Jayden chucks at him, he feels relatively secure.

Halfway through English, Evie appears, and after the lesson they walk to the cafeteria together.

'So, no fillings for me.' She grins. 'What have I missed?'

'Jayden being an idiot and . . . Charlie came to Aunt Violet's this morning.'

'Charlie, your brother?'

'Yeah. He said he wanted me and Nina to live with him.'

'Cool.'

'Not really. Aunt Violet said a bunch of stuff about responsibilities and kids being expensive and some things about his dad I didn't get and now he's gone back to London.' Duke doesn't say anything else. He doesn't share how upset he is but he can hear the wobble in his voice.

'You're better off without him.' Evie offers him a crisp and he shakes his head.

'We're not, though. I don't care if living with Charlie makes us too poor to buy books because there are libraries. I . . . I just want to be back in my own bedroom, with Billie and . . . and I don't care what Charlie's real dad was like or what he did, it doesn't mean he'll turn out the same, does it? I like Charlie. I really do. He's a bit like how I might be when I'm grown up.'

'The ghost of Christmas future.'

'Yeah.' Duke smiles. Evie loves reading as much as he does.

'Tell him then. Change his mind.'

'I can't; he never picks up the phone.'

'Do you know his address?'

'Yeah, it's Baker Place. I remember that because of—'

'Sherlock Holmes.'

'Yeah. I guess I could write to him.'

'He'd ignore that as well. You must go and see him.'

'When? How?'

'When, now, and how is by train.'

'But I . . . I can't just get on a train.'

'Why not? Would you rather do double maths?'

'Well, no. I haven't done my homework but . . .' Duke tries not to look as horrified as he feels. If Evie thinks it's possible, perhaps it is. She knows lots of things that Duke doesn't. She said that's because she hasn't led a sheltered life like him and is street-smart, although Duke knows all about road safety and the green man at the crossing so he thinks he's street-smart too but he's going to *London*.

Alone.

Evie unzips her back and pulls out a white envelope. 'I didn't hand my trip money in this morning because I missed tutor time so . . .' she offers it out to him. 'Come on.' She senses his reluctance. 'Charlie could be packing for New York this very second. If you don't go now it might be too late.'

'But how . . .' His head is spinning.

'Give me your phone.'

Evie shows him how to check the train times and then the bus. 'See, if you go to the end of Mendip Street, there's a bus due in fifteen minutes. Get off after five stops and you'll be at the station. Then you want a single ticket to St Pancras. Charlie will bring you back with him, I expect.' She powers his phone off. 'That's so the police don't trace you.'

'Police?' He feels a bit dizzy.

'Don't worry, you'll be in London before the end of school and Charlie can ring Vile Violet and tell her you're with him. I'll cover for you here. I'll tell Miss Greenly you were sick so the office sent you home. She'll never check.'

'But . . .'

'You'll miss the bus if you don't go now.'

Duke squeezes his eyes shut, wishing he was as brave as Sam in *The Lord of the Rings*.

All The Things You Are.

Courageous. Adventurous. Leaving.

He takes the envelope.

'Thanks, Evie.'

'Go out of the school the back way, past the rugby field. There's a gap in the fence; no one will see. Go. Quick.'

And although his legs feel shaky, he runs.

*

Duke is panting as he climbs onto the bus. He's only just made it here in time. He's so scared the bus driver won't let him on, but he couldn't seem to care less as Duke pays the fare and collects his ticket. He's more confident by the time he reaches the station.

'A single to St Pancras please.'

'Shouldn't you be at school?' The lady peers over her glasses at him.

'No. I . . .' Duke begins to loosen the knot in his tie – why hadn't he taken it off?

'How old are you?'

'Eleven.' Duke straightens his spine. 'I'm small for my age but—'

'You can't travel without an adult unless you're twelve.'

'I am . . .' Duke feels his cheeks burning. 'I will be twelve.'

'Come back when you are then.'

'But I've got money. I need to get to London.'

'Shall I call someone for you? A parent? Your school?'

Duke hurries away.

Outside the station is a cleaner.

'Excuse me,' Duke asks. 'How far away is the next station?'

He chews his gum, leaning on his broom handle as he thinks. 'I reckons about ten miles.'

'Is it easy to find?'

'Yeah.' He gives Duke directions and Duke jots down the names of villages he has to pass through before he's in the next town.

Ten miles. It can't take long to walk ten miles, can it? When he gets to the next station he'll take off his school jumper and tie and tell the ticket officer that he is twelve.

*

The rain is lashing down harder. Duke is soaked, his clothes, his hair, his rucksack feels like a dead weight.

This is awful. Terrible. Horrible.

His shiny black shoes that he'd told Aunt Violet pinched in the shop have rubbed blisters on his heels. He's scuffed the toes as well so he'll probably be in even more trouble than he already is.

He passed through the first two villages okay but then he must have taken a wrong turn somewhere. The piece of paper he'd scribbled directions on is sodden, the writing smudged and he daren't switch his phone on because Evie had said not to and she knows everything.

If she were here, she'd know what to do.

A car approaches. Duke thinks about waving it down but what if it's an axe murderer or a paedophile? Instead, he cowers in a ditch as it passes, the long grass dripping rain down his collar. He stands up after it passes and clambers up the slippy mud, thinking how street-smart he is. How Evie will be proud when he tells her about his adventure even though it doesn't seem very thrilling right now.

It feels awful. Terrible. Horrible.

The sky is bunched with angry clouds. It's already growing dark. Duke doesn't know if it's the weather or dusk sucking away the light and he briefly thinks of turning on his phone to check the time before dismissing it. He feels like he's been walking for a million hours. He's tired and hungry but he knows it will be worth it when he reaches London.

He carries on. He's smiling to himself as his mind wanders. Perhaps one day someone will write a book about his arduous journey, *The Boy Who Saved His Family*, or something. Maybe Charlie could even write it. He'd wanted to be an author once.

He's barely aware of the van pulling in behind him, the opening of the door, until he feels a hand on his shoulder.

CHAPTER TWENTY-FOUR

Nina

The last of the stragglers are mooching down the steps away from the school. Nina chews her gum harder, faster. Agitated. Where is Duke? She tries to ring him again.

'It's still going straight to voicemail,' she says to Maeve, who shrugs helplessly.

A loud clap startles her. 'Nina Johnson. Maeve Kelly. Chop chop. Off you go. School's out and all that.'

'Miss Rudd, I'm just—'

'Making the place look untidy.'

'I'm waiting for—'

'Then wait outside.'

'But it's raining.'

'A bit of water won't kill you. You're not the Wicked Witch of the West, are you?'

'There's only one witch here,' Nina mutters under her breath.

'Would you care to repeat that? Would you like a detention?' Miss Rudd crosses her arms over her chest.

'She said she's got a stitch, miss. That's why we were having a rest but we're going now.' Maeve grabs Nina's hand and tugs her out of the door. They pound down the steps, feet splashing into puddles, shoes and tights soaked.

'You should have said she's a bitch,' Nina says as they huddle under the bus shelter.

'Yeah, that would have helped. She hates you enough anyway.'

'Dunno why.'

'You do antagonise her.' Maeve holds her hands up as Nina glares. 'Don't shoot. I'm on your side!'

'I know, she's just . . . such a cow.'

'Miss Rudd chews a cud.' Maeve laughs.

'You're such a child. Speaking of kids what are we going to do about my idiot brother?'

'Do you think you should ring your aunt? Tell her that Duke hasn't come out?'

'Nah. She'll only blame me and say I was late or something and we were a bit late. He's probably gone ahead with Evie. God, she winds me up.'

'She's funny. I told Jayden to leave Duke alone in the canteen the other day and she came up to me as I was heading back to class after lunch and thanked me for sticking up for Duke this morning. She said "we can't let the boys think they're in charge. You go, girl," and actually held up her hand.'

'What did you do?'

'I was so surprised I high-fived her.'

'I'd have told her to piss off.' Nina hides her shame behind her anger. She should do more to help Duke but she feels all this fury bouncing around inside her that she can't harness and he's so easy to take it out on. She's such a bitch sometimes. No wonder he didn't want to walk home with her.

Maeve nudges her. 'Penny for them.'

'I was wondering if I was always this horrible, before Mum and Dad died.'

'Yeah, pretty much.' Maeve grins. 'But I love you anyways.'

'I feel . . . furious all of the time.' Nina can feel it now, bubbling away under the surface, heating her blood despite the chill wind blowing rain towards them.

'You have changed, but that's only to be expected. You've had such a lot to deal with. Dad was only saying—'

'Your dad was talking about me?' Nina feels the hardening in her stomach soften a little.

'Yeah. He was saying how well you're coping.'

'I dunno if I am. I . . . I dream about them almost every night.'

'I think that's normal.'

'Is that how you felt when you lost your mum?' It occurs to Nina that they've never talked about this before. Maeve didn't have a mum when they'd met at five years old and it seemed normal to her but it isn't normal and she feels guilty now that she's never given her best friend the opportunity to talk.

Maeve shrugs. 'I don't really remember it I was so young. I don't really remember *her*.' Her voice thins a little. It still hurts her; is this how it will feel to Nina in five years, ten, twenty? Can a lifetime take away the stinging pain she feels that hasn't even begun to ease? It's approaching two months since she lost her parents and she can still remember the tone of their voices, their smell. 'Sometimes . . .' Maeve clears her throat. 'Sometimes I think I have memories but they've just come from photographs really and stories Dad's told me about her. You have real memories, Nina. Happy ones to hold on to.'

If there is a sliding scale of grief, Nina wonders what the

tipping point would be. Does the regret of losing someone you never really got to know outweigh the hurt of knowing exactly what you have lost?

She rests her head on Maeve's shoulder and for a while they are quiet, listening to the tyres of the passing cars slosh in the puddles. Watching an array of coloured umbrellas hurry past. They make no move to leave despite their damp clothes.

'What . . . what else did your dad say about me?' Nina asks.

'He said you've grown up a lot.'

'Really?' She can feel her smile stretch.

'Yeah. He says we both have.'

'Now you're older do you think he'll get a girlfriend? Settle down again?'

'I dunno. He's always said he'll wait until I leave home but . . .' she shudders, whether through the cold or revulsion Nina does not know. 'It'd be so weird having a woman around the house. Imagine if it was someone like Miss Rudd.'

'What if it was someone you knew? Someone you liked?'

'Like who?'

'Dunno. Just thinking out loud. Everyone deserves to be loved, don't they? Happy?'

'Speaking of being loved. Ryan and Lenny—'

'Nah. Boys of our age are too immature. I'm not into Ryan. Are you—'

'Lenny's okay. He makes me laugh. Who's your ideal man then?'

Nina feels anxiety instantly itch at her skin. She thinks about the advice website.

Be honest.

She has a desire to rake her nails down her arms and so she

shoves her hands in her pockets as she says, 'If I tell you something, promise not to freak.'

'I promise. Unless you fancy my dad or something.' Maeve laughs as if that is the most ridiculous thing ever.

Nina's phone begins to ring. She's grateful for the interruption as she takes it from her pocket. It's Pippa.

'Nina? You need to come to mine. You need to come, now.'

CHAPTER TWENTY-FIVE

Duke

Duke hadn't known what to do when the policeman had stopped him.

'What are you doing wandering about the middle of nowhere in the rain, young man?' he'd been asked.

'I'm going to London to see my brother.'

'Walking there, are you?'

Duke had tried to explain about being big enough to catch a bus but too young to catch the train even though his mum had said he was an old soul and he had enough money for the tickets but it all came out in an incoherent jumble. In truth, Duke was cold, hungry and horribly, horribly lost.

He had been led to the police car where a policewoman wrapped him in a blanket as he'd shivered and asked if he was under arrest.

'No. But we need to speak to your parents.'

Duke had begun to cry. 'I don't live with . . . they're not . . .' but he couldn't catch his breath and force out the words.

'Is there an adult we can call?' he'd been asked gently, and he'd switched his phone on, explaining he'd turned it off like Evie had said so he couldn't be traced, and had scrolled through his brief list of contacts. He'd thought Evie could probably talk them into letting him go but she didn't exactly sound like an adult. He hadn't wanted them to speak to Violet and Charlie never picked up and so he'd given them Pippa's number.

The policewoman had tried to distract him with talk of school while the policeman had stepped away to make the call but Duke had seen through her ploy. The same techniques Mum would use when Duke had wanted something he wasn't allowed or asked questions she didn't want to answer.

He'd kept his eyes trained on the policeman, trying to lip-read.

'Are you watching that new series with dragons on Netflix?' the lady had asked.

'We don't have a TV,' Duke had replied, although perhaps they did now. There was one in Aunt Violet's lounge but she only seemed to switch it on for the news.

'That's unusual for kids these days.' The lady had looked at him differently then, with more sympathy, like he lived in a cult or something.

'I don't mind, I like books,' he had said. She'd asked him who his favourite author was and when he'd told her 'J. R. R. Tolkien' she'd totally impressed him with her knowledge of hobbits.

'You've read the series?' Duke had been delighted.

'Seen the films,' she admitted.

It's only when they've been talking about Middle-earth for a few minutes that he realizes he hasn't been watching the policeman. The policewoman is better at diverting Duke's attention than Mum ever was. He's a little bit impressed, although he now has no idea what's been said on the phone.

The policeman gets back into the car and starts the engine. Duke doesn't ask where they are going; he's afraid and then relieved when they pull up outside of Pippa's. On the kerb, waiting with folded arms, are Aunt Violet and Charlie. Duke climbs slowly out of the car, not sure who to turn to, but then he sees Pippa and he runs to her instead.

'Let's get inside; we'll get everything sorted out,' she says as she leads him towards his old house.

'So,' says the policeman, once they are all crowded into the lounge, 'who is responsible for Duke?'

Charlie begins to talk but Aunt Violet raises her voice louder. Pippa tries to calm them both but it's impossible.

Nobody but Duke notices Nina slink in.

'Okay—' the policewoman raises her hand '—obviously it's been an incredibly difficult time for your family and I am sorry for your loss. Of course, services don't have to be involved if amicable and acceptable arrangements are made but you don't seem to agree on where the children should live and the fact Duke ran away indicates he's not currently happy. I think I should call—'

'No. Wait.' Charlie steps forward. 'Please, can Aunt Violet and I have a few minutes to talk in the kitchen?'

The policewoman looks to Violet who nods and then they both leave the room.

Nina wraps her arms around Duke and he's about to tell her he's pleased to see her too when he feels her squeezing him tightly, too tightly, her fingernails pinching his arms.

The words she whispers in Duke's ear are cold and hard.

They spin around his brain until they begin to make sense and then for the second time that day he wants to cry.

CHAPTER TWENTY-SIX

Nina

Nina knows she is hurting Duke and she is glad. She digs her nails into his upper arms, tightening her grip when he tries to wriggle away. Her mouth finds his ear. Her words hissing angrily,

'You're such a fucking idiot. Now we'll probably be taken into care and split up.'

He stops struggling, his body slack with shock. She pushes him roughly away. He staggers backwards, landing heavily against the sideboard. The wedding photo of Mum and Dad wobbles before toppling over with a smash.

Before Nina can stop him, Duke has righted the frame and is sweeping the fragments of broken glass into his cupped palm.

'Ouch.' Duke turns to her, his finger dripping crimson blood.

She watches as the police officers exchange a knowing glance, one of them reaching for her walkie-talkie before hurrying from the room, head down.

Nina had thought living with Aunt Violet was as bad as things could get. Now she thinks things are going to get a whole lot worse.

CHAPTER TWENTY-SEVEN

Charlie

Charlie pulls out the chair opposite to Violet's and studies her while she sits. He expects to see anger on her face, confrontation at the very least, but instead she looks tired, broken, but his resolve doesn't weaken. He feels the surge of adrenaline prickle under his skin. This is the way he feels in his business before a negotiation. In control, confident of the facts.

'After speaking to you this morning I caught the train to London. I haven't been back long. I spoke to a solicitor.' He watches the surprise register and gives her a second to absorb this before he follows it up with, 'Obviously the fact that Duke has run away under your care will strengthen my case now but I wanted to see if it was possible for me to adopt Duke and Nina. She told me that would be too confusing for them having a brother who is also their father. Instead, she's advised me to apply for Special Guardianship. That way—'

'You have parental rights.'

'Yes. And Nina and Duke have some stability.'

'They have stability with me.'

'But they're not happy.'

'They're not happy because their parents have died, Charlie.'

'I've lost my parents too,' he says.

Violet's fingers stretch before she curls them into balls as though stopping herself reaching across the table to comfort him.

'Charlie, you wanting Nina and Duke could be a reaction to your grief—'

'It isn't.'

'And then if you change your mind—'

'I won't.'

'If this is just about the house we don't have to sell—'

'It's not. It's about Nina and Duke and . . . and about me too. All of us.'

This time it is Charlie who reaches across the table. He takes Aunt Violet's shaking hands in his own. 'Tell me why you want them,' he says.

'Because—' her eyes fill with tears. 'Because I just couldn't bear another regret.'

Charlie doesn't try to fill the silence. He knows she has more to say and so he waits.

'Me and Ronnie. We were very different.' She doesn't have to tell Charlie this as she sits there in her sensible work suit and her lace-up shoes. 'But I always felt such a responsibility towards her, being the eldest. She was always the favourite and . . . I don't know, I think I felt a certain amount of resentment when Mum and Dad moved abroad all these years ago, as though I was expected to look after her.' She pulls out a tissue from her bag although she isn't crying. 'When she fell in love with your dad . . . I knew it would all end in tears. I told her. I *told* her he'd bring heartache and he did. Over and over. So many times I picked up the pieces and so many times she went back to him. I was emotionally exhausted. My own relationships never worked out because Ronnie always came first. Whenever she had another crisis, I'd drop everything and be by her side.'

'Is that why you never had a family of your own?' Charlie asks.

'Yes. No. I don't know. Maybe she was an excuse. I've never felt that maternal pull that women talk about.'

Charlie lodges this in his mind to bring up later if needed.

'When Ronnie finally left your dad I thought things would be calmer. I could put myself first but then . . . You . . .' Her eyes flicker towards the scars on Charlie's wrist and he feels them burn in response. 'I hated him. *Hated*. It was me who gave her the money, you know, to spend the summer in Cornwall to give you both a break but then she met Bo and I . . . I was furious. I didn't think she'd want another relationship again. Let alone with a deadbeat musician.'

'He was a good man.' Charlie knows the difference between a good one and a bad one. 'And he loved Mum.'

'I know. He adored her and she him but all I could see was more drama. He was so desperate to make a living out of music and I thought he'd run off and leave her to follow his dreams and I'd be left to pick up the pieces again. We fought terribly. All the time. I gave her an ultimatum, him or me, and she chose—'

'Love,' says Charlie. He recognizes that choice; he had faced it himself once many years before and had turned away from it. He too knew all about regrets. 'He had the chance to make it, you know. Marty from the band told me. He was offered a job with a touring band, which would have led to huge things but he chose Mum.'

'He chose love.' Violet is crying. 'And they were devoted to each

169

other, weren't they? I wish I could turn the clock back. I've missed her. I've missed my sister.'

Charlie fetches a glass of water. Stands behind Violet with an awkward hand on her back until her shaking sobs subside.

'I don't want to lose Nina and Duke. I want a relationship with them.' She blows her nose, distraught.

'They don't have to live with you for you to have a relationship with them,' Charlie says gently. He has misjudged Aunt Violet. They all have.

'I thought I could provide some structure but perhaps I've been too strict. I didn't want them to run wild like Ronnie had.'

'Mum was happy. Perhaps she didn't have the career and the smart clothes and the perfectly decorated house but she – they – were happy. It's what I want for Duke and Nina. For all of us. Including you.' He takes her hand again.

'I don't know, Charlie, you're so young.'

'I'm thirty-three.'

'Now you're making me feel old. What about New York?'

'While I was in London I spoke to Simon and told him I'm not going and . . .' This is the first time Charlie will have said this out loud. 'I've handed my notice in at the agency. I'm serious about this. Aunt Violet, I want Duke and Nina to move back here, and I want you to be part of our lives. A family.'

It takes an age for her to answer. Her eyes flicker around the kitchen before landing on the cork board. The photos.

'If that's what Nina and Duke want to do then okay,' she says. 'Okay.'

They stand and hug, Charlie feeling as though Violet has given him something infinitely precious and she has, although they were not hers to give.

In the hallway they meet the police officer.

'Can I have a word,' she asks them and they talk for several minutes.

In the lounge Charlie notices the blood-stained tissue Duke is pressing to his fingers, the broken glass. Horrified, he rushes over to his brother and gently removes the tissue, checking the cut.

It's stopped bleeding, thankfully.

'Am I in a lot of trouble?' Duke asks in a small voice. 'Do I have to go and live in a children's home now?'

'No. You just need to go to Aunt Violet's.' Charlie takes a long nervous breath. 'You both need to go to Aunt Violet's to get your things because you're moving back here with me. If you want to, of course.'

He has barely finished his sentence when Duke's arms are around him and they are hugging, both crying. He rests his chin on the top of Duke's head and raises his eyes to Nina's, seeing the scepticism in hers.

'I know I've let you down,' he says, 'but this time it'll be different. This time—'

'Whatever.' Nina picks up her bag and slings it over her shoulder. 'Are we going then or what?'

'I . . .' Aunt Violet clears her throat. 'I thought I could cook something nice while you're packing and we can have dinner together before I drive you back here. We can talk properly, about your mum. If you'd like?'

'Whatever,' Nina says again. She's angry, confused, but Charlie also knows she's scared.

He untangles himself from Duke and walks over to her, waiting to speak until she looks at him and when she does, he says, low and quiet, 'I promise I will not let you down again,' and he means it.

He watches from the window as his siblings climb into Aunt Violet's car. He can't help smiling, knowing they will be back soon. He pushes his glasses up onto the bridge of his nose, his lenses suddenly coated in a rose-coloured hue.

He has a million things to do before they return – shop . . . there's nothing in for breakfast; the house is filthy; he'll make up the beds with fresh sheets; collect Billie – but he doesn't mind any of it.

That's part of being a family, isn't it? Chaos, responsibility, doing things for other people. He's looking forward to it all. The years to come before the children leave home, strengthening their fragile bond.

What Charlie doesn't yet know is that, by September, only six short months away, their household of three will become a household of two and he will be heartbroken, once more.

CHAPTER TWENTY-EIGHT

Duke

Duke texts Evie:

IT WORKED!!! Living at home with Charlie FOREVER & didn't even spend all of your trip money!

Evie – **You are a GENIUS!**

Duke – **I'm a happy genius!!!**

CHAPTER TWENTY-NINE

Nina

Text to Maeve:

So, Charlie's changed his mind AGAIN & we're living at home with him

Maeve – **Cool!**

Nina – **Whatever. He'll probably change his mind AGAIN**

CHAPTER THIRTY

Charlie

Charlie raps on Pippa's door, bouncing up and down on his toes. 'C'mon, c'mon.'

As she answers, he says, 'Emergency, I need your help.'

'Are the children okay?' Her voice is high, worried.

'They're fine. Sorry.' He is stricken. 'But I forgot to buy any food for their packed lunches. When I was here for that short time before they went to Violet's Nina sorted herself out. But now Duke's at school too. I'm such an idiot. I bought cereal and main meals and completely forgot about lunch and we need to leave for school in—' he checks his watch '—five minutes.'

'You'd better come in and have a rummage.' Pippa stands back, tightening the belt on her dressing gown. With her hair in plaits and face free of make-up she looks barely older than she had at school but of course so much has changed. He feels a sudden stab of longing for simpler times.

Charlie hurries towards the kitchen, notices the half-eaten slice of honey-soaked toast on a plate. 'Now, your breakfast will be cold. I'm sorry.'

'Charlie, it's okay.'

'It isn't. It's my first morning as official carer to the kids and I've already messed things up.' He feels he has such a lot to prove.

'It's not a disaster. Take a breath and don't make this about you, Charlie. It's fine. Let's find them something to eat.'

He opens the fridge. Pulls out a couple of yoghurts.

'Nina doesn't like yoghurt and Duke isn't keen on the peach flavoured one; there should be a strawberry one somewhere.'

'Got it. And sandwiches? Cheese? Can you even put camembert in a sandwich?' He sniffs it.

'It isn't suitable for vegetarians. Why don't you go and comb your hair? I'll rustle up something for them both.'

'Christ, do I look that bad?' Charlie rushes to the bathroom, dismayed at his reflection in the mirror. It's quarter past eight and he looks as though he's just rolled out of bed. This time last year, he had negotiated a seven-figure deal for a debut author over a breakfast deal, virtually unheard of. Now, he can't even get two kids ready for school in time. He runs his hands under the tap and does the best he can to smooth down his hair.

Back in the kitchen, Pippa pushes two containers into his hands. 'Green for Duke, red for Nina. I'll text you a list of things they like then you can pop into Tesco on your way back.'

'Back?'

'From the school. Nina walks with Maeve still but you *are* taking Duke?'

'Oh, right. Yes, of course.' He flashes a smile and hurries back over the road.

*

'Where's Nina?' he asks Duke who is sitting at the bottom of the stairs. If there was an Olympic medal for how slowly someone could tie their shoes, Duke would win.

'She's already gone to meet Maeve.'

'But her lunch? Did she say anything before she left?'

'Yeah—' Duke's unties his laces and begins again '—but you're probably better off not knowing what it was.' He stands. 'Shall I go on my own?'

'No. I thought I'd walk with you. We can take Billie?'

Billie wags her tail, yes please. She is definitely the most excited to be back home. Nina has virtually ignored him and Duke had followed him around silently, as though afraid he will disappear.

They walk down the path. They are not quite into March but the snowdrops and daffodils are pushing their heads through the soil and the sight of this new life gives Charlie hope that his relationship with his siblings can bloom. He tries to engage Duke in conversation but his brother's answers are monosyllabic.

'I thought after school we could play some music? I notice you didn't take your saxophone to Aunt Violet's? We could—'

'I don't want to play anymore.'

'But Duke, you're so talented. Why?' But instead of answering, Duke shrinks into Charlie's side as three boys rush past him, knocking him on the shoulder. Charlie narrows his eyes as he watches them sprint across the playground but then he catches sight of Nina.

'Nina!' He waves frantically. 'I've got your lunch.'

Her face darkens as she strides towards him, snatching the container out of his hand.

'You're, like, totally embarrassing,' she spits before she stalks away, cutting off his apology.

The bell sounds, shrill and loud.

Duke runs towards the school, slowing as he reaches a girl who smiles as he approaches.

And now Charlie is alone.

By the time he's unpacking the shopping he's exhausted, and it's only half past nine.

Charlie FaceTimes Sasha as soon as he thinks she'll be awake.

She isn't.

'Sorry.' It's his most frequently used word of the day.

'It feels like I've only just gone to sleep.'

She rolls over and drags a pillow towards her – the pillow his head should currently be resting on – and props her phone against it.

'How's the apartm—'

'When are you flying out?'

They're getting right down to it then.

'The thing is, Sasha, I'm not. The kids need me here.'

Sasha doesn't say she needs him too. He isn't sure that she ever has.

'And that means? For us?'

He pictures the engagement ring, no longer in his pocket but in the bottom of his bag. 'I don't know but . . . Give me some time to figure it out? I can come visit. Aunt Violet can help with the kids, and Pippa, and you can come over here and . . . it isn't as though your placement is forever and you might not even like it there, Sash. You might not stay.'

'But I might love it.'

More than me? he wants to ask, but he doesn't.

*

It's been eight long, tough weeks but somehow they've stumbled into May, settled into a routine of sorts. For the first few days Charlie had visions of a family breakfast around the table, chatting as they crunched cornflakes, buttered toast, but Nina, it seems, isn't a morning person. She isn't an afternoon, evening or night-time person either or perhaps she just hates Charlie. He knows he's broken the scant trust she had in him when he left them with Aunt Violet, and he appreciates it will take time to repair it. Time is the one thing he has in abundance. He still hasn't decided what he's going to do career wise but bonding with Nina and Duke is his priority right now, however impossible it seems.

'Don't forget Nina is at a sensitive age,' Pippa had said a few nights ago over a glass of non-alcoholic wine after she'd bailed him out again, teaching him to sew Duke's name tag into a new PE kit after Duke had lost his.

'You want a sharp needle,' she had instructed, trying not to smile as he'd tested each tip on his finger, grimacing each time. 'You know what we use the blunt ones for?'

'What?'

'Nothing. They're pointless.' She'd laughed.

'*Needless* to say, I didn't find that funny.' He'd sucked a droplet of blood from the end of his finger.

The atmosphere had changed as she'd showed him how to stitch, their heads close together. There'd been a moment where he'd actually smelled her hair, fresh and clean, and he'd fought the impulse to tuck it behind her ear.

He was just lonely, missing Sasha. That's all.

He'd straightened up. 'Think I've got it now.'

'Good. You know you can get fabric markers? You could have just written Duke's name?'

'And you didn't tell me this before because you wanted to see my fingertips bleed?'

'No.' There'd been a beat. 'Because it's nice to feel needed.'

He'd wanted to tell her that she was needed, that they all needed her, but he hadn't wanted her to feel burdened so he'd snapped off the cotton with his teeth and then said, 'I wish Nina needed me.'

'She does. She just doesn't know how to express it.'

'I don't remember you being like her at fifteen.' Charlie had taken a gulp of his drink. 'Christ, this stuff is rough.'

'Yeah, but she's been through a lot and, taking into account puberty and hormones and—'

'Should I talk to her about periods?' Charlie had suddenly wished there was alcohol in the wine.

'Christ, no. Why would you just bring that up?'

'In case they suddenly start and she's scared.'

'They started almost two years ago for her.'

'Oh. But I should probably let her know I'm progressive and she can talk to me.'

'But she doesn't talk to you about those things and it'll just embarrass her. She can open up to you when she's ready. In the meantime, make sure she has enough allowance to buy her own toiletries. I can check in on her.'

'Allowance? Umm, I've been meaning to look into that. Thanks.' He'd been grateful because Nina was an enigma.

Duke, on the other hand, doesn't leave Charlie's side, even sitting in on some of his FaceTime calls with Sasha, which means Charlie knows the touristy spots Sasha has visited, what she eats, what Broadway shows she has seen but he doesn't know how she *feels*. She always seems to be rushing somewhere and Charlie can't wait until they can properly catch up.

Sundays are Charlie's favourite day. Aunt Violet comes over for lunch – she cooks so it's always the one meal guaranteed to be edible – and then they all watch a movie together on the flatscreen TV Charlie had bought.

Netflix is an endless wonder to Duke and even Nina is pleased although she tries her best to hide it.

Charlie is out of his depth but determined to learn. At night he lies in the bedroom Mum and Bo once shared and reads books on parenting. He's learned about the importance of allowing the kids to ask any questions they have and he tries not to wear expressions of anger or frustration.

He picks up his coffee from the bedside table, which is still littered with Mum's things. Her dog-eared copy of *The Time Traveler's Wife*, a pair of silver hooped earrings. He hadn't wanted to sleep in here but a week on the sofa bed in the lounge had sent twinges of pain up his spine. The room is pretty much as Mum and Bo had left it, as though they might return at any moment. Charlie has a few clothes heaped in the corner, piled on top of the suitcase that Sasha had couriered back to him from New York. A stack of his own books. He hasn't been able to focus on reading since New Year. It's a good job really that he doesn't have manuscripts to read for work at the moment.

It's eleven o'clock – six o'clock in New York. Sasha will be finishing work, going out to eat with her new colleagues. It's inexplicable that city life continues without him. Here the pace is slow but Charlie quite likes it.

His phone rings: Sasha.

'Hey!' He's delighted to hear from her. To see her face fill his screen. 'Did you get my message?'

'Yes.'

'I know it's a long way to come back—'

'I'm not coming back, Charlie.'

He feels a stir of uneasiness. Is she referring to the upcoming difficult weekend where he needs her by his side? There's a finality in her tone.

Neither of them speak but they don't have to. She knows what she rang to say. He understands the silence.

'Where's Duke?' she asks eventually.

'He's in bed. Alone at last.' He waggles his eyebrows up and down but she doesn't break a smile.

'I can't do this anymore, Charlie.'

'This?'

'Me here. You there. It's been two months now.'

'But you won't be there forever and then . . .'

'It isn't you, it's me.' She trips out the tired cliché but they both know it isn't him or her.

'It's the kids, isn't it? You want me to choose between you and my brother and sister?'

'It's not just the kids, Charlie. We had so much in common, the same goals, but now we don't and . . . and strip all that away and what's left? We aren't moving in the same direction anymore. I never thought you'd do something like this. I feel I don't know you at all. Not the real you.'

Charlie runs his fingers over the scars on his wrist. Who is the real him? The fragile boy, the scared man. The facade that he had worked so hard to build, the successful literary agent with the immaculate flat and polished appearance crumbles to dust, leaving behind a spectacle-wearing boy with frizzy hair, self-consciously hiding the scars he carries on both the inside and the outside. It is this boy who whispers 'please' without knowing what he is pleading for.

He thinks of the small, hard ring box. Unopened and now unwanted. The glittering diamond he thought was a substitute for those three words he couldn't say. He can't even say them now because deep down he knows he hasn't proposed to her, not because he hasn't been able to find the right time but because, he now realizes, she may not be the right person. Bo hadn't joined the James Patrick Ensemble; he had given up his dream because he knew unequivocally that Mum was the one but Charlie has never had that certainty.

'I'm sorry,' Charlie says and he is. Without him she could have found the love that she deserved and perhaps now she can. 'Will you be okay? Financially? I can still contribute to—'

'I'll be fine. It's not as though there's rent to pay.'

'But we're still supposed to cover the bills. It isn't fair on you to have to pay them alone.'

'Charlie, I appreciate the thought but you've enough on your plate. I'll be fine. I've already discussed it with Dad and worked it all out.'

They end the call with a goodbye wrapped in a 'take care and we'll still be friends'. But friends cheer each other on and she hasn't even mentioned the reason he wanted her to come home for a couple of days.

Because he thinks he knows why he, Nina and Duke haven't gelled together properly. He wanted Sasha's support when he tried to fix it.

CHAPTER THIRTY-ONE

Duke

Duke doesn't really know what 'May Day' is but all he cares about is that he has a day off from school today. 'I don't know what to wear.' Duke turns to Billie who is sprawled on his bed but she isn't much help.

Duke could ask Charlie but he doesn't.

He doesn't want to bother Charlie with anything in case he thinks Duke is too much trouble and decides to go to New York. Charlie has been especially sad these past few days and Duke is scared he regrets taking him and Nina on. That he'll announce he's leaving any minute.

They've now been living together for two months. It doesn't feel entirely right. It doesn't feel entirely wrong either, not like living at Aunt Violet's had.

Charlie thinks that after today they'll all feel better. Duke had heard him talking to Pippa: 'We need to say goodbye to the past before we can embrace the future. Realize properly that it's just the three of us moving forward now.' *Closure*, Charlie had called it. Duke's sure he got that from a book.

Billie rolls over onto her back, legs sticking in the air, and Duke tickles her tummy. Her fur is wiry and coarse and she's still a bit thinner than she was before she went to live at Pippa's but she, at least, feels the same. Too much has changed recently.

Through the wall, Duke hears Nina crashing around her room, a song he doesn't recognize blaring through her speakers. She never listens to jazz anymore. None of them do.

Duke stares out of his window. The sky is light blue, dotted with fluffy white clouds. Does that mean it's going to be warm or are the clouds ready to scatter showers? Mum always seemed to know. He rummages through his wardrobe. He's never been to a funeral but he knows you're supposed to wear a black tie but he doesn't have one. Does that matter if this isn't a real funeral? They still haven't found Mum and Dad's bodies but they're having a memorial – a celebration of their lives, Charlie called it.

'Do you have any questions?' Charlie had asked when he'd told Nina and Duke his plan. He was always asking if they had any questions. Duke has a list but he keeps it in his head because he knows Charlie cannot answer them.

1. When will Mum and Dad be found?
2. When will Jayden stop picking on him?
3. When will he grow as tall as the other boys in his year?

'No questions,' Duke had said and Charlie had grinned that big fake grin that he had never worn before he became the children's guardian. Duke wishes he'd chill out. Be the Charlie that he used to be, a bit cool, a bit sulky, a bit funny. Infinitely better than the stranger he's become who asks if they need anything every thirty seconds and smiles too much.

Duke pulls on his favourite stripy T-shirt and red hoodie.

Downstairs the others are waiting by the front door. Nina in black skinny jeans and tight top.

Charlie's wearing a suit and tie. He looks at Duke and then Nina and says 'Just a sec,' running upstairs to return minutes later in beige chinos and a burgundy checked shirt.

'Let's grab our instruments,' Charlie says.

'No. I'm not a performing monkey.' Nina crosses her arms.

'Today isn't about what you want,' Charlie says, but he follows it up with his false smile. 'Today's about Mum and Dad.'

'We can hardly ask them what they want, can we?' Nina says.

'I don't want to play either.' It isn't really that Duke doesn't want to. He really, actually, can't. Each time he thinks about playing his saxophone, his throat does a funny shrinking thing and he can't swallow.

'Why don't you bring your instruments and if you don't feel like playing nobody will force you,' suggests Pippa as she heads towards them from the kitchen.

Nina tuts but she fetches her clarinet anyway. Pippa is the peacemaker. The constant. She's here most days. So far, she has taught Charlie to:

1. Sew (after Jayden stuffed his PE shorts down the toilet and Duke pretended they were lost)
2. Wash their clothes properly (the first time, Charlie made Duke's school shirts pink. He says nobody in London has a washing machine and all use a laundry service but Duke knows London has a population of 9 million and NOT ONE WASHING MACHINE?!)

186

3. Make a meal plan (because for the first week they ate pasta every night because Charlie said he couldn't cook because he always ate out in London. No ovens, Charlie?!)
4. Laugh. She made Charlie do a proper-not-a-fake-laugh when they played Uno and he lost because he didn't know the rules (no games in London either . . .)

Charlie carries Duke's sax and his own guitar, the picnic in a rucksack on his back. Pippa is laden with blankets. They walk quickly because they're late. Charlie had put a tray of vegan sausage rolls in the oven but forgotten to switch it on. They'll be the last ones there.

'How are you feeling? Any questions?' Charlie asks for the millionth time. He keeps reading manuals on parenting because he knows he's really not very good at it. Duke wishes he'd read a cookbook instead. Most nights dinner is burned. Bring back the pasta.

'Who will be there again?'

'Well, us, of course. Aunt Violet. Nina's friend Maeve is coming with her dad, Sean. There's some of your old home-ed crowd. Bet you'll be pleased to see them and tell them about school?'

Duke's throat tightens. He hates school – *hates* it – but he hasn't told Charlie this because he's scared that if Charlie thinks he has to home-school Duke it will definitely become too much for him.

'There'll be Dad's boss and a couple of people from the factory. Marty from the band is coming if he feels well enough. Will Evie be there?'

Duke nods, still too choked to speak. Evie wasn't sure if she should come because she didn't know Mum but said she'd show up because she is his friend.

Friend!

He's able to swallow again. 'And Sasha?' Duke knows Charlie asked her to fly over and, although Charlie hadn't said she would, Duke thought they both wanted to surprise him, but it isn't a nice surprise when Charlie says,

'I'm afraid we won't be seeing Sasha again. We've broken up.'

One of the blankets slips from Pippa's grasp and they wait while she bends over and picks it up, shakes it out. Nina helps her fold it, then she stacks it on top of the others. When she stands up again, her cheeks are pink.

'But I liked Sasha.' Duke's voice is louder than he intended but his world has shrunk again. It's not that he knew her very well but she was another person in his world and now she, too, has gone.

'You didn't even know her,' Nina says under her breath.

'Did you break up because of New York?' Duke asks.

'It was for various reasons,' but Charlie didn't offer any of them to Duke in the way that Mum would when she tried to convince Duke there were other reasons to him wanting a snack. Thirst. Boredom. Tiredness. But sometimes Duke just wanted a biscuit. He thinks grown-ups look for too many reasons sometimes. Why can't they just stop analysing everything?

Duke glances to Pippa; she'll tell him if she knows but she's staring at Charlie, a shocked expression on her face, and Duke thinks she must have really liked Sasha too.

Charlie hitches the rucksack higher on his back. 'You know one of the best things about being back?'

'No.' Duke hopes it's him and Nina.

'The air. It's so fresh. I really only walked to and from the tube in the city and . . . I guess I didn't notice it so much when

I lived there, but it wasn't clean. And this view.' He sweeps his arm around as though Duke hasn't seen it infinite times.

Changing the subject.

Again.

They are almost at the top. Billie is straining to rush ahead. They're away from the road so Duke unclips her lead. She races off, Nina close behind.

They pause when they reach the peak of Briar's Hill. Charlie takes off his jacket; his cheeks are pink. Duke bats away a buzzing fly as he scans the area. It's weird seeing so many people here. The grass is covered with a patchwork of red, green and blue picnic blankets as though this is a party. Charlie begins to greet everyone but Duke hangs back, feels Pippa's hand in his. 'A celebration, remember?' she whispers, and Duke's feet reluctantly follow her even though he doesn't feel like celebrating.

Duke tries to talk to the home-ed crowd but he doesn't really belong anymore and so he sits apart from them, nibbling at a vegetarian Scotch egg. It isn't until Evie arrives that he begins to relax.

'Sorry I'm late. Have I missed the speeches?' She flops down beside him and helps herself to a sourdough sandwich, peeling back the bread to see what's inside.

'Speeches?' The word strikes horror in Duke's heart. Is he expected to say something?

'The eulogy, I think it's called?'

'I dunno.' He kicks himself about how many times Charlie had asked him if he had any questions and he had said no.

But Evie's question is answered when Charlie stands and claps his hands. 'I just want to say a few words.'

'Is that your brother?' Evie whispers. 'You look alike.'

'Firstly, thank you for coming. It's been difficult to know

what to do; we didn't feel a conventional service was appropriate given Mum and Bo's bodies haven't yet been recovered. And they were never one for formal occasions. Duke, Nina, do you want to join me?'

Duke can't think of anything he'd less like to do but everyone is watching him, so he reluctantly stands next to Charlie, Nina to his left. He feels he might topple over backwards with fear but Billie bounds over and sits on his feet and her weight helps him stay upright.

'We chose to come here because this is where we came for picnics as kids, not all together; there's a bit of an age gap between me and my brother and sister although you can't really tell.' Charlie pats his face and everyone laughs. 'We all have very happy memories here and we thought it might be nice if anyone wants to share their own memory of Mum or Bo. I'll start. We first met Bo in Cornwall. Mum and me were . . . taking a break and on the promenade were the scruffiest bunch of musicians I'd ever seen. Sorry, Marty!' Charlie holds his hands up in apology and Marty shouts, 'Kids spend a fortune on the vintage look now. We were ahead of our time.'

Charlie shakes his head, a smile on his face. 'Anyway, they began to play "Summertime" and Mum decided to join in – not from where we were standing, of course; she ran upfront, sharing a microphone with Bo and . . . I don't know. I think Simon Cowell would describe it as magic happening and . . . you could see it was special. They had chemistry right from the start. When the song had finished we began to walk away. Bo launched into Janis Joplin and shouted, "You're taking a piece of my heart," but that wasn't true. I think he gave his whole heart to her in that moment, as she did to him. They belonged together and, if there's one consolation about this whole sorry situation, it's that they never had to live without each other. I really don't think that they could.'

Charlie sits back down cross-legged and Nina and Duke do the same. Duke lowers his head, swallowing back his tears.

'I'd like to share something about Ronnie, my sister,' Aunt Violet says, fiddling with the edge of a blanket. 'It's not really a story but a memory. I was three when my parents brought Ronnie home from the hospital and I loved her for about five minutes until I realized how much she cried and how much attention she was getting. "Take her back," I demanded but my dad said he couldn't and . . . and I'm glad they never did because I grew to love her so much and I . . . I . . . I'm sorry I can't do this.' She sits down and Pippa pulls her into a hug.

'When I first met Bo,' Marty speaks now, 'I took him to my local and we sank pint after pint of real ale. He had his guitar case with him and I asked him to play me something. He swayed as he stood, he'd had far too much to drink, but he played "All Along the Watchtower" by Hendrix, and man, the hairs on the back of my neck stood up. When he'd finished I told him how good he was. "Yeah, but the other bloke was better," he'd told me. "What other bloke, Hendrix?" I'd asked him. "Nah the bloke over there." He'd pointed to a mirror. He'd caught sight of his reflection and because he was so pissed he hadn't realized it was himself.' Everyone laughed, even Violet.

'My turn,' Pippa says. 'I was brought up by my grandmother because my dad was in the army and Mum lived abroad with him but they wanted me to be schooled in the UK but I never felt I missed out on having a mum and dad present every day with Ronnie and Bo living next door because they really made me part of the family. It was Ronnie and Bo who were there for me after my grandma . . . Anyway, I miss them very much.'

There's a few more stories until silence falls. There's something Duke wants to share but he's shaking at the thought of speaking in front of a large group.

He closes his eyes and his mind rolls back as he remembers one picnic where a wasp had stung him. He had screamed and screamed. Mum had held him on her lap, wiping his tears and singing in a low, comforting voice.

All The Things You Are.

Brave.

'Can I . . . Can I say something?' He looks to Charlie who nods. Duke doesn't stand. He doesn't speak. He feels Evie squeeze his hand, whisper, 'You've totally got this.' He takes a gulp of water before he can force out the first few words. 'Mum and Dad taught me a lot,' and once he's started it gets easier. 'Not fractions or German or anything because now I'm at school I know I'm rubbish at all that but they taught me the most important thing of all. Music. If I think about us playing now I feel happy and sad but . . . just thank you for the music.' Someone laughs at this but Duke isn't sure why.

Afterwards it is Nina who speaks. 'I never got to say goodbye and so I want to play a song for them now. The first time I heard a clarinet it was on "Stranger on the Shore" and Dad later taught me it.' She plays it now. Duke closes his eyes and tries to pretend he is at home, in the music room, with Mum and Dad listening, but the wind on his face reminds him that he is outside and that they are not here.

Afterwards, Charlie takes his guitar and performs 'There Will Never Be Another You'. He has a good voice. 'Do you want to play something?' Charlie asks Duke when he's finished.

No.

No.

No.

Just the thought of playing makes Duke's tummy feel as though there's one of the dandelion clocks in there that Mum used to get him to blow to tell the time, its fruits scattering in all directions. Frantically whizzing around.

He knows what time it is now. Time to run away but his feet are stuck to the grass.

'Duke? Shall we do a song together?'

Charlie looks at him with such hope. Duke really doesn't want that look to morph into disappointment.

'Umm. Yeah. I can try.'

They confer, the three of them, settling on 'Summertime'. Not feeling strong enough to play anything with real meaning.

Duke is shaking, his fingers, his hands, his knees. Their music is out of time, out of tune. Jamming together used to come so effortlessly for him and Nina but now it's strained. Forced. Duke comes in a fraction of a second too late, Nina early. Duke wonders whether it's because they are out of sync as a family that's throwing them off. 'You're an old soul,' he can almost hear Mum say; 'you always think so deeply.' This relaxes him a little but not enough to salvage the song. His throat closes and he has to stop playing and they are not even halfway through. He lowers his sax and his head and waits for Charlie and Nina to finish. When they do there is a smattering of applause they don't deserve. Nina begins to dismantle her clarinet, Charlie packs his guitar back into his case while Duke stands sadly watching them.

'Don't worry. It looks really hard to play,' Evie says. 'Can I have a go?' He hands his sax over, and watches while she places her lips around the reed and blows. Despite his sadness, he laughs when she can't squeeze out a note.

The afternoon drifts by and when the air begins to chill everyone swaps goodbyes. Nina hugs Maeve and then she actually allows Aunt Violet to hold her but only for a moment before she wriggles free. Aunt Violet turns to Duke and he thrusts his hand out quickly, offering a handshake, and everyone laughs. Maeve holds her palm up and Duke high-fives her.

He picks up Billie's lead from the grass and she looks at him, a worried tilt to her head, but when Duke loops the lead around his shoulders rather than fixing it to her collar she lets her mouth droop open, her tongue lolling out as though she is laughing.

He begins a slow walk, throwing a glance over his shoulder to see if the others are following. Charlie and Pippa are flapping grass off the picnic blanket before they begin to fold it. Nina is sharing a hug with Maeve's dad – Mr Kelly. Duke watches as she turns her face into his neck and Duke wonders if he smells the same as Dad did and he feels a hard sweep of longing. He crouches to pat Billie to stop himself from running over to Mr Kelly too and demanding a hug. He thinks how lucky Nina is to have a substitute dad almost. No wonder she doesn't want to let him go.

Duke has Charlie and Pippa and Aunt Violet but that's not many people in his life, although there's Evie, he supposes, and she's as good as ten friends. Billie licks his hand – *don't forget me* – and together they walk down the hill, towards the house that, while still a home, is missing its heart.

Billie darts off to sniff rabbit holes, bushes, pieces of litter and Duke dawdles. The others catch up with him and they walk silently together. There's an odd almost-smile on Nina's face and Duke doesn't understand what she has to be happy about, today of all days.

Once they're inside, Nina pelts up the stairs. Duke shrugs off his coat and Pippa takes it from him and hangs it on the peg. He's about to tell Charlie and Pippa how sad he feels and ask them if they want to play a game but then Pippa says 'I'm going to head off, Charlie. I've got a headache.'

'I'll walk you home,' Charlie says like she lives a million miles away and not literally next door but then, if she isn't feeling well, he supposes Charlie is just being kind.

They leave and Duke is left in the hallway.

Alone.

He trudges up the stairs. Nina's door is ajar. Perhaps she'll want to play a game with him. He peers through the crack. When he sees what she is doing he is horrified.

Horrified.

CHAPTER THIRTY-TWO

Nina

Nina is practising kissing on her hand, in front of her mirror. She supposes she should feel sad after the memorial but she doesn't.

She is in love and the feeling is both new and familiar. It's as haunting as listening to Nina Simone singing 'I Put a Spell on You'. It's butter melting into toast. A candle in the darkness. As exhilarating as a roller coaster and equally frightening too.

From her window she can see Charlie and Pippa walking towards her house. Funny, Nina thought Pippa would be here all evening. She's literally here all the time, teaching Charlie how to cook, how to care for Mum's house plants, how to organise a fridge as though he is some useless Fifties' husband. But then he has been pretty useless and it's not like she minds Pippa being here.

She gives Charlie advice too.

Once, she overheard Charlie asking Pippa how he can get Duke to come out of his shell a bit more as though he is a snail.

'It's about finding some common ground,' she had said.

'But he won't play his sax.'

'Books then?'

And so Charlie had formed the lamest book club ever, just him and Duke. They're reading some ancient story called *Goodnight Mister Tom*, and Nina doesn't understand why because they have a TV and Netflix now. She'd rather watch the film.

Anyway, Charlie hasn't tried to find any *common ground* with her and she's glad.

They don't have any.

She likes being on her own, like now. Sitting at her desk, smoothing out a blank page. She rubs at an itch on her cheek and catches the faint trace of Sean's aftershave. She breathes it in deeply, trying to recapture the feeling of his arms around her.

A spark of possibility ignites but grief tries to extinguish it as she catches sight of a photo of Mum and Dad on her bookcase. She has no right to be happy, no right to any of it and yet still she hopes and dreams and signs the name she wishes were hers over and over again.

Nina Kelly

Nina Kelly

Nina Kelly

It's childish practising a signature that is not, may never be hers but she remembers how alive she felt on the top of that hill, being comforted, and she holds it to her heart as proof that she is loved. She is wanted.

She turns to another page, allows her innermost feelings to spill out onto the paper – a love letter she will never send. I want to . . .

Touch you.

Kiss you.

Taste you.

And then, ashamed of the ridiculousness of it all, the trouble it would cause, she scratches out everything she's written, the nib of her black biro tearing at the paper until her words are barely legible, making as little sense on the page as they did in her head. Still, she tears up the letter into dozens of tiny pieces before letting the fragments flutter through her fingers into the bin. She wishes she could throw away her emotions as easily. She wishes she didn't feel the way she feels. It isn't right.

But still, she closes her eyes to see that face, that smile, those lips she wants to press against hers and she knows it cannot, will not ever happen, and she curls herself onto her bed and cries. The pang of loneliness is so sharp, so fierce, that she stuffs her fist into her mouth so no one can hear her pain.

When there are no more tears to fall she unfolds herself and goes to the bathroom to splash cold water on her face. When she comes back into her bedroom, Charlie is standing over her desk, the piece of paper in his hand with her childish signatures on.

Why hadn't she torn that up too?

She snatches it from him and scrunches it into a ball, glares at him with all the hate she can muster and throws the one thing at him that she knows will hurt him the most.

CHAPTER THIRTY-THREE

Charlie

Charlie hadn't meant to invade Nina's privacy. After he had walked Pippa home, fetching her a glass of water and a couple of paracetamol, he had thought he could take the kids out to dinner, but Evie had rung Duke and invited him over for pizza which just left him and Nina.

Nina's room was empty, the door ajar. He'd wandered inside to wait for her and, as he stood next to the desk, he couldn't help noticing the piece of paper containing two words that struck fear into his heart.

Nina Kelly

Nina Kelly

Nina Kelly

He knew what this was; he'd been at school once. It was a girl practising her future signature. Her married signature.

Kelly isn't a unique name but the only one he knows is Maeve's dad, Sean.

He thinks back to the picnic.

The way Sean held Nina in his arms, her cheek resting against his neck. The seconds that slid by before he let her go.

Is there something going on between them? Anger flares in his stomach. Sean is far too old for his sister; even if he were younger, Nina's age, Charlie knew it wouldn't matter. He would have a problem with anyone laying his hands on her. Even if there's nothing going on and it's all in her head she obviously has feelings for him, thinking . . . what? Sean might marry her?

It is stupid and childish and that makes Charlie think at best Nina is solely harbouring a crush; at worst she had been standing in the arms of a . . . a paedophile, right in front of him too.

He doesn't hear Nina come back in the room. It isn't until she snatches the paper from his fingers and screws it into a ball that he registers she is there, mouth twisted in fury.

'What the fuck, Nina?' Charlie doesn't follow the advice from the parenting books. He knows his face is showing anger and frustration and he doesn't care.

'It's nothing.' Her cheeks are blazing; her eyes too.

'It isn't nothing. Sean Kelly! If he's touched you—'

'He hasn't,' she snaps. 'And so what if he has? At least he *cares* about me.'

'Cares?'

'He listens to me. Asks me how I feel.'

'I'm always asking you how you bloody feel.'

'Yeah, but do you really want to hear the answers?'

'He's a grown man.'

'And I'm not a child. Get out my room, Charlie.'

'You can't talk to me like that.'

'I can talk to you however I like. You're not my dad. Is this how your dad treated you? Or is this how you treated him? Is that why he left you?'

Charlie feels his hand twitch but he doesn't raise it. They glare at each other.

He takes a deep breath. 'Fine then. I'll go and ask Sean what he thinks—'

'No. Please, don't Charlie.' Nina doesn't apologise but she no longer shouts. 'It isn't . . . I just . . . Look, I can promise you there is nothing going on between me and Sean.'

'I . . .' he trails off. If there's a chapter in the parenting book covering this then he hasn't yet read it. 'Okay. I believe you.' She sounds so sincere. 'Look, I was going to ask if you wanted to go out for food? Duke's eating at Evie's. It would be nice for the two of us to spend some time together?'

'Another time? It's been a long day and I'm not hungry. Why don't you go somewhere, Charlie? I'll wait here for Duke. You haven't had a night out since you moved here.'

He doesn't want to go anywhere on his own but she is trying to make amends so he says yes and slips out of the room with the olive branch, his shame and the sordid conclusions he had jumped to.

Charlie has caught a bus into town and walks into the nearest bar. He's been here before when he was sixteen, with Pippa, because they had a reputation for never checking IDs. Then it was a spit and sawdust pub. All dark beams and sticky floors and live music at weekends. Now it's a Wetherspoons but whether through nostalgia or because he can't be bothered to find anywhere better, Charlie orders a Guinness and while the barman is waiting for it to settle, he asks for a whisky chaser. Alcohol hasn't passed his lips for years – and for good reason – but he downs it in one, feeling the burn in his throat, the warmth in his stomach. He sips his pint, licking the froth from his lips before he glances around, wondering if there's anyone here he went to school with, but he doesn't recognize anyone. Even the music is new to him.

He's making a mess of everything.

Should he talk to Sean and ask him outright if anything is going on? He wants to believe Nina but he can't scrub the image of Sean's arms around her from his mind. Mum would know how to handle this but then if Mum and Dad were still here Nina wouldn't be searching for a father figure.

He wishes Pippa were here. She'd know what to do. She seems to know everything, from sprinkling baking soda over the rug to neutralise the smell of Billie to rubbing the chopping boards with half a lemon to remove the stains.

It isn't just cleaning she's helped with.

They'd had a games night and she had taught him to play Uno. She had played the +4 coloured card and had told him that meant he had to find four things, one yellow, one blue, one red, one green, in thirty seconds. He had raced around the room panicking, a red cushion tucked under his arm, a green spider plant balanced in his hands, 'nothing's blue, nothing's blue', Billie at his heels, only realizing when he turned around to find her doubled over in hysterics that she had made up that rule.

He had laughed too. It had been so unexpected, he'd actually placed a hand over his stomach, questioning whether the sound really came from him. Whether he'd make it again. He'd felt a flash of guilt. But then Pippa had placed an arm on his forearm, saying, 'They'd want you to be happy. They loved life.' He'd taken a moment because hearing that, knowing that, didn't make it any easier to have a good time but then she'd shoved him good-naturedly, 'Your turn, loser.' She'd formed an 'L' on her forehead with her fingers, but she did it with the wrong hand so it was backwards.

'Who's the loser now?' He'd shoved her back.

He wishes she were here. He pictures her at sixteen, nodding her head to the beat of the band, swigging from a bottle of orange WKD while he drank the blue. They'd catch the last bus home and then sit on the pavement outside their houses, leaning against their respective fences, reluctant to say goodbye.

To push away the image, he drains his pint and orders another.

'Bad day?'

'Yeah.' He's not in the mood for conversation so he takes his glass and walks away from the woman who spoke but she follows him to the table he sits at.

'Do you mind if I join you? I'm waiting for a friend and I hate being in a bar on my own.'

Charlie gestures to a seat.

'There's not a jealous girlfriend who'll turn up in a minute, is there?'

'No. She dumped me,' Charlie says without thinking.

'No wonder it's a bad day.'

'Oh, that was days ago; it got worse.'

'Thank God for alcohol then.' She raises her glass and Charlie chinks his against hers.

'Sorry. I'm not normally this . . . self-pitying,' he says.

'What are you then . . . normally?'

'In London.'

'Christ. No wonder you're depressed here. This is the best we have to offer in terms of nightlife.'

'I know. I grew up here.'

'Back visiting family then?'

'Something like that. Can I get you another drink?'

'Vodka tonic.' She hands him her empty glass. 'I'm Gina by the way.'

'Charlie.'

Later, Charlie feels the room begin to spin. He's drunk too much but for the first time in a long time he's had fun. Tonight, no one expects anything of him; he can be anyone he wants to be.

Gina's easy to talk to; they've dissected each other's music tastes, favourite foods, debated whether *Die Hard* is a Christmas movie, talked about everything except real life. She laughs at all of Charlie's terrible jokes while twisting her hair around her finger. He knows that she is flirting with him but that doesn't mean he is immune to it. He can't remember the last time he saw naked desire in someone's eyes.

'So . . .' He leans into Gina. 'What happened to your friend?'

Gina shrugs. 'His loss.' Her fingers reach for Charlie's and he feels a jolt of . . . something. 'He's a train driver so perhaps he's been called out on a train-related emergency.'

Charlie snorts. 'Train-related emergency. Like what?'

'I dunno. Rabbit on the track or something. What do train drivers do?'

'Drive trains. Every boy's dream.'

'Was that your dream when you were young?'

'No. I wanted to be an author. How about you?'

'Ballerina.' Gina stands and pirouettes, falling onto Charlie's lap. 'So, what did you end up being?' She runs a fingertip down his cheek.

'That's too depressing. Let's talk about something else.'

'Or let's not talk at all.' She leans in, her eyes flicking between Charlie's eyes and mouth. He licks his lips; he so badly wants to kiss her, and then he does.

And she kisses him back.

The taxi drops them off outside Charlie's and in true movie style they fumble with each other's clothing all the way to the front door. In the hallway he finishes unbuttoning her blouse, and she yanks the T-shirt from over his head. His hip catches the table by the foot of the stairs and the china bowl they keep their keys in crashes to the ground.

'Whoops,' Gina says and they begin to giggle like children but then they are kissing again and he doesn't feel like a child anymore.

He takes her hand and leads her up the stairs but when they reach the landing it's suddenly flooded with bright light.

'Charlie.' Nina's furious voice instantly sobers him up. He sees the horrified expression on Gina's face as she hurriedly tugs her blouse closed to cover her chest.

'How could you?' Nina places both hands against his chest and shoves him, hard. 'With *her* of all people.'

CHAPTER THIRTY-FOUR

Nina

'Miss Rudd. You're fucking *Miss Rudd*?' Nina can't believe her teacher – her teacher who makes her life a misery – is half naked in her hallway. Billie omits a low growl.

'Gina? Gina is Miss Rudd? I don't . . . I didn't . . .'

From his floundering excuses, the shocked expression on Charlie's face, Nina guesses they didn't get as far as surnames.

'You were bringing her back to Mum and Dad's bed?' She is screaming now, partly because she is furious and partly because if she's angry she cannot cry. She refuses to shed a tear in front of Miss Rudd.

Gina.

Duke stumbles out of his bedroom, sleepy-eyed and hair tousled.

'Go back to bed,' Nina orders; she is the adult now.

'But—'

'Now!' Nina yells and Duke retreats, Billie trotting after him. She hears the slam of his door followed closely by the slam of the front door. Gina, at least, has left.

'Kitchen,' she growls at Charlie, stamping after him as he weaves his way downstairs.

They stand on opposite sides of the room, him leaning against the fridge, her the worktop. She can see a light on in Pippa's house; through the window she sees her filling a glass with water.

She focuses on Charlie, 'Coming in drunk—'

'I don't drink,' he says.

'You're pissed.' Does he think she's actually stupid?

'Yes. Now, but . . . normally. I don't drink. I don't do . . . that either.'

'That? Fuck my teachers?'

'I didn't fu . . . Nina, I'm sorry. I made a mistake, okay?'

'No.' She shakes her head furiously. 'It. Is. Not. Okay. You came here, Charlie, and you fought for us. You told Aunt Violet . . . you told the *police* that you were responsible. That . . . *that* was not responsible.'

'I know.' He runs a hand over his chin; there's the scratch of his bristles. He's a mess.

'I don't think you do know. Duke has lost his parents.' She can't think about her own feelings; she has to remain detached or emotions will clog her throat and she will be unable to speak. 'His world has always been small and now it's shattered. You came here, with Sasha, and he formed an attachment to her. The times she visited, video calling, he thought she was part of the family. Then she left, you left and then we moved to Aunt Violet's and then you came back, alone, and now Sasha's gone for good.'

'Yes.'

'And you tell Duke that he won't see her again, you tell him that casually on the day of the *memorial*. Drop it in conversation without any explanation or thought to his feelings—'

'I'm so—'

'And then hours after telling him this you bring another woman home. *A teacher from school.* He needs consistency. Stability.' She does too but she does not voice this.

'I didn't think,' Charlie can't look her in the eye.

'Are you one of these people who can't bear to be single? Are we going to have a parade of women here until you find one you want to keep?'

'No.' He clears his throat. 'No. Absolutely not.'

'Because if you can't commit to us and—'

'I can. I have. Nina, I'm so sorry. Honestly, I don't usually go for one-night stands and, as for dating . . . before Sasha I was single for a long time. Look, I didn't take into account your feelings tonight and I certainly didn't consider that Duke might have been upset that me and Sasha have broken up but in retrospect I can see that he needs . . . we all need things to be constant for a while. No more women, I promise.'

'Do you, though? How can you promise that?'

'Because . . . you both have to come first. Our family has to come first. I'm not saying I'll stay single forever but right now, while we all get used to each other, while we build on the foundations—'

'*Build on the foundations?* Did you get that from a book?'

'Umm, yes. Yes. I did.'

'You don't need a book, Charlie. You just need to think. And not with—' she waves her hand towards his crotch, glad it's dark and he won't see her face flaming '—that part of you. Because if Aunt Violet is the more stable option for us, I'll move us back there.'

'She isn't. I promise, Nina.' He places his hand over his heart. 'No relationships, at least for a while.'

'Good. It's not like I expect you to live like a monk forever but, Charlie, you brought someone you'd just met back to our home, to Mum and Dad's bed.' Nina feels her voice cracking. She can't hold it together much more. 'See you in the morning.' She rushes from the room and towards the stairs with Charlie's 'I promise I won't let you down' trailing in her wake.

Nina can't sleep. She doesn't want to be here, in this house, with Charlie, reeking of alcohol, in Mum and Dad's room. She thinks about texting Maeve to see if she's awake, asking if she can come over, but what would Sean say if she arrived on the doorstep at midnight. He must care to have come to the memorial. Would he comfort her or would he turn her away? She couldn't bear the sting of rejection; tonight she feels so lonely.

She turns onto her side. Through her thin grey curtains she can make out the moon, high and round. She remembers when she used to believe it was made of cheese. She used to believe in so many things but now she struggles to find something to hold on to. She tries to conjure the warm feelings she felt earlier but they are slippery and slide through her fingers as she tries to hold them close.

She needs to sleep.

Tiredness burns behind her eyes. Thank God tomorrow is a teacher training day. No school and no Miss Rudd.

Every time Nina closes her eyes she pictures her teacher and Charlie practically ripping each other's clothes off.

Is that all adults want? Sex. She tries to unpick her feelings, which felt so pure earlier but are now tangled with confusion and shame. She finds a thread that she thinks is love but she's afraid if she tugs on it everything she feels will unravel.

She'll unravel.

She climbs out of bed and finds the piece of paper she'd scrawled over earlier,

Nina Kelly
Nina Kelly
Nina Kelly

She will never be her, the person she longs to be. Even if she were, she would only fuck it up, because that's what she does. Hurt other people. She couldn't even be bothered to say goodbye to her parents when they left on New Year's Eve. Couldn't spare five seconds to hug them, tell them she loved them.

She did not even look at them properly.

Love is a privilege she doesn't deserve.

She will forever be Nina Johnson, lost.

Alone.

If she could go back to one moment in time it would be that New Year's Eve morning, in Pippa's kitchen. If she could make amends now somehow, she would.

She'd do anything.

Nina opens her YouTube app and searches for videos. She scrolls through clip after clip until she finds it, something she can hold on to.

Something she can believe in.

Something that might change *everything*.

CHAPTER THIRTY-FIVE

Charlie

It feels as though something has crawled into Charlie's mouth and died. He reaches for a glass of water but every time he moves his head the pneumatic drill in his brain grows louder.

It's ten o'clock and he's still in bed, partly because he feels so rough and partly because he's avoiding Nina. The humiliation of being caught half undressed on the landing with her teacher is crushing.

There's a light tap on his bedroom door. 'Come in, Duke,' he calls, and he winces as the throbbing behind his temples increases.

'How did you know it was me?' Duke asks.

Because Nina would have thudded on the door, hard and angry.

'Magic.' He tries to smile.

'It smells weird in here.' Duke covers his mouth and nose with his sleeve.

'Yes, that's because I did something very stupid last night.'

'Has Miss Rudd gone?'

'She has and I'm sorry if she upset you.'

'Nina hates her.'

'I know that now. Look, about me and Sasha breaking up . . .

I'm sorry I didn't tell you. Do you have any questions?' Charlie forces a smile.

'Dunno. Are you going to miss her?'

'Yes.'

'Me too. Can I go to Evie's? She said her mum will pick me up.'

'Of course.' Charlie feels relief flood through him. 'Duke—' he calls as his brother turns away. 'I'm glad you've got a friend.'

'We all need a friend, don't we?'

'Yes.'

'But not Nina's teacher, Charlie.'

'No. Not Nina's teacher.'

Charlie waits until the door has closed before he places the pillow over his face.

Later, he has showered and is frying a hearty brunch, a mug of strong coffee in his hand.

Nina sticks her head into the kitchen. 'I'm going to Maeve's.'

'Do you want a lift?' he offers.

'You're probably still over the limit.' She gives him such a scathing look he feels himself shrivel like the bacon in the pan.

'I'm sorry about last night. I meant what I said though. Absolutely no more women. You and Duke come first. Even if Jennifer Lawrence knocks on the door and asks me to dinner.' He smiles at her; she doesn't smile back but he doesn't stop trying, 'I could pick you up later?'

'If it's dark *Sean* will drive me.' There's a challenge in her words and he knows that she is goading him but he's just grateful she is speaking to him at all.

'Good to know,' he says, although he thinks it's anything but.

'Charlie?' she asks uncertainly. 'When was your first kiss?'

He is thrown. He jumps at the spit of oil on his hand and he turns off the gas under the pan.

'I was six. We were in the sandpit at school and she had the red bucket and I really wanted it so she swapped it with my yellow one and I was so happy I kissed her.'

'I mean your first proper kiss.'

'I was thirteen and we'd watched *Pay it Forward* about a kid whose kindness changes the world. She cried at the end and . . . and I remember wanting to take away her pain. Thinking, that if I could, I'd feel it for her. She looked so beautiful. It felt right.'

'And was it . . . right?'

'It was. At the time. Sometimes you have to trust your instincts.'

Charlie sees Nina's face light up and he knows he has said the wrong thing. She spins out of the room and he wants to call her back. Redo the conversation. Tell her she shouldn't kiss anyone until she is twenty. Thirty.

Until she's sure he is the right person.

Tell her that Sean isn't that person.

Pippa looks tired. Dark violet circles under her eyes.

'What do you want, Charlie?' She can't quite look him in the eye. He can't account for her frosty tone.

'How's your head?'

'Fine.' She sounds anything but fine. 'Is there something I can help you with?'

'I just wanted to see how you are—'

'Now you've seen.' She begins to shut the door.

'Yes, and umm, I . . . I wanted to ask you about the freezer. It's quite icy—'

'No shit.'

'And I wondered whether it needs defrosting.'

'I don't know, Charlie. I'm not Mrs bloody Hinch.'

Charlie doesn't know who that is, but he does know something is wrong.

'Have I done something to upset you?'

'You woke me late last night, slamming the taxi door and giggling with . . . whoever.'

'I'm sorry.' He feels that today he has apologised, at least once, to just about everyone. He fumbles to pat Billie who had been sitting on the doorstep at his side, to reassure himself that somebody still likes him but she has squeezed through the gap in Pippa's front door and is now sitting in the hallway, pressing her head against Pippa's legs. 'That . . . last night was a mistake. She turned out to be Nina's teacher.'

'*Miss Rudd?* You brought Miss Rudd home?'

'I didn't know it was her.'

'Does Nina know?'

'Sadly so.'

'That would account for the shouting. You'd better come in.' She opens the door wide and he follows her into the kitchen, which is just like the one next door except everything is in reverse. He sits at the breakfast bar while Pippa makes coffee. He takes a sip and it scalds his mouth and he takes another, welcoming the pain, a penance almost.

'I was drunk last night.' His words settle immediately.

Shocked, she turns to face him. 'But Charlie, you don't drink.'

'No.'

'Not since . . .'

'No.'

She reaches for his hand, traces her finger over the scars on his wrist. His skin tingles under her touch, his heart accelerates. She knows that turning to alcohol isn't something he'd do lightly. 'Do you want to talk about it?'

'Yes. No. I don't know. I'm messing it all up, Pippa.' He tells her about the row with Nina, his fears that she might have developed feelings for Sean.

'It's a crush. It's natural. Maeve's a decent girl and she can only be that if she had a decent father. Sean's done a great job bringing her up alone. I don't think you've anything to worry about. He has a teenage daughter; even if he suspects Nina has developed feelings for him he won't act on them. He's a good dad.'

'Am I . . . am I like my dad?'

'No. Christ, Charlie. No.'

'Nina said some . . . things and I didn't handle it very well. It was all too much yesterday, the memorial, the . . . the memories.'

'Come on.' Pippa picks up their mugs and leads him into the living room.

The bookshelves are empty, books stacked on the floor. There are cardboard boxes on the dining table.

'Having a clear-out?' She can't meet his eye. His stomach drops. 'Pippa?'

She takes her time setting their drinks down on the table. 'After Aunt Violet took your house off the market the estate agent knocked on the doors of all the neighbours, including me. He had a couple looking to buy on this street, she grew up here, and . . .' She swallows hard. 'I didn't want to worry you because I wasn't sure but they came for a viewing and made an offer

215

and . . . I don't know what I'm going to do yet but I need to sort through Grandma's things eventually.' Her hands twist together in front of her.

Because one day she might leave.

It's how he imagines being struck by a bolt of lightning might feel: sharp, shocking and completely unwelcome.

His knees fold of their own accord and he sinks down onto the sofa, head in his hands.

It isn't until this moment that he finally admits to himself that he hasn't come here to ask about the freezer. He doesn't care about the freezer. It was an excuse, all of it. He's a thirty-three-year-old intelligent male. All along he had known how to work a washing machine, how to plan meals. He knew all of it but he didn't feel he had the right to a friendship with Pippa and so he appealed to her good nature to help him because he wanted to spend time with her.

He's a thirty-three-year-old intelligent male but he's an idiot.

He hadn't proposed to Sasha because deep down he knew Pippa was the one.

Has always been the one.

He raises his head. Sees Pippa's distress.

She sits too. The air around them thick and heavy. The house silent.

They say when you're dying your life flashes before your eyes. Charlie isn't dying but he still feels pain. Still sees his memories rush towards him, past him, away from him. He catches one and offers it to Pippa in desperation.

'Nina asked me about my first kiss.'

'Did you tell her about the one when you were six or thirteen?'

'Both.'

'Did you tell her they were both with me?'

They sit on the sofa, their thighs touching. The same sofa they had watched *Pay it Forward* on.

He glances at her, not sure what to say, whether he should say anything at all.

She was his best friend. His first love. His everything.

'I'm sorry,' he says again but this time he isn't referring to last night. 'I treated you so badly.'

He watches the hurt register on her face. 'It was a long time ago and I forgave you. I understood.'

'You always were too good for me.'

'I wasn't,' she says quietly. 'You just always felt you weren't good enough.'

Charlie leans back and closes his eyes. Is she right? He lets his mind roll back and play out his past. Alcohol has brought it all to the surface; the memories and the emotions he usually keeps buried. The pain. It's there in black and white and shades of grey and he feels it all again, everything. The fear he had felt while his dad raged drunk. The helplessness because he couldn't protect his mum. The sense of safety as he'd sought refuge here. The sadness he'd felt as he'd watched his dad pack, leave. The confusion that his love wasn't enough to make his dad stay, make him sober. The resentment when he had to visit his dad in his new flat rather than spend time with Pippa. With her it was the only time he ever felt safe, happy, himself. Right here, he acknowledges that he still feels safe around her. Himself.

'You were never the same after that day, Charlie,' she whispers as she takes his hand again.

It had been a Saturday. He had wanted to take Pippa to Briar's Hill for a picnic.

'You must go and see your dad,' Mum had insisted.

'Why? He doesn't care if I'm there; he barely notices.'

'Because he's your dad and he left me, not you, and . . . he'd never hurt you, Charlie.'

Charlie had been in a foul mood when Mum had dropped him off. Infuriated that Dad wanted to watch the match with him, he really hadn't been interested. He'd sat while Dad fizzed open can after can of Foster's while Charlie dreamed of Pippa. The smell of her hair. The softness of her lips. She'd been his best friend since they were five and he couldn't believe that she loved him back. They were only fifteen but he already had their future mapped out, marriage, a family, everything.

All of it.

And he'd *never* be like his father.

Dad's team had won and he'd roared his delight, climbing onto the glass dining table and beginning a victory dance.

'Get down, Dad. It's not safe.' Charlie had felt like the adult.

Dad had stretched out his hand. 'Don't be so fucking boring. Come up.'

'No. Dad. Please.' Charlie had seen the strain of the glass, the dip. 'You'll hurt yourself. Get down.'

'You're such a killjoy, like your mum.'

'I'm not. I'm . . . your son, Dad. Why don't you care?' Charlie had been close to tears. 'Don't I mean *anything* to you? Don't you love me? I love you.'

Their eyes had met and simultaneously there'd been a crack, a shatter. Charlie had leaped forward, his hands stretched out to catch his dad. He'd felt Dad's foot as it landed hard on his forearm. Felt the tear of his skin as the sole of Dad's boot drove shards of glass into his skin. He remembers the pain. The way he'd screamed and screamed. The blood. So much blood. He remembers Dad yanking off his T-shirt and pressing it to Charlie's wrist, the smell of his sweat and beer mingling with the metallic tang of his blood, which was pooling over the shabby beige carpet.

Charlie had thought he was dying and, from the panic in his eyes, Dad had thought so too but still he hadn't told Charlie that he was sorry. He hadn't told him that he loved him.

There had been a hammering on the front door and Dad had tried to shush him but Charlie hadn't been able to stop screaming. When the police had burst in, Dad had run out of the back door.

Charlie, having been taken to hospital, had somehow felt that it was all his fault.

His wrist and arm were stitched but they couldn't repair the tear to his heart, which widened when Mum told him that Dad had been tracked down and interviewed but wasn't facing any charges for neglect but, nevertheless, he was moving away; he wouldn't be leaving a forwarding address.

It was shortly after this that Mum had taken him to Cornwall – *to recuperate* – and then she had met Bo. Charlie had instantly recognized the love between them and he'd tried to equate that love with the feelings he'd had for Pippa but the one searing thought that pierced his mind again and again was that his love hadn't been enough for his dad; it hadn't been enough to stop him drinking, stay at home, get down from the table, and it wouldn't be enough for Pippa.

He wouldn't be enough.

Back at school after the summer, everyone had eyed the scars on his wrist and rumours had circulated that Charlie had tried to kill himself and he'd never corrected them because the shame of people thinking he'd tried to take his own life was less than the shame of his father not loving him.

'I never told Sasha, you know?' He returns to the present, to Pippa.

'Any of it?'

'No. I thought that she should know, if we were to . . . you know settle down, but I couldn't bring myself to talk about it.'

'She wouldn't have judged you on your father.'

'Perhaps not on that, but on what came after.'

He hears a sharp inhale from Pippa and he knows she is remembering as he is too. How he began to drink, finding the hidden bottles his dad had left behind at home and downing them, draining the Martini that was Pippa's grandmother's and, later, stealing cash so he could buy his own.

'Please, Charlie,' Pippa had begged as she'd found him at the top of Briar's Hill in a pool of his own vomit. 'I can't bear to see you like this. I love you.'

'I don't love you,' he'd said although he did. He'd wanted someone else to feel that their love wasn't enough. He'd wanted to hurt someone the way he was hurting. He'd pushed Pippa away again and again until eventually she'd stopped knocking on his door with that hopeful look in her eyes.

It was Bo who'd intervened after he'd moved in with them. 'Enough's enough, lad,' he had said firmly. 'You're killing your mother.'

Charlie had glared at her, blaming her. If she hadn't driven Dad to drink, if she hadn't told him to leave.

If.

If.

If.

He convinced himself it wasn't his fault. Addictions ran in families. Perhaps if he had children of his own they too would be alcoholics.

It was Mum falling pregnant with Nina coupled with the firm but fair pep talks from Bo that had made him realize he had a choice, a future. It had cleaned him up. He was going to be a big brother and it felt like a fresh start.

He avoided Pippa where he could, ashamed at the way he had treated her, wanting to make it up to her but not sure how, knowing she was leaving soon for university. While drawing his bedroom curtains one night, he saw her, illuminated under the orange glow of a lamppost, kissing someone else.

After she left for uni he was bereft, finding joy in Nina but little else until he left for London using his inheritance from his grandparents to rent a room in a house while he worked as an intern in publishing and then he focused on his present, trying to put his past behind him.

For years he has abstained from alcohol to prove to himself that he is nothing like his dad but sometimes he hates himself for feeling he has something to prove. Last night he drank and felt like the man who had let him down and he still hates himself. He can't win.

'I missed you when you left.' Pippa rests her head on Charlie's shoulder. 'I still miss you.'

He touches her hair; it still feels like silk. He swallows hard; he has so much he wants to say. She gazes up at him, letting him know with her eyes that he hasn't left it too late.

He knows if he were to kiss her she would taste of his past and his present and the future he wants.

He leans into her, she stretches towards him.

'I've never . . .' she touches his face. 'I've never felt the way I have with anyone else but you.'

There are tears in her eyes, his too, because he wants to kiss her, to tell her that he feels the same but he has only today made a promise to Nina to stay single and however much he wants Pippa he just can't be with her.

But, oh, how he longs to be.

'I'm not ready,' is all he can say because although he doesn't believe she will feel any resentment towards the children if he says that they're not ready he doesn't want to say anything that might possibly affect her relationship with them.

They need her.

'But I can wait, Charlie.'

'I'm so sorry, Pippa. I love you dearly as a friend but . . .' he can't finish the lie but he's said enough. He doesn't want her to put her life on hold the way he has put his romantic life on hold because who knows how long it will take to earn Nina's trust back.

Months?

Years?

It isn't fair.

He deserves what Pippa says next, even if it breaks his heart.

CHAPTER THIRTY-SIX

Duke

'Have you heard from Pippa?' Charlie asks casually over dinner.

'Yeah, she sent me a picture of her parents' house in Scotland when she got there,' Duke passes Charlie his mobile.

Nina peers over Charlie's shoulder. 'She sent me a different one.' She doesn't offer to show Charlie, instead stabbing at the congealing mess on her plate that Charlie has reassured them is a vegetable lasagne. Duke takes another small bite. Should lasagne be this . . . crunchy? Crunchy and slimy at the same time. How is that possible? Perhaps even Gordon Ramsay would be impressed, not by the meal but by Charlie defying science.

'Hasn't she sent you any photos, Charlie?' Duke takes back his phone.

'I haven't heard from her but I expect she'll show me herself when she gets back in a few days.'

'She's there for two weeks.' Nina clatters her cutlery on her plate, giving up on her food.

'Is there something wrong?' Duke thinks Charlie should know how long she's away for. What else is Pippa keeping from him? Why had she suddenly decided to visit her parents?

'She isn't sick is she?' Duke reaches for Billie. Is Pippa going to *die* too?

'No, she's fine but—' Charlie glances out of the window, the wet streaks snaking down the panes making patterns '—Scotland has an amazing history you know, we should go one day. You might learn about William Wallace in History.'

'We're doing the Great Fire of London at the moment. Evie got into trouble because instead of answering the questions on the paper we were given she wrote "Instead of the past we should be more concerned with the future of the planet" in capital letters.'

Evie has taught him a lot about the environment; she knows more than Mum even did, but still she wouldn't go away for two weeks without contacting him.

'You and Pippa *are* still friends?'

'Of course.' Charlie gives a fake parenting-book grin. Duke knows he is hiding something but that's okay because Duke is hiding things too.

1. The fact he hates school.
2. The real reason he doesn't play his sax anymore – he had told Charlie he'd grown out of music but it's because whenever he tries to play loneliness crawls up his throat and blocks his breath.
3. That he saw Nina kissing her hand and it was the grossest thing ever.
4. He sleeps with Mum's T-shirt every night and tries not to mind that her smell is fading.

'So, what did you think about the book?' Charlie pushes his own plate away and taps the cover of *The Curious Incident of the Dog in the Night-Time*, their latest book club read. Nina rolls her eyes and leaves the room.

'I loved it.' Duke had raced through the story.

'What was the best bit about it for you?'

'Well, I didn't think I'd like it at all because the dog died—' Duke pulls Billie that little bit closer '—but then when Christopher is trying to solve the mystery it's epic. He's different, isn't he, to other kids?'

'We're all different, Duke.'

Charlie is doing that head-to-one-side tilt to show he's really listening.

'Yeah but—' Duke strokes Billie '—it's like Nina says, I'm weird in a bad way but Mum said I was special and Evie says I'm weird in a cool way. I think books that show we're not all the same are good because it might make readers more, I dunno, tolerant? Is that a good word?'

'It's an excellent word.'

'Because people . . . I think they just really want to be happy but they can be scared of things they don't understand, so if it's explained to them properly then they might be more accepting. Nobody's perfect, are they? Yeah, that was the best bit for me. Having a character who is different to other kids their own age.'

'I think you're right, Duke. Books are so powerful. As well as making us feel happy or sad they make us think about ourselves and the world around us. Imagine being able to write a story that changes someone's life?'

'Why don't you, Charlie?'

'Why don't I what?'

'Write a book? You always wanted to. I dunno what you do all day while me and Nina are at school. It's not like you have a job, is it?'

Charlie's face falls before he rearranges his expression, that fake grin again. 'Looking after you both is a privilege and—'

'Charlie?'

'Yes, Duke.'

'Please stop reading parenting books. Throw them away and write your own book. Change someone's life even if it's only your own.'

'I'm not sure I'd even know where to begin writing an entire book.'

'Begin at the beginning. Everything starts somewhere, doesn't it?'

'But what if . . .?' Charlie tails off, turning towards him. His expression is so *real,* not parenting-book happy or displaying active listening but kind of like Billie when she's not sure if she can do something and she looks to you for reassurance.

'But what if it works out okay?' Duke summons his best piece of advice and that didn't even come from a book. He waits for Charlie to answer but his brother is gazing out of the window, over towards Pippa's house. Duke doesn't know if he's even listening anymore.

Then Charlie gets up and rushes from the room.

CHAPTER THIRTY-SEVEN

Charlie

'What if it works out okay?'

When Duke had said this to Charlie yesterday he'd had to leave the room and compose himself in the bathroom because he became so choked up listening to Duke, gazing at Pippa's empty house, he knew tears were about to fall.

'What if it works out okay?'

His brother may have been referring to writing a book but that simple question had made him pick over the conversation he'd had with Pippa during their heart-to-heart when he had found her sorting her possessions into boxes.

Made him think of a million different things he could have said when she had told him tearfully that she was going to go and stay with her parents and make a decision about her future and by this Charlie knew she meant whether or not she'd sell the house and leave. She said she wouldn't be in touch while she was gone, but Charlie knows now that she meant she wouldn't be in touch with him because she's still messaging Nina and Duke.

Because she cares about them.

Has he made a terrible mistake? Duke's words ring in his ears,

'Nobody's perfect' and 'People can be scared of things they don't understand, so if it's explained to them properly then they might be more accepting.' How is Duke so wise for an eleven-year-old?

Last night, after he'd pulled himself together, he had tentatively tapped on Nina's door, intending to test the water somehow regarding he and Pippa potentially becoming a couple. When she hadn't answered he'd opened the door. She'd been hunched over her laptop. Her head had snapped up when he'd cleared his throat.

'Charlie, what the fuck. Get out!' She had looked around, probably searching for something to throw at him and he had retreated.

It hadn't been the right time.

But it is, perhaps, the right time to consider his own future and this is what he mulls over once the children have gone to school. Duke has made him think about what he really wants to do. He could set up as a literary agent on his own from here, or perhaps move into editing, but then neither of those things appeal to him in the same way anymore. Reading someone else's words when he has a deep-rooted desire to write his own.

Books have a smell, a voice. Charlie has always found comfort in them; to him they are living, breathing things that, if you listen very carefully, whisper more than the story printed on the page. They hold the secrets of the writer; the things they have been through, the things they long to experience – their hopes, their dreams and often their sadness.

As an agent, he never told his authors to write what they know, how much duller the world would be without *The Handmaid's Tale* or *The War of the Worlds*. *Dracula* or *The Hunger Games*. He feels privileged to have witnessed so many books come to fruition. Beginning with the soft sigh of an idea until the vibrancy of an imagination sparks it into glorious technicolour. He championed his authors as the words poured, or sometimes stuttered, from mind to page. He believed in everything he represented; whether it became a bestseller or not, each story had a place in his heart.

He covers his chest with his hand, feels the steady beat beneath his palm. Does he have his own story to tell?

Is Duke right? Should he, *could* he, try and write his own novel? He doesn't have to cast his mind back to question when or why he gave up on his dream to do so – so much in his life seemed to begin and end with his dad. Instead he allows himself to recall the book that made him long to create his own.

Goodnight Mister Tom.

It had been one of those childhood summers; blue skies and fluffy white clouds, days that blended into one another as the stretch of the school holidays seemed endless.

Charlie had been eleven; he'd just completed his last year at primary. It must have been a weekend because his mum was in the garden. Charlie was sprawled on the lawn, which was yellowing with thirst, the tickle of the grass against his bare legs, in his ears the buzz of bumble bees as they'd hovered around the lavender bush, which smelled of comfort.

He'd barely moved for two days, engrossed in the tale of William who was evacuated during the war to the home of elderly Tom. To this day, Charlie remembers the horror that nipped at his heat-pink skin as he'd read about William's cruel mother and the neglect the boy had endured. During one harrowing scene he had dropped his book and rushed to his own mother, wrapping his arms around her legs as she'd aimed the hose at the heat-cracked soil in the borders, droplets of water cooling him as she'd turned around.

'Hey—' she had put one arm around him '—what's up?'

'Just . . .' Charlie hadn't quite known how to express the range of emotions the characters had made him feel. He'd realized then that words were an incredibly powerful thing. That he couldn't have been the only one touched by the story. The thought that there was a unity among readers had been comforting. It had given Charlie a sense of belonging to a secret club that non-readers could never be a part of and would never understand. That was when he'd decided he wanted to write his own book one day. To make readers feel. To bring people together.

He had let go of his mum's legs and looked earnestly at her. 'I'm just glad you're not mean,' he'd said.

'Charlie.' She'd switched off the hose and crouched down, looking him in the eyes. 'I can promise you that I will always do the best for you that I possibly can.'

And she had. Charlie can see this undoubtedly now.

Charlie sees the similarities between him and William, plucked out of their ordinary lives and placed down somewhere else entirely. Him ending up in a hospital bloodied and bandaged. Perhaps he has many stories to tell.

He opens his laptop and flexes his fingers and tries not to think like an agent: what's popular; what's marketable. He doesn't want to write psychological thrillers with predictable twists or police procedurals with jaded detectives.

He wants to write of unrequited love, of hope, of sorrow and loss and joy.

'Begin at the beginning,' Duke had said.

When was that? The first time he had kissed Pippa in the sandpit. Their first date? Charlie offering to take her for lunch. 'I'll meet you there,' she had said and he hadn't understood why until he'd walked into the restaurant.

She'd worn a black dress, her hair bundled on the top of her head, lips glossy. She had never looked more beautiful.

'I didn't want Gran asking questions,' she had said shyly as he'd straightened his tie, presented her with a baby pink rose, ignoring the curious glances of the other diners. They were oblivious to everything but each other. Not caring that it was broad daylight, not a candle in sight. That this was in fact a greasy spoon. To them it was everything. They had ordered bacon sandwiches because they could eat with one hand, the fingers on their free hands linked together.

It had been the most romantic meal of his life.

He writes. Allowing the words to stream from him, wishing he could speak the way he writes, honest, unfiltered, from the heart. He writes until Billie places a paw on his knee, reminding him that it's time for her lunchtime walk.

He scans over what he has written. They are not good words, not yet, but there's something there, a promise, a possibility, and he thinks that one day, with time and patience, they might eventually be . . . something.

For the past two weeks Charlie has let all his feelings pour onto the page. All the emotions he feels but cannot share with Pippa because she doesn't want to speak to him. She sends daily updates to the children though. Long messages which Duke and Nina share with him each night over dinner while he sits with a fixed grin on his face and agrees that yes, Edinburgh castle is impressive. Glasgow Contemporary Art Gallery looks fun. Loch Ness is beautiful but he doesn't believe in monsters. He doesn't know what he believes anymore.

Today the words aren't flowing. He's exhausted. His sleep broken, dreams full of Pippa. He leans back on his chair, yawning as he gazes out the window. Heart stuttering as he sees Pippa walking up the path. He rubs his eyes, wondering for a split second whether he has imagined her but Billie is already racing to the door, tail wagging furiously.

'Hi. Good trip? How were your parents? I saw the photos that—'

'Charlie.' Pippa cuts off the nonsense that tumbles from his mouth. 'Can we go for a walk? I need to speak to you and I don't want to do it here with the kids due home from school soon.'

Pippa doesn't tell Charlie what she wants to talk about just yet and he doesn't ask. Instead, he texts Nina and asks her to walk Duke home today and then they move in synchronicity, heading for Briar's Hill where they climb to the top and sit on the ground, not flopping down like they used to when they were young, but lowering themselves carefully onto the grass that is patchworked with brown, thirsty patches. May is unseasonably hot. He can't remember the last time it rained.

Charlie steals a glance at her. The gentle breeze flutters the hair around her face, her eyes fixed on the horizon.

How could he have ever thought he could live without her?

Falling in love with Pippa for the first time had happened so close to the accident at the dingy flat his father had been living in since he had separated from Mum.

Too close.

It anchored Charlie's feelings for Pippa to that time. Thoughts of his father evoking bittersweet memories of Pippa, thoughts of Pippa bringing back into sharp, painful focus his raw and conflicted emotions, love and lust, grief and guilt.

When he was in hospital following a blood transfusion, weak and confused, Charlie was too immature to fully process and experience his intense feelings – anger and sadness and loss – and so he shut them out. He shut everyone out – his mum, Pippa.

She is here now though and Charlie has no idea what she wants to say.

'I talked everything through with my parents and I've made a decision.'

Charlie's chest tightens painfully.

'I've handed in my notice at work. I . . . I've accepted the offer on the house.' She draws up her knees and rests her chin on them.

Charlie quells the panic that rises, mentally calculating in his head how long she might still be here for. He has never bought or sold a property but he has friends who have. With banks and solicitors and mortgages and surveys, the process takes months.

'I'm leaving as soon as I can, Charlie,' Pippa says. 'Once I've found a home for everything in the house I'm going back to Scotland until the money comes through and then . . .'

His mouth is dry; he licks his lips before he asks, 'And then?'

She shrugs. 'I don't know. You know . . . you know the way I feel about you and it's hard, too hard to see you every day. It took me a long time to get over you before. I don't know if I ever really did and . . . I know you care, Charlie but . . . it's not enough.'

Stay. The word rises from his heart until it's in his mouth, on his tongue. *Stay.*

He wants to tell her that she means everything to him, that if she leaves he has no purpose. He wants to apologise for being weak and indecisive but explain that he feels the decision is not his alone to make. He wants to beg her to wait until Nina is ready, Duke.

He wants to say sorry.

233

He forms the words in his head before he says them but they are all inadequate, inappropriate, mistimed and misjudged.

And can they really make it work when they couldn't before?

So much has happened between then and now that Charlie isn't sure either of them knows the way back to the way they were, the people they were, young and in love and full of hope. But she knows him in a way that no one ever has before, and, whereas Sasha only ever had part of him, Pippa loves him as a whole.

What is he going to do?

He needs to make a decision based on facts not feelings. It is still unbearable to recall Nina's anguished screams when the police officers came to the door on New Year's Day, he remembers the feel of Duke clinging to his legs. He recalls the utter bewilderment on their faces, their disappointment as he left them with Violet and their relief when he returned. He has seen, little by little, day by day, the frowns disappear from their faces, Nina even smiles occasionally now when she thinks Charlie isn't looking. But then, in an instant, their expressions can darken as they remember that their parents are never coming home again. He is there at night as they wake from nightmares. He is there to offer comfort and security and reassurance.

The cold, stark truth is that Duke and Nina need him far more than Pippa does. He has to put them first because that's what being a parent is, isn't it? Second place. Always. He feels terrible for the pain he has caused Pippa but takes his own needs and locks them away once more. Perhaps in the future he will get them out, dust them off, examine them from all angles, wondering if now is the right place, the right time for him. He has already found the right person.

But he has to let her go.

'I think . . .' Their eyes lock and he sees the hope on her face but he cannot deny her his honesty in the way that he had before. 'If leaving is the right thing for you then you should.' The confusion on Pippa's face clears as she understands what Charlie isn't saying – that he can't be with her – and instead, her face falls into an expression of immeasurable sadness. She wrings her hands in her lap. His chest hurts and it feels as if she is holding his heart, squeezing it in her fingers, her grip growing tighter.

He feels the distance between them widen although neither of them has moved. Loneliness ripples through him but hasn't it always been this way? Keeping everyone at arm's length? Charlie feels he has always been waiting for the next loss. For someone else to leave him. There's a justification in his sadness. An 'I-told-you-so' woven through his pain. 'I think . . .' Charlie stumbles over his own inadequacy. 'I think in a different time, a different place, we could have been blissfully happy.' He speaks tentatively. Carefully placing every word but she looks so utterly hurt, so utterly bewildered, and he knows what he is saying is no consolation but he wants her to understand. If it weren't for the circumstances, if it weren't for Nina and Duke then perhaps, but love cannot be enough. It has to have a shape, a future. They sit on top of the hill where they shared their first taste of alcohol, their first and only cigarette and their hopes and dreams with the unacknowledged truth heavy between them.

It, whatever *it* is, is over.

They sit quietly, soaking up the last of the afternoon's warmth the way they used to after school, not quite ready to part.

He wants to say those three words that he has not uttered since he said them to his dad but they steal the saliva from his mouth and, besides, it wouldn't be fair to tell her this now. He realizes, belatedly, that he has spent his entire life looking for someone who will love him unconditionally, someone who doesn't judge him by the scars on his wrist, by his frizzy hair and glasses. With Sasha he was asked for more than he could give but Pippa doesn't want him for a lifestyle or to fit a five-year plan; she only wants him, and that in itself is terrifying. Now he's found that love, he's petrified of losing it. Of losing her.

His mind lurches wildly between wanting to let her go to needing her to stay.

'I don't want you to . . .' He takes a deep breath. Charlie's heart-sick gaze meets Pippa's. She looks to him with sad eyes, waiting for him to finish his sentence but he can't fill it with the words she wants him to say. 'I don't want you to get cold.' He stands and offers his hand to pull her to her feet. 'Let's go.' He is trying to rebuild the impenetrable wall he worked so hard to erect but it's crumbling with every desperate word he says and he knows that not only is he ready for this, he wants it.

He wants her.

Forever.

'I'll come and tell the kids,' she says, but she doesn't get a chance.

Because when they get home, Duke and Nina have news of their own.

CHAPTER THIRTY-EIGHT

Nina

'So . . .' Nina begins excitedly as Charlie and Pippa walk through the door with Billie. 'They're giving out awards at the Jubilant June Showcase and . . . guess what! I'm getting the "Most Improved Student" prize out of the whole of my year and that's not even the best bit. I've won a hundred and fifty pounds of New Look vouchers!'

Nina can't quite believe it. It's the best thing to happen to her since forever. Even though it will be embarrassing to stand on the stage and accept her award in front of everyone she can't wait to go shopping and buy some new clothes.

'And . . . get this . . . it's Miss Rudd who put me forward! Miss Rudd! That's because I've seen her boobs and she has to be nice to me so thanks, Charlie. You almost shagging my teacher did me a favour in the end.'

She doesn't know what else to say to Charlie. How to explain that it isn't only the vouchers causing her euphoria. When Miss Rudd had kept her behind to tell her it had been the first time that they'd been alone since that night.

'Thanks,' Nina had been shocked. 'Thought my dick of a brother would make you hate me forever.'

'Charlie isn't a . . .' A flush had crept around Miss Rudd's neck. 'You shouldn't use language like that. He cares very deeply about you. That much was apparent after the . . . unfortunate incident. And I don't hate you, Nina. I think . . . I think you remind me a lot of myself at your age and—' she'd twisted her silver ring around on her middle finger '—it might seem like I'm hard on you but that's because you have so much potential and you don't always put enough effort in. I want you to do well. This is my first teaching job in a secondary school and perhaps I haven't always got it right.'

Nina had seen a softness in her teacher that she hadn't seen before.

'I guess I haven't either. I could try harder.' She'd smiled and was just walking out the door when she'd turned back. 'What did you mean about Charlie? You know? After—'

'He came to see me at school. Was very apologetic. He wanted to make sure that I didn't hold his behaviour against you.'

'He had my back,' Nina had said softly.

Miss Rudd had smiled. 'He had your back.'

Remembering this now, Nina throws her arms around Charlie and then realizes it's the first time she's ever wanted to hug him so she squeezes him tighter.

'Thank you,' she whispers in his ear. 'Thanks for this and for . . . everything.'

'I haven't done anything really,' he says.

'You have.'

It isn't only that he came to the school without telling her to make sure she'd be okay. He's given up his flat, his job, Sasha and promised he won't have another relationship until they've found their feet as a family, until the time is right. Finally, Nina feels herself beginning to trust him. They're starting to feel like a real family. For the first time in ages Nina can't feel her arms itching to be scratched.

She feels . . . something akin to happiness.

But then Duke thunders downstairs with news of his own.

Only he's not quite so happy.

CHAPTER THIRTY-NINE

Duke

It has been a terrible, horrible, awful day.

'What's up?' Charlie asks as Duke throws his arms around Billie, burying his face in her fur.

'Nina?' Charlie asks when Duke doesn't answer.

'Dunno. He walked home with Evie.'

Pippa's hand is warm and soft on the back of his neck but then it's gone and it is Charlie gently helping him to his feet. Leading him to the sofa, Billie at his heels.

His brother crouches down in front of him. 'I can't help you if I don't know what's wrong.'

'Nobody can help me,' he says dramatically.

Charlie glances at Pippa before saying, 'A problem shared is a problem halved.'

'But it isn't though, is it? You haven't got to do it.'

'Do what?'

'I've got to perform in the Jubilant June Showcase. I didn't even know there was one. Nobody told me that everybody in my year has to do something. Two weeks! I've got two weeks. It's too soon.' Duke feels sick at the thought. *Jubilant June*. More like Jeering June with everyone booing him off stage. 'I can't *do* anything. I don't have a talent.'

Charlie raises his eyebrows. 'You can play sax and piano.'

'I can't do music anymore, you know that. If I could then I couldn't do our kind of music anyway. Everyone would *laugh* at me.'

'He's right,' Nina says. 'If he took his saxophone in he'd be annihilated and the other kids would probably break it for kicks.'

'I'm sure they—'

'They would, Charlie. They would.' Duke feels a mad fluttering in his stomach. 'But it doesn't matter because I can't play. Pippa?'

'Whatever you do will be brilliant, won't it, Charlie?'

'Of course. I'll help you figure something out.'

'I've got to go to work now, Duke,' Pippa says, 'but text me and let me know what you decide to do.'

After she leaves they bounce around ideas.

'Ventriloquist?' Charlie suggests. 'I'm sure Nina has an old doll or—'

'A *doll*. I can't go on stage with a *doll*.'

'Juggling?'

'I'd drop the balls and everyone would *laugh*.'

'Have you got a yo-yo? You could do tricks?'

'No. But what about normal tricks? Frodo from *The Lord of the Rings* said magic is everywhere.' Duke looked around as though he might see some.

'That would be cool.'

'Help me practise, Charlie? And you, Nina?' She's glued to her phone again.

'I'm watching YouTube.'

'You're always watching YouTube.'

'You're always annoying.'

'Annoying. Jinx.' Duke said 'annoying' at the same time as Nina so now she can't speak.

She shrugs and heads upstairs.

'Come back,' he calls. 'I'll release you from the jinx,' but she's gone.

'Charlie, you have to—'

'Duke, breathe. Everything will be okay.'

'But I don't know any tricks and magicians have to have *flair* and I don't think I have any *flair* and—'

'Calm down, Duke. We'll think of something else then.'

And then they did, and it was brilliant.

Absolutely bloody brilliant.

CHAPTER FORTY

Charlie

'Yes. You can laugh,' Charlie says to Billie as he constructs and then abandons another paragraph in his novel. She is watching him intently, her tongue lolling out of her mouth.

He is exhausted. Yesterday, when Duke had come up with the idea of choreographing a routine for the talent show with Billie they had both thought it was brilliant.

It really wasn't.

Billie might be trained to sit and stay but, despite hours of practice, they couldn't get her to roll over, high-five, or anything else.

'I think she's too clever?' Duke had said.

'Clever?'

'Yeah. She knows that when she's learned it, she'll stop getting treats for trying.'

In the end they had stopped trying.

Decided that perhaps magic was the thing after all. Charlie had texted Pippa once Duke had gone to bed: **sorry it got rather hectic and you didn't get a chance to speak to the kids to tell them you're moving.**

I'll talk to the kids before I go.

He sends another message, **Can we talk?**

She hadn't replied.

Today he has messaged her again, and again. Knocked on her door, called her name despairingly through her letterbox not sure what he wants to say but knowing he has to say *something*.

Eventually his phone trembles a message.

Give me some space, Charlie. I need to learn to be without you.

It is another punch in the gut. Charlie wants to reply that she's just had space in Scotland, but he respects her and wants her to be happy so switches his phone off before he can say anything to make it worse, although how much worse it can get he does not know.

The days pass slowly. Charlie hangs on to the hope that somehow he and Pippa will fall back into their friendship. He gives her the space she needs, deleting the heartfelt texts he regularly composes rather than sending them. Drags himself away from her door whenever he finds himself poised to knock on it. His heart hurts, he spends as much of his time gazing out of the window like a lovesick teenager hoping for a glimpse of her as he does writing.

The cursor on the blank screen winks on and off, taunting him.

It's impossible for Charlie to focus on his manuscript. How can he write about being brave and taking chances when, next door, Pippa is preparing to leave, and he is letting her?

Desolate, he types another sad sentence and then immediately deletes it, wishing he could write his own ending to the story of his life. His own happily ever after.

Charlie folds Duke's magic cape after he's left for school. For the past two weeks Duke has practised his act and although he hasn't exactly nailed it, it isn't the disaster it was. He's performed to his 'audience' each night, Charlie clapping enthusiastically, Billie looking bemused, Nina glued to her phone, watching something on YouTube.

Charlie thinks Duke will be okay. Better than Charlie is doing right now. The scant sightings of Pippa entering and leaving her house haven't been enough. He knows he's being selfish but he cannot bear it any longer.

He texts her,

Hey

And waits, and waits. He's made the first move, now it has to be up to her.

It's another hour before the doorbell rings. Charlie opens the door. His breath catches in his throat.

Pippa stands on the doorstep, uncertain and afraid, and he feels a desperate hope begin to swell inside of him until she begins to speak.

'I've just brought back a few things you left at mine.' She holds out a bag but Charlie knows that really she is holding out her heart. Offering him one last chance. He sees it in her eyes.

'Come in. Please.' He steps backwards and takes the bag from her.

'I think we've said all there is to say, don't you?' Her arms are crossed; she's hugging herself, whether to keep her emotions inside or to keep Charlie's out he does not know.

She begins to turn and a cold, sharp fear grips him.

'Wait. Please.'

She shrugs as though it doesn't matter to her either way but she steps inside, the corners of her mouth flickering into a brief smile as Billie bounds to greet her.

Pippa sits at the kitchen. Outside of the window, heavy clouds threaten rain once more. He fills the kettle, spoons coffee into mugs, 'I've really missed you these past couple of weeks. I'm glad you popped round,' he says but when he turns, Pippa is on her feet, heading back down the hallway. He races after her.

'*Popped round?* I can't do this,' she says. The expression on her face is disbelief but more than that. Charlie has never seen her look so hurt. 'I *can't* just have a casual coffee as though we are friends. We are *not* friends, Charlie.'

'I know.' And he does know this because if she were just a friend he wouldn't have the fierce desire to cup her face in his hands, to lower his lips to hers. Unable to fight the urge, this is what he does now.

The kiss sates his soul the way that water quenches an endless thirst. It is nourishing, life-affirming.

Perfect.

'Charlie?' Her voice is a broken whisper as she pulls away. His name a question.

He can't give her answer, can't promise her a future. There is only here and now. This. He lifts her into his arms, carries her upstairs, lays her on his bed.

There's an urgency as they undress each other, Pippa yanks his T-shirt over his head, he pulls down her jeans. He wants to be on her, in her. She wraps her legs around his waist, her nails digging into his shoulders as she cries his name.

It is over quickly. Too quickly.

Charlie hugs her tightly to him, feels her cheek press against his chest. He wonders if she can feel his heart and whether she knows every beat is for her. He wants her again.

Slowly, he begins to kiss her as though they've got all the time in the world, although they both know that they haven't.

Later, Pippa sleeps peacefully in a way Charlie thinks she has not slept in days judging by the black bags that circle her eyes. She feels safe, held by him. He knows this because he feels it too. That security.

He is tired, exhausted by emotion, but he can't stop thinking.

Desperately searching for a solution that would mean he can have it all. Pippa's love, Nina's trust. That he can somehow convince his siblings that it's different with Pippa. She won't disappear the way Sasha had, evoking memories of the way their parents had suddenly vanished from their lives. She's more than the quick fling that was nearly Gina. Who does he put first? Nina and Duke? Pippa?

Himself?

There are many different kinds of love.

This . . .

This is real.

Charlie watches her as she lies beside him, the gentle rise and fall of her chest. The sound of soft breaths. Clouds obscure the afternoon sun but still it pushes through the window, casting a small circle of light over her heart which he knows beats for him. He doesn't want to break it and the thought that he might drapes a heavy blanket of sadness over his other emotions.

The clock ticks.

Time marching forward.

Time running out.

Now that he has found love, now that he is certain of it, it is, perhaps, too late but still Charlie carefully cradles the feeling on the palm of his hand, knowing it is something rare and fragile and beautiful and not quite wanting to release it. Pippa is blissfully unaware, her face slackened with sleep, the taste of her still on his lips. The inevitability of goodbye is torturous but he has made a promise to his family. His family who he has let down in the worst kind of way, never forming a relationship with his siblings, even though, he thinks, he is not the worst kind of person.

Or is he?

It has been years now since the accident in his father's flat and the memory is as hazy as the muted recollection of a dream. Not entirely tangible and open to interpretation. But whether it was or wasn't his fault doesn't change the fact that the fabric of his universe had been ripped apart at the seams and, afterwards, things were never quite the same. However hard he had tried to repair the tear with clumsy stitches, looping the coping techniques he had been taught over and over his pain until it was barely visible, he hadn't felt any better. Endlessly he had questioned who he was, what he felt. How had his life been built on a lie?

He had thought his father loved him.

The counsellor he had seen had tried to reassure Charlie that his father had made his own choices. Chosen to drink. Chosen to dance on the table. Chosen to leave while his son received an emergency blood transfusion at the hospital.

It didn't seem possible his father had chosen all of these things and yet, somehow, it was, and Charlie had never really been able to stop analysing it all. Even into adulthood he found himself constantly scrutinising his reality, reaching out to touch it with his fingertips, trying to fathom what was real and what wasn't.

She.

She is real and his battered heart isn't quite ready to let her go.

Pippa sighs and rolls over onto her back, her head lolling to one side, her blonde hair fanned across the pillow.

Charlie dips his mouth towards her ear, the smell of her coconut shampoo drifting towards him as he whispers his secrets; the hopes and dreams he had for them.

He tells her it all.

Everything.

And that is how he unequivocally knows she is the one.

He trusts her in a way he hasn't quite trusted anyone in years and years, not since that inimitable day when the glass had slashed at his arms and the scant faith he still had that his father was, deep down, a good man had disappeared.

He gently brushes her hair back from her face; her skin is warm and soft.

I love you, he thinks, although he cannot voice this aloud. He feels the shape of the words stuck to his tongue, heavy and cumbersome, but every time he is on the cusp of releasing them the memories of the last time he uttered those three words causes his chest to tighten painfully and his heart rate to increase.

He doesn't regret what has happened here today but it hasn't changed to cold, stark facts.

He feels a sting at the back of his throat.

The light changes in the window. Rain patters against the panes as the sky cries ceaseless tears.

He hotches down the bed and curves his body around hers.

When she wakes, in his bed, in his arms, will she think he's changed his mind?

Has he?

It's almost time to make an impossible decision, which will end in heartbreak.

Charlie's heartbreak.

Pippa is going to leave unless he makes her a promise that will be impossible to keep.

He thinks of the threads that tie him to this house through his tangled past and his complicated present and, for a single blissful moment, he imagines cutting himself free. Floating between his family and her. Which way would the wind blow him?

There are many different kinds of love and if he has to choose one . . .

He *has* to choose one.

Today.

Now.

Can love be enough?

Will his brother and sister forgive him if he tells them he's fallen for Pippa? They both know her well. Love her. He thinks, perhaps, that Duke will accept it, be happy even, but Nina? He can picture her dark eyes flashing with anger. It doesn't matter how fond she is of Pippa, she will feel betrayed, and he knows this because he has felt that too in the past. The resentment that his mum put Bo before him, at the time after his father left when he needed her the most, is enduring. If he sours his relationship with his sister now, when they're just starting to bond, it will forever taste bitter.

Pippa begins to stir, begins to wake.

He cannot let her go.

Cannot let this go.

If there is a chance that Nina will understand he has to try. He'll talk to her, explain the way he feels, has always felt, and hope that she understands.

'Charlie?' Pippa touches his face.

'I'm ready,' he whispers. A delighted smile spreads across her face.

'But,' he explains to her that he isn't sure if the children are ready. 'I'm going to talk to them properly, tonight. I'll come over tomorrow and—'

'No.' She sits up, clutching the sheet to her. 'Meet me in Joe's instead.' The greasy spoon where they'd had their first date. 'It was the beginning of us and if we have to end—'

'We won't.'

'But if we do. It feels, fitting somehow.'

'I'll be there.' He'll take her flowers. A bouquet this time that includes roses to show her that he remembers the past but also that he's not looking to recreate it. They can build something new and fresh.

'See you tomorrow.' She doesn't offer a time and he doesn't ask. It will be noon. Just like before.

He kisses her deeply as she leaves. Paces the hallway until the children get home, running through conversations in his mind. Structuring reassurances, thinking that he's an answer for every single concern.

Never, ever, guessing for a moment the fireworks that lie ahead.

CHAPTER FORTY-ONE

Nina

'Good day at school?' Charlie literally pounces on her when she gets home.

Nina shrugs. 'It was all right.'

'Can we talk?' He's rubbing his fingertips together, an anxious expression on his face.

'In a bit. I've got homework to do first.'

'Yes, of course.'

She takes the stairs two at a time before he can call her back. She guesses he's been reading that bloody parenting book again.

Whatever.

His newfound words of wisdom can wait.

She hasn't got homework at all but there is something she can't stop watching. Something she can't get out of her mind.

She thinks she has found her dad.

Before she has even settled herself on the bed, she has opened her laptop. Is replaying the YouTube video for the millionth time trying to make sense of the grainy images.

Is it her dad?

It has been torturous keeping this to herself but she hasn't confided in anyone. Charlie and Duke have been obsessed with the stupid magic act and although she normally shares everything with Maeve, she hasn't been able to share this. Not wanting Maeve to look at her with sympathy, shatter her hopes because it seems preposterous to think that her dad has survived the cold and choppy sea and chosen not to come home and yet . . .

She studies the footage again on her laptop, it is impossible to tell.

In front of the camera the small girl with the bouncing pigtails thrusts out a cornet speared with a flake. 'I scream—' the person recording shakes with laughter '—ice cream.'

'I scream,' the child insists, emphasizing each word before letting out an ear-piercing shriek.

'Shut-up-shut up-shut-up,' Nina mutters as though she might silence the toddler, might be able to hear the busker who is almost out of shot.

She plays it again and again, hoping that this time it will be different but the bloody child is still bloody screaming.

Nina slams the laptop lid shut. Unbidden, her nails begin to rake at her skin and so seconds later she opens the YouTube app on her mobile to occupy her fingers.

She can't clearly see the man in the background strumming his guitar, can't hear him playing, but there's something in his stance, something so familiar it makes her heart ache.

A headache is forming behind her eyes.

Is it possible her dad survived but has forgotten who he is? She googles amnesia and reads that the most common cause are head injuries, alcohol and traumatic events. Could her dad have hit his head on a rock when the boat capsized? He had the alcohol and the traumatic event in the bag.

Nina's longing that her dad might be alive is tightly bound in strands of logic that he can't be. Nevertheless, she tries to unpick her hope, but it's all tangled together and she just can't do it alone. She cannot bear the weight of this any longer.

She uncrosses her legs and stamps out her pins and needles before heading to find Charlie. He wanted to talk to her about something anyway.

She hears the shower running, decides to wait in his room – Mum and Dad's room – for him.

There was a time she would have hurled herself into their bed for Sunday morning cuddles with them. Rushing in with her stocking when she'd woken in the early hours to find that Father Christmas had been. Reading intently from her favourite storybooks while Mum breastfed Duke who was forever hungry. Now she slowly lowers herself onto the edge of the mattress and glances around the room.

The mustard-yellow chair by the window is heaped with Charlie's clothes, the wardrobe still full of her mum's dresses, her dad's shirts. Make-up and jewellery on the dressing table have been pushed to one side, bottles of Charlie's aftershave and his hairbrush stand among handfuls of loose change. Nothing has been removed as far as Nina can tell. It's as though her parents could step back into their lives at any given moment and Nina thinks how hard this must be for Charlie. Mum's dressing gown on the back of the door being the first thing he sees when he wakes, the last thing before he closes his eyes.

He cares.

He could have packed her parents' belongings away, donated them to charity, but instead he surrounds himself with them. She doesn't know how he can bear it. It's hard enough downstairs with her dad's carved wooden figures and her mum's vinyl records. At least she has her own room, her own sanctuary. Charlie sleeps in the place they last slept.

Nina runs a hand across the pillow where Mum had once rested her head. She feels something hard underneath her palm.

An earring.

Nina holds it to the light, the silver glinting in her fingertips.

Charlie has had a woman here, in this bed – her mum's bed, but when?

Nina remembers these sheets hanging on the washing line, not the way Mum would peg them so that they didn't crease in the middle or drape on the grass, but bunched up too closely, not enough air around them for them to dry properly. Nina remembers telling Charlie he had hung them wrong; was it only yesterday? Yes, she's certain it was. Whoever has been in this bed, who's left this earring, did it today.

'Nina?' Charlie stands before her, hair damp, towel wrapped around his waist, droplets of water glistening on his shoulders.

'What the fuck, Charlie?' Nina jumps to her feet.

'What—'

'What the *actual* fuck?' Nina thrusts the earring in front of his face, reminiscent of the bloody child in that bloody video holding out her cornet.

I scream.

Nina screams now. 'So while me and Duke have been at school, you've been . . . you've been *fucking* some tart in my parents' bed. Showering off the smell of the skank, were you?'

'It wasn't like—'

'At least I know it wasn't my teacher this time because she was in class with me. It isn't Sasha because she's in New York. So, who is she Charlie? Who's worth lying—'

'I haven't lied—'

'You promised.' Nina swipes angry tears away with the heel of her hand. 'You promised me that you wouldn't see anyone until Duke has adjusted. Until we've adjusted but you . . . you . . . three women in the past few weeks. You just can't help yourself, can you? Is that a stable environment for an eleven-year-old to grow up in? Is it?'

'Please, Nina. Let me explain—'

'There's nothing to explain. I trusted you. We trusted you. You said you'd put us first. You're a waste of space, Charlie Johnson. I don't need you and Duke certainly doesn't need you. Why don't you just bugger off back to London? We'd rather be with Aunt Violet than you.'

'You don't mean that.' Charlie touches Nina's shoulder. It makes Nina's skin crawl. She shakes him off.

'I'm going out.'

'Please don't. I need to—'

'Well, I need to be as far away from you as possible. Go fuck yourself, Charlie.'

She storms out of the bedroom, slamming the door behind her, trying not to think of all the other times she had slammed this door in the past.

'Mum, everyone gets more pocket money than me. It isn't fair.'

'Mum, everyone is staying at the party until ten o'clock. It isn't fair.'

Nina throws herself onto her own bed now, burying her face into her pillow to drown out the sound of her sobs. Charlie doesn't love them. He's lied to them. The first chance he has he'll probably leave them and then where will they go? Not back to Aunt Violet. As much as she's grown closer to her aunt – and, not that she'd ever admit it, she really enjoys their Sunday lunches together, Violet

256

teaching Nina to whisk the batter for the Yorkshire puddings, to beat the custard so it doesn't go lumpy – she doesn't want to live with her again. She wishes she were old enough to take care of her and Duke. She wishes they weren't reliant on someone else.

It isn't fair.

She's sick of feeling so alone.

It's time to find out whether she has to be.

Nina ignores Charlie when he taps on her door so softly. She nips the tip of her tongue in-between her teeth in concentration as she carefully draws a liquid eyeliner across her top lids. She dusts bronzer across her cheekbones and slicks her lips with a brave scarlet, which isn't quite how she feels but she wishes it were. It's warm but despite the bold lipstick choice she isn't quite ready to bare her arms. She slips on a sheer black blouse and after examining her reflection she undoes the top three buttons, squirts perfume onto her cleavage.

She doesn't want another row with Charlie so she pads quietly downstairs, slips out of the front door and runs until she reaches the corner and then she slows to a walk so she isn't a hot, sweaty mess when she arrives at Maeve's.

Sean opens the door. Nina feels a blush creep across her neck as though he can read what's on her mind.

'You look nice, Nina,' he says as she steps inside. Self-conscious, she wonders if she should have worn one of her usual shirts. This see-through top suddenly feels too obvious. Too immature. She doesn't want to be seen as a little girl anymore. She is here tonight to share how she feels.

Instead of dashing up to Maeve's room, she follows Sean

into the kitchen and perches on a stool at the breakfast bar. She watches him as he opens the fridge and takes out a box of eggs.

'Have you eaten?' he asks and she feels his concern drape around her like a blanket. Her shoulders relax a little.

'Yes,' she lies. Her nervous stomach has no room for food.

She fumbles around for something intelligent to say but as she watches him crack eggs into a bowl she's overcome with emotion and a small, anguished cry escapes her throat.

'Nina?' Sean wipes his hands on his jeans and rushes to her side.

'Sorry. It's just . . . the way you cracked eggs. My dad used to do it that way too, just using one hand. I've never seen anyone else do that. Sorry.'

She's embarrassed at her falling tears and annoyed that even now, five months later, the most unexpected gesture can cause a wave of grief to crash over her. Sean pulls her into a hug and she rests her cheek against his chest, feeling the beating of his heart, wondering again what he would think if he knew what was in hers. Discreetly she tries to wipe away her tears, hoping that her carefully applied eyeliner isn't streaking down her face.

'Nina?' It is Maeve's voice now, questioning.

'Sorry.' She pulls back from Sean. 'I was just having a moment.'

'My cooking's enough to reduce anyone to tears, isn't it?' Sean says.

Maeve rolls her eyes and Nina wants to tell her that she shouldn't do that. She shouldn't be irritated by her dad because one day he might not be here. She's snivelling again. She slides from the stool and tells them she's going to the bathroom.

'See you in my room, yeah?' Maeve calls after her.

Once Nina has repaired her face, she finds Maeve cross-legged on her bed, picking at the skin around her fingers. She raises her head as Nina flops down beside her.

'Did you want to go out?'

'No.'

'You're all dressed up. Aren't you bored of hanging around here all the time?'

There's nowhere else Nina would rather be than here, in this house, but she doesn't share that. Instead she says,

'I've got something for us,' as she lifts a bottle of stolen vodka from her bag and sloshes some into two of the empty mugs that litter Maeve's dressing table. Nina knocks hers back, her throat burning as the alcohol slides down, washing away the rawness from the angry words she had hurled at Charlie. She slugs another generous measure into her mug wanting to forget about her brother altogether. Needing Dutch courage for what lies ahead later that night if she gets the opportunity, of course.

'Anything you want to tell me?' Maeve asks.

'Umm. No. What?' Maddeningly, Nina feels herself blushing again. Is Maeve wondering why she chose to stay downstairs with Sean rather than come upstairs to find her?

'You're knocking it back a bit?'

Somehow Nina finds herself pouring her third drink; Maeve has barely touched hers.

'I think I've found my dad,' Nina blurts out. Having made the decision to finally tell someone earlier she can't keep it inside anymore. She opens YouTube on her phone and passes it to her best friend. Nina studies her as she watches the clip, her face inscrutable.

'It could be anyone?' Maeve says after she has played it through several times. 'The coastguard said there's no way anyone could have survived.'

'But what if this *is* him? What if he hit his head on a rock and has amnesia and doesn't know who he is?' Nina again feels the burn of vodka as it hits her stomach.

'That seems a little unlikely. Surely if you don't know who you are you'd go to the police and they'd figure it out? Nina, you have to let this go.'

'But . . .' Nina passes the phone back to Maeve. 'Look again. You've known Dad for ten years. You know his stance.'

'He's blurry and out of focus. Sorry, Nina. I don't think this is him. Didn't you say it's normal to think you see someone after they die?'

'Yeah. Sixty per cent of people do, according to Google, but this isn't imagined. He's right here.' She taps her phone screen with her nail. '*He's* here. And . . . and maybe if he survived then Mum did too.'

'What does Charlie think?'

'Charlie's an arse.' Nina drinks straight out of the bottle now. The room is beginning to sway. She wishes she had eaten something.

Annoyed that Maeve doesn't believe her she changes the subject. For the next couple of hours, they chat about nothing, the way Darren McKay asked out Sophie Clarke. Laugh that, despite nominating her for an award, Miss Rudd still can't look Nina in the eye since she saw her boobs.

Nina drains her drink.

Again.

'I feel a bit sick.' Nina clutches her stomach. Bile burns her throat as she swallows.

'I'm not surprised with the amount you've drunk.'

'I haven't drunk that much,' Nina says, although the bottle is nowhere near as full as it was when she opened it. 'It's because I haven't eaten.'

'Want me to make you something?' Maeve asks. 'An omelette?'

Nina thinks of Sean again. Cracking the eggs with one confident hand.

'Nah. Let's go to the chippy.' Nina stands. The floor rocks beneath her feet and she slumps back onto the bed.

'I'll go – you wait here. Curry sauce?'

'You know me so well,' says Nina although that isn't the truth. Maeve doesn't know the longing in her heart. The love she feels but she just can't tell her. It would change everything.

Nina must have slipped into sleep because she jolts awake and feels the drool seeping down her chin. She unfolds her stiff body and staggers downstairs, into the kitchen. The walls are rolling in, the floor tilting left to right. She reaches out a hand and grips the worktop to steady herself. Her vision blurs in and out of focus. She thinks she's alone but then realizes she isn't.

And her alcohol-fuddled brain tells her that perhaps she doesn't have to be alone ever again because as she focuses on the lips she so desperately wants to kiss she feels something.

A connection.

She doesn't stop to think about whether the warmth she feels is down to the vodka because she tells herself how is it possible to like someone for such a long time and for them to not like you back?

She lurches forward. Presses her mouth against lips that begin to move against hers before they become unwilling. She is shoved roughly away.

'Sorry . . . I . . . sorry.' Mortified she turns and stumbles towards the front door, a blast of warm air grazing her cheeks as she falls out into the front garden. She begins to run.

'Nina! What were you thinking?' Sean's voice snaps at her heels but she doesn't turn around. 'What the hell are you playing at?' he calls. She doesn't stop running but she can't escape the feeling of rejection.

Humiliation has sobered her up by the time she reaches home. She quietly opens the front door, creeps down the hallway. The door to the lounge is open. Charlie is sleeping in her dad's armchair, but he is not their dad and he does not love them. He just loves himself and . . . sex.

She treads careful footsteps, avoiding the third stair, which always creaks. Her room is tidy, her bed made. Charlie must have done it after she went out. She unzips her rucksack. It's virtually empty, Charlie had taken her PE kit to wash. She brushes the thought of this kindness away, tipping her bag upside down and shaking out her schoolbooks. She slides open her drawers and hurriedly throws things into her rucksack.

It is gone 1 a.m. by the time she stumbles out into the street but she doesn't care she's broken curfew.

She doesn't care about any of it.

She's never coming back.

CHAPTER FORTY-TWO

Charlie

Charlie wakes, his body stiff and uncomfortable. He's been in the armchair all night. He'd fallen asleep waiting for Nina to come home. There's a crick in his neck that twinges with pain as he moves his head. He kneads one shoulder with his fingertips before massaging the other. Nina must have snuck past Charlie last night when she came home. He feels a mixture of annoyance and exhaustion. He understands why she didn't wake him – they'd only have had another row – but she could have, at least, thrown a blanket over him.

Is this how all parents feel, Charlie wonders, as his tired legs trudge upstairs. This constant gnawing ache that you're getting everything wrong, or is it just him, out of his depth?

It's a mess.

He has to meet Pippa in the café in approximately five hours and he hasn't even talked to the kids yet, wanting to gauge Nina's reaction before he approached Duke.

He doesn't blame her for exploding when she found the earring. Her trust is as fragile as a butterfly's wings. Gossamer-thin and easily broken.

There's still time to explain everything though.

Tentatively he taps on Nina's bedroom door. She doesn't tell him to come in but she doesn't yell at him to go away either and this, he thinks, is progress.

He presses his ear against the door.

He can't hear anything except the frantic beating of his own uneasy heart.

'Nina?' He knocks again, louder this time, thinking that perhaps she is still asleep.

Charlie chews his thumbnail, wondering what to do.

Part of him feels if Nina is acting like a child she should be treated like one and shouldn't get a say in his private life but he remembers how hateful the world can feel when you're a teenager and he wants Nina to feel he is on her side.

His knuckles rap once more before he pushes the handle down and steps inside the room.

For a second he's taken aback. The room is exactly as he'd left it yesterday evening. Bed made. Tidy. For a second he wonders if Nina was up early, slipped out before he woke, but she's never bothered to straighten her duvet before.

Something isn't right.

He scans the room, noticing the pile of schoolbooks on the floor where he had left her rucksack yesterday after he had taken her PE kit to wash. Where's her rucksack?

He feels hot. It feels horribly intrusive to rummage through her drawers but he does it anyway. He thinks there are a couple of pairs of jeans and some tops missing.

She's run away.

Charlie is overcome with a helplessness so fierce it saps the strength from his legs. He sinks onto her bed.

She's run away.

Is he that terrible to live with? That unbearable? Is this all because of the earring?

He calls up her number on his mobile. The photo of him at eighteen holding his brand-new baby sister lights up. She doesn't answer.

'Nina, call me immediately,' he garbles onto her answer service. 'You're not in trouble, I promise.' Even as he says this, he recalls the expression on her face when she found the earring in his bed and he knows that, to her, his promises are empty. Easily broken.

'Duke!' He runs out onto the landing. Bursts into his brother's room. Duke sits up and clutches his covers to his chest. His sleepy eyes widen as a look of fear clouds his face.

'What's wrong?' Immediately he thinks the worst.

Charlie tries to smile, not wanting Duke to panic. Not wanting to bring back memories of the last time Duke was wrenched from sleep because this is not like when his parents were missing.

His parents were dead.

Nina is fine; she has to be.

Anxiety rattles against Charlie's ribs and he places a palm over his chest and draws in a deep breath.

'When was the last time you saw Nina?' Charlie asks

'Yesterday when she came storming out of your bedroom. Why?'

'I'm just not sure where she is.'

'If she isn't here, she'll be at Maeve's.'

Relief washes over Charlie. 'Of course she will be. I'm going to get her. Get dressed. I'll meet you in the car, hurry up.'

*

Charlie parks outside Maeve's house. There is no one framed in the window. Sean's arms aren't around Nina the way they were at the memorial, not that he can see anyway. He tells himself he's being ridiculous. Nina has a crush, that's all. It's apparent from the way she's scrawled Nina Kelly over and over, practising her signature in case Sean ever marries her. It's a childish fantasy. She hasn't come here to be with him.

She's come here to get away from Charlie.

'Stay here,' he tells Duke. If Nina causes a scene, which he fully expects her to do, he doesn't want Duke to be caught in the middle.

'But I—'

Charlie silences his brother with solely a look and it's the first time he's felt any small success as a parent. Because of this he's a little more confident as he raps on the front door.

Maeve's eyes are bloodshot, as though she's been crying or has had very little sleep.

'Where is she?' Charlie demands. There is no good cop to his bad cop but he's come here for his sister and he isn't leaving without her.

'I don't know.' Maeve tries to close the door but Charlie pushes against it with his hand, barges into the hallway. 'Maeve, she's fifteen. Underage. Where is she?'

'She's not here.'

'Where's your dad?' Charlie feels a sudden, sick dread plummet to the pit of his belly.

'He's gone to Tesco.'

'Right. Good. Well, you must know where Nina is. She's your best friend?' Charlie's eyes flicker to the stairs and then back to Maeve's face.

'You can check my bloody room if you'd like.'

Charlie strides up the stairs before she can change her mind, Maeve trotting after him.

He pushes into the first room. An adults' room. Sean's room. Minimalist. A double bed in the centre but no sign of his sister, thankfully.

'My room's down here,' Maeve says but Charlie ignores her, throwing open the next door to a room that contains a desk and a stack of boxes, clothes spilling out them. Women's clothes. Maeve's mother's clothes, he realizes with a pang of guilt. He forgets sometimes that it isn't only his family that has experienced tragedy.

He silently follows Maeve as she leads him to her bedroom.

'See. You can check under the bed and in the wardrobe if you want.'

Feeling faintly ridiculous, Charlie does both of those things.

Nina isn't here.

'But she was here? Last night?' he clarifies.

'Yes,' Maeve says quietly.

'Can you think of anywhere else she might have gone? Anyone else she might have gone to?' Charlie asks her a string of other questions and she replies to all in a series of shrugs.

'Maeve, please. I'm going frantic.' If she'd gone to Pippa's then Pippa would have called him. He can't think of anywhere else she might have stayed overnight.

Maeve covers her lips with her fingers and Charlie thinks she is pushing the words she wants to say back inside her mouth.

'Please tell me. Did something happen last night? Something I should know about?'

Maeve stares at the carpet. There's a splodge of purple nail varnish shining among the cream pile.

'You're her best friend. She's been gone all night. I know she doesn't have any money. She could be . . . she could be . . .' He sinks down on Maeve's bed. 'I need to know she's safe?' He is one step away from dropping to his knees and pleading. 'Where is she?'

'I . . . I don't know but she . . .'

Maeve glances out of the window, the branches of the oak tap-tap-tapping against the glass.

Tell him – tell him – tell him.

'Please. I need . . .' He longs to be a writer but he cannot find the words.

'She thinks she saw her dad. On a YouTube video. Busking in Cornwall.'

'How on earth—'

'She was searching for footage of Colesby Bay. She's probably gone to find him.'

'What?' Charlie can't take it in. He feels the world slipping away from him. He drops his head into his hands. The mattress beside him dips as Maeve sits; she places her arm around him and he lets her head rest against his shoulder.

Nina thinks she's seen Bo.

Why would she even think that?

Because Nina believes Bo is alive.

It is then the door bursts open. Maeve jumps to her feet as Sean storms into the room.

'What the actual fuck?' His eyes are stone. He grasps Charlie's arm and wrenches him to his feet.

At first Charlie can't comprehend what's going on, his mind in Colesby Bay picturing Nina lost and scared, but then he realizes he is a grown man alone in a teenage girl's bedroom and he sees the inappropriateness in this and why her father is concerned, in the way that he has been concerned over Nina's crush on Sean. Before he can set Sean's mind at rest he has been dragged down the stairs.

'Wait!' Charlie digs his heels in but he is sliding down the hallway, being manhandled out into the front garden.

'You are never to set foot inside of my house again.' Sean roughly shoves Charlie so he tumbles to the floor.

'You've got it wrong.' Charlie staggers to his feet. 'I've no interest in Maeve. Please believe me. I know it's easy to jump to the wrong conclusion. I thought you were interested in Nina once—'

'You thought *I* was interested in *her*?' Sean releases a laugh that is edged with cruelty. He leans forward and growls, low and quiet, inaudible to anyone but Charlie, 'Tell your sister to stay away from us. She's not fucking welcome around here anymore.'

Then it happens in a split second. Charlie reacts to hearing his sister dismissed as though she's nothing. Cast aside from what she regards as her second family. Sean's hands connect with his chest. Charlie's fingers automatically curl into his palms. He draws back his elbow and propels his fist into Sean's face. Hears the crunch of knuckle on bone. Feels the warmth of Sean's blood splattering onto his wrist.

His pulse pounds in his ears; he is horrified. Sean may have been furious at catching Charlie in Maeve's room, Charlie angry with hearing his sister cast aside, but it should never have come to this. He catches sight of Maeve, her hands clasped over her mouth in shock.

He turns and stalks away.

Nina isn't here.

She's run away.

Charlie is going to find her.

CHAPTER FORTY-THREE

Duke

'Are you okay? I wish you hadn't seen that,' Charlie says as they are screeching away from Maeve's house. 'Violence is never the answer, Duke.'

Duke twists around in his seat. Maeve is helping Sean to his feet. They grow smaller and smaller, until they could be Lego figures standing on the lawn of a Lego house. None of this quite seems real. Duke rubs his eyes. An hour ago he was fast asleep and now . . . this.

Duke steals a glance at Charlie, seeing his brother in a whole different light.

'Duke?' Charlie asks again. 'Are you all right?'

'That was . . . that was bloody epic.' Duke forms fists and air punches – 'Pow. Pow. Pow. Can you teach me how to fight, Charlie? I never knew you could?' He had prayed every morning before school for an end to Jayden's bullying, never realizing that the answer was living in his house. Cooking his dinner. 'Charlie, that was totally amazing.'

'Duke. It really wasn't and I can't teach you to fight because that was the first time I've ever hit someone and . . .' Charlie releases his right hand from the steering wheel and shakes it. 'It hurts.'

'Not as much as you hurt his face.' Duke keeps his fists close to his face like a boxer and jigs up and down on his seat. 'I wish I'd recorded it.'

'It isn't something to be proud of,' Charlie says.

But imagine if Duke had captured it on film. Showed it to Jayden. Just the threat of Charlie might be enough to keep him at bay.

'Why did you floor him anyway?' Duke asks.

'He said something about Nina and—'

'Did he call her weird?'

'No.'

'A freak?'

'No.'

'Did he—'

'It doesn't matter what he said.'

But it did to Duke. Was it worse than the names he was called every day? If it wasn't then surely Charlie should protect him too.

'Charlie.' Duke lowers his hands onto his lap. He's going to tell his brother everything. All of the things he'd been scared to say before, scared that Charlie wouldn't be able to cope with the thought of home-schooling Duke. That, if he knew the truth, he'd run off to London and leave them again with Aunt Violent but now . . . Now he knows that Charlie cares. Properly cares. He can see that from his bruised knuckles. From the droplets of Sean's blood on his sleeve.

His brother *is* bloody epic.

But before he can speak, Charlie is talking again.

'When we get home I'm going to ring Aunt Violet and see if you and Billie can stay there tonight. I need to go and find your sister.'

Duke had almost forgotten that they'd gone to Maeve's in search of Nina. 'Where is she?'

'She's run away.'

'Run away? Why?'

'Nina's gone to . . . She thinks . . .' Charlie drums his fingers on the steering wheel. 'She just needed some space but I can fix it, I promise. I'll bring her home.'

'What if you can't find her?' Duke feels a bit sick. The world is a big place. What if he never sees Nina again? Sure, she can be annoying and mean but . . .

'I'll find her,' Charlie says quietly.

'I want to come.'

'You can't.'

'Why not? If she's left because of all the shouting yesterday then it's you she's run away from, not me?' But Duke isn't quite sure that is true. Has he been a bad brother? He knows he embarrasses her. What if all the shouting was about him?

'It's . . . complicated. Anyway, you like Aunt Violet now?'

'Yeah. We had a good talk about vegetarianism last week. She really listened to me. I told her how cows were slaughtered.'

'I thought she looked a bit green during lunch. She didn't each much of her roast beef.'

'Perhaps she'll stop eating meat too.' It was cool that Charlie ate veggie meals most nights now. 'Anyway, she's okay now I've got to know her. Not that I'd want to live with her again or anything,' Duke shoots a worried glance at Charlie.

'It's only for one night, I promise.'

'Okay. Actually, can I stay at Evie's instead? It's the talent show tomorrow and I need to practise. Last Sunday, when I asked Aunt Violet to choose a card, she kept telling me what it was before I'd had enough chances to guess.' He's sure that Derren Brown must have needed more than twelve guesses when he first started out.

'Okay. I'll call her. At least you'll get a decent meal tonight. Bet her mum's a better cook than me.'

'Everyone's a better cook than you.'

'Hey! You don't have to—'

'But her mum could never lay anybody out with one punch.' Duke grinned at Charlie, suddenly feeling better. Wherever Nina had gone, whatever she had run away from, Charlie would make it better.

Duke had piled his favourite things onto his bed along with his school uniform, which definitely wasn't one of his favourite things. It was difficult to know what to take not knowing when Charlie would be back. He'd laid out his wand and his cape just in case he had to go to the end-of-term show from Evie's house although he hopes that a missing sister will be enough to get him out of it. He wonders if Charlie can write him a note?

Dear Miss Greenly
Duke's sister has run away and he is too sad to do magic.

Would that work?

Duke sits at his desk and pulls out a piece of paper and a pen. It's nice paper – left over from when Mum made him write thank you notes after Christmas, thick and not the normal boring white but a creamy colour, which is funny because it's made of elephant poo, which Mum said was better for the trees. It's not the colour of poo, and it doesn't smell like it so Duke doesn't mind using it. He has almost finished his letter when Charlie pops his head around the door.

'I've spoken to Shannon, Evie's mum. She's looking forward to you going. If we hurry, you won't be too late for school.'

'Okay.' Duke carefully folds the paper and tucks it inside an envelope. 'Can you give this to Nina, please?' He hands it to Charlie.

'Of course. Try not to worry, Duke. It will all be okay.'

'Will you be back for my show tomorrow night?'

'I'll try to make it.'

'But you might not be?'

There's a pause before Charlie says, 'I can't guarantee I'll be there, Duke, I'm sorry. Sometimes . . . sometimes if you think you might not be able to keep a promise it is, perhaps, better not to make it in the first place and then you don't betray a trust.' Charlie's voice breaks.

Duke wraps his arms around his brother and gives him a hug.

'It's okay. It's okay. The show will be rubbish anyway. I can always do my bit for you and Nina when you've found her,' he says to try and make Charlie feel better but, for some reason, this only makes his big brother begin to shake.

Duke thinks that he might be crying.

CHAPTER FORTY-FOUR

Nina

Ten and a half hours. It has taken ten and a half hours to get to Colesby Bay.

Nina had hoped hitch-hiking would be like in the movies – not the horror ones, of course, where the driver turns out to be an axe-wielding maniac – but from one of those feel-good stories where a family picks up a stray on the side of the road and takes them to both their destination and their hearts. In films, the hitch-hiker and the driver end up sharing lemon sherbets and confidences, healing from past hurts before singing along to bright pop songs on the radio.

It hadn't been like that at all.

The first car that stopped had been full of teenage boys. She had tentatively stepped forward when the driver had wound down his window but when she smelled the alcohol on his breath, heard the cry of 'Show us your tits' from the backseat, she had scuttled away from the road and hid in a bush until they'd gone. That wasn't even the lowest point. There was the salesman with the creepy moustache who'd told her he could get a discount on the mattress of her dreams and tried to put his hand on her knee.

There was the middle-aged woman she had assumed she'd be safe with but who had ranted about her 'fucking husband' who stuck his 'fucking tiny penis' into her 'fucking best friend' and how she wanted to burn her friend's house to the ground while they slept, and did Nina think that was a good idea? Nina hadn't been sure if she'd been serious but when she'd opened the glove compartment to fetch the crying woman a tissue she had seen a new pack of three disposable lighters and she'd asked to be dropped off at the next lay-by. Finally, she'd been picked up by a lorry driver who had ignored her for hours as he'd munched his way through a six-pack of sausage rolls, the flakes of pastry settling on his comedy moustache, but at least he hadn't tried to touch her knee, see her boobs, or implicate her in a murder. He had dropped her off at an industrial park on the outskirts of town and she had trudged the rest of the way on exhausted legs, the morning sun already belting out heat.

Now she is here she isn't quite sure what to do, but she's hungry. Not one person had offered her anything to eat or drink.

She checks her purse. She has £11.27 pence on her. Mentally she runs through what she might have in her savings account; she bought that black top last week and splashed out on a Mac lipstick the week before, diving into the Christmas money that she hadn't felt like spending earlier this year. Could she risk using a cashpoint? In films the police always seem to trace missing people from their bank cards or mobile phone signal. Is that true? Hitchhiking wasn't exactly like in the movies but then Nina supposes she hasn't seen enough films to know. That's what comes from growing up without a TV. She thinks she's safe to use her cashcard. No one has probably noticed she's even missing yet and, if they have, Charlie will likely think she's at Maeve's.

The memory of what happened there last night springs humiliated tears to her eyes.

Nina, what the hell are you playing at? Sean had snapped but Nina hadn't been playing.

It was not a game.

But is it love, this ache in her heart? She is questioning what a few scant hours ago felt unquestionable.

Real.

Solid.

She just doesn't know anymore. She remembers the horror in Sean's voice as though nobody in their right mind would want to kiss her back and everything feels wrong.

Dirty.

Despite the warmth, she wraps her arms around herself and tries to get her bearings.

Colesby Bay conjures images of a picture-perfect village but this thriving tourist town is larger than she remembers. Along the harbour yellow and orange bunting flaps in the breeze pushing the smell of fresh fish towards her. Her stomach rolls. Bile rises up her throat along with the remnants of last night's vodka. She rushes away from the fishing boats before she's sick.

There's a cobbled alleyway, an A-board at the entrance proclaiming 'the best scones in Colesby Bay' and this is where she heads. The café is dark and empty, the view from the table by the window, a brick wall. Nina scans the menu before wedging it back between the bottles of ketchup and mustard and she wipes her now greasy fingers on her jeans. She orders a mug of tea and deliberates between a bacon sandwich and a full English while the waitress tat-tap-taps her impatient pen against her pad. Realizing she needs to make her money last as long as possible

Nina disappoints her growling stomach with the cheapest thing she can find instead.

Her drink is sloshed before her. Nina tears open the tiny packet of sugar, some of it spilling onto the plastic tablecloth as she tips it into her too-strong-tea. The toast is oozing with melted butter, which drips down her chin as she takes a hungry bite. She hadn't spent the 25p extra on jam but this is still one of the best breakfasts she's ever had. She can literally feel it settle her stomach, soaking up the last of the alcohol. She presses her finger onto the stray crumbs and pops them onto her tongue until her plate is clean. Then she wraps her hands around her mug and tries to formulate a plan.

The waitress slaps a bill in front of Nina and while Nina is counting change from her purse she says,

'Can I ask you a question? I'm looking for a busker.'

'Step outside the door and you can't walk a hundred metres without falling over one,' the woman replies.

'This is someone specific.' Nina opens YouTube and shows the clip to the woman.

'I've never seen him but I know where that was filmed; it's by the lifeboat station.'

'Are you sure?'

'Yes. Look, there's a bunch of flowers taped to the railing behind that little girl. There's always a bunch there. Four people drowned here at New Year.'

Nina washes down the lump in her throat with the dregs of her tea. 'Thank you,' she manages to say, rummaging for a fifty-pence piece she lays as a tip.

'Silly buggers,' the woman says. 'Went out on a boat at midnight in sub-zero temperatures. Would have been dead in minutes. They never had a chance.'

Nina swipes her precious coin back off the table and carries it with her anger back out into the alleyway where she sinks down onto the cobbles, rests her head on her knees and takes deep, slow breaths, feeling the toast fighting to claw its way free of her stomach.

Silly buggers.

She wants to march back into the café and tell the woman she is wrong, but she can't.

Slowly she rises to her feet.

They never had a chance.

The woman has only said the same thing as the coastguard and the police. It isn't news to Nina and yet it has hit her in a way it hasn't before. Resignation is a heavy weight she carries back to the harbour. What now? She can't just go home and give up though. Not when she's come all this way.

Would have been dead in minutes.

Nina shakes her head, not caring what she looks like, wanting to rid herself of the woman's voice. Instead, her mind is filled with Sean.

Nina, what the hell are you playing at?

She begins to hum 'So What'. She wants to drown out the waitress, Sean.

Everything.

Music straightens her spine and strengthens her legs. It lifts and encourages her.

She remembers her dad surprising her with a clarinet. Teaching her how to gently twist the pieces into place.

'Be careful. It's not as tough as it looks on the outside,' he had said. 'Things rarely are.'

But she is. She feels stronger now as she walks towards the lifeboat station. Filled with purpose.

If her dad is here, Nina will find him. She clutches hold of that thought as tightly as the seagull clutches in his sharp orange beak the stray chip he had swooped onto the pavement to retrieve.

Nina reaches the place where the video was filmed but it isn't what she was expecting. Ridiculously, she had hoped that everything would have remained static. The child frozen in time, holding out her ice-cream cone. The busker singing an endless song. Disappointment is crushing. It's like when Dorothy whisked open the curtain in *The Wizard of Oz* and the sight before her was so unexpected, Nina actually felt Dorothy crumple through the pages of the book.

Nina feels herself crumpling now, crumbling, turning to dust where she'll merge with the sand. Disappear with the waft of a breeze, carried over oceans. Forever searching.

To anchor herself she holds on to the rusty railings and when she's taken a few deep breathes she examines the flowers that are bound to the iron with a frayed piece of rope. They aren't roses, which were Mum's favourite – does that mean Dad hadn't been here? Hadn't left them? They are dying, the purple petals curling brown scatter under her touch. There's still some green in the stalks though, so she doesn't think they are necessarily very old. Nothing would last long in this heat without a drink.

Nobody could last long in those freezing temperatures.

That's what Alan, the coastguard, had said.

She wonders if he's working today. If he'll remember her. She waits until she's sure the tears that threaten to fall have been contained and then she heads into the lifeboat station.

'Hello?' she calls.

'Hello.' It *is* Alan.

Her heart lifts and sinks when he doesn't recognize her. How can it be that he had been present at the most significant time in her life and he does not know who she is?

'I'm Nina. I met you New Year's Day. My parents . . .' She falters.

'Ah, Nina. Of course. How are you? Are you here with your brothers?'

'No. I'm alone. Look—' she pulls out her phone, swiping past her notifications, which shout of eighteen missed calls from Charlie, and she shows him the clip. 'They've found two of the others but not my mum or dad and this looks like my dad and I thought he might have, they both might have . . .' she garbles, trailing off when she notices that the confusion on his face turns to pity as he realizes what she has hoped.

'Nina, I'm so sorry but—'

'I shouldn't have come.' She turns and runs away from his words, away from the truth.

They never had a chance.

She is not giving up.

Nina drifts, dazed. Heading back into town without knowing exactly where or why. She passes a pub, the Crow's Nest, a 'live music every evening' sign outside. She picks her way through the garden packed with pink-shouldered tourists, past the wooden picnic benches laden with pints of fizzing cider, the sweet smell attracting the wasps. The grass is patchy and littered with cigarette butts. She steps inside and waits a moment for her eyes to adjust to the gloom before she approaches the bar.

'Got any ID?' the harassed-looking barman with a red mohawk asks.

'I'm not here for a drink. I'm looking for a man.'

'A little young, aren't you?'

'A musician?'

'The worst kind, darling.'

'My father. You have live music here every night? Look.'

She pulls out her mobile, opens YouTube. Stupidity is a needle pricking her skin as she sees the red battery flashing in the top right-hand corner of her screen. She hasn't brought her charger.

The screen turns to black while the video is still loading. The barman wanders off to serve someone else. She shakes her handset as though she can dislodge a smidgen of life left in the battery but it won't switch back on.

Nina, what the hell are you playing at?

Sean had made her feel like a child last night and this is the way she feels again.

Small.

Vulnerable.

Insignificant as she is shouldered out of the way by a man waving a twenty-pound note who demands a pint *pronto, mate*. Desolate, she wanders back outside. Everybody has somewhere to be. Dads that march with purpose back to their families, a clutch of cornets in their hands, ice cream dribbling onto their fingers. Parents rushing after toddlers grappling with inflatable balls, flamingos, dolphins that are almost larger than them. The group of teenagers heading into the arcade, change jangling in their pockets. Nina feels invisible as they stream past her, nobody giving her a second glance.

*

It is early evening. The weather has turned in an instant as though someone has switched off the sun. She hasn't found him.

Still hasn't found him.

Her feet are sore from the miles she has walked. Her voice hoarse from the number of people she has asked about her dad, feeling the same sharp pang of missing him each time she described him.

She's stuck. She hasn't got enough money for a train and she doesn't fancy hitch-hiking again. Without being able to access the contact list on her phone she can't look up anybody's phone number; besides, who could she ring? Who would care?

She should go home but home is where the heart is and Nina's heart is broken. She curls onto her side on a wrought-iron bench on the promenade. The slats are uncomfortable but Nina is too tired to care. She tucks her rucksack under her head and drapes her jumper over her shoulders. A shadow falls across her and she sees an elderly couple clutching steaming fish and chips, grease soaking through white paper wrappings. Her stomach grumbles. Perhaps if she moves to make space for them to sit they'll share their dinner with her but before she can move the lady complains it's too cold and the man tells her they can eat in their car.

Nina shivers. The last chink of perfect blue sky has disappeared behind black clouds that scud across the sky.

The wind throws stray ice-lolly wrappers and scrunched-up plastic bottles across the beach; the ocean smashes waves against the sand. The donkeys are led up the ramp – no more rides today – hanging their tragic heads, the jangle of the bells on their brightly coloured harnesses barely audible over the upcoming storm.

The abrupt change in weather has scattered families back to their caravans and hotels.

Nina watches the angry sea. How frightening must it feel to be swept away by the current, how helpless and hopeless must her parents have felt as their mouths filled with freezing salt water, their lungs. What went through their minds? Each other? Her parents were the most devoted couple she'd ever known. She had found their public displays of affection embarrassing. The way they still held hands despite being married a zillion years. How the way Dad would kiss the tip of Mum's nose told her that he couldn't live without her each time she made him an unexpected cup of tea. Or were they perhaps thinking of her? Duke? Charlie?

It seems impossible that her dad would have left her mum and swam to shore to save himself and yet if Mum were alive too what was the chances of both of them having amnesia, really?

There are so many things Nina wants to know and she thought that coming here would give her the answers but now all she has are more questions.

Her lack of sleep last night forces her eyelids closed. She barely registers the first scatter of rain.

'Nina?' A hand on her shoulder, shaking-shaking-shaking. 'Nina?'

She prises open her eyes. Bursts into tears at the sight of him.

'You're here. You're really here.' She touches her face, his face, to make sure she's not dreaming.

She isn't.

He is really, really here.

CHAPTER FORTY-FIVE

Charlie

Charlie experiences an overwhelming onslaught of guilt and relief as Nina stares up at him, raindrops coating her lashes. He also feels something else.

Love.

'You're really, really here.' She stands and throws her arms around his neck. She's shivering. He doesn't know if this is with cold or fear or relief but he takes off his jacket and wraps it around her shoulders, remembering the pink fleece blanket she'd be wrapped in as a baby, the weight of her in his arms.

He can't drive her straight home – she's soaked through and needs a hot bath and some dry clothes. He needs some food. He's missed both breakfast and lunch. At the thought of lunch he remembers, with a jolt, that he was supposed to meet Pippa and, once more, feels torn in two. Instinctively he wants to call her and explain their missed date but right now his sad and bedraggled sister's needs must come first. Should come first. There's a sadness as he realizes that this perhaps is his answer. It isn't the right time for him and Pippa.

Again.

But there is a sickness deep in his stomach at the thought of hurting her. As soon as he gets the chance he'll talk to her properly. Honestly. It's the least that she deserves. They'll get through this, somehow. All love needs is to be believed in.

'Let's go and find a hotel.'

Nina nods, her face pale and worried. Charlie puts his arm around her, wishing he could have shielded her from whatever she has been through in these past twenty-four hours. There's time later to ask how she got here, if anyone hurt her, and the thought that they might have done, that some scumbag might have laid a finger on her, squeezes Charlie's stomach muscles, plays an ominous beat on his heart. He flexes his fingers, feeling the sting of his knuckles as he curls them into a fist. He'll kill anyone that has hurt her. This he knows undoubtedly.

Charlie slings Nina's rucksack over his shoulder. His own, with the few items he had hurriedly packed, is in the boot of the car. Despite the rain they walk at a slow pace. Nina's exhaustion is apparent with every weary step. At least he got a scant few hours' sleep last night.

The first few places they pass have 'FULL' signs swinging violently in the wind.

Charlie steers Nina down a side street, away from the sea-front. It is at the end of this road they see a red 'VACANT' sign glowing in a window.

A homely-looking woman answers the door. The smell of baking drifts down the hallway, which is lined with wooden crosses. She wipes her hands on her apron as her gaze flickers disapprovingly between Charlie and Nina.

'Do you have two rooms? One for me and one for my sister?'

Once their relationship is established they are welcomed inside.

'I've only got one room but it's a twin. How long are you staying for?'

'I'm not sure.' Charlie doesn't want to distress Nina by saying he wants to leave as soon as she's dry and warm and rested.

'Holiday, is it?'

'If we can go straight to the room that would be great, thanks, and do you have a menu?'

'It's breakfast only but . . .' she looks at Nina and softens. 'I can heat up some soup when you're settled?'

'That would be perfect, thank you.'

The room is basic but clean. There's a shelf containing four bibles and three teddy bears. A picture of Jesus hangs above each bed. Charlie has fetched the car and parked it outside and when he returns Nina is still in the bath so he takes the opportunity to ring Shannon, Evie's mum.

'How's Duke?'

'He's fine. How are you? Any sign of Nina?'

'Yes, I've found her.'

'That's wonderful. Do you want me to fetch Duke so you can tell him yourself? They're watching *The Lord of the Rings*. That Gollum is terrifying but they don't seem bothered.'

'No. Don't disturb him.' Duke will have a million questions and Charlie doesn't have the answer to any of them. 'Can you tell him everything is fine and I'll be in touch again tomorrow and let you both know when we'll be home.'

After they've said their goodbyes Charlie is about to try Pippa – he has a missed call from her – but then Nina comes back into the room wearing a cheap white towelling bathroom, a towel twisted on top of her head. Her damp clothes bundled in her arms. Charlie takes them and drapes them over the radiators he has already switched on. He raises his gaze to the window, the panes streaked with rain. It's slowing now, the torrent a light pitter-patter. The clouds are no longer dark and angry but light and fluffy, the sun smiling as she gathers strength again – nothing to see here – as if the storm had never existed. He searches for a rainbow but he cannot see one.

Eventually he turns. Nina is sitting on the edge of the bed, her hands shoved into her sleeves. She is fragile and he must be gentle with her so that she does not break. He sits beside her.

'Whatever you ran away from . . .' He hesitates. The promise that he can fix it falters in his throat. What if *he* is the problem? What then? But he thinks of Sean – *Tell your sister to stay away from us. She's not fucking welcome around here anymore* – and he wonders by the sting of his knuckles whether he has already fixed the problem or made it wholly worse.

Charlie waits for tears, a confession of infatuation, but instead Nina says, 'I wasn't running from anything. I was running *to* something. Someone. Dad. I thought he was alive, Charlie. I . . . I thought I saw him.'

Maeve had told Charlie that Nina believed she had seen her dad but hearing Nina say it herself so convincingly is breath-snatching.

'Where's your phone, Charlie?'

Wordlessly, he hands Nina his mobile.

'There's a clip on YouTube. I'll show you.'

He feels sick. He can hardly bear to look at the footage that might give concrete shape to the vague, amorphous doubt he had, even as he filled out the court forms, that Bo and his mum aren't really dead. What kind of a son is he? He had given up on

288

them the way he had given up on New York, Pippa, the novel he wanted to write, his career.

Everything.

'Charlie, *look*.'

He forces himself to take the handset, study the film. The blurry and out-of-focus busker, drowned out by the infuriating 'I scream' child. He rewinds it back to the beginning.

It's not him.

He watches the way the guitarist raises the neck of the instrument.

It might be him?

It can't be. Logically. Rationally. Statistically. It cannot be him.

'I'd convinced myself he was alive because I so badly wanted him to be. I went to see Alan the coastguard, and he said . . . Oh, first I met this waitress in a café. She'd heard about it . . . Them . . . She said. She . . .' Nina is hiccupping her words out.

'Shh.'

Charlie puts an arm around her and she rests her head on his shoulder. 'It's like losing him all over again,' she whispers. 'I believed it was him because I wanted to believe but it isn't. I feel so stupid. So alone.'

'You're neither of those things, Nina,' Charlie says with conviction. 'I'm here. Will always be here. I promise.'

There's a tap on the door. When Charlie opens it he is greeted by a waft of tomato soup.

'Thanks so much.' He takes the tray and carries it over to the small round table by the window. Nina perches on one rickety chair and he takes the other.

The bread is crusty and white and Charlie dips it into his bowl until it's soft and orangey. He pops it onto his tongue and a memory comes. Him at thirteen, in bed with tonsillitis, feeling miserable because it was the end-of-term disco and he'd wanted to go with Pippa. David Ashton had been staring at her across the classroom during maths and flicking elastic bands at her when the teacher wasn't looking. Charlie knew this meant he fancied her. If Charlie had been at the disco then he and Pippa would have stayed together, laughing at the teachers, the music, thinking they were too cool for it all. Without him there, Charlie had worried Pippa might kiss David and he felt a twist of jealousy. That was the first time he remembers his feelings for her changing from best friend to something else, something more.

Mum had brought him his lunch in bed – Heinz tomato soup and bread – and to this day it always tastes of comfort to him. Of being loved. Looked after.

Lost in thought, Charlie has almost emptied his bowl. He nods towards the plate and Nina shakes her head so he reaches for the last piece of the bread.

'What happened to your hand?' Nina touches his knuckles with a light fingertip.

'I just . . . I'm an idiot. Clumsy.' He rips off the crust and pops it into his mouth and makes a show of chewing so he doesn't have to talk.

When he's finished, he says slowly, tentatively, 'Nina. What happened last night? At Maeve's? I know something did. I went there looking for you this morning.'

'Oh God.' Nina looks at him with horror. With embarrassment. 'I'm such a fool.' She begins to cry. 'I thought it was love. I . . . I still think it's love. But it . . . it . . . Charlie, it *hurts.*'

Charlie reaches out across the table to comfort her, his beautiful, brilliant sister. All along he had thought that he was the brave one. Giving up his London life, his career. Sacrificing everything to move back to a house that held both the best and the worst memories. Dealing with the practicalities with stoicism, never letting his stiff upper lip tremble. He's spent years closed off to his feelings, going through the motions, mistaking what he had with Sasha for enough. It wasn't enough to be treading the same corporate path, to want the same things, and when he actually felt something real and solid and sustainable with Pippa, he pushed her away, keeping his heart safe. Since his dad had fled when he had needed him the most, his past has consisted of a hundred excuses why he couldn't allow himself to fully love and recently he has created a hundred more. If he's honest, his previous inability to commit to Pippa wasn't just because he has convinced himself that Nina and Duke will be against him having another girlfriend but borne out of fear. Fear of feeling like . . . like Nina feels now.

'Here.' He hands her the box of tissues from the windowsill. She plucks out one and blows her nose.

He could have told Nina and Duke about Pippa before now but he had chosen not to. Made excuses. Meanwhile, Nina has purposefully made herself vulnerable, opened herself to potential rejection. That takes real courage. He watches her now, wiping her streaming eyes, her tender heart beating sadly on her sleeve, and knows that she is far stronger than he.

Love is a risk and it has taken his fifteen-year-old sister to show him that sometimes you have to take a chance, make a leap of faith. Jump and hope that open arms will catch you. Love is potential and faith and pleasure and pain. It is all of those things and so much more.

Charlie doesn't quite know what to say to her now but she is waiting for him to speak. He doesn't want to tell her that the man she thinks she loves never wants to see her again. He doesn't want to lecture her about the age gap, the inappropriateness of the idea that a forty-year-old man could be with a schoolgirl. He sees the enormity of her emotions and he doesn't want to belittle them.

Instead, he takes both of her hands in his.

'I know your feelings for Sean are—'

'Sean?' Nina screws her face, confused. 'You think I . . . Sean? It's Maeve. I love *Maeve*, Charlie, and I've ruined *everything*.'

CHAPTER FORTY-SIX

Nina

Speaking of her love for Maeve gives it a weight. A form. Nina watches as it flutters around the room before it settles onto the table among the crumbs. She can almost reach out her hand and touch it. Releasing it from her chest where it has been a heavy load has brought her a momentary lightness but, as she waits for Charlie to digest her words, to speak, the pressure builds once more.

She tries to pull her hands back from Charlie's, but he tightens his grip, his palms slick around her fingers.

'So . . .' he glances at the puddle of sunshine that now streams in from the window. Despite the warmth, magnified by the glass, Nina feels cold as she waits for his words, for his judgement.

Why can't he look at her?

'Charlie? Say something?'

'You . . . you and Maeve?' His voice is an octave higher than usual.

'You're disappointed. Ashamed.' She snatches away her hands.

'Nina . . . I'm . . . relieved,' he says gently, leaning forward, stretching out his arms and turning his palms upwards.

'Relieved?' She places her hands back inside of his. Feels his fingers curl around hers.

'I thought you were . . . Sean.'

'Sean?' Nina's disgust wrinkles her nose. 'He's ancient. Why would you think that?'

Now it is Charlie who looks unsure, embarrassed. 'Because after the memorial I found that piece of paper in your room where you'd practised your signature as Nina Kelly – Sean's name.'

'Maeve's name.' Will he understand? She needs an ally. A friend. A brother. He doesn't know her well – this is apparent from his suspicion about her and Sean – but she can tell he wants to deepen their relationship when he asks,

'Tell me everything then. You and Maeve.'

'You really want to hear? You're not . . . not . . .'

'We do have lesbians in London, you know.'

'Charlie!'

Nina doesn't quite know how to explain it all, how to figure it out, but she thinks perhaps if she talks about it, they can figure it out together.

'It started when . . .' The memories jostle and tumble inside of Nina's mind, trying to rearrange themselves into an order that makes sense. 'It started when I snuck out of the house late one night for a double date with Maeve and Ryan and Lenny. I got dressed up and was so excited but I realized as I ran towards out to the meeting point that I couldn't care less about Ryan; the person I was excited to see, the person I'd got ready for, was Maeve. I remember how much it hurt when I got there to find Lenny's arms around her. I was . . . jealous. I wanted to be the one holding her.' Nina remembers this moment with clarity.

'But you didn't tell her?'

'I couldn't. I . . . we've both grown up together and sometimes I look at her and . . . it's not always easy to look past the five-year-old girl to see the woman.' Nina pauses. 'Yeah, I think I needed to know she was seeing me for who I'd become. Sean too. It was important to me he saw me as an adult, someone responsible who could hold an intelligent conversation, a suitable partner for his daughter, not a stupid girl with a crush.'

'It must have been hard to keep your feelings to yourself.'

'Almost impossible. Sometimes our hands would brush against each other and I'd feel this jolt and I'd look at her and think "You must have felt that too." How is it possible she didn't? But then I'd think what are the chances of her being gay as well, but I thought . . . or perhaps I hoped, she might be, but there was definitely a shift in our relationship. I dunno. It happened gradually. Things felt different between us. Zingy, you know?'

Charlie nods. 'I know how zingy feels.'

'I began to think how crazy would it be if Maeve did feel the same, if she was scared of telling me in case she ruined our friendship. What if we spent years not telling each other how we felt? How stupid would that be? Being in love with, being in a relationship with your very best friend; that's all anybody wants, isn't it?'

Charlie's eyes glisten with tears and Nina gives his hands a squeeze of gratitude for the emotions he is feeling for her right now. His understanding.

'Only I've messed it up. I've messed everything up. I didn't mean to lose my temper with you. I'd been watching the YouTube clip that I thought was Dad over and over and was more convinced each time it was him. I wanted to show it to you, ask what you thought. You were in the shower so I waited in your room and, when I found that earring, I was so . . . pissed off with you having sex with a random in Mum and Dad's bed. So confused.'

'We do need to talk about that; it's not exactly what you think, but not now. I am very sorry that I upset you though.'

'I *was* upset partly because you'd promised me that you wouldn't bring another woman into our lives – Duke's life – until we'd all got used to each other but partly because . . . I was jealous, I suppose.'

'Jealous?'

'Yeah. You had someone and I . . . I felt so lonely and . . . scared. What if you disappeared back to London again and left us? Who would I have? I decided that I'd tell Maeve how I felt. I got all dressed up like she hasn't seen me in my sweats without make-up before.' Nina remembers her excitement, her trepidation as she slowly walked to Maeve's house, rehearsing how she would tell her. Wondering if Maeve did feel the same or if it was all in her head. 'When I got there I was so nervous I couldn't face her straight away. I sat in the kitchen with her dad instead, trying to sound grown-up and intelligent, wanting him to see me as an adult. As more than just his daughter's friend. As a potential partner for her. I still think he sees us as kids. God knows what he thinks of me now.'

Charlie tightens his jaw, the muscle clenching. Nina pauses, thinking he might speak but he doesn't. She carries on,

'Anyway, I went up to Maeve's room and showed her the clip – she didn't think it was Dad – and . . . and I got drunk, partly to block out the disappointment that Maeve didn't think it was Dad and partly because of . . . everything.' She can still feel the burn of the vodka as it hit the back of her throat, the burn of humiliation as she remembers what happened next. 'It's all a bit of a blur.

I wanted chips so Maeve said she'd go and fetch some. I think I slept for a few minutes. I remember waking with drool down my chin – very attractive – and for a second not knowing where I was. I went downstairs to the kitchen, I was really disorientated and then I saw her.'

Nina closes her eyes. Maeve must have run to the chip shop and back because she was breathless, her cheeks pink, her red hair escaping her scrunchie and she had never looked more beautiful. It was what came next that was ugly. Nina cringes against the memory. She had lurched herself into Maeve's arms, pressing her lips against hers.

'I kissed her and . . . I think she kissed me back, at first, but then there was a noise behind us and she shoved me away. I turned and saw Sean glaring at me and I ran out of the door. He followed me and shouted, "Nina, what the hell are you playing at?"' Nina covers her face. 'He sounded so angry, and Maeve . . . Maeve didn't say anything then, or since. She hasn't been in touch at all. Charlie, I . . . I repulsed her.' Even now, remembering this pinches the air from Nina's lungs. Once home Nina had texted Maeve – **Sorry. I love you** – but Maeve hadn't replied. Nina had placed her heart in the palm of Maeve's hands but she hadn't closed her fingers around it. She hadn't tried to hold on to it at all as it floated away. She hadn't wanted it.

She hadn't wanted her.

She tells all of this to Charlie, who holds her as she cries, and afterwards she is so exhausted by her tears, her emotion, she crawls under the covers.

'Sing to me,' she whispers.

Charlie sits on the edge of her bed and strokes her hair the way Mum used to do to her, still did to Duke right up to the accident, and probably once did to Charlie. Before he even opens his mouth she knows what he will sing.

'All The Things You Are'.

He calls her inspirational. Loyal. Kind. And the words bypass her ears and land gently on her battered heart.

Her eyelids are drooping. Heavy.

She doesn't make it to the end of the song.

Nina wakes in a strange bed, in a strange room. She checks the time, it's only 10.30. How long has she been asleep? Two hours? Three? It all comes flooding back and when it does she feels, not shame, but something else. Supported. Understood. Things might never be the same for her and Maeve again but, although she might have lost her best friend, she has gained a brother. For the first time she feels she can rely on him. She listens now for his breathing but the room is silent. She rolls over, the orange streetlight outside pushes through the thin curtains illuminating the empty bed beside her.

Confused, she sits. Glances towards the bathroom. It's in darkness, the door open.

Charlie has gone.

CHAPTER FORTY-SEVEN

Duke

Duke's mobile rings. There's only four people who would ever call him and one of those is in the room with him. He thinks it's probably Charlie but deep down he hopes it's Nina.

It's Pippa.

Duke's stomach performs a backflip the same as it did when he'd heard middle-of-the-night knocking on his door last New Year's Eve. The same as it did on the first day of school. The flip that tells him that even if he hopes that things will be okay, they won't.

He's tentative when he answers the call, expecting bad news.

And it is.

CHAPTER FORTY-EIGHT

Charlie

There are so many things in Charlie's head as he marches along the seafront, each step taking him further away from the B & B. Further away from Nina who was in such a deep sleep he doesn't think she'll wake until morning. He had felt so many emotions as he sang the same song to her that Mum used to sing to him when he was small. Love comes in many forms. He knows this now undoubtedly. Love is unconventional. Unpredictable. It is there in an unexpected cup of tea, a home-baked cake, a smile.

A song.

It is there in a handful of change pushed into a child's hand, not so he can go to the arcade and keep out of his mother's way, but so he can find a distraction in the flashing lights and enticing machines. So he can forget, just for a short while, that one of his parents didn't love him enough to stay. But he doesn't know if this is true anymore. Love can be separated. Compartmentalised. Pushed away and locked away.

He leans his forearms on the railings and gazes out to sea. The water is dark, the sky an orange-streaked salmon. The promise of a hot day tomorrow.

It's still early, the pubs haven't yet closed. He doesn't blame Nina for falling asleep. Her night of hitch-hiking is still something they need to talk about but right now she needs to rest. He'd left her a note telling her he's gone for a walk but he's been stalking at brisk pace for half an hour now and it is not enough to calm him.

He needs a drink.

He glances up at the cliffs, remembers the café that has long since closed, the fizzy Coke in a bottle. He craves that sweetness now. The bubbles.

A cider.

There's a pub ahead – the Crow's Nest – and this is where he heads. He doesn't need the board outside to tell him there is live music. He hears it, the woman singing something he doesn't recognize.

Inside he leans against the bar and waves a ten-pound note. The barman with a red mohawk pulls him a pint. He takes one sip, two, three.

There's a smattering of applause and an announcement from the small stage behind him.

'Now for all you jazz fans. Put your hands together for Woody.'

A different voice singing.

A man's voice.

A voice he knows.

If I were to pick a name it would be Woody Shaw.

He doesn't need to turn but he does anyway, in slow motion. The rest of the world falling away. There are no tables and chairs. No customers. No chatter. There is only himself.

And Bo.

His stepdad.

It's like looking at him through one of the fun mirrors on the pier. He looks the same but different. Not different because of his now long hair and thick beard, the strange clothes and shabby black Vans on his feet or because he has lost weight, but different because the man he knew – the man he *thought* he knew – would never have abandoned his children.

Charlie staggers backwards, the corner of the bar digging sharply into his spine. His mind hops from theory to theory, trying to process the impossible sight before him. Bo must have hit his head. Have amnesia. But as Bo's eyes sweep the room and land on his, Charlie knows this not to be true.

Bo stops playing. Ceases to sing. A look of utter horror spreading across his face.

He recognizes Charlie.

There's a crash as the microphone stand topples to the floor as Bo staggers against it, before he pelts towards the door, the guitar dangling from the strap banging against his hip as he runs away.

CHAPTER FORTY-NINE

Nina

There's a notepad on the bedside cabinet. She can make out Charlie's scrawl. Nina angles the paper towards the window and reads by the fading daylight.

Gone for a walk.

She wonders if she should get dressed and go and find him.
She hates to think of him alone.

CHAPTER FIFTY

Charlie

'Wait!' Charlie's feet pound against the pavement. 'Wait!'

Bo is older. Slower. Encumbered by his guitar but still it's several minutes before he stops suddenly and turns, holding his instrument like a shield. Exhaustion and shame written all over his face.

'What. The. Fuck.' Charlie leans forward, his hands on his knees, panting hard. He is almost incoherent. Breathless, not only because of the run but because he is choking with rage. 'What the *actual* fuck?'

Bo is a statue, motionless, speechless, too shocked to find an explanation or too embarrassed to give one, Charlie isn't sure which.

A couple sharing a bag of chips skirt around them. The man glancing back over his shoulder, perhaps feeling the anger radiating from Charlie. He places a protective hand on his girlfriend's lower back and hurries her away.

Charlie jerks his head towards the beach and Bo follows him down the steps to the place where they used to build castles together, build memories. But they are not the same people. This is not the same sand. The golden grains that Charlie would dig his toes into have long since been blown away, washed away. Does anything last forever? Charlie thinks the blistering hate he feels in this moment will endure.

They perch on uncomfortable rocks. Bo setting his guitar down with a care that he hasn't shown his children.

'You're not dead then?' is all Charlie can think of to say.

'No.'

'We *grieved* for you. We *cried* for you. We held a memorial, for fuck's sake.'

'I'm sorry. For what it's worth.'

'What exactly are you *sorry* for? Bringing Mum here New Year's Eve? Taking her out on the boat? Meeting her in the first place?' Charlie thinks Bo should be sorry for all of those things and more. 'Or for letting us believe that you were . . . that you are . . .' Charlie swipes away furious tears. 'Is Mum alive?'

The answer barely audible, 'No.'

There's an unbearable pain in Charlie's chest; it's like losing her all over again. He takes a moment before yanking his phone from his pocket and ignoring his notifications, and jabs open his photo app. Thrusts his handset towards Bo.

'Remember him. Duke. Your son?' He chooses another picture. 'And her. Nina. Your daughter, who is here by the way.' Another. 'Both of them with Billie. Remember? You had a dog. A life.' He whispers now. 'A family.' He shakes his head. Unable to process any of it.

Bo places a hand on Charlie's knee and Charlie wants to slap it away. He wants to hold it tightly. He wants to rest his cheek on Bo's palm, let Bo feel the bristles that sprout from his chin, ask him if he remembers teaching Charlie to shave all those years ago. Whether he remembers any of it; the day Charlie stood next to Bo at the altar, both of them awkward in suits and ties, and handed him a thin gold band along with his mother. How Bo had written his own vows and promised Charlie that he'd always look after her, always look after them.

'It was my fault,' Bo says. 'We were on such a high after the gig. We felt so young and reckless and I wanted to sustain that feeling. We'd had too much to drink and when Fingers suggested going out on his boat to watch the fireworks it was—'

'Stupid.'

'Yeah.'

Charlie waits out the silence. Both wanting and not wanting to know the raw and painful details of that night. Details that he will pick over in the coming days, months, years.

'When I think of that night it's all so hazy. A blur.'

'Did you hit your head?' Charlie's voice is as small as he feels. He hates the childlike desire that rises in him as he asks. An explanation that Bo can offer that he can clasp to his chest and pretend to believe it because he wants so badly for it to be true.

Yes, it was the tooth fairy who left a shiny fifty-pence piece under your pillow.

Yes, it was Santa Claus that filled up your stocking.

Yes, I hit my head and had amnesia so I'd forgotten who I was until you walked into the pub.

'No,' Bo says.

Charlie feels his hopes shatter against the rocks.

'It's hard to recall because . . . because it was dark and terrifying and it all happened so quickly.' Bo squeezes his eyes closed and Charlie knows from the expression on his face that he is back there, the water sucking him under. 'It was rougher than we'd

306

thought. The boat capsized and . . . I heard her calling for me but I couldn't find her, and then she went quiet.' Bo's hands wrap around his throat. 'The salt water . . . it was freezing. I ducked under the surface, Hal was screaming for help. I knew he couldn't swim. He was right by me. If I'd stretched out my hand I could have reached him. Taken him to the boat, which wasn't far away. He could have clung on to it but . . . I left him. I turned away from my oldest friend and I left him to drown so I could find your mother. You know she was everything to me, Charlie lad. *Everything.*'

'And did you? Find her?' Charlie is willing for the impossible. A different ending to the story.

'I did. But . . . but it was too late. She was already . . .' Bo is shaking. His hands. His body. His voice. 'I tried to hold on to her. To bring her back but the current . . . She slipped from my grasp and it was dark. So dark. I can swim – you know that – but I couldn't fight against it.'

'How did you survive?'

'I don't know, lad.' Bo's tortured eyes meet his. 'I ask myself over and over why me and not her? Why was I spared. I'm not a religious man but . . . why?' He looks to Charlie for the answer, no longer the parent. No longer dependable but unsteady and uncertain. Broken.

'Why didn't you come home?'

'After I was washed up I was too shocked to think straight. I walked until I came across a caravan park. I thought I could fetch help but it was locked up for the winter. I was exhausted and I couldn't see any other signs of civilization so I broke into a caravan and yanked down the curtains and wrapped them around myself. I thought the cold would kill me and I thought I deserved it because . . . because . . . she . . . your mother . . .' Bo huffs out air. 'I . . . I was numb I suppose is the best way to describe it. Numb.' He nods. 'I had a fever and I'm not sure how long I was there. I ate stale biscuits I found in the cupboard and there was water. All the time I hated myself. I thought you'd all hate me. Blame me. When I ventured out I discovered I was only a few miles up the coast. I walked back here, to Colesby Bay. I intended to ring you, honest to God I did, but . . . Charlie, I wasn't right . . . in the head . . . the thought of Nina and Duke's grief. Your grief. I . . . I just couldn't bear it. She'd always been the parent, not me. I . . . I didn't know how to do it without her. I was protecting them.'

'You were protecting yourself.' It is the sad, simple truth.

Bo shrugs. 'Perhaps. I couldn't see a future without her. I didn't want one.'

'And yet here you are. Surviving.'

'Yes. Surviving, lad. Not living. Existing. I got by with eating scraps, leftovers from the chippy. No one knew me. It was Fingers who had friends here and he . . . well, he's gone too. I was the only one left, Charlie. The *only* one. That had to mean something, didn't it? What if . . .'

'What?'

'You wouldn't understand.'

'Like I understand any of this?' Charlie forces a hollow laugh because he knows the occasion calls for it. 'Try me.'

'I thought what if I'd been spared to . . . to . . .' He nods towards his guitar.

'To make it as a musician?' Charlie is incredulous Bo has even thought this.

'I had a chance once—' Bo begins.

'To be in the James Patrick Ensemble, I know. But you gave it up because Mum was your dream but now she's gone—'

'I only have nightmares.'

'You should have come home.'

'I thought you'd all blame me. I blamed myself.'

'Mum once told me that accidents happen. It's what you do afterwards that counts.'

What will Charlie do after this? Whether it was an accident meeting Bo, fate, it has given him his life back. Freed him from the responsibility of Nina and Duke. Perhaps he'll go to New York after all, take Pippa. He's found it so hard being a substitute parent and yet, for some reason, the thought of leaving Nina and Duke is crushing.

'Charlie, how can I explain to Nina and Duke when I don't even understand? I don't know why I survived. Why I—'

'Perhaps you were *spared* to bring up your children?'

Instead, Charlie had felt obliged to step in and now that his time with them is coming to an abrupt end he doesn't think it is obligation that has kept him there. There is a part of him that wishes he had never walked into the Crow's Nest. Never found out the truth.

'How are they?'

'Do you care?'

'Of course I do. I never meant to—'

'Abandon them—'

'Stay away this long. Are they happy?' Bo's voice is level but his tone is brittle, as though he might snap as easily as one of the strings on his guitar.

'Happy? They think both of their parents are dead.'

'You know what I mean. I . . . I thought I'd mess it up. I knew you'd be better at raising them than me.'

'How did you know I'd stick around?'

'Because you're a good lad.'

'Then you don't know me at all because when they needed me, at the very worst time of their life, I left them too. I'd say like father like son, but you're not my father, are you?'

'Where are they? Who—'

'Violet took them but then I went back to look after them because I made a promise to Mum on New Year's Eve that I'd look after them. I couldn't leave them. I know what it's like to be left. You decided you weren't cut out for parenting like my dad wasn't cut out for parenting. He left me. You left me.' Charlie's voice thins until he feels it crack. 'You could have come home but you made a choice not to.'

'It's not the same,' Bo reaches out to touch Charlie's shoulder but Charlie shrugs him off. 'This isn't because of them. Because of you. Your dad didn't leave because of you neither.'

In front of Charlie is the crashing ocean but all he can hear is his dad smashing through the glass table; here there's the darkening sky but all he can see is the blood pouring from his wrist.

'We're not talking about him, we're talking about you,' Charlie says.

'We need to talk about him if you seriously think—'

'There's nothing to say. I nearly died and Dad . . . he ran away.' His eyes meet Bo's and Charlie can feel the anguish in his, the throb behind them.

'Oh, Charlie. Your dad was an alcoholic, not because of Mum and not because of you.'

There's a long stretch. Charlie knows they should be talking about the future and yet it is the past that has defined him. Bo is his only link to that. This might be the only chance to rake through it.

'I told my dad I loved him,' Charlie whispers. 'That was the last thing I said to him. That was the last time I ever said that to anyone because what does it mean? Nothing.'

'Everything,' Bo says gently. 'If "I love you" are the last words you ever hear from a person then you can rest easy that you've given meaning to their live. Purpose. Whatever choices he went on to make after that are on him, not you. It wasn't your fault.'

'Do you think? All this time . . .' Charlie's tears leak down his cheeks, Bo's thumb wipes them away. 'I thought I wasn't enough. That . . . I wasn't worth staying for. I always felt such shame that I was so . . . so unlovable that he . . .' he covers his face with his hands. Can feel his body tearing in two with the force of the release of years of pent-up sorrow.

Eventually, Charlie roughly wipes his face with his sleeve. Although he is sad and angry he also feels more at peace than he has done for a long time.

'There's so much to sort out. You and Mum have recently both been declared dead. Your life insurance has just paid out and the mortgage is in the process of being paid off. I guess we'll have to pay it all back somehow.'

'Perhaps—' Bo readjusts his weight and it's only a slight shift but Charlie notices the distance that has opened up between them '—it's . . . easier, cleaner, if I don't come home.'

'What? You must. Don't do this to Nina and Duke. Don't let them feel that they weren't enough to keep you. Don't let them feel the way I've felt all of these years.'

'They would only think that if they knew I was alive.'

Bo's words hang before Charlie bats them away. 'You can't

expect me to keep something like this a secret? From them? From everyone? It's not only immoral. It's illegal. Bo . . .' Charlie leans forward. 'If you've ever loved me. *Please* don't put me in that position.'

There's a beat. Charlie feels his heart hammering in his chest while he waits.

Bo nods. 'I won't put you in that position, Charlie lad. Where are you staying?'

'A B & B near the harbour. It's about a half hour walk. I've got the car there.'

'Go and get the car. I'm going to walk up to the Cliff Top Café – it's where I've been sleeping rough – my things are all there. Don't wake Nina. Just fetch the car and come and meet me there.'

'I can walk up with you and—'

'It's not far—'

'Or you could come to the B & B and—'

'Charlie.' Bo stands and brushes the sand from his jeans. 'It's better this way.' He pulls him into a hug. 'I love you all. I know I haven't acted like it but . . . I'm going to fix it. Everything.'

'Okay.' Charlie isn't happy they aren't staying together but he doesn't want to upset the fragile equilibrium. 'I'll be with you in about half an hour. Don't . . .' *Run away. Disappear. Leave us.*

'I love you, Charlie lad.' Bo covers his heart with his chest before he turns and walks away.

A stitch burns in Charlie's side as he jogs back to the B & B.

His fingers are trembling as he starts the car. He begins to back out of the driveway but his anxious foot presses too hard on the accelerator. There's the blare of a horn, a squeal of brakes. Charlie waves an apology and edges forward to let the car pass.

He sets off at a slower pace, through the town, past the pubs, the smokers huddled under infra-red heat lamps. The chippy with the snaking queue. The couples sitting on the harbour wall, holding hands. He shifts down a gear as he begins the ascent to the Cliff Top Café. Headlights sweeping the blackness. He parks the car at the top, leaves the engine running and the lights on.

'Bo?' He jogs over to the empty shell of the building where he had spent so much time when he was at Colesby Bay as a teenager. He steps inside, his feet crunching on broken glass. The windows have been smashed and there are patches in the roof where he can see the sky. Moonlight pushes its creamy light inside and Charlie sees the counter where he'd push a tower of teetering coins towards Jenny, his favourite waitress, who would tell him to choose either a yellow, blue or red straw while she levered the lid from a bottle of Coke.

Red, he always chose red.

The inconsequential details suddenly feel important.

'Bo?'

He picks his way over upended tables and chairs, past the remains of a bonfire, and he pushes open the door to the toilets. It's darker here, the small opaque windows not letting in the light, but Charlie can see enough to know that, wherever his stepdad is, it isn't here.

'Bo?' Charlie makes his way into the back room. He had sat here once, while Jenny dabbed disinfectant-soaked cotton wool onto his knee before covering his graze with a plaster. She had given him a lollipop – lemon, no lime – as though he was five and not fifteen.

There's a mattress on the floor. Two bin bags in the corner. He pulls out shirt after shirt. Not the sensible white work shirts Bo would button up each morning but brightly coloured with swirling seventies patterns. A pair of faded jeans. Is this it? Is this really all Bo owns now or had there been more?

Charlie hurries outside, screams into the night, 'Where are you?'

His eyes scan the area, the car headlights picking out a mound on the edge of the cliff. Charlie runs towards it. Drops to his knees. The wind whipping his hair around his face. Salt pushing into his mouth.

A pair of battered black Vans. And a box of fudge.

'No!' Charlie's cry is deep and primal. How could Bo have jumped, left them? Had he been planning it when he'd been talking to Charlie? Had Charlie caused this? He remembers telling Bo that it will be a mess to sort out, that the life insurance had paid out, the mortgage had been settled.

'I'm going to fix it. Everything.'

Was this . . . was this his *fix*?

'If you've ever loved me. Please don't put me in that position,' he had begged.

'I won't put you in that position, Charlie lad.'

There is something wrong. Something missing. Charlie can't quite place it.

How could Bo have done this? Left him? Left them? Charlie is shivering violently, his teeth harassing against each other; he tastes blood where he has bitten his tongue. He remembers the warmth of Bo's embrace. The way he had told him he loved him.

But now . . . *this*?

When Charlie had opened up about his dad, Bo had said, 'If

"I love you" are the last words you ever hear from a person then you can rest easy that you've given meaning to their live. Purpose.' Was that what he was trying to tell Charlie half an hour ago? That Charlie had given meaning to his life. Purpose.

A memory, Charlie at sixteen playing 'Misty' on the piano, Bo leaning against the doorframe, mug of coffee in his hand.

'You're so talented, Charlie lad. I'll make a guitarist out of you yet.' He had handed Charlie Mum's guitar and picked up his own. Bo had begun to strum 'Fly Me to the Moon' and Charlie had joined in, their fingers working in harmony, their voices.

His guitar.

Bo had left his clothes in bin bags but Charlie doesn't recall seeing his guitar. He rushes back into the café. Searches every dusty corner for Bo's instrument. It isn't here.

Back outside he peers over the cliff once more. There is nothing except furious waves bashing against rock. The water murky. He can't see any splintered wood. He can't see a guitar.

His fingers automatically seek out the scar on his wrist, thinking of the way all of his peers thought Charlie had tried to take his own life. He hadn't though, had he?

Has Bo?

He just doesn't know.

Exhaustion crashes over Charlie, dragging him to his knees.

He cries then, for Nina and Duke who have known loss all too intimately for their tender years. He cries for his fifteen-year-old self and then for now. He has lost a different father, in an equally unfathomable way. He cries for Bo who loved his mum far more than he loves his children. He cries for his mum who is not here to take the pain from her children and weave it into something else. Something better.

He cries for them all.

He is shivering when he eventually drags himself to his feet, clutching the box of fudge tightly to his chest.

Charlie takes one last lingering look at the café before he whispers, 'Goodbye.' There are so many different paths Bo could have taken that would not have led to this. What can he do to ease Nina's pain when he tells her this impossible, unthinkable end?

Don't tell her.

Tell her.

Call the police and let them take over. Find Bo and then what? He comes home and Charlie goes back to his old life?

He starts the car and begins the descent back to the B & B.

What is he going to say?

What is he going to do?

CHAPTER FIFTY-ONE

Nina

Nina's sleep is long and deep. She had briefly woken last night and contemplated finding Charlie after reading his note but then she'd slipped under once more and now it's nine o'clock. Charlie is setting a tray upon the round table; it must have been the clink of china that roused her. Nina studies him as he arranges the tea and toast. He hasn't shaved. Behind the lenses of his glasses his eyes are tinged with pink as though he has been crying or hasn't slept well. Possibly both. He is a world away from the groomed man who had come to babysit six months ago.

'Morning,' she says tentatively.

'Morning, Nina. Sleep well?' He doesn't look at her. Is he angry? It's hard to tell.

'Yes, thanks. I woke and saw your note but then I was flat out again. I didn't even hear you come in. Did you have a nice walk?'

'Nice?' He sits down and lets out a noise, which isn't quite a sigh but it isn't a laugh either. 'It was . . .' Charlie turns his attention to the window. 'I went to the pub and . . . I met a ghost.'

Nina pads across the room and sits opposite Charlie. 'A ghost?' Nina is worried. Has he even slept at all?

'A ghost from the past.'

'Charlie, you're scaring me.' She takes his hand. 'Look at me, please.'

He turns his bloodshot eyes to hers. 'Are you happy, Nina?'

'Happy?'

'I know you miss Mum and Dad and now there's all this stuff with Maeve but living at home, with me, am I . . . am I enough?'

'Charlie, you are everything.' She watches as his eyes fill with tears. 'You . . . you put up with my shit and you're always there.'

'I don't always get it right. Sometimes it's so hard to make the right decision. Sometimes—' he squeezes her fingers, a desperate look on his face. 'I always thought that somehow parents had all the answers but I don't. Sometimes I don't know what to do.'

'But you show up,' Nina says. 'You came here, after me. You . . . you show up and, sometimes, Charlie, that's enough. Knowing there's someone who will always be there even if they're a crap cook and can't iron.'

He nods. Draws in a deep breath and lets his shoulders drop.

'Now what's all this about ghosts?' Nina gently probes.

'I was revisiting some childhood haunts and thinking about what's most important to a kid.'

'The person who is always there,' Nina whispers and they sit, holding hands as the tea cools and the butter hardens. They don't move until there's a knock on the door telling them that checkout is at noon.

They have eaten cold toast slathered with sweet-strawberry jam and Nina has dressed, long sleeves covering her scars even though the sky outside is cloudless. It's going to be a scorching day.

'Are you ready to go home?' Charlie asks.

Nina fiddles with the buttons on the cuff of her shirt until she pops it open.

'I wish I could stay here.'

'Because . . . because of the YouTube clip?' Charlie asks quietly.

'No. I know that Dad's . . . that he isn't here but it gave me a purpose, coming here. Something to do. Somewhere to be. At home . . . I think Maeve hates me and there's nothing—'

'Don't say that,' Charlie says fiercely. 'There's us. We need you. Me and Duke.'

'You don't need me, Charlie. You've got purpose. You're writing your book and Duke . . . he's probably glad I ran away. Glad to see the back of me. I . . . I haven't been very kind to him lately.' She hasn't supported him. She won't blame him if he hates her. Everything is such a mess. Instinctively her fingers slip under the sleeve of her shirt needing that release, her nails poised to draw blood, but, before she can, Charlie holds something out to her.

An envelope.

'I'd forgotten but Duke asked me to give you this.'

'What is it?' She takes it, trying to ignore the itch on her skin that is desperate to be scratched. She examines the childish scrawl of her name. Turns it over in her hands, trying to guess what is inside. Is it weighted with anger that she's been a terrible sister? Is it light with joy because she's left?

Charlie shrugs. 'I don't know but I'll leave you to read it in peace. I'll go for a wander. I won't be far away.'

Nina both wants and doesn't want to know what Duke has written. She recalls the last time he had written to her, a 'sorry' note from Father Christmas when she had woken up to find not the make-up set and hair straighteners she had wanted in her stocking, but sheet music and a home spa kit. She had been old enough to know there wasn't a Santa but she had gone along with their annual ritual of laying out a mince pie and a glass of milk and a carrot for Rudolph, for Duke's sake.

In the morning, after they had opened their presents, Duke delighted he'd got *The Lord of the Rings* Lego he had asked for, she'd gone for a shower. Back in her bedroom, she'd been dressing when she had noticed a note on her bedside table that definitely hadn't been there before.

> *I am sorry I didn't bring you the make-up and hair straighteners you asked for but I think you are pretty enough without them. Lots of love from FC xxx*

For a long time she had treasured that note, keeping it in her shoebox of special things, like the cinema ticket from the first time she was allowed to go alone, and notes Maeve had passed her in class. Last year the box had been overflowing and Nina had carelessly chucked loads of things away including birthday and Christmas cards from her parents that now she would give anything to have in her possession again. Had Duke's note been one of them?

She swallows hard, emotion already rising in her throat as she carefully slides her finger under the seal, trying her best to preserve the envelope. Whatever the letter says she wants to keep it intact. It will be a reminder that she is loved, or a reminder that she isn't.

> *Dear Nina,*
> *I am sorry that you've run away and it is all my fault. You said on New Year's Eve that if I ate the cookie dough then*

someone would die and I didn't believe you but I will always listen to everything you say now, I promise. I know I am weird and annoying and too sensitive and all of the other things I am. I am going to try really hard not to be. If I could magic away all of the things you don't like about me I would but you are right, I am rubbish at magic and everyone will probably laugh at me when I do the show but I wouldn't mind being laughed at if it was by you.

Our house was always full of noise, do you remember that, Nina? Laughing and singing and then shouting when you argued with Mum and Dad (I know that was because of the hormones and not your fault.) Now it's too quiet.

I miss the music. I miss a lot of things. Mum. Dad. You. Do you remember when we used to play 'I Wan'na Be Like You' and we'd waggle our bums like Baloo as we danced? It was always my favourite song. I loved Mum singing 'All The Things You Are' and telling me I was brave and funny and kind all the things I didn't feel I was but, really, I just wanted to be like you. I still want to be like you, my big sister who really is brave and funny and kind.

Don't leave me.

Please come home, Nina. You used to say we had too many people in our house and not enough space but now we have too much space and not enough people.

I miss you.

Love Duke xxx

P.S. Billie misses you too.

Nina reads the letter twice more before pressing it against her aching heart. How can Duke think the boat accident is his fault for eating the cookie dough? He's stupid, stupid, stupid and she misses him so much. She begins to cry. Eventually, her tears spent, she eases the letter back into the envelope and smooths it flat onto the bedside table. She splashes cold water onto her face before she heads out to find Charlie.

It's not yet midday but it's sweltering. The sunflower sun pumping out heat. She can smell the glistening tarmac on the road, fighting against the scent of hot doughnuts She's only been walking for a few minutes but sweat is sticking her shirt to her back. Her fingers play with her cuff; she wants to roll up her sleeves but is scared to show off her scars but then she remembers Duke's letter, how he thinks of her as brave, and she pushes up the fabric, exposing her skin. Exposing herself.

Her feet lead her towards the promenade. Near the steps that lead down towards the sand is a busker with a guitar. Her heart stutters with hope before falling back into static despair. The man is not her father although he holds himself the same way. She thinks he is probably the blurred image on YouTube. She wonders if she will ever stop seeing Dad. Her mum. Perhaps she will always see them in every couple that dances, hear them in the melodies of songs, sense them encouraging her in everything she will do.

Charlie isn't far away. He's sitting, unblinking eyes fixed on the horizon. Nina doesn't know what he is seeing but she doesn't think it's the lapping waves or the children building sandcastles, parents sunbathing, congratulating themselves for holidaying in June, pulling their kids out of school before the end of term, saving a fortune. Knowing that come July every stretch of sand will be speared with windbreaks, spread with colourful towels.

Nina notices the box of fudge next to her brother. Her stomach clenches with anger the way it did that New Year's Day when they'd rushed here to try and make sense of the senseless and Charlie had bought sweets on the way home.

Her parents are dead.

The thought that had spun as fast as the waltzers on the pier that day, eliciting the same sick feeling, returns now.

This is not a holiday and yet again he has been shopping for souvenirs.

She feels the bond they have formed these past twenty-four hours stretch tight. She doesn't want it to snap. Charlie is all she and Duke have. She might not understand him, but she wants to at least try. He came here for her. That means something.

Nina sits at the opposite end of the bench; between them is the unspoken and the unexplained. She glares at the box with its 'Wish You Were Here!' postcard of the pier at Colesby Bay.

For a time, neither of them speak, watching the frothy trail of a speedboat as it slices through the water. Eventually, Nina asks, 'What's with the fudge, Charlie?'

'Your dad used to buy me it all of the time.'

He doesn't elaborate. In front of the railings that lead to the beach a woman raises her camera towards a seagull soaring through the brilliant blue sky. She shields the screen from the sun with her hand and smiles – the perfect shot – before looking around for something else to capture. What would she see if she aims her long lens at Nina and Charlie; strangers sitting awkwardly, together but not? A holidaymaker, souvenir sweets to take home to his family? A girl deep in thought, wondering what fun to have next? Or would she strip away the layers and see the boy trying to recapture the taste of his childhood, a girl who desperately wants to repair her cracked heart. A fractured family who want to come together, but don't quite know how.

Charlie suddenly turns to her as though he's made a decision. Nina sees the tears in his eyes.

'That summer, when my mum met your dad. It was . . . well, it was a very confusing time for me. My own dad had . . . you know, and I was . . . scared, I think it's fair to say. Scared that everyone in my life would leave me. That Mum and Bo would run away together or Bo would disappear and leave Mum broken-hearted. The way she looked at him . . . that love was something I had never seen before and I could see that, despite everything we had been through, he made her happy, was devoted to her, but I still had this constant, low-level anxiety. Fear of abandonment, my therapist said later. I wanted to protect Mum, be the man of the house, as it were.' Charlie nods as though affirming to himself that, yes, this is the way it happened. 'I cornered Bo when he was on his own and ordered him to leave us alone. I told him that I knew he'd hurt Mum and it was better if it ended now. He walked away and I remember feeling . . . relieved it was so easy to get rid of him but also devastated he had gone and it would just be me and Mum again. He came back few minutes later with a box just like this one.' Charlie picked up the box on his lap and rattled it. 'He asked "Do you know what this is?" "It's fudge," I replied. "It's more than that. It's a mistake. It's thought to have originated when a confectioner 'fudged' a batch of caramels and this was the result, but you see, Charlie, it's delicious, try a little."' Charlie offers the box to Nina and she takes a piece, letting its sweetness tingle her tongue. 'Bo said. "Things that can seem like the worst mistake often, usually, work out for the best. Remember that, Charlie lad. I might seem like a bad decision for your mum but I adore her and, as long as she's around, I'll be around too. I promise.'"

Nina doesn't look at Charlie; she can hear from his cracked voice he is crying.

'And . . . and he was, around for as long as she was. Nina . . .' Charlie shuffles up until he is sitting next to her, slipping one arm around her shoulders. 'Sometimes I don't know what I'm doing. I've made mistakes, I know. But if I had a choice whether I could go back to my own life or stay I would stay. I would choose you and Duke every single time. I do . . . I do choose you. We've all made mistakes but sometimes—' he taps the lid of the box '—we just have to trust that things will work out.' He reaches into his bag. 'I have something for you. Well, it's yours. Something you threw away.' He hands her the wooden fish he had made for her all those years ago.

'I'm here for you, Little Fish.'

Joy spreads through her. He remembers.

'I trust you, Big Fish.' She elbows him gently, placing the fish on her lap.

Their hands both reach for a piece of fudge at the same time, their fingers connecting, their hearts too.

It is almost noon by the time Charlie and Nina are ready to leave. The landlady hovers on the landing outside of their room, duster and polish in hand, vacuum cleaner propped against the banisters.

'Do you think we'll ever come back here?' Nina asks.

'To this B & B?' Charlie chucks their bags into the boot.

'To Colesby Bay.'

'I don't know. Perhaps. I always lose something when I come here, but then I find something too.'

Nina doesn't ask Charlie what he's lost and found this time. She hopes he's referring to the tension that was between them, which has disappeared.

'Home.' She fiddles with the stereo once Charlie has started the engine, pairing her phone, choosing a playlist of seventies pop.

Charlie checks his watch. 'We've seven hours before Duke's talent show; we should make it.'

Nina thinks of her younger brother and the letter and the way he has adapted to everything. He was supposed to be the one who couldn't cope with change and yet he has, far better than she has, adjusted to her constantly fluctuating world. She steals a glance at Charlie; he's softly singing along to Bread's 'Everything I Own'. She has been unfair, telling him he can't date. Unreasonable. He has given up so much for them already. She has used Duke as an excuse when what she was really worried about was herself. What might happen if Charlie fell for someone who she hated. If he fell in love with someone who wanted her own children. A life away from them, their home. But she can't dictate love. She pictures Maeve the night they kissed, her cheeks flushed, hair glinting red under the light.

'Charlie, about that earring,' she begins.

'It wasn't what—'

'Please. Let me say this. I don't want you to be lonely. It isn't fair to say you can't date, but there must be rules.'

'Rules?' The corners of Charlie's mouth twitch into a smile.

'Don't laugh. You can't just bring randoms home.'

'Randoms?'

'You know. Women you pick up in pubs.'

Charlie laughs, 'Nina. Seriously. I'm flattered you think I'd find it so easy to pick up women but—'

'You managed it with Miss Rudd. *Gina.*'

'I was . . . it doesn't matter how I was. You think I'm that smooth, though?' He pretends to brush an imaginary speck from his shoulder.

'Well, you managed it again unless you've started wearing jewellery.' Nina leans closer to Charlie, studying his earlobes.

'It was Pippa's earring.'

'Pippa's. Oh, that's a relief. Wait. How did it get into your bed?'

'She was in my bed.'

'But then where were you . . . oh.'

'Oh, indeed.'

'But . . . Pippa. *You* and Pippa. How long?'

'You remember I told you about my first kiss? It was Pippa.'

'The one where you were six or thirteen?'

'Both.'

'But that was years ago.'

'It was.'

'And now you're like . . . thirty-three?'

'I am.'

'Fuck. Charlie. All this time you've . . . loved her?'

'In my defence, I didn't know until recently that I still did. I pushed her away.' Charlie glances at Nina, suddenly serious. 'You're not the only one who gets scared at the thought of people leaving. After my dad . . . left—' Nina notices his knuckles whiten against the steering wheel as he says this '—I was lost. Confused. Not sure what love was or why mine wasn't good enough.'

'Oh, Charlie. You . . . you're just as fucked up as me.'

'Family trait.' He flashes a smile. 'Do you think it's too late for me?'

'Well, you're an idiot but at least you know that now. Tell her.'

'You won't mind if she and I become . . . an us?'

'Mind?' Nina can't even remember the first time she met Pippa; she's just always been there, part of the family. Unwavering. Dependable. Driving them to Colesby Bay without hesitation the day the awful news came in. 'I can't think of anything better.'

Charlie smiles and cranks up the air conditioning. 'It's hot, isn't it?'

'That's because it's . . .' Nina clicks off the stereo and launches into a rendition of 'Summertime', her hands beating out the rhythm on her thighs. Charlie joins in, not with the low, muted voice she's heard him sing with but with a clear confidence. They take it in turns to pick songs, both immediately knowing the lyrics, the soundtrack of both of their childhoods. From the upbeat tempo of 'On The Sunny Side Of The Street' to the laidback 'Autumn Leaves' they sing them all.

Together.

Later, Charlie says,

'We've forty-five minutes before the concert starts. If we go straight to the school we can grab front row seats?'

'Charlie?' she asks. 'Can we go somewhere else first please? It's really important.'

CHAPTER FIFTY-TWO

Duke

After school, Shannon, Evie's mum, collects Duke again because Charlie still isn't back from rescuing Nina.

'He has rung to say he's on his way though,' Mrs Marshall says.

'Will they be back in time for the concert?' Duke asks but Mrs Marshall doesn't know.

At Evie's, they dump their bags and coats in the porch, kicking off their shoes, before racing upstairs.

'Do you want to practise your act?' Evie says.

Duke tries, but the handkerchiefs he attempts to pull out of his sleeve get stuck and he still can't quite master opening the secret compartment in his top hat without it being obvious.

'Perhaps you should make it a comedy act?' Evie suggests but Duke knows that weird isn't the same as being funny. Everyone will be laughing at him tonight but it won't be kind and encouraging but hard and spiteful. Duke can't take much more of school. Tonight will be the straw that broke . . . whatever back it broke, a donkey? Duke pictures a donkey with red and white stripy straws coming out of his body but even the thought of this doesn't make him smile.

Downstairs, Mrs Marshall dollops shepherd's pie onto plates. It's made with Quorn so Duke isn't sure if she should still call it that because it doesn't have any lamb in it. It's delicious but Duke can't eat because his stomach is already full of nerves. Instead, he asks for the recipe for Charlie so Mrs Marshall at least knows he likes the taste.

He feels sick, all his worries banding together and marching around the inside of his body. He feels their tiny feet in the pit of his belly, feels them moving under his skin.

'Let's get back to school, then.' Mrs Marshall scrapes the leftovers into the bin. Duke wishes he could join them, hiding under the potato peelings and the browning banana skins. Bin Boy, he could be called, and . . .

'Duke?'

'Ready,' he says. Even though he is not.

There's a gap in the red velvet curtains that sweep across the stage and Duke peeps through it. The school hall is almost full, the hard grey plastic chairs his class had lined up earlier groaning under the weight of the parents. His eyes sweep over the audience. There is no one here for him. Once, he'd have had almost a whole row of people watching him; Mum, Dad, Nina, Pippa, sometimes Charlie, but then if Mum and Dad *were* still alive he wouldn't have Charlie and if his brother had come it would be Charlie *and* Sasha because she wouldn't have left him because of them. Now he thinks of it, if Mum and Dad were still alive he wouldn't be here, at this stupid school, about to make a fool of himself again.

He clutches his magic wand tightly in his fist and wishes he could make everyone disappear. Or that he had the ring from *The*

Hobbit, which grants the wearer invisibility, then no one would be able to see him.

There's a woman crouching in the aisle at the front, camera poised to film her son or daughter. She's wearing a blue floaty dress that touches the floor. Mum had one the exact same shade, the colour of a cloudless sky, and Duke remembers the softness of it against his cheek as he cuddled up to her, the summer meadow smell of it.

He misses her so much.

Before he drops the curtain he sees Aunt Violet squeezing between the rows to take her seat but it just isn't the same.

Jayden, Luke and Brandon swagger onto the stage in baggy tracksuit bottoms and huge T-shirts, thick, bright gold chains looped around their necks. And they call him weird, Duke thinks.

Luke starts beatboxing, Jayden and Brandon running to the front of the stage, fingers splayed, arms going up and down in time to the beat like one of those lucky ornamental cats that sits in the windows of Chinese restaurants.

'Our teacher ain't fly we think he's a sucker,

'He thinks that he's so cool but he's a mother—'

The power is shut off, the hall plunged into darkness save for the slivers of light leaking through the heavy curtains. Miss Greenly hurries on the stage and ushers the boys off.

The rest of the acts are okay. Some kids forget the words, forget their dance steps. They still get a round of applause. This should make Duke feel better but it doesn't. What if he's the only kid no one claps for? The show is nearly over. Again, he peers around the side of the stage, eyes seeking out Nina and Charlie. They *still* haven't come. Duke wonders if they've gone straight home. Forgotten about him.

Evie is the last act before him – penultimate – Duke learned that word today during dress rehearsal when Evie refused to take part. She said she had a sore throat and wanted to save her voice until tonight but Duke knew that was a lie. Even he doesn't know what her act is. She crouches and sets up a small projector. The white wall behind her fills with the photos of a battery farm, featherless chickens shoved together in tiny cages.

The lights go out again and Evie is ushered off, shouting, 'Meat is Murder,' as she goes.

Duke's name is called.

He can't do this.

His name is called again.

Light-headed, he shuffles onto the stage, careful not to trip over his cape in the semi-darkness. There's a movement to his left, a shadow rushing towards him, his magic wand is whipped away and, instead, something cold and hard is thrust into his hand, something looped around his neck.

The lights glare once more. Duke stares at the saxophone – his saxophone, which he clings on to. In front of him, Nina is adjusting a microphone. To his side, Charlie raises the lid on the piano, flexes his fingers.

What's going on?

Duke can't possibly play.

He remembers his parents' memorial on Briar's Hill. How he'd tried and failed.

Nina glances at him and he shakes his head; he cannot do this. She hurries over to him and hugs him tightly, whispering in his ear. 'It wasn't your fault, Duke. Eating the cookie dough didn't cause anything. I'm sorry you ever thought it did. I love you.'

Until that moment Duke hadn't realized how much his stomach

felt like the snow globe Dad had bought him when they had visited the Natural History Museum. A blizzard of guilt and regret swirling around inside of him.

It wasn't his fault.

The relief settles on him. Tears build as she rushes back to the mic and clears her throat. 'This school is full of losers,' she speaks loudly. 'Cruel kids who think if you aren't like them there must be something wrong with you. Kids who pick on those who are a bit different. Kids who are mean to others because they're scared that if they aren't doing the bullying they will become the bullied. But . . . it's okay to be different. The weirdest people are often the most interesting. The most talented. Those of you who have ever called someone a name, hurt them, laughed at them, you . . . you should be ashamed. I'm ashamed because this is something I've been guilty of in the past. Not anymore though. I'm trying to be a better person. To be more like the kindest person I know.' She smiles at Duke and gives an encouraging nod and he knows. He knows what she wants him to do.

But can he do it?

If Nina believes that eating the cookie dough hadn't caused the accident then perhaps he does deserve to feel the joy of music again but deserving to and being able to are entirely different things.

Last time they had played together up on that hill it was a mess, out of time, but then they were out of sync as a family. Now, as he sees the love in Nina's eyes, in Charlie's, when he thinks of what they've been through together, he knows.

They *can* do this.

But still he's scared.

He raises his instrument, places the reed between his lips. His whole body is shaking, his hands, his knees, even his stomach is rocking from side to side.

He waits.

Charlie strikes the first notes, not the toned down, subdued version he and Nina had played last New Year's Eve, but the full-on happy *Jungle Book* one. Duke's mind is blank but his body remembers what to do, how to play. Nina sings, carefree, jigging out the beat, Charlie nods his head as his fingers fly up and down the keys, Duke taps his feet. By the end of the first verse the audience is on their feet dancing, proper Baloo-like, wiggling their bottoms as they swing their arms from side to side. It is, Duke thinks, bloody epic.

They're not out of time the way they were at Mum and Dad's memorial but perfectly in sync and that's because, finally, they feel like a united family.

There are many different kinds of love, Duke realizes. The one he has for his family is certain and strong but the way music makes him feel, a fizzing Catherine wheel spinning around his stomach, is another. He has missed it so much.

This is, Duke thinks, what he wants to do forever and he wishes his mum was here to support him because he has no idea how to make his dreams come true.

The song finishes and the audience bursts into applause. Duke closes his eyes and lets the symphony of appreciation crash over him. Nina takes his hand, Charlie takes the other and they bow – not in the timid way he had practised in front of the mirror after his magic trick, but raising his head confidently.

'More!'

Duke glances stage left and Miss Clarke, the drama teacher, gives a nod.

This time Duke slides onto the piano stool. Charlie runs backstage, returning a few minutes later with an acoustic guitar. Nina takes her place behind the microphone. They don't need to communicate with words, knowing what they're going to play.

'All The Things You Are,' Nina sings, her voice like the honey Duke drizzles on his porridge. It's the slowed down version. The one Sarah Vaughan makes sound sad but Nina doesn't make it sound sad. It's raw and hopeful and full of longing.

After the song has finished, Duke swivels around on his stool to face the audience, his legs too wobbly to support him. The spotlights blur his vision and for a single perfect moment he imagines he sees his parents on the front row.

They are clapping louder than anyone.

And then his vision adjusts and they are gone.

After the concert there's a drinks reception.

'Duke, you were wonderful!' Miss Clarke approaches them, glass of wine in hand. 'You all were.' She smiles at Nina and Charlie. 'This is my brother. Tell him.' She nudges the man standing next to her in the ribs. He offers his hand to Charlie.

'Hello. I'm Graham Clarke from The Aringford Music Academy. We're a private school with an emphasis on encouraging musical talent and wow—' he turns to Duke '—you certainly have talent. We're open to scholarship applications right now but we haven't seen anyone of your calibre. If you want to apply you'll have a very good chance—'

'You'll get in!' Miss Clarke says.

'It would be unfair on the other candidates for me to say you'll definitely be offered a place—'

'But it's what he means.' Miss Clarke places her hands on Duke's shoulders. 'The place is yours if you want it.'

'Can I, Charlie?' Duke feels himself inflate with excitement. He crosses his fingers behind his back hoping that Charlie won't pop his balloon of happiness.

'We'll come and have a look around.' Charlie pulls out his phone. 'What's your address?'

Duke feels himself begin to deflate, his hope seeping away as he hears that the school is seventy miles away. He's told that he can board but he knows that means sleeping in a strange bed in a strange place and there's already been so much change this year.

Jayden, Luke and Brandon charge past him, leaving a trail of sticky orange squash in their wake. Tears prick his eyes. He can stay here and be miserable or leave and follow his dreams but his dreams seem too enormous to him. He wishes he'd performed magic instead tonight.

'Hey,' Nina whispers, 'don't worry; we'll figure something out.'

Duke shakes his head sadly. 'I can't go, I'll miss . . . Billie too much.' Duke doesn't say he'll miss his sister, his brother; he doesn't have to. Their eyes are glistening too.

'We'll talk about it,' Charlie promises. 'At home.'

'After you've been next door and spoken to Pippa, Charlie,' Nina says sternly.

Duke remembers his phone call of yesterday. 'Pippa rang to explain she is leaving and to say goodbye to me. She said she'd called you both but you didn't pick up.'

'Has she already left?' Charlie grasps both of Duke's shoulders that he tries to shrug.

'I dunno. I've been at Evie's, haven't I?'

'Christ. Let's go.'

As they rush to the car, Duke thinks about the importance of holding onto the things you want. People. Dreams. He thinks how far away Scotland is. He thinks, that perhaps, seventy miles won't seem so far after all.

Charlie screeches to a halt outside of their house and runs straight to Pippa's front door. Duke doesn't need the darkened windows to tell him it is too late – the wind chime she had made from her grandmother's beads that always hangs by the front door is missing.

She has gone.

CHAPTER FIFTY-THREE

Charlie

Charlie is leaving.

He loads his case into the boot of the Beetle before he turns to face his brother and sister.

He will miss them.

'Are you sure you two will be okay?' he asks.

'They'll be fine.' Aunt Violet wraps her arms around their shoulders and pulls them in to her. They lean against her.

He pats Billie goodbye and then opens his arms. His siblings run into them. He squeezes them tightly, dropping a kiss on each of their heads.

'I love you.' The words he has been unable to say slip naturally from his mouth, leaving a sweet residue on his tongue.

They tell him they love him too as he slides behind the steering wheel, and smooths out a crumpled piece of paper on the passenger seat. It's the address of Pippa's parents in Scotland. After a frantic search, Mrs Miller who lives opposite and had been friends with Pippa's grandmother had given it to him.

'You're going to bring her home?' She'd gripped his hand with her gnarled one.

'I . . . I hope so.'

'Right from when you were bairns you were meant to be. In and out of each other's houses. Friends. That's the best basis for any relationship. Me and my Edgar were the best of friends too. Married forty-five years before he passed.' Her eyes fill with tears. 'You must come over for a cup of tea when I'm back.'

Loneliness is everywhere but he's only noticing it now.

It's a long drive. Country roads lead onto motorways, which lead to rutted tracks until at last, tired and hungry, he is there.

He knocks tentatively on the door. Holding his breath as it swings open. It's not Pippa, but her mum.

'Hello.' He's not sure if she remembers him. He hasn't met her many times over the years. 'I'm—'

'Charlie.' She sighs. 'You'd better come in.'

She shows him into the kitchen and then leads him to the lounge. 'Follow me.' They trudge upstairs.

'You have a lovely home,' Charlie says but he's confused. He isn't here for a tour. She shows him the master bedroom, the study and then the spare room. The neatly made bed and the empty wardrobe and then he understands.

'She didn't come here?'

'No. She's not going to either. She's gone to "find herself", whatever that means.'

'If she calls—'

'She's had her mobile disconnected.'

'I know. I've been trying to ring her. But if she calls can you tell her to contact me? Tell her that I'm sorry.'

Pippa's mum nods, once, and Charlie trudges back to his car.

Behind him he doesn't hear the door slam but senses it gently close.

He wonders where to go, where she could be. The world is a big place and it's impossible to guess. His only hope is that wherever she is, she's happy.

He makes the long journey home, tears trickling down his cheeks.

He doesn't wipe them away.

At home, Aunt Violet greets him with a sympathetic smile and a hot meal. It's later, after she's left and Duke has gone to bed, that he's alone with Nina.

He pours his heart out to her and then her to him. She tentatively tells him of her plan for tomorrow, asks him what he thinks. He hugs her tightly.

Proudly.

CHAPTER FIFTY-FOUR

Nina

There are many different kinds of love. The romantic, all-consuming I'd-actually-die-if-I-can't-be-with-you kind, and the security of you're-my-best-friend-and-we'll-always-have-each-other's-backs type. Nina feels both of these for Maeve.

She waits for her now as she has a thousand times in the past but this time her stomach trembles with nerves. She has no idea from the scant texts they have exchanged what Maeve is thinking and this is new and uncomfortable. Ever since she was five she has *known* Maeve, every look, every expression. Has been able to read between the lines of her messages, recognizing instinctively a hidden sadness, an undisclosed fear. The kiss has shunted their relationship into new territory and Nina very much hopes that, after today, there will still be a relationship, even if it isn't the one her aching heart would choose. She can't bear to lose Maeve from her life completely. Charlie thinks it's a good thing she is here today, for clarity if nothing else.

It'll be okay.

It is cooler. The light pattering of summer rain has chilled the air. Nina wraps her arms around herself as she waits on the solitary bench, the dampness in the wooden slats seeping through her jeans. No one comes to this tiny pocket park, the space too small for dog walkers, the lack of play equipment too boring for kids. It all feels rather clandestine, not like their usual meetings in town where they'd amble around the shops, arms linked, trying on clothes they could never afford. They would slurp caramel frappuccino and laugh at each other's creamy moustaches, devour plates of French fries and then worry they were fat. It all seems so inconsequential now, the things they used to stress about. A few months ago their biggest concern was their GCSEs, whether they'd put on weight and if they'd ever achieve the perfect eyebrow arch. Now it was being an orphan, the uncertainty of the future and . . . this. Whatever *this* is.

It'll be okay.

Nina gazes up at the rainbow curving over the trees, the thin strips of colour shimmering in the hazy sunlight and she remembers the adventure of seeking out the pot of gold, Mum ambling behind, Duke in a baby sling across her chest.

'Hurry-up. Hurry-up,' she had called. 'Before it disappears.'

But the end of the arc was always just out of reach, disappearing in front of her eyes, the sky again a flat blue, as though the rainbow had never been there at all, and Nina could never quite understand how something could be there and then suddenly not. She hasn't believed in pixies and treasure for a long, long time, but love? She still believes in love.

Maeve approaches her now. The sight of her causes Nina's breath to catch in her throat. The sun illuminates the gold streaks in Maeve's hair, a halo-type glow around her head. For a moment Nina is caught between past and present, unable to anchor herself in either. Her mind's eye seeing Maeve, pigtails bouncing, grinning a gap-toothed grin as she raced up to her in the playground.

The joy she felt when she was five years old mirrors the joy she feels now.

It'll be okay.

Maeve settles herself on the bench next to Nina, but not close enough. There is no touch of their thighs, no brushing of shoulders. They don't speak. Time blurs as they watch the clouds drift. Once they'd have pointed out images, the dragon with outstretched wings, the pig with a curly tail. Once, everything wouldn't have felt so . . . awkward.

'I'm sorry,' Nina says at last, and she is. Sorry for everything. All of it.

'I had no idea.' Maeve can't quite look her in the eye, her lashes downcast. 'When you kissed me—'

'Can we just forget it ever happened?'

'I don't think we can, Nina. No.'

Nina feels the tears swimming in her eyes. The skin on her arms itches to be scratched but this time she knows the hurt she caused on the outside can never outweigh the hurt she feels on the inside. She clenches her hands into fists, digging her nails into her palms in an effort to prevent her clawing at her skin anyway.

'You were drunk. Did you kiss me because you were drunk?'

Nina is unsure what to do, what to say. Maeve is handing her a get-out-of-jail-free card but she's hesitant to take it. She has a choice, to explain her clumsy advance as a moment of madness, one caused by too much alcohol and too much emotion. She can say that she was trying to block out the thought that her dad might be alive but choosing not to come home. She can say all of these things and more, of course, but she's been denying part of who she is for such a long time now she's not sure she

343

can continue to, but if living as her true authentic self causes an irreparable tear in her relationship with Maeve, is that a chance she is willing to take?

'I did kiss you because I was drunk.' Nina stares at a dandelion puffball blowing in the breeze. She wants to pluck it from the ground, blow away the seeds and make a wish to turn back time. To travel to before that awkward night in Maeve's kitchen. No, before that. To New Year's Eve where, at least if her parents were still leaving, she would have kissed them goodbye. Goodbyes are important. 'But only because I wasn't brave enough to kiss you when I was sober.'

'I thought you fancied my dad.'

'Sean? Why?'

'You just seemed different round him. Weird.'

'I wanted him to see me in a different light. Not as a child he'd known since I was five but as a woman. As a prospective partner for you. If you can't be friends with me anymore, Maeve, I understand but . . . I promise I won't do it again. Can we . . . Can you try to forget it ever happened?'

Nina shoves her hand between her knees and crosses her fingers. Don't let this be goodbye.

It takes an age for Maeve to speak, and when she does she says,

'I don't want to forget it, Nina, because . . .' There's a breaking of Maeve's voice. Nina waits while her friend gathers her composure, hardly daring to breathe. 'Because . . . because I think I might feel the same.'

Nina inhales sharply. Could it . . . could it possibly be true? Maeve's despairing eyes meet hers and Nina wonders whether she should just tell Maeve they should forget what they think they feel, spare her the pain their situation is so obviously causing her.

'How long . . . how long have you known, that you're . . .' Maeve sweeps a tear from her cheek.

'Gay? I think somehow I've always known. I've never felt . . . anything else. But I guess I knew for sure that night we sneaked out and went on a double date with Ryan and Lenny. When he walked me home he kissed me and I . . . I slapped him.'

'You hit Ryan?'

'It was instinctive. I didn't think. It felt so wrong. Not just because he was the wrong boy but . . . but because he *was* a boy. I told him I'd never fancy him but I couldn't tell him why. I couldn't tell you why. I thought you'd look at me differently. Wonder if I fancied you, which I did of course but . . . It was a real turning point for me. That night.'

'Poor Ryan.'

'I know. He was . . . nice. He said he wouldn't tell anyone I'd slapped him; he was worried it would make him seem repulsive, and I said he could tell Lenny we'd kissed because . . . that's what boys and girls on dates do, isn't it?'

Maeve gently lifts Nina's arm and traces the scars with her fingertip. Every nerve ending in Nina's body tingles with anticipation, a desperate hope swelling inside of her. Maeve lowers her head, her mouth brushing Nina's skin.

Nina holds her breath, waiting. Wanting.

Maeve lowers Nina's arms and takes both of her hands.

'What happens now?' Nina asks.

They gaze into each other's eyes and both lean forward at the same time.

Their lips meet. It isn't a passionate kiss – there's time for that later – but there's a gentleness in its hesitancy. It's a let's-take-this-slowly and a I-promise-I-won't-hurt-you.

An it'll-be-okay.

SIX MONTHS LATER

CHAPTER FIFTY-FIVE

Charlie

Charlie untangles the fairy lights while Nina pulls decorations from a box. It is their first Christmas without their parents which they'll get through the way they got through celebrating each of their birthdays for the first time without Mum and Bo lighting candles on cakes, singing 'Happy Birthday' – together.

'I made this at preschool.' She dangles a star made from clay, which is painted, for some reason, purple. She loops it onto the branch of the tree, which is already dropping needles onto the carpet, but it's worth it for the smell of pine that's currently over-riding the stench of Billie after she went swimming in a pond. 'And this—' she holds another ornament up '—is unidentifiable. It must be one of Duke's.'

'Rude,' says Duke. 'I'm a genius. Do you know how I know that?'

'Because my teacher says so,' Charlie and Nina chorus together, with an eye roll.

Duke is home for the Christmas holidays, the same but immeasurably different. The first few months of boarding at the music academy could have gone either way. When Charlie had dropped him off in September tears had streaked down Duke's cheeks as he had begged Charlie to take him home.

'Give it until the end of term and then if you hate it, you can leave. I promise.' Charlie had quickly swept his brother into a fierce hug, resting his chin on the top of Duke's head, holding him tightly until Charlie had stopped crying his own silent tears. He was broken-hearted at the thought of their household of three becoming two but he knew this was the best thing for his brother.

It had been disconcerting at first, Charlie watching the clock, his days no longer measured by the restrictions of the school run but stretching long and lonely until Nina arrived home. He had tried to focus on his novel but in-between writing he had wandered from room to room, remembering the house as it was; Duke sprawled on the bed in his room – for Charlie always thought of it as Duke's room now – reading a book. Mum and Bo making music in the dining room, and Charlie would ruminate over where Bo might be now, if he was still writing songs, thinking of them. Charlie fritters away hours on YouTube, searching for 'jazz musicians', 'Colesby Bay', 'buskers'; he no longer believes that Bo jumped that night on the cliff or perhaps this is what he wants to believe.

Everyone has their own version of the truth, don't they?

Duke's calls home have been a highlight for Charlie. He'd stand at the window, mobile clamped to his ear, noticing that each day the leaves were shifting away from green, gliding through a spectrum of yellow, orange and red and as he'd listen to Duke chatter about his new friends, his new teachers, about how everything was bloody brilliant, he knew undoubtedly that although something might seem like the end, often it's a new beginning. After Nina had snatched the phone from his hands so she could hear Duke's news, he'd continue to stare outside, into Pippa's garden, Pippa's window. The new owners haven't yet moved in. He wonders if the ache for her in his chest will ever dull.

Charlie wakes early on Christmas morning. After pulling open the curtains, he returns to bed, lies on his side, Billie folding herself into the curve of his knees, and he watches the sky work through its palette of greys. He remembers the Quality Street Christmases of old, him sitting cross-legged on his mum and dad's bed – this bed – tearing open the presents from his stocking. His dad covering his ears in mock horror as Charlie blew into his first harmonica. Rather than making him sad, the memory makes him smile.

He gets up and pulls on his dressing gown. Bangs on Duke and Nina's doors.

'Wake up. Santa's been.'

He wants to make the most of every second of the day. He regrets not coming home last year. If he had known then it would have been Mum's last Christmas he would have been here, pulling crackers, wearing the flimsy paper hats that make everyone look silly. But hindsight is a sad and tragic thing and, although Charlie had missed his chance then, he makes up for it now.

Charlie carves his first turkey that is dry and unappealing, while Nina sieves the lumps from the gravy. Duke lays the table. From them all there are intermittent tears over memories of last Christmas and gratitude for this one. Charlie treasures it all; the terrible jokes, the fighting over the crispiest roast potato, accusations over alleged cheating during Monopoly, the heated debate over whether *Home Alone* or *Elf* is the best festive film, for he knows now not to let moments slip by unnoticed and unappreciated. Not to take for granted that there will always be another time, another place, because sometimes there just isn't. But there is the good, the bad, the happiness, the sorrow for this is what being a family is. Drama and accusations. Laughter and support. Too much noise followed by long stretches of silence.

Forgiveness.

Love.

It had snowed overnight and on Boxing Day, rather than languishing on the sofa, they meet Aunt Violet and take Billie for a long tramp over the hills. With gloved hands they scoop up snow and fashion a snow dog, with pebbles for eyes and twigs for whiskers. Billie barks furiously at it and, when it doesn't reply, she wees on it, turning its white legs to yellow. At home, they invite their neighbour, Mrs Miller, over. Duke snaps chocolate into chunks while Nina heats milk. Charlie pulls fluffy marshmallows into tiny pieces. Once they have warmed their hands they gather in the music room and sing, not carols, but something they write together. The lyrics incorporating all of their hopes and dreams for the next twelve months, Duke with his music, Charlie with his writing. Nina wants to take A level psychology 'to help people struggling with their feelings understand themselves a little better' although she still feels the tug of the creative side to her. She's undecided about her future career but Charlie has reassured her that that's okay. Unknowingly, today, they have been forming new traditions they will carry out year after year.

*

It is New Year's Eve. In retrospect, Christmas was perhaps easier than Charlie had thought, but today is impossibly hard. It's a day full of memories of lasts.

The last kiss.

The last goodbye.

Nina checks her watch. 'This was the last time I ever saw them,' she cries.

Charlie feels a tightness in his chest. It wasn't the last time he had seen Bo and he feels horrible. He turns away from her tear-stained face, towards the window, and focuses on the hypnotic drip, drip, drip from the icicle clinging to the eaves. Eventually it will melt to nothing and another will form, unaware of the inevitability that it, too, shall perish. Does not knowing something make it all right? Is blissful ignorance the key to happiness? Charlie does not know. Again, he wonders if he should tell Nina and Duke the truth but he is terrified it will break them when they are only just beginning to heal. Tear their family apart when it has finally come together.

He says nothing but he feels no lightness in his silence. Guilt and shame are heavy loads to carry.

The doorbell rings and Nina unfolds herself from the sofa – 'I'll get it.'

From the hallway he hears Nina crying, a soft voice comforting her.

Charlie waits.

Eventually she comes back into the room, hand in hand with Maeve. Rather than disappearing upstairs, they arrange themselves on the sofa – Nina's legs over Maeve's lap, their fingers entwined. It's a day for being together.

The intimacy between them shines a spotlight on Charlie's

lonely heart. 'Shall we watch a movie?' he asks, not in the mood for another game.

'*The Lord of the Rings*?' Duke says, ever predictable, ever hopeful.

'No way. We've seen that three billion times since Charlie bought the TV.' Nina throws a cushion at him.

'*Die Hard*?' Charlie suggests.

'Is it a Christmas movie, because, if so, then no.' Duke strokes Billie who is not so much curled on his lap but crammed into the space between his legs and the chair where she really doesn't fit.

'It's not a Christmas movie,' Charlie says as he lines it up.

'It totally is, and Christmas is over,' Maeve says.

'So, you won't be wanting any of these?' Charlie slides out a brand-new tub of Cadbury Heroes from under the sofa.

'Chuck me a caramel.' Duke cups his hands ready.

'Errgg too gooey.' Maeve pulls a face. 'Got a Dairy Milk there, Charlie?'

'I'll have a fudge,' says Nina.

'You don't like flying, do you?' On screen, John McClane utters his first line when the doorbell rings again.

'I'm not getting it. I don't want to disturb Maeve,' Nina says.

'Same but with Billie.'

Charlie complains good-naturedly about missing his favourite film as he heads towards the door. He pulls it open and is glad it's him who answered it as he finds himself looking at the face he never thought he would see again.

His world tipping on its axis, again.

CHAPTER FIFTY-SIX

Duke

As much as he loves his new school, Duke has been happy to be home for the holidays but there is something unsettling about today. As though they are all waiting for something to happen. He tries to focus on the movie but his mind drifts back to last year, making cookies with Pippa, playing 'I Wan'na Be Like You', with Nina, for Sasha. It is disconcerting the way people can come and go. Mum and Dad were here, and then suddenly they weren't. His throat closes and the caramel feels too thick to swallow as he remembers the way he'd hugged them goodbye. He draws in a shaky breath and tries to recall the way Mum smelled but he can't. He remembers there was perfume but also there was the smell of cookies drifting from Pippa's oven.

He holds Billie tighter; her rough tongue licks his hand in an I'm-still-here way.

Momentarily he wonders who is at the door this time. He casts his eye to Nina and Maeve, hears Charlie in the hallway.

All the people he loves the most in the world are here and he'd spoken to Evie earlier.

There is nothing to worry about at all.
He tries to relax but still there's that ominous feeling.
That sense of waiting, but for what?
Or who.

CHAPTER FIFTY-SEVEN

Nina

As Charlie disappears to answer the door, Nina twists open the wrapper of her sweet and places the fudge on her tongue. She's never been that keen on them before but she finds them strangely comforting now, linking the taste to both her brother and her dad.

'Things that can seem like the worst mistake often, usually, work out for the best.'

This she knows is true from the way Maeve leans her head on Nina's shoulder, the despair following that drunken kiss long forgotten.

Everyone makes a mistake, don't they? It's what you do afterwards that counts.

Sean doesn't exactly welcome her with open arms on the odd occasions she goes to Maeve's house – they spend most of their time here – but each time she sees him he is a little less hostile; he doesn't want to lose Maeve.

Momentarily she wonders who is at the door but she doesn't really care. She breathes in the smell of Maeve's shampoo.

She has everything she needs, right here.

CHAPTER FIFTY-EIGHT

Charlie

Charlie feels a twitch of exasperation in his stomach as he strides towards the front door; whoever is interrupting *Die Hard* better have something important to say, but then he remembers last New Year and suddenly his annoyance mutates into fear. His fingers grip the handle but he's afraid to open the door, remembering the policemen on the step, with their 'We're sorry to inform you' and 'Is there anyone we can call for you?' He begins to shake. If it had been any other day he'd have answered before the second, insistent knock without thinking but it's as though this date is now forever bound in tragedy.

He steels himself, keeping his eyes lowered while he pulls the door towards him.

'Charlie.'

He steps backward in shock, his head pounding with possibilities. Probabilities.

'I . . .' he cannot form the words.

'Can I . . . Is it all right if I come in?' It's the question of a stranger, an unwelcome visitor, but this is not a stranger.

This visitor is not unwelcome.

He is soaked with relief that she is here.

'Pippa, please . . .' he falters. Not sure what he is asking. *Love me. Never leave me. Forgive me.* 'Come in, come in.'

He leads her into the kitchen, all the time formulating the words he wants to say that even in his own head sound inadequate. He purposefully keeps it light. Afraid to ask her why she is really here. Afraid she will leave. 'Do you want coffee?'

Do you want me?

'Yes, please. I've brought . . .' she looks unsure as she hesitantly offers him a plate of cookies.

'Round food.' He remembers.

'A full circle.'

A circle has no beginning and no end. The pressure throbbing inside of Charlie's head begins to ease. Whatever this is, he doesn't think it's her seeking closure, a goodbye.

'How is everything? Did you set up as a sole literary agent?' she asks. It isn't what Charlie wants to talk about but he doesn't want to rush it. He doesn't want to rush her.

'No. I'm having a go at writing my own book.'

'Charlie, that's amazing. How's it going?'

'It's been a bit like pulling teeth but I've finished the first draft. Edits next and then I'll send it out to try and bag a deal, I guess.'

'Exciting!'

'Terrifying.' It is only now Charlie realizes how daunting the prospect of releasing his carefully crafted words into the world is. He thinks about the submissions he would receive on a daily basis and wonders whether his responses should have been quicker, kinder, but the sheer volume of emails he'd receive didn't allow for the luxury of detailed feedback. It's so much responsibility cradling someone else's dreams in your hands but he remembers the thrill of discovering a new writer, nurturing their career, and wonders what editors will think when they read his opening line, 'There are many different kinds of love.' He hopes they will want to read on.

'It's hard to share. To be . . . vulnerable,' Pippa says, and Charlie knows they are no longer talking about his book. 'Are the kids—?' She glances around the room.

'They're in the living room watching *Die Hard*.'

'Still on Christmas films?'

He grins. 'It's not a Christmas film.'

'It totally is.'

'Maybe you're right.'

'Yippee-ki-yay.'

She smiles and Charlie's heart turns over inside of his chest.

'That's not the only thing you were right about,' he says quietly. Their eyes lock, the atmosphere heavy once more.

Pippa looks away, crosses to the kettle and pulls mugs from the cupboard. She is not yet ready to talk, or perhaps she is not yet ready to listen. Charlie waits until the drinks are made and they are sitting at the table, close enough to touch each other, but not.

'How have you been?' he asks when what he really wants to know is where she has been and who with.

'After I handed in my notice I went to Birmingham.'

'To stay with friends?'

'Yes, friends. Not Rick.' She knows he is really asking about her ex. 'And then I went to see my parents.'

'I looked for you.'

'I know. They said. And then I went to Colesby Bay.'

It is Charlie's turn to speak but he doesn't know what to say. He takes a sip of his coffee to wash down his confusion. Pippa knew that last summer he had looked for her and yet she didn't contact him, instead going to Colesby Bay.

'Why?'

'I wanted to go back to the place . . . last New Year. It was the start of everything and I wanted it to be the end of everything too. I stood on the same beach and it was supposed to be my closure. My goodbye to you but instead . . . I get it, Charlie. I understand why you didn't turn up to meet me that day and then wouldn't pick up my call. I get why you're so guarded. I know that you think your dad made a choice to leave you and, to an extent, your mum and Bo did too by getting on that boat. I know you're scared of getting hurt but I also know you're scared of being the one to cause the hurt. The way you put Duke and Nina first is . . . it's everything . . . hurtful and commendable and understandable and . . . it's lovely. You're lovely. And I don't know if—'

'I love you.' He reaches across the table and takes both her hands in his. It is the simple truth. He sees the emotions that flicker across her face, hope, happiness and then apprehension. She tries to pull her hands away; she is waiting for the 'but'. 'I love you,' he repeats the phrase and it doesn't feel awkward or unnatural or any of the things he feared it might. 'I always have, Pippa. You were the first girl I ever kissed and I want you to be the last. I was going to tell you that when we met in Joe's greasy spoon but then Nina ran away and I had to go and find her. I should have called but it was all so hectic. I thought I'd explain everything when I got home but you had already gone. I'm sorry.'

'No . . .' Tears glisten in her eyes and he feels his face crumple. 'No. Don't apologise for putting them first. You're a good man, Charlie. A kind man. I can wait until you're ready. Until they're ready.'

'I told them about you, about us. I had to before I went to Scotland.'

'What did they say?' She wears such a look of uncertainty.

'Nina said I was a fucking idiot for letting you go. Duke . . . pretty much the same but with less swearing. They love you. I love you.'

Those three words trip off his tongue with ease. 'I want you in my life. We want you in our lives.'

Pippa stands, her chair legs scraping against the floor, and for one single, terrible moment Charlie thinks that she is leaving but instead she sits on his lap, winds her arms around his neck and kisses him hard. He buries his hands in her hair, pulling her to him.

'Charlie!' Duke calls from the lounge, breaking them apart. 'You're missing the best bit.'

'I'm really not,' he whispers before pulling Pippa to him again.

It is near the end of the film when Charlie and Pippa head into the lounge, lips swollen from kissing. It is Charlie's favourite part – John McClane is saving the day, saving his marriage – but Charlie doesn't mind when Duke switches it off. For the first time he feels like the hero of his own story.

'You're back.' Duke rushes towards Pippa but Billie gets there first, turning happy circles, joy wagging her tail into a blur. Pippa bends her knees and strokes Billie's head with one hand, while, with her other arm, she squeezes Duke to her.

Nina sits up straight, shifting slightly away from Maeve, but Pippa has already noticed their closeness.

'It's good to see you.' She looks Nina directly in the eye. 'Both of you. Together.' She smiles and Nina grins back, her hand finding Maeve's once more. She's still worried about being judged, not yet wholly comfortable with who she is, but Charlie and Duke make sure she knows that whatever challenges she might face, here she is loved, she is accepted, and ultimately isn't that what everyone wants?

Love.

Acceptance.

'I go to boarding school now,' Duke garbles his news. 'It's not just any other school, it's a music school. I got a scholarship because my teacher—'

'Says I'm a genius,' chorus Charlie and Nina.

'Is that so? You'd better play for me then.'

They all traipse into the room next door. Duke picks up his sax. 'Come on then.' He glances between Charlie and Nina.

Wordlessly, Nina switches on the mic while Charlie deliberates between the guitar and the piano. There is none of the awkwardness of last year. Charlie not wanting to play in front of Sasha, not wanting to play at all. Music is a part of him, his link to Mum, and he is grateful for it.

They play 'Minnie the Moocher'. Billie weaving between them in her four-legged-dance. Maeve picks up a pair of maracas, Pippa a tambourine, and they both sing the chorus. Maeve's pitch is perfect. Pippa is flat but she sings unashamedly and Charlie loves her for it. They switch to 'My Baby Just Cares for Me' and for this Nina sings purely for Maeve, their eyes locked. Maeve and Pippa sway from side to side, waving their mobile phones like lighters. Afterwards, Charlie rests down his guitar and sits at the piano, Billie at his feet. He plays and sings 'What a Wonderful World'. It feels apt.

He knows there are many different kinds of love but there are also many different kinds of family. He used to think 'blended' was a bad word but now he sees it for what it is.

A choice.

Nina, Duke, Maeve, Pippa and himself might not fit the convention of what a family should look like but . . .

Billie rests her head on his knee in a don't-forget-me way, as though she can tell what he's thinking.

They are bound by love and loss and shared memories, hopes and dreams.

They are, Charlie affirms as he looks around the room, his past, his present, his future.

His everything.

They are all he needs.

EIGHTEEN MONTHS LATER

EPILOGUE

Charlie

It's scorching hot, only the whisper of a breeze blowing in from the sea, gently lifting and dropping the orange and yellow bunting strung across this pretty cobbled street. Even with the throng of tourists, Colesby Bay is idyllic.

Vanilla ice cream dribbles down the cone and Charlie licks it from his fingers. Next to him, Nina slurps at her lolly, pastel-coloured hundreds and thousands clinging to her lips. Billie, her nose now peppered with grey fur, bumps her head against Charlie's leg – *save some cornet for me.*

They pass a stand of postcards outside of a shop with candy-coloured buckets and spades in the window.

'We must send a postcard to Violet while we're here,' Charlie says, before they round the corner and see him.

Busking.

Charlie's breath catches in his throat as Nina clutches his arm tightly.

'How does he have the guts to do that?' she asks again, watching her younger brother as he captivates the passers-by with his saxophone, the flat cap by his feet glinting with coins.

At thirteen and a half, Duke is a world away from that shy and unsure eleven-year-old he'd been when Charlie first got to know him properly.

'You've so many friends now,' Charlie had said when he had collected Duke at the end of term. It had taken ages for Duke to say his goodbyes.

'Yeah, Evie will always be my best friend though. It's good that people like me, but you know . . . I like myself nowadays and that's the key isn't it, to happiness? Liking who you are.'

'You're so very wise.'

'Mum always said I was an old soul.'

You can see this now. Strands of 'Unforgettable' drift from his sax. Duke has his eyes closed; he doesn't just play the music, he feels it.

'I can't believe it's the first day of our holiday and he wants to work,' Nina says.

'Playing music isn't exactly work,' says Charlie.

'And this isn't exactly a holiday.' Pippa stretches out her arm and tilts her hand so the diamonds in the platinum band on her ring finger sparkle in the sun. Bringing Nina and Duke on their honeymoon isn't conventional but then they aren't a conventional sort of family. Besides, time is precious. Nina will be heading off to uni in September to explore psychology even though she's still not completely sure what she wants to do yet. There's a creative side to her that also needs fulfilling.

Every moment is one to treasure.

Duke finishes the song and takes a bow, thanking everyone for listening.

'I can't believe it's been two hours,' he says as he crouches down to put his instrument back in its case. 'What's the plan now?'

'Shall we drop the sax back at the hotel and then head for the beach?' Charlie asks.

They stroll, Billie stopping to sniff everything.

It is down one of the side streets that Nina freezes. 'Oh. My. God.' She clasps one hand over her mouth and, with the other, she points.

Charlie's eyes follow her finger and when he sees what's in her field of vision he takes a step backwards, in shock.

'Charlie!' Duke exclaims.

'It's brilliant!' Pippa claps her hands and rushes over to the bookshop. There, in the centre of the window, is a huge display of books. Charlie's book.

'It's still so . . . I can't quite . . .' Charlie rakes his hands through his hair. He's been published a week now and he still isn't over his astonishment and surprise whenever he sees his novel. He hopes this feeling never wears off. As a literary agent he was used to sharing his authors' happiness, but he never imagined it could feel . . .

'It's bloody epic,' Duke says, rushing inside.

There's a table by the door, piled high with hardback copies. Charlie traces the gold embossed title with his fingers – *All The Things You Are.* It could never have been called anything else.

He opens the cover, reads the dedication that brought a lump to his throat when he wrote it, still brings a lump to his throat when he reads it.

For Mum, who made us all the things we are. We miss you every day.

'No dogs in here.' A stern-looking woman with round metal glasses hurries over to them.

Nina picks up a book and points to the back cover with a grin before pointing to Charlie. The woman's eyes flicker between his author photo, and his face.

'You're . . . you're Charlie . . .'

'Johnson.' He uses the same surname as his siblings now.

'So, the dog in the book, is she based on . . .?' She crouches and fusses Billie behind her ears.

Charlie smiles. He doesn't tell her that the dog isn't based on Billie. It is Billie. He doesn't tell her that the book, a supposed work of fiction, isn't really. It's him. Them. Their lives.

'I love the family in your book. Wouldn't it be wonderful if there was an old-fashioned family like that who played music rather than watched TV? Who actually liked spending time together and put each other first?'

'It would,' says Charlie.

'I hope you write a sequel. I want to know what happens next. Hopefully they live happily ever after. Can you sign some copies while you're here? Perhaps hang around for a while and chat to the customers?'

'I'd love to,' Charlie says, 'but not today. We've a date with the beach. I'll pop back later in the week.'

'You can stay here if you want to,' everyone reassures Charlie as they head out of the door.

'Nah. I actually like you all and want to spend time with you and put you first.' He smiles.

Pippa kisses him hard. He slips his arms around her waist.

'We'll be here all day at this rate.' Nina rolls her eyes. 'How about we give you two newlyweds some space. Me and Duke will drop the sax at the hotel and grab some towels and meet you at the steps in forty-five minutes?'

'Cool. I can grab a quick shower while you talk to Maeve for the millionth time.'

'I wasn't thinking of calling her,' but the smile on her face says differently.

'You were too.'

'At least somebody loves me.' Nina nudges Duke with her elbow as they head off.

'Somebody loves me too. Have I told that my teacher—'

'Says you're an annoying genius?'

Charlie smiles as he watches them leave. Pippa says, 'Actually there's a shop I'd like to check out. Can I meet you there too?'

'If you're sure?' Charlie doesn't offer to go with her. There is something he wants to do as well.

He waits until Pippa has rounded the corner before he turns and walks at a brisk pace. Every now and then he has the sensation he is being watched and he throws a glance over his shoulder, but he thinks it's because he doesn't want anyone to know where he is going.

What he is doing.

And then, he is there.

The Crow's Nest.

Outside there is still a blackboard stating, 'Live Music Every Night'.

Charlie weaves through the drinkers in the garden and steps inside the gloominess. He almost expects everything to be exactly the same, Bo on the small stage near the door, the barman with his red mohawk taking orders, but the stage is empty and behind the bar are two young girls, deep in conversation.

'I was wondering if you can help me?'

'Toilets are for customers only.' The girl barely glances his way.

'It's not that. It's . . . I'm looking for a musician. He was a regular. Woody? Does he still play here?'

'Never heard of him.' The girl snaps her gum.

'How long have you worked here?'

'A year. People move on though, don't they?' She shrugs before turning away.

Charlie buys a Coke. It doesn't come in a bottle with a red stripe straw but the sweetness on his tongue, the bubbles on his nose, still take him back to childhood.

He savours it. Dragging it out until it's time to head to the steps to meet the others. As he walks, Charlie has the sensation of being watched again.

Nina and Duke are already waiting. Charlie feels a hand on his shoulder. He turns around.

'Hey you.' He kisses Pippa.

Again, he feels eyes on him. He lets go of Pippa and turns a slow circle. Through the swarm of happy holidaymakers he notices a man stalking away, a guitar strapped to his back. His gait is familiar, but the sun is bright and everything is shadowed.

Charlie shields his eyes and studies the retreating figure. The man has one hand to his face; is he scratching an itch, wiping away tears?

Is it him?

We believe what we want to believe.

For a few seconds Charlie watches him as he hurries towards the outskirts of town, growing smaller.

Family is a choice.

Charlie turns back to the others. 'Last one to reach the sea is a loser,' he says. He hesitates before he moves, giving Nina, Duke and Pippa the chance to pass him, but it's Billie, despite her ageing years, who hurtles down the steps first, barking in excitement as her paws sink into the sand.

Pippa and Nina kick off their flip-flops, hitch up their sundresses and hurtle towards the sparkling waves. Duke sprints past them, forming an L-shape on his forehead. Charlie slows, stops, watches as one by one they splash into the ocean, kicking up a spray of water, Nina and Pippa shrieking that it's cold, Duke grabbing his sister around the waist, threatening to dunk her under. Billie turns happy circles, her fur sodden. Charlie places his hand on his chest, feeling each beat of his joyous heart.

'Come on!' Pippa runs to him, wraps her arms around his neck and presses her salty lips against his. She takes his hand and presses it against her stomach. 'The sequel,' she whispers in his ear.

Charlie doesn't understand.

'You know? The woman in the shop said she couldn't wait to find out what happens next, and neither could I. I . . . I went to Boots and bought a pregnancy test. I had a feeling but . . . this—' she lays both her hands on top of his '—this is what happens next.'

'Charlie, you're the loser!' Duke shouts and before Charlie can gather his thoughts, gather his words, Pippa is leading him into the sea. He can't stop smiling.

Charlie is the last one to splash in the waves, but he feels he is the winner as he watches them all. His happily ever after.

He is a brother. A husband. Soon to be a father.

There are many different kinds of love.

Right here, right now, he feels them all.

READER LETTER

Hello,

Thank you so much for reading *From Now On*, my third 'Amelia Henley' book! I do hope you enjoyed it, and, if you did, and have a few moments to pop a review online, I'd be immensely grateful. It really does make such a difference.

https://www.amazon.co.uk/Now-Amelia-Henley-ebook/dp/B09TQWSQ4M/ref=sr_1_1?crid=3T0PAO8CZGE3X&keywords=amelia+henley+from+now+on&qid=1652372165&sprefix=amelia+henley+from+now+on%2Caps%2C76&sr=8-1

The character of Charlie came to mind at the beginning of the pandemic when I spent a lot of time thinking about life, and how it rarely goes to plan. Originally, Charlie was eighteen and about to embark on a new adventure when life forces him to take a different direction after the sad and sudden loss of his parents. I began writing it from entirely Charlie's point of view but it didn't feel right. About halfway through I lost interest in the story and decided to scrap what I'd written altogether and begin again. This time with Charlie being so much older, living his own life, about to move abroad with a woman who doesn't want children, with little relationship with his two half-siblings, Nina and Duke.

I immediately fell in love with Nina and Duke and wanted to see the events unfold through their eyes too, examine their relationships with those closest to them, not only family, but friends and romantic interests. To make the novel a real exploration of love in all its forms. (*Love Actually* was the perfect title, but, you know . . .)

I adore the Johnson family (including Billie!) but it's time to let them go and focus on Joe and Emilie, the stars of next year's book. I do hope you join me again and in the meantime do come chat to me on social media.

Amelia x

https://twitter.com/MsAmeliaHenley

https://www.instagram.com/msameliahenley/

https://www.facebook.com/msameliahenley

ACKNOWLEDGEMENTS

Huge thanks to my wonderful publishers, HQ Stories, especially Lisa Milton and my fabulous editors, Manpreet Grewal and Melanie Hayes. Donna Hillyer for the copyedit. There are so many people behind the scenes working on each book and I'm grateful for them all from the cover designer, marketing, PR, production, to distribution and retailers.

As ever, a big thank you to my agent, Rory Scarfe, and the team at The Blair Partnership.

Thank you to Cathy Ashley from the Family Support Group, who patiently answered all of my questions around guardianship. Any mistakes are purely my own.

I'm so thankful for the support and encouragement I receive from the wonderful online bookish community. Spreading the love for a story on social media, reviewing and recommending books is really instrumental to its success. A special shout-out to Wendy Clarke and 'The Fiction Café'.

Love to Natasha Haddon, who has been an immense support, right from hosting my first book launch for my debut.

My friends, particularly Sarah and Natalie. My family, especially my mum, sister Karen, and Rebecca (Mrs Jensen!).

Tim, I love you dearly.

My children, Callum, Kai and Finley, who, however big they grow, are always the centre of my world.

And, of course, Ian Hawley.

BOOK CLUB QUESTIONS

1. Were you shocked when Charlie uncovered Bo's secret? Was he right to keep it?
2. What do you think really happened with Bo at the Cliff Top Café?
3. Charlie carried a lot of resentment towards his mum; could you understand this? Do you think she knew and, if so, why didn't she broach the subject with him?
4. Sasha is very focused on her five-year plan. Do you think having such specific goals is a good thing or can it stop you enjoying the present moment?
5. Nina is a very confused fifteen-year-old, both about love and about whether she wants to be a psychologist or something more creative. What advice would you give to your fifteen-year-old self?
6. Pippa fell in love with Charlie in the sandpit at age six. Do you think young love can be everlasting? Were they always destined to be together?
7. Charlie sacrificed his career in New York – was he right to do so? Would you have done the same?

8. Why do you think Violet takes on the children? How could she have handled things differently?
9. Billie seems to instinctively know when something is wrong. Do you believe animals can sense these things?
10. What would you like to happen to the Johnson family in the future?

**Turn the page for an exclusive extract
from Amelia Henley's debut novel,
The Life We Almost Had, the beautiful and
emotional love story of Anna and Adam**

Available to buy now!

PROLOGUE

Seven years. It's been seven years since that night on the beach. I had laid on the damp sand with Adam, his thumb stroking mine. Dawn smudged the sky with its pink fingers while the rising sun flung glitter across the sea. We'd faced each other curled onto our sides, our bodies speech marks, unspoken words passing hesitantly between us; an illusory dream. *Don't ever leave me*, I had silently asked him. *I won't*, his eyes had silently replied.

But he did.

He has.

My memories are both painful and pleasurable to recall. We were blissfully happy until gradually we weren't. Every cross word, every hard stare, each time we turned our backs on each other in bed gathered like storm clouds hanging over us, ready to burst, drenching us with doubt and uncertainty until we questioned what we once thought was unquestionable.

Can love really be eternal?

I can answer that now because the inequitable truth is that I am hopelessly, irrevocably, lost without him.

But does he feel the same?

I turn over the possibility of life without Adam, but each time I think of myself without him, no longer an *us*, my heart breaks all over again.

If only we hadn't…

My chest tightens.

Breathe.

Breathe, Anna. You're okay.

It's a lie I tell myself, but gradually the horror of that day begins to dissipate with every slow inhale, with every measured exhale. It takes several minutes to calm myself. My fingers furling and unfurling, my nails biting into the tender skin of my palms until my burning sorrow subsides.

Focus.

I am running out of time. I've been trying to write a letter but the words won't come. My notepaper is still stark white. My pen once again poised, ink waiting to stain the blank page with my tenuous excuses.

My secrets.

But not my lies. There's been enough of those. Too many.

I am desperate to see him once more and make it right.

All of it.

I wish I knew what he wanted. My eyes flutter closed. I try to conjure his voice, imagining he might tell me what to do. Past conversations echo in my mind as I search for a clue.

If you love someone, set them free, he had once told me, but I brush the thought of this away. I don't think it can apply to this awful situation we have found ourselves in. Instead I recall the feel of his body spooned around mine, warm breath on the back of my neck, promises drifting into my ear.

Forever.

I cling on to that one word as tightly as I'd once clung on to his hand.

I loved him completely. I still do. Whatever happens now, after, my heart will still belong to him.

Will always belong to him.

I must hurry if I'm going to reach him before it's too late. There's a tremble in my fingers as I begin the letter, which will be both an apology and an explanation, but it seems impossible to put it all into words – the story of us. I really don't have time to think of the life we had – the life we almost had – but I allow myself the indulgence. Memories gather: we're on the beach, watching the sunrise; I'm introducing him to my mum – his voice shaking with nerves as he said hello; we're meeting for the first time in that shabby bar. Out of order and back to front and more than anything I wish I could live it all again. Except that day. *Never* that day.

Again, the vice around my lungs tightens. In my mind I see it all unfold and I feel it. I feel it all: fear, panic, despair.

Breathe, Anna.

In and out. In and out. Until I am here again, pen gripped too tightly in my hand.

Focus.

I made a mistake.

I stare so intently at the words I have written that they jump around on the page. I'm at a loss to know how to carry on, when I remember one of the first things Adam had said to me: 'Start at the beginning, Anna.'

And so I do.

Speedily, the nib of my pen scratches over the paper. I let it all pour out.

This is not a typical love story, but it's our love story.

Mine and Adam's.

And despite that day, despite everything, I'm not yet ready for it to end.

Is he?

CHAPTER ONE

Anna

Seven years before

The date I met Adam is forever etched onto my mind; it should have been my wedding day. I tucked my hair behind my ears; rather than being strewn with confetti, it was greasy and limp. Unwashed and unloved.

The plane taxied down the runway before it rose sharply into the sky, a frothy white tail in its wake. Out of the window was nothing but cloud, as thick and woolly as my thoughts. Each time I remembered the way I'd been dumped, virtually at the altar, my face burned with the shame of it.

Goodbye.

I wasn't sure if I was saying farewell to England or to the man who had broken my heart.

Fingers threaded through mine and squeezed. Tears threatened to fall as I gazed down at my ringless hand. Ridiculously, one of the things that had excited me most about my honeymoon had been the anticipation of the sun tanning my skin around the plain gold band I'd chosen. Knowing that even if I removed my jewellery to go into the sea, the thin, pale strip of skin circling the second finger of my left hand would act as a clear indicator that I was married.

That I was loved.

'Stop thinking about him.' Nell clicked open her seatbelt as the safety light went out, and signalled to the cabin crew for a drink. I smoothed out the creases in my floaty linen dress and it struck me I was wearing white. Miserably I fiddled with the neckline, not embroidered with tiny pearls that shimmered from cream to lilac to pink under the lights, like the dress I had picked out. It was hard not to cry again remembering the perfectness of that day. Mum covering her mouth with both hands when I glided out of the changing rooms and twirled in front of the many mirrors. Everywhere I looked I had beamed back at myself.

'That's the one,' Mum had whispered like we were in a church, not a bridal shop, but I didn't need her to tell me that. I knew it was the one.

It was such a shame *he* wasn't the one.

'It won't always hurt this much,' Nell said; not that she'd know. She was usually the one breaking hearts, hers was still intact. 'You've had a lucky escape. He wasn't good enough for you. Besides, twenty-four is too young to be married. This isn't the 1950s.'

'If it were the 1950s, I'd have been married years ago and popped out a couple of kids by now.' My throat swelled at the thought. I might have been young but I couldn't wait to be a mother. Would I ever have children? I'd thought my future was mapped out, but now all I had was doubts and fears and a mountain of wedding gifts to return.

'I can't see you slicking on lipstick and tying a ribbon in your

6

hair five minutes before your husband gets home. And that's after a day cleaning windows with vinegar and beating carpets.'

'I know who I'd like to beat,' I muttered darkly.

'I'll drink to that.' She flashed a smile. 'And from now on, the only vinegar will be on the chips he told you that you shouldn't eat.'

'He was worried about my health.'

'Bollocks was he. He was worried you'd realize you're a normal-sized, goddess of a woman and leave him for somebody who didn't keep calling you chubby. Anyway, let's not give him a second thought. I'm ready to get this party started—'

'Nell—'

'I know, I know.' She caught sight of my expression. 'This isn't what you wanted. I'm not the one who should be here and you've no chance of joining the mile-high club now—'

'Nell—'

'But. You can either spend the next ten days crying by the pool or try and make the best of it. I know you loved him, Anna—'

'Nell Stevens.' Her concerned eyes met mine and I knew she was worried she'd pushed it too far. 'I just want to say... thank you. Not just for persuading me to come but... for all of it.' Nell had dropped everything when I had called her at work, sobbing uncontrollably two weeks before my big day. She had kept me stocked up on vodka and ice cream while she phoned around the guests, explaining it was me who had had a change of heart. It was Nell who had talked me out of confronting Sonia Skelton when the rumours about her and my fiancé surfaced, and her who confiscated my phone at night so I couldn't drunk-text the cheating scumbag at 3 a.m. She allowed me to retain some dignity, on the outside at least. Humiliation still stung each time I thought of him, and I thought of him often, but oddly my feelings around him were tangled in a mass of embarrassment and regret, underpinned with a slow, simmering anger. I'd wasted three years of my life. Honestly, I wasn't sure it was him I actually missed or the idea of him. If you have to ask yourself 'is it love', it probably isn't, is it?

Our foreheads touched and again her fingers entwined with mine. There was no need for words until our drinks were delivered. Nell dived on the miniature bottles with a 'woo hoo'.

'You've a lot to be grateful for.' She unscrewed the gin and fizzed tonic into my glass.

'Alcohol?'

'That goes without saying. But the travel agent didn't have to let you change the name on the ticket. Now you've got someone to rub sun cream on your back without expecting to get laid, and someone to hold your hair back when too much Sex on the Beach makes you sick.'

'I'm not going to have sex on the beach or anywhere else… Oh.' I realized she was talking about the cocktail.

'You never know. We might meet two nice boys.'

'No boys.' I swigged my drink, bubbles tickling my nose. 'No boys ever again.'

I raised my glass, arm hovering in the air until she raised hers.

'This will be the adventure of a lifetime,' she said and we chinked. She turned out to be right.

But rather than flying away from something, I was flying towards something.

Towards him. To Adam.

I just didn't know it then.

8

By the time the coach dropped us off at our hotel on the Spanish island of Alircia, it was nearly midnight but I still called Mum to let her know I'd arrived; she'd only worry otherwise.

'We're here.' I tried to keep the sadness out of my voice but Mum heard it anyway.

'It'll get easier, Anna,' she said, but I knew being alone hadn't got easier for her. 'Better with no one than the wrong one.'

'I know.' I *did* know. I'd accepted his proposal for myriad reasons: because of what I'd been through, was yet to go through, but none of them the right reason. The only reason.

Love.

I told Mum I'd speak to her soon. Nell and me hovered near the pots of exotic plants and flowers, waiting for the driver to empty the luggage hold; Nell plucked a bright pink bougainvillea and tucked it into my hair.

'It's so beautiful here,' she exclaimed, but I barely registered the fairy lights twisted around the thick trunks of the palm trees that circled the pool. We wheeled our suitcases towards reception to check in. I was hot and exhausted. The gin I'd drunk earlier had left a residue on my tongue. A throbbing in my temples.

'Check this out!' Nell, typically, had abandoned her luggage and was sauntering into the bar. 'Nightcap?'

'I'm shattered.' I was struggling with her case and mine. 'I just want a shower and my bed.'

'Spoilsport.' She said it lightly but I felt a pang of guilt. I knew she'd used all her annual leave this year and had taken this time off unpaid to support me. The least I could do was let her have a drink.

'I suppose because it's all-inclusive it would be rude not to,' I said.

I stayed with our things, stifling a yawn and hoping Nell would order us shots as she sashayed to the bar. Instead of something we could knock back quickly, she returned with two glasses brimming with orange liquid and stuffed with pink parasols, cocktail sticks spearing glacé cherries.

'I asked for something fun,' she shouted over Madonna who was 'True Blue'. What was it with Spain and their fascination with English Eighties music?

I took a sip. 'Jesus. We'll sleep well after these.'

'You think? I can only taste the orange. You're such a light-weight. Hey, one o'clock.'

'God, is it? No wonder I'm so tired.'

'No. Look. At one o'clock.' Nell jerked her head to her left. 'He's checking you out.' I couldn't help but look and when I did, I felt... I don't know, a sense of déjà vu. Familiarity. He was tall, dark and awkward, sipping beer from a plastic cup, and alone. He seemed to be alone. He caught my eye and smiled. I turned away.

'No boys, remember?' I said to Nell.

'I've you listed as being on your honeymoon?' the young receptionist with jet black hair and bright white teeth asked.

'Yes.' Nell peered at his name tag. 'Miguel.' She draped an arm around my shoulders. 'If we could have our key. My wife and I are eager to go to bed.'

Pretending we were married was preferable to going into why I wasn't and Nell knew I did have that terribly British urge to constantly explain myself, but the emotions that surfaced when I heard myself described as someone's wife zapped the last of my energy. All of a sudden it all caught up with me. The journey, the alcohol, my lack of sleep. My vision darkened and my ears began to buzz. Wishing I could sit, I rested my head on Nell's shoulder, lulled by the tap-tap-tap of Miguel's keyboard as he checked us in, words drifting in and out of reach ... *breakfast... sun loungers... excursions.*

'Let's go, darling.' Nell dropped a kiss atop of my head. Simultaneously I straightened my neck and wiped my mouth for traces of drool before I thanked Miguel and forced my feet to move. I could feel eyes burning into my back as we headed outside where the air was still warm and chirruping crickets welcomed us to their island.

The music grew fainter as we searched for our accommodation, using the scant light from the screens of our phones to make out the numbers on the whitewashed walls. Inflatable swans and flamingos rested on balconies, a signpost to the apartments with kids in them. Towels and swimwear dangled from retractable washing lines.

Stars speckled the sky and through the blackness, to our right, the sound of the waves lapping against an unseen shore. The warm air smelled of the beach.

'This is us,' Nell said. She unlocked the door and flicked on the lights. 'Oh God. I'm sorry, Anna.'

I pushed past her, wanting to see what she saw. A 'Just Married' banner was strung across the lounge, rose petals scattered on the floor. On the coffee table, a bottle of champagne and two flutes.

I was a bride without her husband. I began to cry.

'Excuse me,' a voice behind me said and I spun around, wiping my eyes.

It was the boy from the bar.

Adam. It was Adam.

Want to read more from Amelia Henley?
Then don't miss her latest emotional and uplifting read,
The Art of Loving You

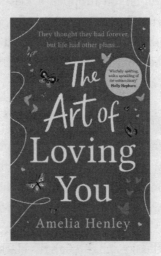

They were so in love . . .
And then life changed forever . . .
Will they find happiness again?

Libby and Jack are the happiest they've ever been. Thanks to their dear friend, eighty-year-old Sid, they've just bought their first house together, and it's the beginning of the life they've always dreamed of.

But the universe has other plans for Libby and Jack and a devastating twist of fate shatters their world.

All of a sudden life is looking very different, and unlikely though it seems, might Sid be the one person who can help Libby and Jack move forward when what they loved the most has been lost?